Minders are watching Luke as he seeks to find a former love.

Minders

Minders

The boy, the dog, and the hawk.

By

Rob G. Lerner

Cover by PJ Hines

Pomanjer Publishing Inc., LLC

Copyright

ISBN-13: 978-0692388341 (Pomanjer Publishing Co., LLC)

ISBN-10: 0692388346

Published February 2015   )))(((Pomanjer Publishing Co., LLC

About Pomanjer Publishing Co., LLC

Pomanjer Publishing Co., LLC, publishes fiction and non-fiction books that speak to our hearts and catch the idiosyncratic attention of the Pomanjers.

Contact information:

Pomanjer Publishing Co., LLC
P.O. Box 986
Vienna VA 22183

Minders

By

Rob G. Lerner

Cover by PJ Hines

Book two of *The Changers Series*, *Minders* continues the story begun with *Changers*. Friendships are in tatters because of consequences of choices made in *Changers*. Luke unexpectedly learns of the whereabouts of Iowa and tries to see her against advice of more temperate minds and his own promises. What follows tests his love, loyalty, and belief in the young woman. Minders asks whether what is important is real and challenges the reader to draw the distinction between opportunity and temptation.

About the author

Rob G. Lerner, tempered in the western states, resides in Virginia with his wife and son, whose favorite bird is a great blue heron that frequents the nearby creek. Rob, an armchair mountain climber who aspires to be a Formula One racecar driver, has been crafting fiction for years. When not in the fictional world, he explores classical music and Renaissance art. Rob can be reached through the publisher, Pomanjer Publishing Co., LLC.

Previously by Rob G. Lerner:

Changers

Book one of *The Changers Series, Changers* concerns five young friends who discover a secret power – the ability to assume the form of an animal. It is a wonderful power, but its use proves to have significant consequences for their friendship, their community, and ultimately the Changer legal system. (2013)

The Boy Who Loved Dolphins

Timmy is a young boy who feels alienated from his parents. His beloved grandfather fills his head with wild tales of life beneath the sea. Things take a strange turn when a group of wild dolphins adopts Timmy, who comes to know the value of a real, if imperfect, family. (2012)

To Alex

Contents

About the author...vi

Chapter One...1

Chapter Two...9

Chapter Three 13

Chapter Four 18

Chapter Five 24

Chapter Six..28

Chapter Seven..35

Chapter Eight 40

Chapter Nine...44

Chapter Ten 51

Chapter Eleven..57

Chapter Twelve 60

Chapter Thirteen...65

Chapter Fourteen..71

Chapter Fifteen 75

Chapter Sixteen...79

Chapter Seventeen 83

Chapter Eighteen 87

Chapter Nineteen 90

Chapter Twenty 97

Chapter Twenty-one 102

Chapter Twenty-two 110

Chapter Twenty-three 118

Chapter Twenty-four 125

Chapter Twenty-five 131

Chapter Twenty-six 136

Chapter Twenty-seven 141

Chapter Twenty-eight 146

Chapter Twenty-nine 153

Chapter Thirty 158

Chapter Thirty-one 163

Chapter Thirty-two 170

Chapter Thirty-three 174

Chapter Thirty-four 178

Chapter Thirty-five 182

Chapter Thirty-six..188

Chapter Thirty-seven 197

Chapter Thirty-eight..205

Chapter Thirty-nine 213

Chapter Forty 223

Chapter Forty-one..231

Chapter Forty-two 235

Chapter Forty-three 243

Chapter Forty-four 250

Chapter Forty-five 257

Chapter Forty-six..261

Chapter Forty-seven 268

Chapter Forty-eight..273

Chapter Forty-nine..282

Chapter Fifty 287

Chapter One

Luke was tall and thin. His smooth, regular features were complemented by his carefully ironed clothes and his thick, dark hair, which was fairly short and neatly trimmed. Because of his firm handshake and direct, confident manner when he presented himself, people who didn't know him often thought he was older and more experience than he was, perhaps a young businessman fresh from graduate school rather than a junior in high school. Luke was also the first of the Cygnets – or what used to be called the Cygnets before they went their separate ways -- to learn that their friend and former Cygnet, Iowa, who had attended the same middle school as the other Cygnets, was still alive. To be honest, they really didn't think she was dead, but sometimes it was hard not to fear the worst when no one had heard from her since she disappeared that night three years ago.

"You won't believe what I heard," he said as he stood in front of the school lunch table where Press and Dana, young ladies who were also juniors and former Cygnets, were having lunch. Luke wasn't wasting any time on formalities. He was too excited by the information, and he also knew that if he wasn't quick, Press would ignore him or talk over him before he had a chance to say what needed to be said.

Press and Dana paused and looked up at Luke. Normally, Press would have ignored him, but his strange demeanor momentarily caught her attention. Dana, on the contrary, was polite, and she looked up to hear what he had to say.

"You're not going to believe it," he began when they turned toward him. "I'd ask you to guess, but there's no way you'd guess right."

"Okay, so we can't guess right," said Press, her cold, athletic face glowering at Luke. Even though she was sitting down, it was clear that she was tall and muscular.

"I'm not kidding. This is so amazing, this is…"

Press turned away. She retrieved a large, green canvas bag from the floor and plunked it on the table in front of her and began rummaging through it for her lunch.

Dana pretended not to notice Press' rudeness. She regretted that Luke had chosen this time to reveal his news, because she knew that Press would react exactly as she was reacting now. "What is it, Luke?" she asked, smiling and pretending that she and Press were interested.

"It's amazing, and you're not going to believe it. Are you sure you don't want to take a guess? No? Not one? Okay, here it is: Iowa is alive. Can you believe it? It's amazing, right? Can you believe it?" Luke was normally calm and quiet, but his enthusiasm and his big, infectious smile surprised Dana and made her chuckle, which she tried to hide from Press. She wanted to be nice to Luke, but at the same time she didn't want to antagonize Press and then listen to her badmouth Luke after he was gone.

"Really?"

"I never really thought she was dead," Luke continued. "I knew she was alive. Something in me said she couldn't die, not without someone else knowing about it. Okay, I know what you're going to say, but there's more. You're not going to believe this, either."

Luke was about to disclose the additional news, but he paused when he noticed Press glowering at him and disdainfully chewing her food. After she swallowed, which seemed difficult and uncomfortable, she picked up a small bottle of orange juice and drank the entire contents without taking a breath or turning away from Luke. Banging the bottle down on the table, she tilted her head to one side and stared at him for a few seconds. "So, she's alive," she finally said, breaking the uncomfortable silence. Her voice was flat and emotionless, and she was making it clear that she was irritated by Luke's unwelcome appearance and not interested in his meaningless, trivial news.

Dana, who still looked like a sweet, chubby middle school student, smiled at Luke and pretended not to notice Press' ill manners. While she agreed with her closest friend on most things, she was nevertheless pleased to hear that Iowa was among the living (like Luke, she never truly believed the girl was dead), and besides she still liked Luke. Dana felt that Luke had taken responsibility for what had happened three years ago, and, unlike her friend Press, didn't try to shirk responsibility by blaming the others.

Luke noticed Dana's smile and, taking it as an invitation, pulled a chair out from the table and sat down next to Dana and almost directly across from Press. While it was clear that Dana didn't mind Luke's company, it was equally clear that Press did.

"Yes, she's alive, and isn't that amazing?" Luke asked, looking at each one in turn and still grinning from ear to ear. "We haven't heard a thing from her in years, and, as far as anyone knew, she could have been dead, kidnapped, or whatever. But I didn't believe it, not for a second. Do want to know something else? I know where she is."

"Did she phone you?" Dana asked, recalling another time when Iowa disappeared and phoned Luke to announce her return. "Or did you see her?"

"Neither. And you won't believe how I found out." Luke was about to tell them where Iowa was and how he found out when Press interrupted him.

"I don't know why you think we care about Iowa's disposition or how you stumbled across this 'amazing news,' as you call it," she said. Her voice was stern and her eyes narrow.

Luke wasn't entirely surprised by Press' attitude. He knew how she felt about Iowa (she had made her feelings quite clear over the years), and there was little doubt in his mind that she wasn't fond of him, either. But in his excitement to pass on the good news, he had mistakenly thought that the past would be forgotten, or at least forgiven, and that Press would be pleased to hear about Iowa. Sure, there were bound to be some troubling memories, but after three years and a good deal of maturation – and after nearly a lifetime of being close friends – Luke couldn't understand how Press could continue to feel and act as she did.

"Luke," Dana interjected, doing her best to keep the conversation pleasant while trying to keep peace with Press, who would doubtless hold her accountable for everything she said to Luke. "I think the underlying issue here is that we aren't Cygnets anymore. Everything has changed. I'm glad Iowa's alive – and I really hope she's doing well – but it's kind of hard to get excited when she's been gone for so long. We're not the same people we were then. Do you know what I mean?"

Luke's smile immediately vanished. He might have expected such a statement from Press, who seemed quite happy the Cygnets had fallen apart, but not from Dana. She had always been friendly to everyone, and none of the Cygnets had been more loyal to the group and its members than she, and so for her to suggest that the Cygnets were finished – that their individual friendships were finished – was shocking (even if it was pretty much the case), and it made Luke wonder if she had changed because of Press' influence or if he had ever truly known Dana.

"No," he said, shaking his head and gazing at Dana's pleasant face. "No, I don't believe you mean that. We're still friends regardless of what happened years ago, and Iowa is still our friend even if we don't call ourselves Cygnets anymore. She's special to us just like…"

"Special to you, maybe," Press interjected. "You had a crush on her. But you didn't care what she thought about the rest of us, which wasn't very much. If she cared for us, she wouldn't have kept disappearing without telling anyone except you."

Luke felt like screaming at Press. He wanted to tell her that everything she accused Iowa of doing over the years, she herself did (except for disappearing). He wanted to tell Press (and Dana, for that matter, since she was so enamored of Press) that she could be mean, controlling, and insensitive, and that if any of the Cygnets were unfriendly, it was she. But Luke controlled himself. Over the years, there had been too many harsh words between people who should have been close friends.

"Do you remember why she left?" he asked Press, glancing at Dana. "The Smiths, that's why. They were the horrid people who were going to take her to another state after her parents died. Can you imagine what might have become of her had she let that happen? You know as well as I do that we would never have heard from her again if she hadn't run away. Think back. Do you remember how scared she was when they informed her that she was leaving with them?"

"Apart from the Smiths being her guardians, all the rest of it was only what she claimed. There was no proof to any of it, and you bought it hook, line, and sinker."

"No, I believed her because she was my friend. When a friend tells me something, I am going to believe it. If you told me…"

"If I were your friend, I wouldn't tell you something like that. Friends tell friends the truth, and they don't tell a pack of lies just to get sympathy. She couldn't tell us a single reason why they were 'horrid,' as you say. And it's a joke to think that she couldn't have communicated with us, even if they took her to the other side of the world. What, no phones, no Internet, no post offices? Do you think they were going to tie her up and tape her mouth shut so she couldn't speak to us? Friends? Friends? The only one she seemed to like was you, although this friend of

4

yours practically gouged your eye out when she was mad at you. Don't you remember that?"

"That's not fair...," Luke stammered.

"I agree. It's not fair. But that was Iowa. She was our best friend when she needed us, but we were nothing to her when she didn't. We were less than nothing: We were like those stupid sticks we used to play with. It was no different when she disappeared. She didn't tell anyone she was leaving, and she didn't tell anyone when she returned, except for you, and that was only because she needed you to make us forgive her."

Dana placed her hand gently on Press' forearm to calm her down. "Luke, Press has a point. I don't agree with everything she said, but you have to admit the way Iowa behaved toward us...do you remember all those terrible jokes she played on us? Remember the time she floated in the lake, pretending to be dead? Remember how scared we were and how she laughed when she saw our faces? Look, I'm really glad she's alive, and I truly hope she hasn't been hurt. But if she were to come back today, things wouldn't be the same as before. We're not the same people we were then. I don't think any of us want to be..."

"Dana," Luke interrupted, a little more forcefully than he had intended. "I know we're all different people now. But it doesn't mean that our friendship is over, and it definitely doesn't mean we can't be happy to have found Iowa again. Maybe some things have changed, but I will never abandon you and Press..."

"The feeling's not mutual," Press said and pulled her arm away from Dana.

Dana smiled at Press to calm her down and then turned to Luke. "I'm sure you're going to speak to her, and so you can give her our best, that's all."

Luke turned his body toward Dana. "Aren't you at least interested in where she is? Maybe you'd feel differently about her if you knew."

"Fat chance," Press mumbled.

"Press, please," Dana said quietly without looking at the girl. "All right, Luke, where is she?"

"She's at a refactoring facility. She's been there all along. That's why she never sent a word to us. You can't communicate with anyone when you're in one of those places, and so there's no way that should have told us what happened. Don't you see? It wasn't her fault."

Press was silent while she gathered up the wrappers and napkins from her lunch. Luke and Dana quietly watched Press, each expecting her to say something harsh or unkind. She didn't disappoint them. When Press was finished placing all the refuse in a neat pile in the center of her lunch tray, she pulled her green bag over her shoulder and turned to Luke. "I suppose that's one way of looking at it," she began and then stood up, grasping both sides of her tray at the same time. "But where was she when we were all caught? I don't recall her giving herself up, do you, Dana? So, she's at a facility. Do you know when this happened, before or after that night? My guess is after – after, that is, she left us holding the bag." Turning away from Luke and looking directly at Dana, she informed her friend that she would be at the library after class.

Luke and Dana watched Press leave the lunchroom. Turning back toward Luke, Dana told him that she had to go, too. "I'm not mad," she said to Luke, smiling as if the old friendship was as strong as ever. "But Press is right about some things. Iowa wasn't there that night. Maybe, if she had been, we might be a little more sympathetic. I don't know, Luke."

Luke looked at the table and shook his head slightly. Looking back at Dana, looking at her neatly combed hair and the small, dark mole on her left earlobe, he couldn't help wondering if something else was going on. There were bound to be some memories of Iowa that weren't entirely pleasant, but Dana had always been kind and forgiving and, as far as he knew, liked Iowa as much as any of them.

"I don't know where Iowa was that night," Luke began quietly, "and I'm not going to hold anything against her on the basis of what I don't know. Can't we forget all this and just be happy that we found one of our oldest and dearest friends? Do you remember what we promised each other? We promised to remain friends forever, through thick and thin. I'm keeping my promise, and I know Iowa is doing the same."

Dana was staring off at something in the distance. She was silent for a few moments before turning back to Luke. "I have to go to class," she finally said. "It was nice talking to you, and I hope things are well with Iowa." She picked up her tray and left in the same direction that Press did. She glanced back at Luke while emptying her tray in the garbage can, and then exited the cafeteria.

Luke remained at the table for a few more minutes. While he sat thinking about what Dana and Press had said, a couple of students sat down across from him. Neither one of them knew Luke, much less wanted him in on their conversation, and so they turned their shoulders to him while they arranged their lunches on the table and continued discussing something started before they arrived.

"My mom won't talk to him anymore," one of the girls was saying quietly to the other. She was leaning toward the other girl, tilting her head in such a way that her long, black hair fell over her shoulder, partially obscuring her face, to prevent Luke from hearing what she said. Luke could hear both of them clearly, however, and for some reason instead of giving them their privacy, he remained at the table and pretended not to hear what they were saying.

"They got into this big fight about something. I don't know what it was, because my sister and I weren't there at the beginning. It was something about a woman, which Daddy denied, and, when she repeated the accusation, he called her a loony tune. That did it. Mother ran into the bedroom, slammed the door and locked it, and Daddy left the house. He came back a little latter, but instead of going into their bedroom, where Mother was still wailing up a storm (you could hear her all over the house), he went into his study and shut the door. He didn't come out until the morning when we were eating breakfast. Mother was much calmer then."

"So what happened after that?" the other girl asked. She was bigger than the first and, because her hair didn't hang below the tops of her ears, she couldn't even pretend to hide from Luke's ears.

"Nothing! They acted as if nothing happened. They told Sis to mind her own business when she asked about it. The funny thing is, they don't speak to each other anymore. They sit at the dinner table with us, they'll laugh at our jokes and ask us about our day, but they won't say a word to each other, at least not directly."

"Not a word?"

"Not a word. If Mother wants something on the table near Daddy, she'll ask me for it and pretend that he is somewhere else. Last week, he tried to speak to her after dinner (they were in the other room and didn't know Sis and I could hear them, or him), but she refused to talk and stormed off to her room. It used to be his room, too, but he's not allowed to come in there anymore, except when she's not there and only to get his clothes."

"It must be hard on him."

The girl with the long hair laughed. "You can't imagine. But now he's stopped trying and refuses to look at her, even when they're passing each other in the hall."

"So, what's going to happen?"

"Nothing, I suppose, unless someone starts talking."

Luke finally got up and walked to class. Even though he had one of the best pieces of news of his life, he was disheartened and, if his next class wasn't so important, he would have gone to the school nurse for a sick pass to go home.

Chapter Two

Immediately after dinner, Luke went to his room and closed the door. Stretching out on his bed, his hands behind his head, he tried to understand why Dana and Press were so resistant to Iowa's reappearance. Perhaps resistance wasn't the right word, but it was clear that they weren't interested in Iowa's wellbeing and didn't want to contact her, if such a thing were possible. Not surprisingly, Press was adamant. She had always been a little hard to get along with, and there were a couple time when she and Iowa nearly came to blows, but not because of anything that Iowa did. Press wanted everything her way, whether it was the rules of a game or the time when the Cygnets would meet. Press was also a little jealous of Iowa, because the Cygnets tended to look to Iowa for direction, not Press, who as a star athlete at school was used to having people follow her lead. Even if she were glad that Iowa was alive, Press could hardly be thrilled that Iowa might return and take up where she left off.

Dana was a different story. She seemed to like Iowa as much as everyone did, even when Iowa played practical jokes she didn't like. Iowa wasn't a cruel person, but some of her jokes pushed the limits of friendship (one time, she told everyone to meet in the field near the lake, and before the meeting informed everyone but Dana to meet at the lake instead. When Dana accidently stumbled on them, Iowa insisted that Dana must have forgotten the change and then laughed the whole thing off as a joke. Iowa was only trying to get a slight rise from the girl, who was rarely flustered or angry, but it was clear to everyone, Dana included, that Iowa truly liked and admired Dana – indeed, whenever she seemed to have gone too far and Dana's normally pleasant expression changed, Iowa would apologize profusely and would be the soul of kindness to her throughout the rest of the week. So, while it wasn't surprising that Press would resist Iowa's reappearance, if it came to that, Luke found it hard to understand Dana's resistance, unless it had something to do with Press and her influence. But even this didn't make sense, for Dana had always been her own person and would never have let anyone control her. Maybe things changed after the

Cygnets broke up, and maybe she was what she seemed to be at lunch, that is, a little too eager to please Press.

Luke shut his eyes. As the darkness engulfed him, he put aside the conversation with Press and Dana and tried to imagine what Iowa might look like today. Since he had never forgotten her (and, if needed, he had two pictures of her in one of his drawers to draw from), it was easy to visualize her soft lips, large eyes (the irises were daylight blue in the center with a nighttime shade around the edges), and golden hair, which shimmered in the daylight and fell over her forehead and shoulders, forcing her to clear her eyes with the back of her hand or with a sideways motion of her head. Her shoulders were narrow and her body trim, curved, and elegant (unlike Press' rigid, muscular frame), and when she looked at you, her entire body had a way of amplifying her dazzling smile. While refining Iowa's image, it occurred to him that he never had any doubts that she was alive or that someday he might be able to stroke her long, silky hair. Of course, Press was right that Iowa disappeared without informing anyone, but she was wrong to assume that Iowa failed to do so out of indifference or disrespect to the Cygnets. Iowa wasn't like that. She loved and respected Press and the others, and, if her jokes were a little rough at times, it wasn't because she didn't like the Cygnets or was taking their friendship lightly. Observing Iowa standing in front of him, her soft hair floating across her cheeks and forehead, Luke agreed with Press on at least one point: There was a bond between them that wasn't shared with the other Cygnets. The Cygnets were connected by love and friendship, and yet there was something additional between Luke and Iowa, and this accounted for Iowa's decision to reach out to him and not the others when she reappeared a few years ago. Yes, he added, Iowa stabbed him under his left eye with a long stick, but it was an accident and not, as Press often claimed, a deliberate attempt to blind him. The young woman glowing in the light in front of him would never do such a thing.

Luke stretched his neck from side to side and then arched his back and shoulders. Snuggling back in the bed, he tried to recover the glowing image but it quickly faded the instant he moved his back, and he was unable to conjure up anything resembling Iowa. After a few seconds teetering on the verge of sleep, he started to think about the Cygnets, which of course included Iowa. The Cygnets…it suddenly seemed like a silly name, but when it had been bestowed on the five children (by none other than Iowa herself), it meant something serious and meaningful. Iowa, the tall, thin girl with glasses (when she wore them) and sharp elbows, adored swans, and to her these pristine white birds epitomized all the positive aspects of nature –love, friendship, unity, respect for the environment – and she used the name to describe this tightly-knit group of friends. Everyone one of them loved the name, Press included, and before long the term Cygnets was as identifiable with each one of them as their own names. When they went to the lake in the woods, which was as often as possible, they often dreamed of floating across the mirror-like water, eyeing the dark, impenetrable forest surrounding the lake, and watching the white clouds develop and dissolve in the clear sky. The idea of living like a swan, of setting aside the harshness of human life, and existing freely and unthinkably while gliding on an endless stretch of placid water was irresistible, which helps to explain why four of them, when they were able to change, had chosen to be swans.

Turning back to Iowa, Luke recalled one of the last times he had seen her, which was one of the last peaceful days the Cygnets had before changing tore them apart. It was late summer, and the sun was sinking below the horizon and casting its warm rays across the blue sky, the dark waters of the lake, and the perpetually green leaves of the surrounding trees. Feeling its pleasant warmth on his bare skin (he, like the others, was wearing a bathing suit) and inhaling the tree-scented air, he turned and noticed Iowa standing on a large rock near the lake's edge. He couldn't remember where the other Cygnets were at the time (they must have been deep within the woods, because the only sounds he could recall were the tinkling leaves and hush of the water), but he didn't care because Iowa was watching him, her arms at her sides and a gentle smile creasing her lips. She didn't say anything, and Luke, who was silent, too, couldn't help looking directly at her, observing how the breeze played with her soft hair, tossing it across her face after which she brushed it out of her eyes with the back of her right hand. It was at that moment, in the hushed silence that surrounded them and promised to bring them even closer together, that Iowa's smile broadened and she whispered his name. "Luke," she whispered again and, opening her arms to him, she seemed to be asking him to step closer to her. Luke could feel himself smiling, he could feel himself being drawn to her, but no sooner he had taken one step toward her than he noticed sounds emanating from the woods behind him, voices that echoed throughout the trees and quickly got louder and louder until he could finally place names to the individual laughs, shouts, and screams.

"Luke, Iowa!" he heard repeated several times until the other Cygnets surrounded him and Iowa and demanded games that included everyone.

Luke would have replayed the image of Iowa beckoning him over and over, but his mind began to wander back to the Cygnets and then to Press and Dana, and then to the day that Iowa called him after having been missing for nearly a year. This was the first time that she had disappeared, and she spoke to him before speaking to anyone else on her return because, as she told him, she missed him and she wanted him to reach out to the others to ask them to take her back. He couldn't refuse helping her, especially because the sound of her voice was more beautiful than her hair and could emit sounds that were as alluring as Siren songs, although it wasn't easy because of Press' anger over the fact that she had told no one, not even Luke, that she was leaving. They accepted her back, but only after she taught them how to change. Yes, it was the changing that brought them back together and, for a time, enhanced their closeness – made them Cygnets once again. But it was also the changing that eventually disrupted their seemingly rock-solid friendship and led, as if it had been inexorably determined by the stars, to that terrible night…

Luke didn't want to think about changing or the breakup of the Cygnets. Draping his right arm over his eyes to keep the bad memories from penetrating his thoughts, he recalled how he discovered the most wonderful thing in the world, that Iowa was still alive.

Chapter Three

Under different circumstances, Luke might have been ashamed of how he acquired the information, but because this was such wonderful information, he excused his behavior and actually smiled over his subterfuge. It happened Friday.

It was late in the afternoon, and most of the students had already gone home or were attending a basketball game in the school's gym, which was located at the back of the building next to the athletic field. Luke, however, was at the opposite end of the building, in one of the classrooms near the school office. The last class of the day had ended over an hour ago, but Luke had stayed behind in the lab to complete one of the assignments, having received permission to stay after class and been given a key to lock up when he left.

Upon finishing the assignment, Luke put away the lab equipment and placed his paper in a tray on the corner of the teacher's desk. Taking one last glance at the room to make sure that he hadn't forgotten anything, he locked the door and walked over to the school office where he was supposed to drop the key into a metal lockbox outside the office's main door. He was just about to drop the key into the box when he heard someone from inside the office mention Iowa's name. There was no mistaking the name for anyone else (he had never come across anyone with a similar name), and for a moment the rush of past memories made him stop and, standing just outside the office door, listen to what was being said about her.

"Iowa is doing fine," he heard a woman's voice exclaim. Luke didn't recognize her voice, but he thought that she might be one of the school counselors because of the firm, confident way in which she spoke.

"She's moving onto the next level, then?" another woman said. Luke knew this voice. It was the school principal.

"Oh, definitely. You know, it's amazing how well she took to treatment."

"I am impressed. I didn't hold out a lot of hope for her. Given her condition when she was found, I was certain that she would remain an animal for the rest of her days. Afterwards, when she began showing some signs of recovery, I was equally convinced that her recovery wouldn't be complete, that at best she wouldn't be allowed to leave the facility. Well, she surprised me. She surprised all of us, I think." The woman paused for a moment, as if she was mulling something over. "But are you sure…"

"There's no doubt about it."

"So, what are the next steps?"

Luke heard a loud noise behind him. Startled, he turned around and saw one of the janitors dragging a large, gray trash can down the hall before disappearing into one of the classrooms. The noise seemed to echo throughout the school, and by the time the janitor disappeared, Luke's heart was beating rapidly. Normally, such a banging noise wouldn't have bothered him (he might not even have noticed it), but he was suddenly afraid that someone would come out of the office and find him standing there, listening to the conversation. Turning back toward the office, Luke listened carefully to make sure that no one was speaking about him before he picked up the thread of the conversation again.

"That shouldn't be a problem," the principal said. "It's a natural step. Once again…wait a minute. Did you say that she's still at the facility?"

"Yes," the first replied. "If you look at the last paragraph on page five, where it talks about living quarters, you'll see that she's now residing permanently at Lordan Zoo."

"I'm sorry. I've only had a chance to skim the report. I meant to read it carefully this afternoon, but we had a number of minor fires to put out, if you know what I mean. I am pleased you could take time out of your busy schedule to come here this afternoon."

"Please, it wasn't a problem at all. But let me correct what I was saying. She seems quite happy and well-adjusted there, and as long as she continues…I see no… Besides, there is a real need for services…"

The voices were becoming harder to hear, as if the women had moved farther back into the office or were whispering because of the sensitivity of the information. Clearly, the first woman had indicated that Iowa was going to stay at the zoo for an indefinite time, but why and in what state (was she behind bars like all the other animals there?) he couldn't tell. Casting aside the rest of his inhibitions about eavesdropping,

Luke quietly inched closer to the door and turned his head at angle so that he could hear the conversation better.

"…one of the best in the country."

"Should a decision be made…well, is there someone here that she could stay with, if only on a temporary basis?"

"No, I don't see that happening. Ms. Royce will be responsible for…education, which is also noted in the report. Right now, we aren't seeing anything that would necessitate a return...at least not at this juncture."

Luke shuddered at the mention of Ms. Royce, formerly a science teacher at his middle school, now an administrator at his high school, and the arbiter of the Cygnets at their so-called trial. It was Ms. Royce who determined that the Cygnets were guilty of behaving recklessly and punished every one of them, except Iowa, accordingly. Iowa, of course, was nowhere to be found when Ms. Royce and the others in the community surrounded the lake and captured the worst offenders while requiring the others to report to her office the following day at school. Luke actually liked Ms. Royce and, even though she had been critical of his behavior and held him largely responsible for certain things, he knew that she was fair and forgiving – she never seemed to hold a grudge. Still, she had a habit of turning up when least expected, as if out of the blue, and he knew that if he were caught doing something wrong, it could mean additional disciplinary measures.

"I understand, although I am also a little disappointed. You see… By the way, are the Smiths still involved or have they relinquished control?"

"Page seventeen…"

Luke could hear the sounds of paper being shuffled, suggesting that the first woman was finding the page for the principal.

"Yes, yes, well, thank you. You will continue to provide updates, or am I to get these from Ms. Royce?"

Before Luke could learn the answer, he could hear the screech of chairs sliding back on the hard linoleum floor and, within seconds, the sound of footsteps coming his way. Luke immediately straightened and reached over to the box to deposit the key. Somehow or other in the process he lost control of the key and dropped it on the floor, where it bounced, tip first, several times before finally landing in the middle of the open doorway. The tinkling of the key against the floor shattered the silence in the hallway. Afraid of being discovered, Luke lunged for the key, which for several long moments resisted all his efforts to retrieve it. When he finally imposed his will on the object and dropped it into the box, it clanged loudly against the bottom as if it were announcing its presence – and Luke's – to everyone within earshot.

By the time the women reached the office door where Luke had been standing, Luke was gone and the large, main door around the corner had just banged shut. Neither woman noticed anything amiss.

"So then you'll keep me updated?" the principal was saying as she shook the other's hand.

"Yes, of course. But I wouldn't expect her return any time soon. She's…"

"I understand. Maybe if I were in her shoes…"

"Indeed."

Moments before he fell asleep that night, Luke couldn't help laughing at the manner in which the information fell into his lap. When he stopped laughing, he slowly came to the realization that since Iowa was so close, he might actually be able to see her again. The idea of seeing her again had never entered his mind either when he heard the women talking or when he tried to explain the details to Press and Dana, and yet because the facility was relatively close (maybe forty or fifty miles away), it should have been obvious to him from the start that it offered a wonderful opportunity to renew his friendship with her.

Luke could see himself walking into the facility and meeting Iowa, who had been waiting anxiously for him to arrive. Throwing their arms around one another, they stood motionless for several moments, quietly sniffling and refusing to say anything, as if words were inferior to the feelings they were experiencing. When they finally took a step back, they couldn't take their eyes off one another, neither one quite believing that this precious moment had finally arrived. Luke observed Iowa's soft mouth and the way in which its corners curved slightly upward, as if in a perpetual smile, and then he noticed her bright, blue eyes, which were filled to the brim with moisture that at any second could overflow and rush down her cheeks. Luke tried to touch her soft cheek, but she pulled back and he noticed that her once soft features were now hard and firm, her lips taut. He whispered her name, as if that might soften whatever had hardened inside her, but she took a step back and folded her arms, glowering at him. It had been a long time since he had seen her, and he realized that if she were angry about anything, it was the fact that he hadn't reached out to her since she disappeared. Before he succumbed completely to sleep and began dreaming about coming home after having ice-skated across a vast, snow- and ice-covered lake, Luke promised himself that he was going to speak to Dana one more time. This time, however, without Press.

Chapter Four

The Cygnets were a group of five young people (Luke, the only male in the group, Iowa, Press, Dana, and Lu) who had been close friends almost since kindergarten. It was unclear what initially attracted them to one another, but over the years they developed a strong relationship based on familiarity, common interests (a love of the outdoors and an appreciation of animals, especially swans), and a belief that they would grow old together. For a short time before the end, they were also united by something that differentiated them as people from everyone else they knew – they were Changers.

Changers were people who could transform or change their bodies (and all the organic material they were wearing) into animals. Actually, most people can change into animals (complete with fur, feathers, or whatever), because we all possess a strange, little-known genetic trait for molecular malleability that has been passed down from the moment hominids began differentiating themselves from other animals. But this genetic trait or capability is rarely exercised, because few people are aware of its existence (there are a fair number of scientists today who continue to deny the feasibility of molecular malleability) and, even among those with a vague notion of the possibility, fewer still understand that to exploit this capability requires only a certain amount of training and preparation. To put it simply, changing is a mental process that enables the transformation of human substance into animal substance, enabling the Changer to acquire all the physical attributes (size, shape, color, texture, etc.) of a particular animal. If, for example, someone understood the process and had the proper instruction, he could lie down on his side and in seconds turn into an African lion, if he so desired. Having changed, this individual would not only be physically indistinguishable from all other African lions; he would also possess the African lion's sense of smell, its strength and endurance, and its ability to hunt down and kill other animals. But, unlike an African lion, the Changer could revert to human form and substance anytime he chose to do so, provided that he hadn't been the animal so long that he no longer remembered the essential differences between animals, human beings, and his own self. Changing is not without its limitations.

Iowa told the Cygnets about changing, and she encouraged them to experience a new and wonderful life as an animal. She learned about changing from her father, who changed into a swan on his deathbed; but it was her mother who taught her how the process worked and helped the girl understand some of the limitations of the process. Sadly, Iowa's mother died before she had a chance to explain all the downsides to changing, and by the time that Iowa had mastered the process of changing from human to swan and back again, she possessed only a rudimentary notion of what she was doing and what would happen as a result. Iowa didn't understand that if it weren't properly controlled, changing could produce the same kind of deleterious effects that an addictive drug has on reason, behavior, relationships, and even lives. Although Iowa did understand that the transformation of human substance generally meant a Changer could only be one kind of animal (having changed into an African lion, one could not become a gold finch or a collie – one was either an African lion or a human), it never occurred to her that even this minor limitation could have disastrous, unforeseen consequences. Indeed, Iowa didn't understand how changing would eventually destroy the Cygnets and their relationships with one another.

Once Iowa had given the Cygnets the benefits of her knowledge, she encouraged all of them to become swans, just as she had become shortly before her mother's death. She didn't insist (that was something Press might have done), although she did her best to highlight the beauty of the white bird and, since they were all at the edge of the lake, she demonstrated the gracefulness of its swimming and the sheer joy it experienced swimming across the lake and floating effortlessly with the gentle movement of the waves. The display was practically irresistible, especially since the Cygnets were already mesmerized by her ability to change into something radically different from her normal self, and in no time they all followed her lead, splashing on the surface of the lake and paddling and floating from one end to the other. Everyone, that is, except Luke. Luke appreciated swans, and he wholeheartedly agreed with the name Cygnets for their group, because he believed that it accurately represented their aspirations. But he didn't want to become a bird, and so he abstained from changing during the first hours of the Cygnets' transformation into swans and, instead, sat at the edge of the lake, watching his friends flap their wings and play on the water and noticing how changing was bringing the others closer as friends and Cygnets.

No one knew that this was the beginning of the end of the Cygnets. While the others came to the lake each day to change and spend their afternoons frolicking in the water, Luke stayed home or, if he came, watched the other Cygnets from a distance (he usually sat on a rock about ten feet from the water's edge) as they played their games and gradually excluded him from most of their interactions. Initially, he didn't feel like he was being excluded (this is surprising, since there wasn't any way that he could interact with a group of swans in the same way that he could interact with the same group of Cygnets), but after a while he began to resent the fact that the others often ignored him and went to the lake without telling him, which never would have happened before they changed into swans.

Angered that the Cygnets were rarely speaking to him, one evening he turned into a dog. Luke justified his change by telling himself and the others that he liked dogs better, but from practically the first moment he changed, he discovered that the distance between him and the Cygnets had grown even greater (dogs are even less capable than humans of interacting with swans). He wasn't asked to leave the Cygnets, but since he couldn't participate in their special experiences, he quickly found that he had nothing in common with them, nothing to share when they sat down in the lunchroom at school to discuss their experiences (all they wanted to do was share their common experiences as swans). Saddened by his increasing alienation from his closest friends, Luke tried to develop new friends by showing some of the boys at school how to change, which was also designed to let the Cygnets know that he didn't need them anymore.

Iowa's mother told her that no one was supposed to know about changing. Iowa, who had reasonably assumed that no one apart from her parents knew about changing, was determined to keep the precious knowledge a secret, and so she instructed each of the Cygnets not to tell a soul about the capability, not even to let anyone suspect that they had a secret that was worth exposing. Luke, angry and failing to understand the significance of this secret, didn't tell any of the boys to keep mum on changing and so in no time several additional boys, none of them Luke's friends, became Changers.

One night, when the moon was full and its soft yellow light rested on the still waters of the lake, the Cygnets (minus Iowa) were gently paddling near the edge of the water. The lake was unusually quiet that evening, the trees surrounding the water were enveloped in dark shadows, and as Press, Dana, and Lu enjoyed floating on the black surface of the water beneath a simmering moon, a pack of ferocious dogs slowly inched their toward the edge of the water. Luke wasn't among the pack and, in fact, he didn't know it existed, much less what it planned to do to the swans. Luckily, the dogs were stopped before anyone got hurt (one of them bit Press but, contrary to her claims, the bite was minor and hardly broke the skin), because somehow or other several of the town officials (who, it turned out, were not only Changers themselves, but were also the authorities responsible for policing and adjudicating the activities of the Changers in the area) got wind of what was going to happen and managed to control the situation before it went any further.

The dogs were all apprehended and were sentenced to two years of refactoring (rehabilitation for Changers) and prohibited from changing for a period of ten years. The three girls were apprehended, too, since they had been changing without adequate supervision, and they were sentenced to two years of counseling and prohibited from changing for five years. Luke, on the other hand, was taken in human form on his way to the lake. He knew the Cygnets would be there and wanted only to revive his friendship with them. Of the Cygnets, his sentence was stiffest – after all, he spread the word about changing – meaning that he was required to undergo counseling (the mildest form of refactoring) for five consecutive years, required to work at a local animal shelter during the same period, had to wear at least one item of clothing made from synthetic materials at all times (because only organic materials can change, changing with synthetic materials could cause complications and embarrassment), and finally was prohibited from changing until he was thirty-five.

One of the most unfortunate outcomes of the situation, according to Press, was that Iowa had not been apprehended with the rest of them. She had been on the water with the other Cygnets earlier in the evening, but she was gone by the time the authorities arrived, and no one had heard from her since that time. Press and all the other Cygnets (except Luke) not only blamed Iowa for what had happened (if she hadn't taught them how to change, then none of the subsequent troubles would have happened, and the Cygnets would have remained close friends), but they also felt betrayed by the fact that she alone escaped and wasn't punished – and, furthermore, she didn't have the decency to apologize to the Cygnets or even send a word explaining her absence. "It was just like her," Press once said, "to disappear when there was trouble. She escaped punishment and left us hanging."

Iowa didn't leave anyone hanging, however. The reason that she hadn't been apprehended was because she was at the opposite end of the lake beneath the thick, overhanging trees and shrubs. No one could see her from where they were, and she hadn't been aware of what was happening to the Cygnets at the other side. The Cygnets were also unaware that a couple of young boys found her a few days later and she eventually ended up at the Lordan Zoo (which is also a refactoring, or rehabilitating, facility where Changers were taught how to become human again), where she lived from then on. Luke was right when he told Press that while undergoing intensive refactoring at such a facility, Changers cannot communicate with the outside world.

Because of the silence, only a few people knew about Iowa's surprising progress at the facility. During her first six months there, she mastered the animal forces that were gradually taking control of her human substance, which for most Changers usually takes three years, if their mental faculties aren't too far gone when they arrive. During the next six, she augmented her earlier lessons by learning how to take control of one's human substance in extreme situations, when one's ability to resist one's animal nature is at its weakest (in a sense, this is the difference between walking calmly to an exit during a fire and panicking, running in any direction that presents itself). By the time she had reached the third year, she had made such amazing progress that she was taught the principles of changing, so that she could control every aspect of transforming human substance into animal substance, while understanding the limits to which the human mind and body can change without permanently altering what it is to be human. It was rare for a Changer as young as she was to be allowed to progress so quickly, but from the very first moment she arrived she showed great promise and an even greater desire to make amends for what she had done. It was even rarer for someone so young to be accepted as an equal in the Changer community and vested with all the responsibilities and authorities that only the older, more experience Changers possessed.

It was that one particular evening that put an end to the Cygnets. The authorities, under the direction of Ms. Royce, prohibited the remaining Cygnets from speaking or associating with each other for a period of one year. This should have been the worst part of their punishment, since the Cygnets had been the closest of friends for years, but the prohibition turned out to be a blessing in disguise. None of the Cygnets wanted to speak to each other, given their humiliation at being apprehended and forced to undergo treatment (the authorities preferred this term to 'punishment,' since the latter term sounded a wee bit draconian); and none of them cared one year later when Lu and her family moved out of state. Unlike Iowa, Lu sent the remaining Cygnets a terse note regarding her departure, at the same time pointedly omitting to add a return address. That was that, and as far as any of them knew or cared years later, she was living happily ever after on the other side of the country. Midway through the second year, however, Press and Dana managed to put aside their differences and soon became as close as ever, perhaps closer. They didn't try to include Luke, but over time their resistance to him softened somewhat (at least on Dana's part), and they spoke to him occasionally, just as they did when he brought them the good news.

Chapter Five

"It's not like we went to jail or have a criminal record," Luke insisted when Dana highlighted some of the reasons that Press didn't like Iowa and didn't relish the idea of seeing her again.

It had taken Luke over an hour to muster the courage to call Dana, and, when he had finally got her on the line, he had nearly forgotten all the troubles and all the injured feelings that had for years characterized the relationships of the former Cygnets. Naturally, he didn't speak as freely as he once did, but he did feel that he could now talk to Dana honestly, without Press lurking somewhere nearby waiting to control the discussion or to turn against Iowa.

"No, of course we don't. But we all had to go through the embarrassment of getting caught, and we are constantly being watched by Ms. Royce and the others, who are probably licking their chops – no pun intended – over the possibility of punishing us for something else." She, too, felt warm speaking to him, although the feeling wasn't strong enough to ease all the anger and frustration that she had grown accustomed to since that night.

"You don't mean that," Luke protested. "You sound like Press."

"I suppose not. But you have to admit that having Iowa back could dredge up a lot of bad memories."

"I don't believe that, either," Luke said quietly. "We'll certainly remember the past, but when we're all together, there's simply no way that we won't remember all the good times and that we'll be happy together like we used to be."

"You're dreaming."

"If we let Press control things, it will be a nightmare."

"Be nice, Luke. You like Press as well as I do, and you know that she was hurt by all the things that happened. It's hard for her, that's all. She's a good person at heart, and she wouldn't for the world wish ill of Iowa. But that doesn't mean that she'll welcome her with open arms. It doesn't mean that we'll ever be friends again, at least not like we used to be."

"That's not you, Dana. I know it's not. You feel the same way about Iowa as I do, but you're afraid to say so, especially when Press is around. Come on, if anyone can think for herself, it's you. Don't let Press tell you how to think…"

"Listen, Luke, nobody tells me how to think, not Press, not you. I told you I still like Iowa, but I just don't know if I could ever see her again. It doesn't matter, because she's in one of the facilities and the odds of us ever seeing her again are slim. Right?"

Luke hesitated.

"Luke, are you there?"

"Listen, Dana, I don't know what happens at the facilities. I don't think the people there rip your head off. Maybe it's just like jail – you're there for a while and then you're released and come home."

"I don't know."

"Well, here's what I know. I want to see her again, even if it's only for a few minutes. I'd like to revive our friendship, but even if we can't, at least I'd like to say I tried. I think you'd like to do the same thing, too."

"No way, if I know what you're thinking."

"No, listen, listen. I want to see her. The facility is only a few miles away. It's an easy trip there and back. But I also think you feel the same, and I want you to come with me. It would be easier if we did it together. It would be like old times, what do you say?"

"Not on your life, Luke. I was never as close to her as you were, and there's no way I'm going to risk Ms. Royce's wrath by doing something so foolish. What if we got caught? Did you even think about the consequences if we got caught? Maybe we would end up at the facility; maybe they would actually put something on our records. Do you want to risk that?"

"Be serious. That won't happen."

"And do you have any idea how we would get there and back in a single day? I don't have a car, and I can't drive. Do you have a car?"

"No, but…"

"Are you going to ask Ms. Royce to give us a ride there? You're out of your mind. I'm sorry. I didn't mean that. It's just that there's no simple way to get there, even if I were to agree to it. And I don't."

"No, no, no, think about it. It's simple. Forget the car. We can…"

"You better not say change. I gave that up when we were caught. I won't risk it. And if you know what's good for you, you won't risk it either. Besides, if you recall, I was a swan, and traveling as a swan would be even slower than traveling on human feet, than hopping on one human foot. Luke, please, put all that out of your mind."

"No, it can be done…"

"I'm sure it can, but not by me."

"No, listen. Don't give in to your fears. The risk is minimal. It's easier than you think, and the best thing about it is that we'll be able to see Iowa. I have it figured out…"

"Luke, please," Dana practically shouted. "I'm not going to do it. I know what you're asking me, and I won't do it. I gave my word to Ms. Royce, and I'm going to keep it. Do you understand me? Furthermore…Luke, I have to be honest. I'm not as eager to see Iowa as you. I feel for her, I'll always remember her fondly – and, truly, Luke, I think Press is wrong to blame her, because nobody forced us to do what we did, nobody held a gun to our heads. We are responsible for our actions. But I'm just not ready to see her now. I'm not sure I'll ever be ready. So even if you had a car, I wouldn't go, not now. Do you understand where I'm coming from?"

"Okay, Dana, I understand. But you know what I don't understand? I don't understand how you can take responsibility for your own actions and yet refuse to see her. She's not to blame for what happened, is she? Can you explain this?"

Dana became silent. At first, Luke was positive that he had made his point effectively. But as the silence continued, he began to fear that he had only succeeded in angering her and that she would hang up any second. He was surprised, however, when she broke the uncomfortable silence, for her tone was calm and pleasant, just what he always expected from her.

"Luke, this isn't about responsibility," she began, and Luke could visualize Dana shaking her head as she spoke. "I don't want to see Iowa, because I don't know her anymore. Do you want to know something? I'm not even sure that I knew her when we were together. Once she started changing, her personality was different and, to be honest, she wasn't the same Iowa that we knew and loved. Press is right that Iowa deserted us. If she were truly our friend, if she truly believed that we were all family, then she wouldn't have done such a thing. Don't you see? She no longer considered us her family, and we shouldn't have been surprised that she left us without saying a word because we didn't know who she was. This is why we were hurt and why some of us are still angry with her. Luke, I'm just not comfortable risking everything to see a stranger."

Luke tried to interject something but Dana immediately silenced him.

"Excuse me, but you don't know her, either. Maybe you did at one time, maybe we all did, but it's been too long and too many things have happened, and there's simply no way of knowing who or what she is today."

"I don't agree. I know exactly who she is. But there's only one way to find out…"

"Luke, I wish you the best of luck," Dana interjected before he could finish his sentence. "I hope everything goes your way. When you come back, you can tell me all about it. I don't think Press will be interested, though."

Luke knew the conversation was over. It was obvious that she wasn't going to change her mind and so, after a few irrelevant pleasantries, the call officially ended. Luke had been positive that Dana would speak differently about Iowa once Press was out of the picture, and yet she said more or less the same thing she said at lunch, even implying that the Cygnets were dead. He was under no illusion that Iowa's reappearance would bring the Cygnets back together as if the past had never happened, but at the same time it didn't seem unreasonable to hope that it would break down some of the barriers between the Cygnets that had been erected that night. What was equally troubling was Dana's refusal to accompany him to the Lordan facility. This by itself dashed his inchoate plan to visit Iowa, although if asked he couldn't have explained why she was pivotal to his plan, why her refusal scuttled it, or why he couldn't go without her.

Luke went to bed that evening brooding over what he believed was a lost opportunity. From time to time, in between periods of anger over Dana's refusal and Press' manipulations, he also considered the anguish Iowa would experience if she knew that her friends, her former friends, had once again deserted her. Although Luke would eventually realize the error of such assumptions, for now the night seemed black and unending and everything else pointless, even his homework.

Chapter Six

Luke didn't see Dana or Press the following day at school. After the last bell, Luke went immediately home. Normally, there were a couple of projects that would keep him late, and there were also times when it was pleasant to spend an hour or two after school in the library, even if it were Friday. But this afternoon, he didn't want to spend one extra second at school, especially if there were the least chance of bumping into Press or Dana, who wouldn't have to say a word to elicit conflicting thoughts in his mind.

In fact, in his eagerness to go home and leave the school behind him, Luke practically jogged the three blocks to his house. Once inside with the front door securely closed behind him, he began singing in a loud voice, carefully articulating every word of an old song, as if to sing it any other way would diminish what needed to burst forth from inside him. "Oooooh," he began in the middle of the song, "the old gray mule, she ain't what she used to be; she ain't what she used to be; she ain't what she used to be..." He sang the lines several times, each time a little louder and a little livelier, although he was forced to repeat the same lines several times because he didn't know the rest of the lyrics or, as a matter of fact, if what he was singing was actually a song or something he heard once, maybe when he was a child in kindergarten or even earlier in day care.

Luke's mother and father had been sitting in the living room only a few feet away from the door, and when Luke burst through the door and began singing, his mother jumped up from her chair in surprise and his father, who had been drowsing on the lounger a few feet away from his wife, sat upright and knocked his glasses (which had been resting on his lap) onto the carpet under the front edge of his chair. Quickly reaching down and fumbling around for them, he was relieved that he found them and put them on before he accidently stepped on them.

For several years now, Luke had been a serious, often dour individual who arrived home quietly and unobtrusively. Naturally, he hadn't always been like this, and the onslaught of the teenage years didn't adequately explain why a happy, exuberant boy turned into a taciturn old man practically overnight. The advent of changing, the incident at the lake, and the punishment and refactoring certainly took their toll on the boy. But there was something else that was at the root of his altered personality, something that was perhaps more fundamental than any of this: Luke couldn't get over the sense that his behavior at the lake deeply disappointed and embarrassed his parents. Because he loved and admired his parents, especially his father, the sensation gnawed at him, particularly after he found out that they were Changers, too, which he discovered when the three of them conferred with Ms. Royce over the terms of his punishment and refactoring.

Luke's behavior at the lake did indeed disappoint them. Luke's father didn't understand how his son could have been so reckless and thoughtless, and he made sure that Luke heard him thank his "lucky stars" that "things" hadn't been worse. But Luke's father eventually had to admit that children make mistakes, and that the world generally doesn't end because of a child's error in judgment. "Children are children," he informed his wife as if she wasn't aware of this fact, "and if they didn't make mistakes, they wouldn't be children. I suppose if mistakes are going to be made, there's no better time to make them." Luke's parents, however, were convinced that he wouldn't repeat his mistakes, and his father was confident that Luke would learn from what happened and would pull himself together to lead a normal, uneventful, and pleasant childhood. And, for a short while, their optimism wasn't misplaced. While Luke wasn't his old self, he nevertheless undertook his refactoring lessons energetically, and he seemed to be well on his way to putting the whole, ugly mess behind him. But a few months into the process, Luke's parents noticed that his buoyant personality didn't return; and, even though he continued to apply himself to refactoring and school, he began to withdraw into himself more and more until he became a stranger that looked exactly like their son.

The once vibrant house, which had reverberated with childish songs, constant chatter, and endless jokes, became dull and drab, and Luke's mother began to despair that she and her husband had lost their vivacious son, possibly forever. On this day, however, Luke's antics revived memories of better times, and Luke's mother, after briefly thinking that Luke was physically ill, began to hope again that he was getting better and that the small house might again see better days. Luke's father, after wondering if Luke was up to something, started to think more or less along the same lines as his wife, although he tempered his emotions in case the boy's happy behavior was a momentary aberration or that he was indeed up to something.

"My goodness, Sweetie," Luke's mother laughed. "I haven't seen you like this in some time."

Luke bounded over to his mother and, gently holding her right hand with his left and putting his right arm around her back, began dancing a waltz to a tune that he made up on the spot.

"Luke, Luke, Luke," she laughed even louder. "What had gotten into your head?"

Luke's father, firmly in possession of his glasses, remained seated and mumbled something to the effect that he was glad Luke was finally back home. Picking up his paper and opening it to an article he had been reading earlier in the afternoon, the man mumbled something else about homework and the "high spirits of young men."

Luke released his mother and guided her back into her chair. Watching her cheerful boy dance alone, she felt happier and looked younger than she had in several long years. Although she wanted to know what precipitated this abrupt change in his personality, she was reluctant to ask him anything about it, fearing that her question might precipitate a relapse. You never know with people's psyches. But as she watched him, she couldn't resist probing him for some information. 'If he's really back,' she told herself, 'one little question isn't going to make a difference.' "Luke, sweetie," she began with some hesitation, "you're so cheerful tonight. Did something happen at school? You don't have any homework for the night?"

Luke plopped himself down in front of his mother's chair and, crossing his legs Indian style, he smiled broadly and said, "No reason. I'm just happy, that's all."

"That's all? Well, you seem awfully happy."

"Okay, mom, I am awfully happy. When's dinner? I am awfully hungry, too."

"No, really, Luke. I am so pleased that you're so…happy. It's been a long time, and I…well, dear, I want you to be happy like this all the time, forever."

Luke reached up and took her soft hands, which had been in her lap. "Really, there's no reason. I guess I decided to forget all the bad things. Does that make sense?"

"It does," she replied. "Thirty minutes to dinner." She smiled pleasantly, knowing that Luke was unlikely to provide any more details and that for the time being it didn't matter

"I'm off to my room until dinner, mother, father. Wish me the best." Luke jumped up and charged to his room and slammed the door shut. Because he hated hearing doors slammed, he opened it up and, poking his head out, hollered, "Sorry."

Having closed his door soundlessly this time, Luke spun around and leaped backwards onto his bed. He hadn't done anything like that in ages, and the thrill of bouncing on his bed, in addition to the clanging sound the springs made when he landed, elicited some early memories he was surprised that he still retained. When he was five or six, he often jumped up and down on his bed with such vigor that his father would demand that he cease immediately or else he would give the boy something to do to work off his excessive energy. Luke knew his father was kidding about the excessive energy, although he realized only later that violently shaking bed rattled knickknacks around the house, which also hindered his father's ability to concentrate on his newspapers, books, and naps. But it was hard to resist, especially when he landed on his back and experienced a delicious feeling of floating on his overly stuffed bed.

This time, after floating and knowing that his father was unlikely to come to his room to put him to work, Luke closed his eyes and thought about Iowa. He had never been angry with her and never once blamed her for what had happened. As he said to Dana or Press, he couldn't remember which, they had all been responsible for their own actions, and blaming Iowa was nothing less than trying to make her responsible for what they did. Maybe it's human nature, but it's also dishonest and disrespectful. He missed Iowa. When she tapped him with her stick just under his right eye (one had to look closely to find the scar), he wasn't very angry and he didn't think that such an action (deliberate or not) merited a break in their friendship. He loved her. Even when she disappeared the first time, when the Smiths came to take her after mother died (her father was already dead), he wasn't angry that she didn't inform the Cygnets and he continued to believe that one day they would start a life together. Perhaps a silly belief for one so young, and yet at the time he couldn't imagine living apart from her.

Observing a thin crack that separated one half of the ceiling from the other, Luke wondered what it would be like living on one side of the crack and being unable to cross to the other side. He thought of Iowa, who was on the opposite side, and tried to imagine what her life was like at the zoo. Even though he had been to the zoo when he was younger, the experience didn't tell him about life inside the cages or about the manner in which Changers were rehabilitated in the zoo. Some of the information he had came from parents and authorities, but very little of it was consistent and some of it simply didn't make sense. He learned a little about the facilities from Ms. Royce, the one person who had first-hand knowledge, but she never described anything in detail. She confirmed that they existed, she explained the purpose behind them, and she noted that no Changer in his or her right mind would want to end up in one of them, given the very real possibility that the individual would never leave.

Iowa didn't deserve it. She wasn't the kind of person who needed to spend her days behind bars with real animals, a source of amusement for parents and children on warm summer days when school was out of session. She didn't need to be subjected to all the efforts to alter her mind so that it functioned again like a human being's, as Ms. Royce described, because she was a human being, not an animal, and she was kind hearted and fun and loving, and nothing like person Press described whenever she spoke of their close friend. If this weren't so, there was no way of explaining why Iowa reached out to him after the first time she disappeared, which occurred before she brought the knowledge of changing to the Cygnets. If this weren't so, there was no sense to her constant support of him even when he chose to be a dog. The others, especially Press, immediately turned against him and demanded that he leave them alone, but Iowa defended him and supported his choice. Luke knew that she was disappointed by his choice, but at the same time he felt certain that she would have stood by him no matter what and that if she hadn't disappeared, they would be close friends to this day.

Tucking his arms behind his head, Luke closed his eyes and told himself that none of it mattered anymore – not the fact that Iowa had been gone for over three years, not the fact that Dana refused to entertain the possibility that she and Iowa could still be friends, and not the fact that

Press couldn't say a single nice thing about one of their best and most loyal friends – none of it mattered anymore, because Iowa was nearby and, for reasons that he couldn't fathom, seemed closer to him than ever before. Three years ago, was it childish to think that he loved her? Three years ago, was it foolish to want to marry her and spend the rest of his life with her? Today, was it equally crazy to desire the same things, especially when he still had over a year left of high school?

Luke was half asleep when he again imagined himself walking through the gates of the Lordan Zoo, following a long, winding path to a special pond at the heart of the grounds, and, shielding his eyes from the sun's bright glare on the water, searching for Iowa, searching for the subtle ripples on the water's glass-like surface that betrayed her presence. It didn't take long to find her. But instead of locating a beautiful, white swan at the center of the pond, he saw Iowa in human form, sitting on a small rock near the water's edge. She was dressed in a long, white dress that hung loosely around her body; and as a gentle breeze came up, the dress pressed against the front of her body while the rest fluttered behind her. Her hair, bright and almost luminous, swept around her head like a nimbus, while her smooth face and blue eyes looked almost exactly the way they did the last time her saw her. She had grown, of course, and yet there was no mistaking who she was – and there was no mistaking whom she was waiting for.

Iowa leaped off the rock the second the second Luke looked at her, flying into his arms and uttering breathlessly, "I knew you would come. I knew you would come. I knew you would come." Luke took her hands and, leaving the zoo as boldly as he entered it, brought her back to town and, shortly after that, to the school, where the Cygnets gathered around her again as if the past had ceased to exist, as if everything that had happened had either been forgotten or had been pushed aside so that it no longer mattered. Even Press was happy to see her again. She held Iowa tightly as tears flooded her eyes, and she insisted that life hadn't made sense while she was gone. Maybe life wouldn't be perfect after she returned (refactoring would certainly continue, as would Ms. Royce's periodic inspections, and they wouldn't be allowed to gather around the lake as they once did), but life wasn't supposed to be perfect, whereas happiness, which was dependent on the inherent imperfection of life, would surround them and brighten the rest of their days.

Luke woke up with a start. Sitting up, he looked around his darkening room. The sun was going down outside, and, as he tried to gather his senses, he heard his mother calling him for dinner. "Luke," she said, "Don't make me come to get you, otherwise you'll have to dance with me again."

"Coming," he replied and stretched his neck and shoulders. As he was standing up, he began to wonder if there was a way he could communicate with her. It would be impossible if she were still a swan, but if she weren't, if she were able to speak or write, then he might at least send her a line or two, get information on how she was doing, where she was at in zoo, and on the best time of reaching her. But maybe that wasn't realistic, he reconsidered, since she probably wasn't in any directory and the only other means of finding this information required visiting the zoo and making inquiries.

"Luke, are you coming to dinner?"

Luke began walking to the door. Grasping the door knob, he paused. 'How would you find her at the zoo? Would you ask for her by name or would you look for the swans? There's got to be a sizeable exhibit of swans. How would you distinguish one from the other? Would she recognize me if she were still a swan? And if she did recognize me, how would we communicate if she didn't change back?'

"Luke," his father called out. "Dinner table, now!"

Luke walked into the kitchen and apologized for being late. The family said a short prayer before eating, while Luke imagined seeing Iowa again.

Chapter Seven

Luke mulled over a number of things throughout the weekend. Late Friday evening, he decided that he needed to speak to Dana one more time, but her mother informed him that she was out with friends and didn't know when she would return. The idea that Dana had friends who weren't Cygnets surprised him (he knew she had friends, but being informed of this fact was tantamount to a slap in the face), but he had the presence of mind to leave his name and number for her to return his call.

After hanging up, Luke leaned back in the oversized lounger next to the phone, the very chair favored by his father for his afternoon naps. Staring into the space in front of him, he began to recall a time when none of them had friends apart from the other Cygnets, when the very definition of friendship meant one's close relationship with the other Cygnets. At one time, the Cygnets actually refused to have friends outside of their group, and yet three years later, Dana not only had several friends but she was also spending entire days and sometimes nights with these wonderful people. Lu and Press probably had a network of close friends, too, although that wouldn't have surprised him quite as much. Lu was quiet and somewhat needy, and it only made sense that living in a town surrounded by strangers, she would develop a network of new friends. Press apparently wanted to divorce herself from everyone except Dana. It was quite likely that since the breakup, she made any number of new connections, especially since she was star athlete.

Dana, though, was different. Of all the Cygnets, she had been the most loyal, the most dedicated to the idea of the Cygnets, and it was hard to believe that she could divorce herself from the others like Press and Lu did. Perhaps he was wrong, but when he remembered their last conversation, he couldn't quite convince himself that she was just like Press and Lu. Yes, she claimed the Cygnets were dead – and yes, she said her friendship with Iowa was as moribund as her relationship with the group – and yet there was something in what she said that seemed to indicate the opposite. Despite her fear of alienating Press, she made it clear that she still considered herself his friend, and there was no reason to doubt her word on that score. No, he told himself, Dana was not at all like Press and Lu, although saying this made him feel a little funny, perhaps a little naive. Luke immediately regretted this suspicion. Reminding himself that he had no reason to doubt Dana, he noted that it was Press' and Lu's behavior (especially Press') that created a doubt in his mind about a close friend. Dana was different.

While Luke waited impatiently for Dana's call, strumming his fingers on the phone, picking up the receiver to make sure it still had a dial tone, and staring at the unit as if that could make it come alive, it occurred to him that it might not be reasonable to expect a call from her that evening. It was late, and, even if she came through the door immediately after her mother hung up, she might be reluctant to call because of the time (she probably thought his parents retired early). Getting up and leaving the phone (patting it a couple of times in the process as if to provide reassurance that he trusted it to put the call through when Dana was ready), Luke reluctantly went to his room where he told himself that a person of Dana's sensitivity would probably return his call Saturday morning or Saturday afternoon, at the very latest. But as Saturday morning merged into Saturday evening, Luke's emotions grew correspondingly strained. At one point in the afternoon, he wondered if Dana wasn't calling because she didn't want to talk about Iowa. At another point in the evening, he suspected that Press got wind of his call and was counseling Dana to ignore him. He might have called Dana again, but by Sunday noon he had begun to think that he had been wrong about her and that she was rude and insensitive for not returning his call. These thoughts grew throughout the day so that by the evening it was impossible for him to call: Luke didn't want to speak to anyone for any reason. Had he called Dana again Saturday morning, he would have reached her mother, who would have apologized profusely for having placed the note with his number on it in her pocket and promptly forgotten about it. Had he called any other time throughout the weekend, he would have reached Dana, who was unaware of his call, who was home all weekend, and who would have spoken to him about his plan even though she still would have refused to participate.

Despite his anger, or maybe because of it, Luke was determined to speak to Dana when Monday morning rolled around. Much calmer after having a solid night's sleep Sunday night, he told himself on his way to school that Dana may have had a legitimate reason for not returning his call and that he would be remiss in not giving her a chance to explain. Besides, what he needed to say was too important to toss aside because she was insensitive or didn't want to speak about Iowa. Sitting in his first class, he added that he needed to find her before Press did, otherwise neither he nor Dana would have a chance to say what remained to be said.

Luke didn't find Dana before lunch. Since he didn't know her schedule, he prowled the halls between classes, but he was either looking in the wrong halls or he simply missed her in the mass of students moving from one class to another. (Naturally, he didn't expect to hold a serious conversation with her in the din between classes; he only wanted to set a time and place to meet where they could talk freely without Press hovering around.) But failing to find her after his fifth class, Luke started to wonder if she were out for the day (sick) and then began to fear that the only place he could find her was in the cafeteria, with Press. During lunch break after his sixth class, Luke went to the cafeteria not to eat but to search for Dana. If she were in school, he reasoned, she would have to go to the cafeteria around this time. He was resigned, however, to the likelihood that Press would be with her (although, if given a choice, he would have chosen to have her sick than sitting with Press), but he was somewhat hopeful that she would understand the importance of what he had to say and would extract herself from Press' claws for a few minutes.

He positioned himself in the far corner near the trashcans, which provided a direct view of the cafeteria entrance and, if he somehow missed her arrival, an almost face-to-face view of everyone emptying their trash. Luke had been eyeing everyone entering the large room for nearly ten minutes when he spotted Dana setting down a tray on the same table that she and Press occupied when he broke the good news. Surprised that he hadn't seen her enter, he was even more surprised that she was alone: Press wasn't visible anywhere. Without searching for Press, Luke immediately walked to the table and stood across from Dana, who had just sat down and placed her lunch in front of her.

"Dana," he began, and hesitated. Looking at her innocent, upturned face, he suddenly felt guilty for the things he had been thinking over the weekend. "Dana, I tried to call…do you mind if I sit down?"

"Oh, yes, please do," she replied in a voice that was every bit as pleasant as her face. "You called me?'

"You didn't know?"

"No, when was this?"

Luke shook his head slightly, suddenly realizing the mistake he made in not trying to call her again. "It doesn't matter," he began and, knowing that he didn't have a lot of time (lunch wasn't very long, and Dana's non-Cygnet friends could stop by any second), he launched into what he needed to tell her. "Look, I understand everything you said on the phone last week, but there's something else I need to tell you that might make a difference."

Dana's eyes narrowed, making Luke a little uncomfortable.

Glancing from one side to the other, as if he had to impart a great secret, Luke leaned toward Dana. "I...I have a plan. It's going to get us to Iowa, and..."

Dana had been leaning toward Luke to share in his secret, but the second he mentioned Iowa she straighten up in her chair and eyed him warily. "Luke," she interrupted, "I thought I was perfectly clear. I'm not going to do it, and I'm not going to get involved with anything that's going to get me into more trouble. Luke, didn't you understand what I was saying..."

Before Dana finished, Press showed up, holding a lunch tray. She stopped at the edge of the table to catch their attention and grimaced, as if it were painful to see Luke again. Persevering in spite of the pain, Press placed her tray on the table, set out her lunch and, after putting her tray next to her under the table, sat down next to Dana and across from Luke. She glanced at Dana and Luke before saying, "So, what am I missing this time?"

"Nothing," Dana responded, "unless you forgot something in the line." She tried to smile, but neither Press nor Luke responded.

"Press," Luke said, carefully and seriously, "I know you don't like me, and so I'll leave in just a minute. But would you mind if I spoke to Dana alone for a few minutes? All I need..."

"Why are you asking me, Luke?" Press responded, acting now as if she didn't care whether Luke was at the table or not. "That's up to her. But, since you asked, Dana and I had planned to meet today at lunch. Hence...," she concluded, motioning to Dana with her left arm. "By the way, I don't recall Dana mentioning you'd be here."

"Press, please," Dana began, trying to keep everyone calm.

"Dana, please," he said, ignoring Press.

She shook her head. "Luke, I've said all that I'm going to say on the subject. We can talk about this, but I'm not going to change my mind."

"Change your mind?" Press interjected. "Change your mind about what?"

"Press, this is between me and Dana. Dana, please, let me speak to you alone for one minute."

"She doesn't need to speak to you privately. Anything she says can be said in front of me."

Dana turned to Press. Her expression was serious this time, and it was clear to Press and Luke that she had had enough of the bickering. "Press, let me handle this."

"What is it, Luke?" Press interjected. "Still mooning over Iowa? That's it, isn't it?"

"Press, stop…"

Dana glowered at her friend, but Press didn't return the look. Instead, she stared at Luke, looking directly into his eyes as if she were trying to read his mind. 'He's in love with Iowa,' she told herself and smiled sarcastically as Luke turned away.

"Dana, please," Luke repeated.

Press was now smiling because she was confident that Dana wasn't going to give into Luke's entreaties. Whatever Luke had to say, he either had to say it in front of her or not at all.

Dana turned to Press and, after a moment's hesitation, said, "I'll be back in a minute. Save my seat, please."

Press' smile immediately disappeared, and she sat up straight as she watched Luke and Dana leave the cafeteria. Dana knew that Press would be angry when she returned, but she also knew that her friend's anger would disappear quickly. Despite her anger and various resentments, Press did have a good heart, even if it wasn't always evident when it came to Luke and Iowa.

Chapter Eight

Outside and away from most of the students, Luke and Press sat down side by side on one of the narrow, cement benches on the side of the building. The day was warm and clear, and as Luke glanced up at the clear sky, he hoped that Dana would have a change of mind after she heard him. She seemed adamant only a few minutes ago, and now she was willing to listen to him privately, without Press' interventions, both of which he felt boded well.

"Okay, Luke," Dana began once they had settled onto the bench. "Press isn't here, so tell me what's on your mind."

"Dana, I...," Luke began hesitantly, clasping his hands between his knees and looking down toward his feet. He couldn't help noticing the sparse lawn and oval patches of bare dirt beneath and around the bench, which were doubtless made by shoes such as his sliding and scraping what once must have been lawn. Turning to Dana, he was encouraged that her pleasant expression returned, and, as he observed her smooth skin and chubby cheeks, as well as her perfectly formed ears, both lobes of which sported a diamond stud, he began to feel comfortable and ready to say what he needed to say. "Look, I'm going to see Iowa." He turned his shoulders in her direction and, sitting on the edge of the bench, noticed the concern that quickly came across her face. "Please, don't say anything until I'm finished."

"I've already told you what I thought about it, Luke."

"I know, I know, but...well, we weren't speaking face to face, and you know as well as I do that it's easy to disguise your feelings and say things you don't mean when you're on the phone."

"I meant everything I said..."

"Please, just hear me out. I know what you said, and I also know that...that you love her as much as I do. You want to see her every bit as much as I do."

"I suppose I still love her, but probably not the way you think. I mean, I love my memories of her, and I love the person she used to be. But, Luke, I was telling you the truth. I don't know who she is now. As far as anyone knows, she could be a vastly different person than she once was. It's been too long, too many things have happened, and, well, we're all different people now. Do you understand what I'm getting at? I don't know; maybe if she were here now, we could…"

"But that's just it," Luke chimed in. He wanted to grasp Dana's small, delicate hands, but he resisted the temptation and leaned back slightly. "She's not, but we can see her and find out. No, please, let me finish. You said you don't know her anymore, but this is our chance to find out who she is, what's happened to her, and all the rest. This may be the only chance we have, and doesn't that make it worth the effort to pursue? Look, Dana, I've got it all figured out. We can see her this weekend. If we go together, everything will be easier and safer. We can be there and back in a day…"

"Luke," Dana said, smiling slightly and patting lightly Luke's right forearm. "This is something you need to do. I'll tell you what: If she comes back, I'll sit down and talk to her, if she's interested. I'm willing to talk to her about anything. I'm even willing to hold out hope that we can be friends again. But, as I told you on the phone, I'm not going to go with you to find her."

"Why not? You just said…"

Dana briefly closed her eyes and put her hands up to stop Luke. "Even if she were our Iowa, I'm not going to help you find her. I gave my word to Ms. Royce not to violate the terms of the agreement. I won't do that for anything. It's my word, and I won't…"

"I gave my word, too, Dana, and I also gave my word to Iowa that I would always be her friend. I'm going to find her." Luke glared at her, and for a few moments she wasn't certain whether he was angry or merely insisting on his point of view. In a sense, it was both, because he couldn't understand how she could refuse after everything he said – how she could still refuse when they were speaking about one of their closest friends. Luke's anger dissipated quickly, though, when he noticed the look of concern that came over her face and, shortly after that, when he recalled how kind she had always been, how willing she had been to stand by him while Press was breathing fire and brimstone. Dana was a good friend, too, and the last thing he wanted to do was to scare or offend her. She was too nice, too supportive. Luke suddenly realized that it was over. He wasn't going to change her mind, and if he continued trying, he would only offend the only Cygnet (apart from Iowa) who was still willing to speak to him.

Leaning back, he smiled as if she had misunderstood his intent. "I'm sorry," he said. "I understand and support your decision. I hope you're not angry with me because I brought this up again. I apologize if I've pressured you in any way."

"I'm not angry, Luke," she said, her pleasant expression coming back. I wish you the best, and I truly hope you find Iowa. Tell me what happens, will you?"

Press was waiting for Dana when she returned. She had finished her lunch and was clearly angry with Dana for speaking to Luke. Without saying a word, she picked up the trash from the table and placed it on her tray.

Dana understood Press' feelings and, as she always did, sought to make peace with her. "I feel sorry for Luke."

Press stopped cleaning up and looked at her. "You feel sorry for everybody."

"Sometimes I do. But there's nothing wrong with that."

"What if they don't deserve your sympathy?"

Dana smiled at Press and began cleaning up her trash, too, although she hadn't finished her lunch. "They do," she added when she was done.

Both girls stood up at the same time and picked up their trays. Dana started walking toward the trash bins when Press stopped her. "I'm not a monster, Dana," she said, tears welling in her eyes. "I know what Luke is going to do. How could I not? He's more like a brother to me than anyone in my family. Sometimes you fight with brothers, you know what I mean? I truly hope it goes okay, Dana, and I hope that Iowa is well and that we see her again. I miss..." Press couldn't say anything else and turned and walked to the trash bins.

Dana and Press walked silently to class together. After leaving the cafeteria, walked down one long hallway, turned the corner, and walked down a much shorter hallway lined with lockers. Press paused in front of her locker and, after fidgeting with the combination lock, retrieved her notebook and textbook. They continued to Dana's locker, where she retrieved her books. The classrooms were only a few feet away and, just as the girls were about to go in different directions, Dana stopped and touched Press on the arm.

"You aren't going to say anything, are you?"

"About what?"

"You know, about Luke and what he might be planning to do."

"Don't you think we're obligated to say something? What if…"

Before Press finished, the school bell rang, signaling that the classes were starting.

"Maybe," Dana responded, and started for her classroom. Stopping again, she turned back and looked at Press. "Maybe, but I'm not going to say anything," she said firmly.

Press smiled. "Neither am I."

Chapter Nine

Luke was sullen by the time he returned home from school. His conversation with Dana had certainly been friendly enough, but he was disappointed by the results and as the school day progressed his disappointment gradually turned to anger. While he was pleased that Dana had softened her stance toward Iowa, he was nevertheless put off by her unwillingness to help him find her. It was true that his plan was little more than a desire to visit Iowa; but he was confident that with Dana involved, they could come up with something that would enable him to visit Iowa and ensure that neither Ms. Royce nor anyone else was any the wiser. She didn't want to participate, though; she refused to participate; and even though she was willing to reap the benefits of a well-executed plan, she wasn't willing to lift her little finger to ensure its success.

Luke was still convinced that he needed Dana's help, and her refusal not only meant that the plan was dead but that there was no plan at all. But as Luke worked through these issues, he gradually came to the conclusion (during the last class of the day) that it wasn't Dana's fault that his plan to see Iowa wasn't going to happen. No, and it was unfair to hold her completely responsible when she actually admitted that she wanted him to succeed. Dana couldn't be the responsible party. It was Press. Press, for some reason, controlled Dana's thoughts like a puppet master, and when the puppet master pulled the invisible strings, Dana jumped and danced and only opened her mouth to voice Press' words.

Once at home, Luke headed directly to his room, telling his mother in passing that he would come out only when dinner was ready. "I'm tired, and I have a ton of homework," he added coldly as he closed his bedroom door behind him. His mother, who was desperate to see her son's spirits rise, was shocked by his lifeless words and harsh facial expression and, later, as she stirred the special sauce for the evening's dinner, she shed silent tears. The poor woman was afraid that her son had suffered a major relapse and would never again assume his formerly loving and cheerful demeanor. Luke's father tried to lift everyone's spirits during dinner by highlighting some of the absurd things he read in the morning paper, and a couple of times he couldn't resist making some feeble puns on the names of some noteworthy but unworthy politicians. Nothing worked, and before dinner was even halfway over, they were all reduced to complete silence, each preoccupied with Luke's problems. Immediately after dinner, Luke went back to his room, while his parents went to the living room where they sat silently wondering when things would finally get better for their beloved child.

In his darkened room (the sun was down by this time, and the only light came from a small, feeble lamp on the far corner of his desk on the opposite wall), Luke fell chest-down on his bed and dangled his long arms over the sides. Burying his face in his pillow, he mulled over Dana's refusal and then Press' angry denunciations (as it seemed to him). It was one thing to dislike Iowa, but quite another to prevent someone from visiting her simply because they disliked their former friend. Why should Press care about any of this? Would it hurt anyone if Dana helped him reach Iowa? Why was it her business, anyway, since the trip didn't involve her and she didn't have to hear any of the details before or after? And Dana…what had happened to Dana to make her so dependent on Press? He was foolish to think that she would change her mind, since it was clear to him that Press had already made it up for her.

Luke slowly closed his eyes and tried to put everything out of his mind. He especially wanted to forget his interactions with Dana and Press, which robbed him of his energy and his desire to do anything productive. He didn't even want to think about Iowa, for that would only fill him with a painful longing for something that he couldn't have. Engulfed in a black void that had neither shape nor dimension, Luke relaxed and within minutes he felt as if he were floating or perhaps suspended somewhere in an infinite space in which there was nothing but the sounds of nature, the whoosh of a gentle breeze, the cooing of rock doves, the chirruping of crickets. While focusing his attention on the sound of the doves, trying to determine the direction from which the sounds originated since they seemed to swirl around him, Luke gradually became aware of the slow rumbling of thunder, which because of its muffled timbre suggested that it was emanating from somewhere over the wooded park that bordered his neighborhood and that stretched out for miles. Once the thunder subsided, a strange, almost suffocating silence (the doves, crickets, and everything else were curiously quiet) surrounded him until, a few minutes later, the wind picked up and began howling and banging tree limbs against his window. The thunder reappeared almost instantaneously, although this time it was much louder and signaled that the storm was coming his way, if not already overhead. But just as the storm's fury seemed the most violent, it suddenly stopped and everything around his was quiet again, as if the storm had an eye that was passing directly overhead.

Luke still didn't open his eyes. He was tired and, knowing that the thunder would reappear in a few minutes, rolled onto his side and angled his back to block some of the light and noise should the storm return. For a few moments, his room and everything surrounding was once more deathly still, until he heard a vague voice saying something from somewhere outside his window. Luke tried to understand what the voice was saying, but it became fainter and fainter until it was almost impossible to hear, as if the speaker were somewhere at the end of a long tube.

Eyes closed, Luke rolled over to his other side to face the window and listened intently for the voice or whatever it was, if it was still there. It was quiet. The storm was finally gone, and he couldn't hear even traces of it anywhere. He began to relax, began to appreciate the solitude, and was ready to go to sleep when the voice came back.

"Luke," the voice whispered. It was a girl's voice, which was faint as if the speaker's strength were ebbing quickly. "Luke," it said again, a little more strongly this time but still decidedly weak, "Luke, Luke, can you hear me?"

The voice quickly became louder and more insistent, as if the disembodied speaker had moved closer to him, perhaps stopping just outside his window. Indeed, as the volume of the voice rose, Luke thought for a moment that he could easily reach outside his window and lift the speaker up by her nose. He might even have tried it, too, but the voice suddenly shrieked "Luke," which startled him because of the strength of the voice and its unexpected familiarity. For the first time since it initially uttered his name, Luke thought that he recognized the voice of the speaker – it was someone he knew, someone who was very close to him – although he couldn't quite identify either the voice or the individual behind it. Luke still didn't open his eyes, although he changed his position to hear the speaker better, for he was now convinced that it had something urgent to pass onto him.

"The name, the name," Luke gasped to himself, "what is the name?" The feeling that the speaker was someone very close to him increased, and yet no matter how hard he tried he couldn't recall the name connected with the voice. "Does it start with a P or an S?" he asked himself, as if the sound of his own voice might provide the answer, but the name still eluded him and the voice didn't volunteer any information. It was as if he were being asked to identify someone from the back of their head. What was even more frustrating was that he wanted to ask the speaker her name, but for some reason he couldn't form any words loud enough for anyone to hear, and he couldn't even move off his bed to reach out the window to grasp the speaker's nose.

"Luke," the voiced continued to cry out, but Luke remained frozen.

Luke might have remained that way indefinitely, listening and fretting over the voice that continued calling his name while struggling and failing to respond, had it not been for a loud crash that opened his eyes and forced him to a sitting position.

"Luke, can you hear me?" his mother called out, knocking on his door at the same time. "Luke, are you all right?"

Luke closed and opened his eyes several times and glanced around the room again. Shaking his head to clear his senses, he turned to the dark door and observed two black marks moving back and forth in the ribbon of light beneath it.

"Luke? Is anything wrong?"

"I'm all right, mother," he finally said without getting up. "I dozed off. I'm fine."

"Luke, I heard something fall to the floor. May I peek in?" Her voice had lost its edge of concern and now sounded cautious, as if she were asking a big favor.

"Okay," he replied reluctantly, unsure of whether he had the strength to endure more questions about his health or what was on his mind.

The door opened slowly, letting in a burst of bright light from the hallway. True to her word, Luke's mother poked her head around the edge of the door, the edge of which she led with both hands, and didn't make any other part of her body visible.

"I'm sorry. I didn't mean to wake you, dear. Oh, your lamp is on the floor. Well, I just wanted to tell you that your father and I are going to bed now. Please don't stay up too late. Righty, righty?"

"Yes, mother."

"Luke?"

"Yes, mother."

"Have a good night, dear."

She closed the door as slowly and deliberately as she had opened it. As soon as he heard the soft thud of the door hitting the door frame, and then the familiar click as the latch snapped in place, Luke fell back on his bed and, staring into the black void surrounding him, began to brood over losing what seemed to be the only opportunity he had of seeing Iowa again. She was almost within reach, he told himself, and yet she could have been in another universe for all the good her proximity did for him, since there was no way he could negotiate the distance without help, and Dana was the only one understood the situation and who therefore could have helped him make the trip. Rolling onto his side and curling into a ball, his eyes filling with hot tears of anger, Luke couldn't resist condemning Press for the failure of his plan and the corruption of Dana. "It's bad enough she blamed Iowa for everything," he said to himself, "but did she have to poison Dana, too?"

Luke was positive that Dana loved Iowa as much as he did, and he was absolutely certain that Dana's hesitation, her cautious willingness to see Iowa if she returned, was the result of being conditioned by Press, who had either browbeaten the girl into agreeing with her or made it difficult to disagree without upsetting her and risking their friendship, or both. 'Why did Press care if Dana still loved Iowa? And what right did Press have to insert herself into Dana's business, his business, anyway? Was she worried that she would have to play second fiddle among her friends if Iowa came back? Why did Press have to stick her nose in everything? Who did Press think she was, and, just for once, why couldn't Dana stand up to her? Why? Why? Why?' Luke rolled onto his side and, propping his head up with his right arm and fist, told the shadows at the foot of his bed that he felt sorry for Dana. "It doesn't matter if Dana's willing to see Iowa, because Iowa will never return if Press has anything to do with it." Luke inhaled deeply and was about to relax and go to sleep when he began to have second thoughts about these conclusions.

"Maybe Press is just not thinking carefully," he conceded. "And Dana, well, Dana is just too nice, and I guess I can see why she feels caught between opposing forces. I don't know why I thought she was completely on Press' side, since she's willing to see Iowa again. Press wouldn't do that, and I have no doubt that…but what's the point? I can't go, and that's that." Luke closed his eyes tightly and tried to think of something else. The thunder was gone, and the only sound emanating from beyond his window came from the breeze, which was now less violent but more insistent. For a few minutes, he focused his thoughts on the wind, imagining string-like tendrils of air swirling around every nook and cranny in search of weaknesses through which to enter the house. But the moment when one of the tendrils identified such a weakness and began tugging at one of the slats on the siding, Dana and Press arose in his mind and challenged him to resolve his difficulties with them.

"Dana's got to give me another chance. I know I can convince her if I can speak to her outside of school, away from Press and everything else that's controlling her thoughts. Especially Press – if she knows I'm speaking to Dana, she'll do whatever she can to wreck things. I can't believe her."

Luke opened his eyes and blinked several times to clear his vision. He remained motionless for several minutes, staring blankly into space until his arm became tired and the side of his head ached. Sitting up and, shaking his arm to improve the circulation, Luke looked around his room but it was difficult to see anything clearly because the shadows had deepened and darkened. The small lamp on his desk flickered on and off several times before going off completely, leaving him in almost complete darkness. Sighing, lamenting both his situation and his thoughts about Dana – and, more than anything else, wanting to see Iowa but realizing its impossibility – Luke laid back down on the bed, pulled a cover over his legs and chest, and tried to sleep.

Within seconds, he opened his eyes and sat up. Glancing around his dark room, he could identify almost all the thick shadows populating the space -- the desk, the dresser, the small bookcase, even the pathetically injured sock on the floor. He could see it all clearly, and he didn't need anyone's help to find the desk or the sad sock's soul mate; he didn't need anyone's help to walk from the bed to the desk, from the desk to the door, and from the door to the bed without stumbling or banging into something.

He didn't need anyone's help even if he were blind and or had to negotiate his way in complete darkness – and he didn't need Dana or anyone else helping him reach the zoo during broad daylight. What was so hard about getting from point A to point B, where A was his house and B the zoo in Lordan? He knew where Lordan was, and he also knew that once in the small town, he could easily find the zoo. There was nothing difficult about it. Maybe, he conceded, Dana could have helped him determine the shortest and most direct route, or maybe she could have done something to keep Press from finding out about his trip and informing Ms. Royce and whoever would listen to her. But he could read a map as well as anyone else, and he was confident that Dana would do her best out of friendship to keep Press at bay until he returned.

"Of course, it would be nice to have company," he said to himself in a voice that nearly echoed in the quiet room. "But if she can't travel as fast as me, she'll be a burden right from the start." Luke added in a whisper after a moment's reflection, "Maybe I don't want her there when I see Iowa."

Luke reached across his bed and turned off the little lamp on his desk, which for some reason had begun flickering again. Snuggling under the covers, he felt warm and comfortable, and, for the first time in days, he felt foolish. He had been too dependent on Dana and, when she refused to agree with everything he said, he mentally accused her of all kinds of erroneous and disloyal things. Dana was still a good friend, and he had no right to think those things about her. She was capable of making up her own mind, and, even if she seemed almost too close to Press, she wasn't controlled by the latter or anyone else, for that matter. Maybe it was okay to be concerned about her relationship with Press and, regardless of what Press said, he and all the others would remain friends no matter what happened. Luke forgave Press just as he fell asleep.

Chapter Ten

By the time Luke closed his eyes, his parents had been in bed for several hours. They were lying silently in the dark, unable to sleep, fretting over their son and his inability to handle the problems that had been dogging him for years. Luke's father was resting on his back and, with his thin arms draped across his hairy chest, staring blindly into the darkness. With her back to her husband, Luke's mother rested on her side, but unlike her husband she kept her eyes tightly closed, as if she were afraid of opening them and seeing something that she didn't want to see. Even though they both pretended to be asleep, Luke's father knew that his wife was still awake because he could feel the bed quiver as she silently sobbed, while the unhappy woman could tell that her husband had not fallen asleep because of the tenseness of his body, which was also transmitted through the mattress. Neither one of them had been willing to expose the other's secret.

Only a few days ago, Luke finally seemed to have shaken off the demons that had been dogging him for years and was once again the lively, outgoing child that had filled their house with joy and love. Naturally, they understood the cause of the boy's malaise (they hesitated to use the word depression because of its negative connotations) that had taken control of him three years ago, but at the time they felt that it was a natural reaction. Any good child, they told themselves, any child with a strong sense of right and wrong, would have reacted in the same way to the embarrassment and humiliation of having done something that hurt people and caused others a significant amount of grief. But as the months passed, and then the first anniversary of the event came and went, and Luke was no better (maybe even worse), Luke's parents began to worry, for they couldn't help feeling that his emotional response to those particular events was excessive, out of proportion to the crime itself.

"Luke should be ashamed," his father once exclaimed in frustration over the lack of improvement in his son's attitude. He and his wife were sitting at the dinner table, while Luke was in his room doing his homework. "Yes, he should be ashamed. He made a mistake, and he should never forget that. But enough is enough, already. He took responsibility, he made amends, and now it's time for him to get on with life. By all means, remember the past – that's how we learn and grow – but now it's time for the boy to stop all this nonsense."

Saying this didn't change anything, and Luke's parents sat the boy down on more than one occasion and tried to reason with him. Luke's father, in particular, tried to make him understand that even though personal responsibility was a good thing (a great thing, in fact), whenever one overdid it, whenever it became self-recrimination, it ceased to be good and became destructive. His father was sitting directly across from Luke. Picking up Luke's limp hand, he looked directly into his son's eyes and said, "You've made a mistake, son, and you've owned up to it. I'm proud of you. But now you're compounding the original mistake by letting it control your emotions. Do you understand what I'm telling you, son?" Luke stared blankly at his father, his mind at work on another matter; and when he didn't respond, the man dropped the boy's hand and stood up. Aiming an index finger at the boy's forehead, Luke's father insisted that the boy change his emotional state. "Lighten up, son," he said, a little more forcefully than he intended.

Having failed in their appeal to reason, Luke's parents, particularly his father, tried to shake Luke out of his funk by appealing to his sense of humor, by making him laugh. He didn't try to make Luke see the lighter side of what had happened at the lake (that would have been grotesque); instead, he appealed to his son's love of the absurd, telling him jokes, funny stories, and anything else that might strike his funny bone – anything that would brighten him up, even for a while.

"Tell me something, son," his father said one evening at the dinner table. "Do you know what a cow would watch if it owned a TV? No idea? Not one? You don't want to guess? Okay, how about the movies? Get it? A cow would watch the movies -- moovies. Cows moo, right? That's pretty funny." Luke's father glanced at his wife, who was smiling faintly and then back at Luke. Luke's expression hadn't changed and, without looking at his father, he continued to make his way through his mashed potatoes and ham. "Okay, okay," his father began again, unwilling to let his son pour cold water on what he thought were decent jokes. "Okay, so maybe it wasn't the funniest joke. I hear you. So how about this? Why don't campers go into their tents during a heat wave? Can't guess? Well, that's because when it's hot, the heat's intense. That's a good one, don't you think? When it's hot, in tents, right?" Luke didn't respond to that joke either, nor did he respond to any of the other countless jokes his father shared over dinner, and after a while his father gave up and sat as silently as his son at the table.

Luke's parents refused to give up, and, instead of reason and humor, they decided to use diversions to brighten their son's mental life. They took him to movies (mainly comedies), they enrolled him in afterschool sports programs, and one time they even invited some of the boys from his school to a party at their house. The latter was a complete fiasco, since Luke wouldn't allow the boys into his room, and he wouldn't come out. After a few months, they were exhausted and disappointed, and it was Luke's mother who suggested that what Luke needed was more time and some space to come up with the right solution to his problems. "He has to find his own way," she said, tears welling in her eyes at the thought of her son suffering even more. Luke's father reluctantly agreed. He was skeptical that anything positive would come from the same approach they tried in the beginning, when they allowed him time to do some soul searching because good boys feel humiliation and guilt.

When they were well into the current year, Luke's parents were disillusioned and almost without hope. They had tried everything, and everything had failed, and Luke's mental abyss was every bit as acute as it had been during the first three months after the event. Luke's father had grown sullen as a result, and there were times when he silently blamed his son for being weak and his wife for coddling the boy. Luke's mother, on the other hand, began weeping more frequently and, in moments of desperation, she pleaded with her son to snap out of it, or at least tell her what to do to help him. "Please, dear," she said one time a few months ago, "please tell me what's wrong. Is it school, is it girls, is it the refactoring? What is wrong with you, Luke? Maybe if I know, I can help. But whatever you're doing, it's not helping. Please, Luke, please." Luke had just come out of the bathroom and, after listening to his mother and watching her clasp her hands together as if she were praying to him, he stared at her as if he didn't know why she was asking him such strange questions. Shaking his head, he stepped around her and went back to his room, noting in passing that he had homework. The woman went to her room, fell on her bed, and continued crying, refusing to stop when her husband entered and sat down beside her. "The boy made a mistake," he said quietly, shaking his head. He didn't know what else to say.

Once again, everything seemed to have changed a few days ago when Luke came home singing and dancing. His parents were overjoyed, and they had every reason to assume that whatever it was that had been eating away at him, it was finally gone or on its way out the door. At least that's what Luke's mother thought (or wanted to believe, since her confidence was based in large measure on her desire to have Luke back the way he used to be). Luke's father agreed as well, especially since he hadn't seen either his wife or son this happy in years, and it didn't seem useful to throw water on her happiness simply because he still had his doubts. But while he had little reason to suspect that Luke would revert to the old ways quite so soon, he was still a little concerned that he and his wife were misreading the boy's happiness and that things could change over time. How or why this would happen, he had no idea, but then how or why it happened so intensely in the first place, he was equally at a loss. Unlike his wife, Luke's father wasn't shocked when his son's new-recovered happiness dissipated, but he was taken aback by its suddenness, and for a short time he couldn't help wondering if he had imagined Luke being better. While Luke's mother spent a great deal of her time in the bedroom weeping over her the loss of her prodigal son, Luke's father got over his disbelief and decided that now was the time to enlist outside help for the boy. He had been reluctant to take such a step – he was the boy's father, after all, and it was his job to take care of him – but because the swiftness of the change angered him (it was finally clear that the boy was not going to help himself) and because his wife was now falling apart because of her son, he realized that neither he nor his son could wait any longer for something that should have been done years ago, maybe at the very outset of Luke's problems.

It should be emphasized that Luke's parents weren't blind or ignorant. They learned about Luke's actions shortly after he was apprehended, and they worked with Ms. Royce to devise a treatment and rehabilitation program that would help their son understand the dangers of changing and profit from the treatment. Luke's parents worked with Ms. Royce not as a patient might work with a doctor, following the doctor's regime and providing detailed information on the positive and negative effects of the treatment, but as doctors sharing knowledge and experience, making recommendations only after a careful consideration by all parties (except Luke, of course). They spoke as Changers to another Changer, although it had been years since they had changed. Nevertheless, they still remembered the allure of changing, and they also understood its destructive elements (changing could be as addictive as an illicit drug), which had ruined the lives of several friends when they were all Luke's age. Luke's parents didn't inform Luke about their own abilities until after Ms. Royce passed judgment (although they discussed the punishment as colleagues, only Ms. Royce was allowed by Changer law to pass judgment). Changing had never been an important aspect of their lives, and so they had hoped that by keeping Luke in the dark regarding changing, he would never learn about the ability and events such as the one that brought Luke down would never occur. They were forced to alter some of their calculations when they found out about Luke's activities, and while they were surprised and disappointed that changing had taken control of him, they were both thankful that Ms. Royce had intervened when she did. On dark nights, especially when thunder rumbled overhead and one could detect the rain by its smell, Luke's father would often wonder what might have happened had Ms. Royce not intervened when she did.

Luke's parents also understood their son's sensitive nature. Once, when he was in grade school, Luke endured several painful ant bites when he tried to rescue a black ant that one of his classmates had dropped onto a red ant pile at the edge of the school yard to observe its dismemberment. So while Luke's parents expected Luke to have a fairly difficult time in the aftermath of the event that occurred three years ago, they weren't at all prepared for what eventually happened to their son. Once again, if it hadn't been for Luke's positive change and then relapse, Luke's parents, especially his father, might not have thrown up their hands and sought outside help. But what could they do? The boy's overly sensitive nature had been dragging him down to a point at which they felt powerless to help, and so they felt that they had no other alternative than to seek help from someone else, someone who was not as involved in Luke's young life as they were.

What neither parent knew, however, was that Luke's recent ebullience was due to the possibility of seeing Iowa again, seeing the girl who mattered more to him than probably anyone else, and that his unexpected reversion to his previous, unhappy mental state was the result of the failure – in his eyes – of his plan to visit Iowa and revive the relationship he thought had been lost possibly forever. Luke never told his parents about his feelings for Iowa, and he never informed them about her possible reappearance and his desire to see her once again (Luke, like others his age, wasn't comfortable discussing love and intimacy with his parents). Unknowingly, he had encouraged them to think the worst and had spurred them into putting plans in place that would have some unfortunate side effects.

Luke's father rolled onto his side, his back facing his wife's back, and closed his eyes, determined to get a few hours of sleep before he took the next step. His wife had been on the verge of reaching over to the man to see if he would pull her closer to him, to give her the warmth and security that she lacked that evening. But when he turned away, she felt as if he were turning away from her (he had enough troubles, she told herself), and so she didn't move and began to cry for both her son and her husband.

Chapter Eleven

"We're going to do something to help that boy," Luke's father quietly insisted the following morning after Luke left for school.

Luke's parents were sitting across from one another at the kitchen table, although both of them appeared to be unaware of the other's presence. Their breakfast was spread out in front of them – eggs, hash browns, and biscuits – but it had been untouched for nearly an hour and was beginning to look unappetizing. Because her husband's words presaged something uncomfortable for their son, Luke's mother bent her head down and began to cry – again, for she had been crying earlier in the morning, too.

Despite the soft, determined tone of his voice, Luke's father felt like pounding his fist on the table and demanding the spiritual forces in the world do something about Luke. 'It's not fair, it's intolerable, and I'm not going to sit still anymore and let it go on,' he told himself. The man started to stand up, but when he noticed the pitiful shaking of his wife's shoulders and witnessed tears rolling down her gray cheeks, he sat back down again and looked at his wife. "We let this go on too long," he said softly, humanely, quite unlike the tone he had only a few seconds ago. "I'm sorry, I waited too long. I…I thought Luke had enough strength and character to…to help himself. But clearly I was wrong. I overestimated the boy's capabilities, and…and maybe I'm responsible for some of his suffering. I don't know, but it's time for me to do something that I should have done long ago, maybe in the very beginning." He lowered his head for a moment and then reached out to his wife, softly grasping her hand which she had placed on the table.

The woman was silent for a minute. Turning to her husband and, with tears still filling her eyes, she smiled wanly and gently squeezed his hand. "Don't blame yourself," she began and fell silent, unable to add that she didn't hold anyone other than Luke responsible for his sorrows.

"No, I should have reached out to someone the very instant Luke became depressed. I thought I could handle everything. I'm a father, I'm a Changer, and I was positive that I knew everything there was about such things. But do you know what's worse? There was a time when I realized that I didn't have the answers, and yet I still tried to cure him without telling Ms. Royce or someone who's gone through this stuff. All those lectures, all those stupid jokes…I can't believe that I was foolish enough to think that any of it would work. What kind of person believes he can command someone to feel better? What kind of person thinks he can laugh it all off? I'm a fool, and because of my folly our son is no closer to being cured than he was the first day after all this happened…" He closed his eyes, tightened his mouth, and exhaled when he opened his eyes.

"You didn't do anything by yourself," his wife said, suddenly feeling stronger. "I could have said something, too. I did say things, but none of what I said did any good. We tried our best…"

"Maybe, but our best hasn't been good enough."

"You almost sound like you're giving up on him." The woman looked at her husband with alarm.

The man hesitated and shook his head. "No, I'm not giving up on him, not just yet."

"We could take him to a psychologist. Some of these people can work wonders. Do you remember Martha's girl? She tried to starve herself to death when she thought everyone in the world was unhappy. I'm sure I can get his number from Martha."

"I think I remember the girl," he replied as if he weren't interested in the suggestion, which he wasn't. "She had dark circles under her eyes, as I recall."

"Yes, that's the one. I'm sure Martha would be happy to help…"

"I'm sure she would," the man interrupted. "I'm sorry, but Luke's problem is different. The girl was delusional. Luke is not. Luke's problems stem from changing, or at least that's at the core of his problems. And we can't tell a psychiatrist that our son is a Changer. We can't risk it; we can't risk spreading the knowledge further than it's already been spread. Can you imagine what would happen if everyone found out how to change? The world would go insane, including all the psychiatrists." He paused and smiled at his wife, as if he felt guilty lecturing her about something she knew as well as him.

"You're right. I wasn't thinking." Her voice trailed off.

"On the other hand," the man said with a wry smile, "can you imagine what a psychiatrist would think if Luke told him about what happened? Our poor son would be locked up quicker than you can shake a stick." He patted her hand. "It was a good idea. But I don't know any Changer psychiatrists, do you?"

"Maybe we could ask Ms. Royce. If anybody knows one, it's her." Luke's mother looked at her husband hopefully, as if there was some real merit in this suggestion.

"Maybe."

Luke's mother closed her eyes for a moment as if she wanted to concentrate on something. She turned her head downward and shook it, after which she opened her eyes and looked at her husband. "What do we do then? I agree, we have to do something."

The man hesitated as if he had something on his mind and needed to consider it more fully before speaking. Reaching across the table, he picked up a cold piece of toast and began mechanically chewing it. After he swallowed, he turned to his wife and said, "I don't have an answer. I only know that we can't help him by ourselves. We need to speak to Ms. Royce. I need to speak to Ms. Royce, because I was the one who let it get out of hand. If only I had reached out to her the very second that this…this state of affairs seemed out of control. Believe me, I didn't know this would happen; I didn't know he lacked the strength… I was a fool…" The man couldn't finish. He closed his eyes and dropped his head, while tears formed at the corners of his eyes.

Luke's mother began quietly crying when she noticed her husband's tears.

Later that morning, Luke's father contacted Ms. Royce and made an appointment to speak to her.

Later that day, Luke stopped at a local market on his way home from school and bought a map.

Chapter Twelve

After dinner, Luke sat at his desk with the map spread out in front of him. The small desk lamp had been fixed and, even though its light was still dim, it was enough to illuminate the map.

On one side of the map was Lordan, which was little more than a tangled web of streets, street names, and places of interest. He located the zoo easily enough, after which he identified the park surrounding it and several long streets that all seemed to converge on the facility. While this was useful information (once in Lordan, he would need to know which street went where), it did nothing to guide him from home to the city itself. Turning the map over and carefully smoothing its creases and edges, he observed more or less the same thing on the back. This section of the map displayed the areas around Lordan, specifically the area between his community and Lordan's city limits. While there were only a few roads on this side, most of which were concentrated on the right side of the map, this side of the map was just as useless as the tangled web in helping him find the best way to go from home to the zoo. Of course, if he were driving a car, both sides of the map would get him from point A to point B quite effectively, or so it appeared. But he didn't have a car, couldn't ask anyone for a ride, and needed to travel quietly and unobtrusively, which would be impossible if he followed busy streets.

Luke closed his eyes, took a deep breath, and then looked at the map once more. One side showed all the city streets, the other a handful of streets entering the city, but neither side offered him the information he needed to get to Iowa and back without being noticed. Turning the map over so that the city faced his desk, Luke began folding the map backwards, reversing the folds to demonstrate its uselessness to him. But before he was half through, having angrily forced some of the folds into place, he noticed a section of the map that was featureless and green. Out of curiosity, he folded the other sections of the map under this square so that the only thing visible was a featureless swatch of green. He gazed at the green section for a couple of moments and, now smiling, shook his head. There it was. It was staring at him all along.

Quickly unfolding the map and placing the relatively blank area outside the city limits upward, Luke noticed that blank area was in fact a wide expanse of federal property, essentially a park that stretched from his neighborhood (starting a few blocks away) to Lordan's city limits and expanded unendingly in either direction (it was bound on the right by a string of roads and highways leading to Lordan). He couldn't believe he had missed it, because this (or a very small corner of it near his neighborhood) was the very park that he and the other Cygnets played in for years, and he knew from experience that the park was uninhabited and that people rarely ventured into it. It only made sense that there were no roads in the park and, if he understood the map correctly, there was one long stretch of land from the bottom of the map to the top (or, on the other side, Lordan city limits) that was bordered, cut off from the roads on the right and everything else on the left, by thick forests. Traveling through this section, one could easily go from his neighborhood to Lordan unseen, unnoticed.

Luke smiled again and, doubling his fist, said, "Yes!" Turning again to the map, he ran the tips of his fingers of his right hand lightly across its surface as if his touch could extract details hidden from sight. He fondled the light green areas, which he knew from the legend were covered by light vegetation; he tapped the various shades of brown and tan, which were barren areas; and he followed a series of tightly spaced lines bisecting the entire map from east to west. Examining the lines more carefully, he realized that they were contour lines and beneath them in two sections (one near the center of the map and one near the left) were the words "Evan's Cliff." Luke had heard of Evan's Cliff (everyone had), although he had never seen it. But as his middle finger followed it from one side of the map to the other, he began to wonder how difficult it would be to scale it – and he would have to scale the cliff if he was going to get from point A to point B, for it bisected everything on this side of the map, including the roads on the right side.

At first, Luke didn't think that the cliff would pose any particular problem. He had climbed any number of outcrops in the park, and, unless it was as high as a mountain (and there weren't any mountains in his area), it wasn't likely to be an impediment to reaching the zoo and Iowa. Luke sniffed and imagined how he would practically fly up the cliff and, once free from earthly constraints, soar the rest of the way to Lordan. But he crashed well short of the zoo when he noticed, just above the cliff line on the left, the numbers "2,120." Sitting upright, his plan now a small pile of burning cinders at the base of the cliff, he stared at the number and said aloud, "What? This can't be right? Evan's Cliff is nearly a half-mile high? That's as high as Mt. Everest." Luke rubbed his eyes and stared at the number, trying first to authenticate the number and then seeking some way to bring the cliff down to size. Nothing worked – the number was the number, even when he looked at it upside down – and when he finally gave up and accepted the cold, inhuman quality of the digits, he slapped that area of the map with the back of his right hand and began refolding the map along its proper creases. "I can't climb that. No one can," he mumbled while he folded the map and placed it back into the drawer.

The map had been spread out on top of several pages of paper yanked from a notebook on the floor. With the map out of sight, Luke reluctantly returned to the pages, notes he had taken in one of his refactoring classes. Staring at the pages, putting one behind the other, one on top of the other, and then stacking them neatly so that their edges matched, Luke tried to make sense of the words and the assignment (a ten-page analysis of the dangers to human society posed by out-of-control animals), but for some reason his mind wasn't working properly, and both the notes and the assignment seemed to be gibberish. The essay was due in two weeks, and this was the first time that he had really sat down to writing. Normally, he would have begun such an assignment a week earlier, but he had been putting off this assignment (ever since he learned where Iowa was) and now, when he had to begin writing, something vague and troubling was on his mind. Pulling out a clean sheet of paper from the notebook on the floor, Luke started to write, rapidly inscribing the title of the paper at the top of the blank page. Because the title of the paper was the same as the title of the assignment, Luke immediately scribbled over it and, dropping his pencil on the desk, put his elbows on the paper and rested his head on his fists.

"I can't believe it," he muttered to himself. "I made it this far, and now I can't find a way…over the cliff, around the cliff, through the cliff to Iowa's place I can't go. Was I just being stupid? Were Dana and Press right that I couldn't do it? I can't climb a cliff nearly a mile high…" Luke closed his eyes and remained motionless for several minutes, seeking guidance from Iowa but obsessing over the impossibility of climbing something higher than the tallest mountain on earth. Over and over the dark lines delineating Evan's Cliff came into his mind, each time chiding him for thinking that he could reach Iowa by himself. When out of desperation he finally opened his eyes to begin his essay, Luke observed what used to be the title of his paper and noticed how the scribbles turned into a thick, black line at the center and then diverged into individual lines a little farther out. He was about to crumple the paper and toss it into his wastebasket when something else occurred to him.

Once again pulling the map out of the top drawer, he spread it across his desk and looked at the lines marking Evan's Cliff. He located the numbers and reconfirmed that it was over two thousand feet high. But when he scanned the map more carefully, he also noted that other sections of the land around the cliff were nearly as high, suggesting that the top of the cliff was merely the highpoint of that section of land, not a strange structure looming overhead as far as the eye could see. In fact, when he compared another elevation mark a little to the south of the cliff, it was obvious that the cliff was not very tall at all, maybe only a hundred feet or so. It was hardly insurmountable. Furthermore, when he examined the lines delineating the cliff, he noticed as he followed the lines across the page that some of them mirrored his scribbles: In the center of the map, the lines were tightly bunched together, creating a single bold, dark line, while near the edges of the page they fanned out, suggesting that at least in these sections the cliff was not so much a sheer face of cold rock but a short and rounded pile of dirt. Luke looked up from the map. Yes, he could do it without Dana's help.

Nothing could be easier or safer. There were no roads in the park, and the open areas were cut off from prying eyes by thick forests. Luke also knew from his days as a Cygnet playing in the park that one could walk through the area for hours, if not days, and never encounter a single person. But even if there were people around, he also remembered how easy it was to find a rock, tree, or bush behind which to conceal oneself, even from such knowledgeable persons as the Cygnets. It wasn't difficult to hide from Iowa, and he recalled one time when she was running furiously around a large outcrop of rocks trying to locate him, never once looking up at where he was resting and observing her movements. Luke smiled the recollection, even though he knew that this "little" incident ultimately ended with Iowa poking him under the eye with a stick. 'Does she still remember it?' Of course, he wasn't going to mention his solution until he returned, because he didn't need Press finding out and blabbing to Ms. Royce.

Smiling, patting the map three times, he carefully folded it and placed it into his geometry book, where no one would find it and where he could pull it out at his convenience and study it. Luke stood up to stretch before continuing with his homework, and while he was standing a melody came to his head along with some lyrics. Lightly tapping his book, he sang quietly to himself,

> "A simple paper map
> "Will guide me there and back
> "Before they raise a shout,
> "Deign a guess or press a doubt."

Chapter Thirteen

Luke appeared to be a little happier the following day. While his wan smiles and long, contemplative silences couldn't be mistaken for any kind of significant improvement, at least he didn't appear to be on the verge of a complete mental collapse and his attitudes, if put in the most positive light, could be counted as signs, though minor, of an emotional improvement. But despite his outward appearance, Luke was inwardly as happy as he had been in years, because he was going to see Iowa. He was careful not to show his happiness, especially in front of his mother, because he didn't want to arouse suspicions and be forced to answer questions about his thoughts, feelings, and whatever else she could devise.

Luke's mother was in the kitchen making her shopping list when Luke came home unexpectedly. He tried to avoid the kitchen (he knew she would be there) when he entered, but the front door always seemed to be sticking at the wrong moment and, when it finally gave way, it produced a loud sucking sound that could be heard throughout the house. When his mother investigated (she hadn't expected anyone at that moment), Luke explained that classes had been dismissed early so that teachers could get their administrative work done. The poor woman had no reason to doubt him – students were periodically released early for this very reason – and she was also convinced that he would never lie to her, even though his adventures in changing were surrounded by a forest of lies. Since it was Friday, she inquired about the status of his homework and, for the sake of hearing his voice, about his plans for the weekend, which, she knew from experience, would entail little more than staying in his room and reading books. Luckily, she had just taken a seat in one of the cushioned living room chairs when Luke informed her that he and Jeremy, a longstanding friend, had a plan to go hiking in the park and that he wanted to spend Friday and Saturday nights at Jeremy's house. Since she and her husband had known Jeremy to be a polite, well-mannered boy (even if they hadn't seen him in some time), she didn't have any concerns about spending the night with this particular boy. More important was the fact that her pathetic boy was finally interacting with someone socially and that he was interested in being someplace other than in his bedroom.

"Well," she began cautiously, half fearful that Luke's request might be a monstrous joke, even though he hadn't told a joke in years (except during the brief interlude of a few days ago). 'But even if it is a joke,' she told herself as she observed her son's handsome, earnest face, 'it has to mean that he's getting better. What happened a few days ago must have been a temporary relapse. I've heard of that happening before. Martha's girl...'

"Mother, is it all right?" Luke asked again, not quite understanding his mother's slowness.

She smiled at him and wanted to reach out to his hand, but he was too far away. "I'm sorry," she said pleasantly, lovingly, "I thought I had answered. Yes, of course, as long as it's okay with Martha's parents. Have you boys asked them yet?"

"Martha's parents?"

"I'm sorry. I meant Jeremy's parents. Did Jeremy ask his parents if it was okay?"

"Yes, he did last night, and they said it was okay as long as you approved. I'll be back Sunday evening, if that's okay. Remember, Monday is Presidents' Day, and so I don't need to be in bed early. Is that okay?"

"Of course, dear," she replied, her careworn smile producing deep furrows around her eyes. She couldn't quite believe the wonderful turn of events – he son was actually going to see friends again – and when she noticed the slight smile on the corners of his mouth, she felt increasingly confident that things were definitely moving in the right direction. "Yes, dear, that's fine. Are you going to have dinner tonight with your father and me?"

"Yeah. Jeremy isn't expecting me before seven."

Luke's mother could barely contain her excitement. When her husband came home a couple of hours later, she met him on the driveway as his car pulled in and, after a big kiss on his rough cheek, she began to tell him about Luke's plans and request. She accompanied him into the house, offering details on Luke's expression and his almost pleasant demeanor. It was then, just before they came through the front door that she paused and told him that she thought there was some real improvement in Luke. "I am convinced that his relapse was an aberration," she added before her husband could respond. "Do you remember Martha's girl? Well, it doesn't matter. You know, I'm thinking that Ms. Royce isn't needed, after all."

Luke's father, however, didn't seem to be as excited as his wife about the news. He agreed that it might be a positive development, but he would have considered the request a little more carefully had Luke come to him with it. He insisted, in a whisper so that Luke couldn't hear (they were in the kitchen now, and the walls in the house were thin), that his reluctance wasn't because he didn't want his son to have friends. On the contrary, it was simply the case that he still had some concerns about Luke's mental state and that he didn't want Luke to become depressed – and there was no question in his mind that Luke demonstrated the classical signs of clinical depression – and become a burden to Jeremy or his family. "And, no," he added, as if his wife had divined another purpose behind his reluctance, "I am not in the least bit worried that our son is a danger to others. Far from it."

Having made his views clear, Luke's father noticed the disappointed look on his wife's face. He smiled at her and tried to think of something that would cheer her up and let her know that he, too, was hopeful that Luke was turning himself around, even if his behavior this time wasn't proof of a long-term correction.

"All right, did you speak to Jeremy's mother and let her know that Luke can be…well, can be a little down at times?"

"Goodness, no, and I am not going to, either. And neither are you. The last thing we want is for Luke to develop a reputation for mental problems. It could hurt his relationships with friends, parents, and teachers, if it got that far."

"Okay, okay, you're right." He relaxed and put his arm around his wife's waist. "I would like to know how things go during this time, but I suppose I can wait until he gets back and hear it from him – if he's talking."

"Yes, let the boys have some fun without parents hovering them."

"I wasn't suggesting that…never mind. I agree with you. Let's let them have some fun."

Luke was a little more talkative during dinner. He responded to his parents' questions about the interests that he and Jeremy shared, the things that they planned to do, and even how his parents were doing. "They're not ill, if that's what you're suggesting."

"No, of course not."

"Jeremy's got a remote-control airplane, and he's going to show me how it works. We're going to test it in the school yard," Luke said between mouthfuls. He sounded genuinely interested by the prospect of testing the plane.

Luke's father was going to warn Luke not to go anywhere near the lake, but he decided that Luke was responsible enough not to need the warning. Still, he was slightly concerned, because Luke was prohibited from visiting that area (part of the refactoring sentence) and because he was certain that it would bring back a wealth of troubling memories.

"You have a good time," his father said for the second or third time. "If you have any problems, you call home immediately. Right?"

Luke looked at his father, and the smile on the boy's face immediately dropped as if his father was alluding to something unpleasant.

"All I meant was that you are going to be gone two days – that's a long time away from home – so if you get homesick or whatever, you give us a call."

Luke nodded in agreement. "I'm not sure about homesickness, but I'll call you if I need to." After dinner, and after cleaning up the kitchen and dining room, Luke went to his room and began packing. It was five-thirty, but he wanted to be ready when it was time to leave the house. He told his parents that when he was done packing, he was going to study until it was time to go.

When the time came to leave, Luke kissed both his parents at the front door and, hoisting his backpack over his shoulder, walked quickly up the street. Jeremy only lived a few blocks from Luke, and it would take a few minutes at most to get there, even with the heavy backpack. It was heavy because of the various items – toothpaste, toothbrush, deodorant, wash cloths and towels, an extra change of clothes and shoes, and so forth – most of which his mother insisted he take if he wanted to be a welcome guest. Luke reluctantly agreed, because he already had several games and sundry items that filled nearly half of the bag. Still, to keep his mother from worrying, and to let his father know that he was following his mother's rules, it was a small thing to do.

The sun was going down soon after Luke left, and by the time he had walked three blocks, there were deep shadows everywhere, and people had already turned on their living room lights, which cast strange, yellow glows outside their houses. 'Like cats eyes,' Luke thought as he rounded the corner, slipped in between a couple of houses, and then entered the park behind one of the houses that marked the edge of a vast area of open land. There were some bushes large enough to conceal a grown man a few feet away from the back fence of the house, and Luke quickly walked over to one of them and crouched out of sight behind it for a few minutes. When certain that no one could see him, he pulled out a pair of leather shoes and a cotton shirt from his backpack, exchanged them for the ones he was wearing, and put the other items into the pack and zipped it up. Next, he retrieved a fat stick from under one of the bushes and used it to excavate a hole that had been filled with branches and topped off with dirt. Finally, he dropped his backpack into it, replaced the sticks and dirt, and made the area look exactly like the surrounding ground. Although the hole was no longer visible, it was still vulnerable to wild animals, but at least he had had enough sense to remove every little crumb of food (remnants of the granola bars that he often took to school) before consigning the backpack to the earth.

Luke squatted back a couple of feet when he was finished, and looked carefully around. It was dark now, too dark to see his backpack's burial mound clearly (it looked completely natural at night), and he felt a slight twinge of worry that if an animal didn't get at it, someone might spot the mound and dig it up for themselves. Looking around as best he could for a few more twigs, he found a handful and tossed them casually over the spot and, finally, stood up, the job complete, as far as he could accomplish it. 'What happens, happens,' he told himself, and, turning around to make sure that no one was within sight, he spotted the black shadows of a small group of trees that were about a hundred feet deeper into the park, and ran directly toward them. Once ensconced in darkness beneath their thick, heavy canopies, he dropped to his knees (the ground was surprisingly soft, because it was covered with leaves) and, after rolling onto his side, changed into a dog that bore a striking resemblance to a golden retriever.

The change had been difficult. He hadn't changed in years, not since the time Ms. Royce apprehended him and the others, and so it had taken several tries before he finally succeeded. Because he still remembered the process (it was like swimming – once you knew how, you never forget), he was not daunted by the failure of the first couple of tries or by the pain, which cut through his body like a slender knife, when he finally achieved it. But even though the pain disappeared nearly as quickly as it had come, he didn't immediately leap to his four feet and, instead, slowly and carefully got up and just as slowly and carefully stretched and limbered all the canine muscles in his legs, back, and neck, after which he shook himself several times. He needed to be sure that everything was still in good working order (why cripple himself before he accomplished his goal?), and so when all the stretching and shaking was finally done and he was certain that he could begin his journey, he lifted his nose briefly in the air, sniffed out the direction he needed to travel, and began trotting deeper into the park.

Chapter Fourteen

The plan was simple. He would travel through the park until he reached Lordan, after which he could pick and choose the streets best suited to reach the zoo. While this wouldn't be the shortest or most direct route, it would offer him the ability to move without arousing suspicions and to hide if that became necessary. Key to the plan was traveling as a dog. Luke understood clearly that he would be in serious trouble if anyone had found out that he had changed, but he was willing to take the risk because he lacked transportation and because he knew that it could take days to walk to Lordan on two feet. But as a dog, he could make the trip in less than a day, and he could use all his special canine senses – smell, eyesight, hearing – to avoid humans, find the city, locate the zoo, and once there meet Iowa. These senses would also enable him to find food and water and eliminate the need to carry a heavy backpack filled with supplies, while his fur and thick skin would keep him warm in the coolest temperatures. Finally, if all went well, he would see Iowa tomorrow morning, perhaps spend the day with her, and return home Sunday evening, as promised. Naturally, he would have to locate his backpack again, but he was certain that it wouldn't take any special canine senses to accomplish that.

Once he was well out of sight of the houses, he stepped out from under the dark canopy of the trees and paused in a wide, moonlit expanse. The full moon cast a silvery light on the uppermost edges of what appeared to be hollows or rocks, and it neatly outlined the top of the clumps of trees to his right, making the shadows beneath the highlighted areas darker and more impenetrable. When he was about thirty or so yards from the trees, standing in an open area surrounded by spotted shadows and strange reflections, the dog paused and again sniffed the cool, night air. He had already discerned the direction in which he needed to travel, but he felt the need to confirm this while at the same time making sure that he wasn't being followed and that he wasn't anywhere near human beings. When he was satisfied that everything was as it should be, he again began trotting toward Lordan, although this time in the open and using the moonlight to help guide him along the way.

Trotting at a comfortable pace, the dog moved effortlessly between shrubs and small bushes, up one grass-covered rise and down another, across wide stretches of barren dirt and then around small bushes, large rocks, and every other kind of impediment he encountered, none of which slowed his pace or caused him to expend an undue amount of energy. Breathing deeply, absorbing the refreshing country air, he could feel his strength increase and his joints become more limber and flexible, as if his very exertions were building his strength and stamina. Every now and then he came up to a small depression in the ground and, unless it was a deep gulley or riverbed, he increased his speed slightly and leaped from one side to the other effortlessly, almost as if he could fly. At one point, he encountered a small stream, hardly more than seven or eight feet wide, but instead of wading through a shallow section, he leaped up and outward and easily crossed it, landing on the far side without slowing his momentum.

The dog continued at the same pace for another thirty minutes or so. Besides the invigorating feeling of his muscles and bones working efficiently beneath his skin and fur, he loved the way the cool air tickled his nose as it swirled around his nostrils before being pulled inward where it filled his lungs and cooled his body. He might have continued luxuriating in such purely animal sensations, his mind blank except for the manner in which these sensations registered on his consciousness, but when he leaped over a medium-sized rock that bore a passing resemblance to the large outcrop near the lake where the Cygnets frolicked, he began to imagine what it would be like being with Iowa again. Envisioning himself in human form, he grasped Iowa's right hand and together they ran toward the lake and jumped into its cool water, never once releasing their hands. Once in the water, they turned and held each other in a tight embrace, during which smiles, tears, and a torrent of words both connected and disconnected passed between them, words that would mean little or nothing to the casual passerby. These thoughts, along with the mindless pleasure he experienced in putting his strong, canine body through its paces, increased his desire to reach Lordan as quickly as possible and, within seconds, he was moving at nearly twice the speed he began the journey with. Such a pace would be difficult to maintain for any appreciable length of time, but he didn't feel bound by normal limitations because his strength and energy felt inexhaustible, while the muscles in his neck, shoulders, and legs encouraged him to push harder, to fly, not jump. And he did seem to be flying when he leaped over a large gulley, his eyes closed and legs tucked beneath him, and felt the air around him holding him up and pushing him onward. He landed with the same grace that propelled him into the air, while the shock of the impact energized his bones and muscles and encouraged him to fly higher and longer. Shortly after this, another opportunity presented itself, this time a long, ragged shadow that was twice as wide and infinitely longer than the gulley. Pushing himself with every ounce of his strength, he somehow managed to clear what appeared to be a black sea from overhead. But as soon as he reached the opposite side, his right front paw suddenly gave way upon landing and, instead of remaining on his feet and continuing his pace, his nose hit the ground and his entire body collapsed under him, causing him to summersault several times until he finally came to a stop against a large rock.

Snorting the dirt out of his nose, the dog then licked the dust and debris out of his mouth and off his snout and lips. He started to get up, but began to struggle because he couldn't put pressure on the paw that had collapsed. Inhaling deeply at intervals, he finally managed to push himself up into a sitting position where, leaning on his left paw and shoulder, he was able to stand up somewhat uneasily on three feet. With his right paw tucked underneath him, he shook his body to remove the dirt from his fur, bouncing a couple of times on his uninjured leg to steady himself, and then stretched out his right leg and gingerly touched the ground. His paw ached, and merely resting it against the soft dirt caused a pinpoint stab that was excruciating. But the location of the pain suggested that his leg wasn't broken.

The dog leaned forward and, steadying himself on his hind legs, raised the offended paw to his nose to determine the cause of the pain, after which he touched the spot with the tip of his tongue to confirm his diagnosis. Using his front teeth, he extracted a rather significant thorn from the paw, which he spat out with a couple heavy shakes of his head to aid the removal. Actually, the extraction took several tries, since the slender portion of the thorn's stalk was all that was left (its large, ragged head had evidently broken away when he stepped on it), and most of that was lodged under the skin, but he managed to extract it anyway without causing further injuries. Gingerly placing his weight on the offended paw, he began to push down until his weight was evenly distributed between all four paws and the pain was completely gone.

Shaking his body once again, the dog sniffed in the direction of the area on which he had fallen, after which he carefully walked around it (to avoid additional injuries) and then continued on his way to the zoo, albeit at a more leisurely pace.

Chapter Fifteen

Nearly one hundred miles across at its widest point, the park was shaped like a broken, lopsided vase, with its intact bottom resting on the Cygnet's neighborhood and the lopsided neck reaching into Lordan's city limits. The broken part was near Lordan, where it splintered at the outskirts of the city, one shard running through the city and thirty or forty shards taking different paths around the town and off to other places and towns. Inside the park there was a long expanse that extended from the bottom of the vase to its neck in Lordan that was bound on one side, the dog's right side, by the thick, black line of forest and on the other, the dog's left, by a much thinner gray line of trees (these were a little farther away and not so densely packed as those on the other side). It was level across most of its interior, although there were more than a few dips and hollows, ravines, rocks and other impediments, while the ground was covered variously with soft dirt, soft grass, and unadorned rock. As long as the dog stayed more or less in the middle of the park, he could be certain that he would be funneled toward Lordan and, with a little luck, to the zoo itself. While this was clear on the map, it was even clearer in his nose, for there were moments when he could detect the caustic smells from the city and, if he angled his nose just right, the exotic scents of large animals not normally found near his neighborhood.

At that moment, there were a few wisps of clouds barely visible along the far horizon, while the rest of the night sky was black and peppered with millions of tiny stars, the brightest of which was so close to the full moon that it nearly touched its shimmering eastern edge. Stretching out in front of him, the vast plain was bathed in the moon's silvery light, making the entire plain look like the surface of the moon, with its ghostly outcrops and cool, heavy shadows that created disquieting images on the ground. When not covered by grass and other vegetation, the ground itself seemed little more than soft, silky dirt, which sometimes exuded a slight puff of gray dust when stepped on just right.

The dog wasn't moving as quickly as he had been only a few minutes ago. His breathing was labored, while his muscles and joints were becoming sore from the running and jumping he had been doing (despite feeling comfortable as an animal, he still wasn't used to all the stresses and strains being put on his body). Shortly after slowing to a walk to ease his discomfort and to give his body a few moments to recuperate, something else began to happen to him – his tongue, which by this time was dangling out the side of his mouth, started to feel dry and uncomfortable, and his stomach was begging for something to ease its knowing discomfort. Once his breathing was back under control (his legs, however, were still a little weary), he shook his body violently a couple of times and licked his lips, which were still dry and taut. Looking around for telltale signs of food and especially water, he noticed about a hundred yards to his left a large, dark area on the ground. He couldn't tell why this area stood out from the others, but when he lifted his nose in its direction, he detected a moist, fetid smell coming from the area.

The dark area turned out to be a small, muddy spot on the ground, which was probably the last remnant of a drying pond. Because of the strength of its smell, the dog had expected to find a puddle of drinkable water somewhere within its boundaries, but after circumnavigating the area several times – each time sniffing different sections of the mud – he couldn't find a single place on its surface that had enough water to moisten his tongue, much less fill his belly. There was nothing but mud, mud in varying degrees of thickness and dryness. After shaking his shoulders and back, the dog stepped closer to the center of the area (stepping carefully to avoid clogging his toes with mud if it ever got that wet and sticky) and surveyed what seemed to be the wettest section. Spotting a couple of bubbles straining to the surface between his feet, he leaned forward and, practically touching one of them with the tip of his nose, inhaled the foul-smelling substance to determine how much water it contained and how far down he would have to dig to get enough to drink. Satisfied that water was within reach, he began scratching the surface of the mud with his right paw, pulling away globs of clay-like dirt, until he excavated a small hole no larger than his head. The hole was dark and difficult to see, except for a narrow strip at its center, which glistened momentarily in the moonlight before fading into the shadow. Leaning forward, he sniffed the inside of the hole, touched the bottom with the tip of his tongue (he used his teeth to scrape the mud from his tongue), and, after adjusting his hind legs (moving them slightly apart), began furiously widening and deepening the hole, using both front paws to pull the dirt and mud through his hind legs to the ground behind him. As the hole got bigger, slight puddles of gleaming water would form, only to be quickly absorbed by the ground. Five minutes later, however, he managed to uncover a small puddle of dirty-brown water maybe an eighth of an inch deep.

The dog quickly put his nose to the surface and began lapping up the brown fluid before it was reabsorbed. The taste wasn't great – it was filled with dirt and debris, and he occasionally encountered something indescribably foul that he gagged out of his mouth – but for a few moments none of this mattered, for he needed moisture of any kind, no matter how vile or polluted. Unfortunately, no sooner had he swallowed a few moist licks of the precious liquid than it was all gone and no amount of digging uncovered enough moisture to wet his tongue again. Reluctantly raising his head and, with one glittering bead of moisture dropping from a whisker into the dark night, the dog glanced around for something to eat, which at the same time would assuage some of his thirst.

Straining his ears and then sniffing the earth, he spotted a mouse a couple of feet away. The mouse was poking its head out of a small hole near a bush and, failing to notice the dog, who stood completely still, not even a whisker moving, decided to venture out a little farther until its entire body except for the tip of its tail was out of its hole. Feeling secure, its whiskers sparkling and quivering in the moonlight, the mouse inched away from its hole in search of something, and it was then that the dog pounced, catching the tiny animal by its tail with his large paw. The mouse struggled to free itself but lacked the strength and, moreover, the dog was too fast, for he reached down with his mouth and, picking up the struggling creature with his teeth and immediately dispatched it, chewing and swallowing it within seconds.

While the mouse eased some of the discomfort in his stomach, there wasn't enough of it to satisfy his thirst, which still demanded his attention. But before he could turn around, the dog spotted another little creature a yard or so from the first. As he did with the first mouse, he leaped and pounced on it, gobbling it down just as quickly and efficiently. He searched for more (two mice were hardly enough), but no matter how hard he strained his senses, these two seemed to be the only ones within reach – the only ones that he could detect. Since there was nothing else in this immediate area, the dog decided to continue toward Lordan, hoping that he would find something along the way.

Sniffing the air to reorient himself, he began walking and then, pushing himself a little hard, trotting toward Lordan and the zoo.

Chapter Sixteen

For a while, the soft dirt and fluffy grasses cushioned his feet and protected his muscles and joints from the shocks caused by running and jumping on hard, unforgiving ground. Although the softness in places slowed him a little, he was nevertheless able to keep a reasonable pace which he hoped would take him to Lordan, or at least the nearest place with water. But as he moved deeper into the park, the soft ground gradually gave way to hard, barren ground that in some places was unpleasant to touch. The surface of the ground now resembled the surface of an ancient painting because of its wide cracks and narrow fissures, which suggested that it had once at the bottom of a large body of water that had dried up. Of course, the forests on either side of him were still visible, although they now seemed out of place, maybe a little absurd, in this hostile region.

The dog had been traveling across the hard ground for some time when he decided to stop and again search for food and water, especially water. Panting lightly, he sniffed the air to remember Lordan's location, and then slowly turned completely around to find something, sniffing the air as he moved and eyeing the ground for signs that something alive was nearby. When nothing seemed immediately apparent, he angled his nose to the ground and checked for signs of both water and life (snorting the dust out of his nose when he got too close to the ground). He checked and double checked the area, and when finally determined that he was wasting his time, he turned and began heading back toward Lordan. The dog hadn't gone more than a few yards when he caught sight of something out the corner of his right eye. It was a vague, grayish streak that seemed to possess an animal-like movement, but when he stopped to look, it was gone and in its place were the dark, barren ground and a black stretch of distant trees.

Moving his nose and shoulders toward the trees, he sniffed for signs of something other than dirt and vegetation. When he couldn't detect anything, he sharpened his senses, especially his sense of smell, to detect the presence of large animals, something more massive than a squirrel or rabbit; and after this effort failed, he searched the distant air for indications that rocks or the distant tree branches had been moved. For a moment, he was certain that he detected something just inside a group of black trees that stood out from the others, but when he concentrated all his senses on that specific area he couldn't find anything except the trees, which were silent and motionless. Thinking that the streak may have been an illusion (at night when the moon is just right, shadows will often dance and flutter and disappear altogether), the dog shook his head and shoulders and resumed trotting across the hard earth toward Lordan, sliding down one slight depression and bounding up an equally slight rise, maneuvering around rocks and strange piles of mud chips, and on and on. The streak, or whatever it was, was soon gone and in the distance toward Lordan a dark line stretched across the horizon.

The dog was moving along the top edge of a long slope when he discerned a faint gurgling sound originating from somewhere in the darkness below. Stopping and craning his ears in the direction of the sound, he immediately lost track of the sound and feared that it, too, was illusion, a figment of a tired mind and body. But when he aimed his nose in the direction of the gurgling, he almost immediately detected the scent of water. Not only that, he could sense that it was fresh water, not the foul-tasting mud that he was forced to drink earlier, and that it would be easy to reach. Testing the air to estimate the distance he needed to travel, the dog trotted down the slope until it leveled off and followed the scent toward its source, which was only a few hundred feet away. The smell of the water made his mouth drool and its drinkability made him desperate to fill his stomach.

The stream was at the bottom of a shallow ravine about two or three feet deep and nearly ten feet across at its widest. It should have been easy to spot the stream in the bright moonlight, but because of the ravine's sides and angles it was completely obscured by a dark shadow, forcing the dog to locate the water by its smell alone. Moving quickly and surefootedly on the uneven ground, he quickly located a small pool of bubbling water no wider than a large man's outstretched hand. The water, which had no visible origin, flowed in a thin trickle from the pool, down a handful of small rocks, and to a point at which it disappeared beneath a large rock perhaps twenty feet away. While the stream was only a couple inches deep, the amount of water it offered was more than he needed and, reaching down, he lapped up the sweet-tasting liquid until his stomach was full and heavy. Slurping up the droplets on his mouth and whiskers, he lifted his head and, arching his nose so that it rose above the edge of the ravine, sniffed the air for signs that he wasn't alone. When he was certain there wasn't any danger, he reached down again and took a few more slurps. Licking his jowls once more and then shaking himself, he turned and leaped up over the edge and resumed his journey.

The water renewed the dog's energy, and he picked up his pace so as to arrive in plenty of time to see Iowa and possibly make plans for the future. While he trotted, his belly warm and heavy, he again noticed the dark line, which was bolder now and stretched from one end of the horizon to the other, neatly separating the earth from the sky. The line was too sharp and linear to be another forest (unlike this line, the tops of the forests were ragged and often slightly blurred), and yet he couldn't think of anything else unless it was another stream. But as he gradually got closer, the line gradually widened until it finally lost its smooth line-like qualities and became a large, dark mass covered with streaks and deformations across its perpendicular surface. This was Evan's Cliff, and it was so high that it cast much of the surrounding area in a long, dark shadow. When he was close enough to recognize it, a small lamp in the back of his mind went on and before him was an illuminated map of the area and the cliff. He had been confident that he understood everything there was to understand about the line that bisected the map, including the effort needed to scale it, and yet as he faced the imposing formation, which seemed to rise out of the earth like the Great Wall of China, he wasn't quite as certain that he would be able to cross it as planned.

It had taken nearly an hour from the moment he spotted the line to come within reach of the base of the cliff. As he approached, he carefully scanned the face for rounded hills, broad alleys, and stone stairs (features that he remembered seeing on the map) and, having failed to find anything resembling such features, routes or paths that would guide him through all its crags and crevasses from the mounds of dirt at its base to razor-sharp line at its summit. Despite its imposing size and the near vertical angle of its face, he assured himself that he could scale it with a minimum of time and effort, although any expenditure of time was suddenly worrisome – and since he didn't know how more traveling time he needed, he couldn't tell how much time he could spend with Iowa. However, the first thing that attracted his attention when he finally came within a few feet of the bottom of the cliff was not the path that would take him to the summit. It was the moon, which was full and radiant (he could see gray craters across its face), even though its bottom edge was obscured by the cliff's topmost edge. In fact, the moon appeared to be resting on the top of the cliff, a few feet back from the summit, which made reaching it seem as easy as reaching the summit.

Snorting and shaking his head, the dog scanned the cliff's craggy face, moving his head from top to bottom, side to side, searching for some weakness that would enable him to touch the moon before it rolled behind the horizon. He was about to give up and move to a different area near the base when he noticed one small section of the cliff that was covered with nooks, crannies, and pathways, the kind of terrain that he knew from the map would enable him to reach the cliff's summit (and beyond) without too much trouble. It was obvious that he would have to push and pull himself up at certain places, but as he studied the height and angle of these features, as well as the height and angle of cliff itself, he came to the conclusion that he could actually scale the cliff long before the moon disappeared.

Stretching his forelegs and then his hind legs, the dog took a couple of steps toward one section of the cliff, and then hesitated.

Chapter Seventeen

Three years ago, he and the other Cygnets (all in human form) were running through the woods, playing a game of tag using long sword-like sticks. Luke was by himself, charging in and around trees, and running as fast as he could. He didn't know how long he had been running, but he didn't feel tired or winded, even when he stumbled and, crashing through a large bush, burst into an open area covered with tall grasses. Even then, he didn't stop or slow down and continued to run as fast as he could, leaping and staggering through the grass, once nearly falling down after he stepped in a small hole on his way to an outcrop of rocks. The outcrop wasn't very big -- it was a fraction of the size of the one confronting the dog -- although like Evan's Cliff there were boulders along its base, as well as paths and ledges across its face that enabled one to reach its top.

Glancing back at the trees, he saw Iowa suddenly burst into the open, running with the same speed and abandon that he had. In that brief instant, he could see her fierce determination not to fall back, to keep up with him, to catch him, while he meandered through the grasses, jumping over one small depression after another, until he came to base of the outcrop. Having put a little distance between himself and her (he was faster and had more strength and endurance), he ran behind a large, rectangular bolder and disappeared.

Iowa followed him around the boulder, around another section of the outcrop, and then around another and another without once catching up to him. She couldn't believe that she had lost him so quickly. She couldn't believe that Luke had vanished around a single corner. Stopping and catching her breath, she turned around several times, glancing at the base of the outcrop and then at the surrounding fields. When all this proved fruitless, she ran to another side of the rocks and surveyed the outcrop and the fields in that direction. Had he truly disappeared? Had she been chasing a ghost? Furious that she couldn't find him, she stood still with her fists at her waist, listening for clues that he might be nearby, or even that any of the other Cygnets might be within shouting distance.

Iowa was about to give up and return to the clearing near the lake, when she heard her name being called. Initially, she couldn't tell from which direction the sound emanated – the voice was low and soft and the speaker seemed far away, as if perhaps the sound had been carried on a gentle breeze – and, moreover, she wasn't entirely certain that her name was the one being called. But after a few moments, as the voice continued to repeat the name, Iowa gradually became certain that the name was indeed hers, even if the direction of the caller was still unknown. Having spent a couple of minutes fruitlessly trying to locate the source of the voice, she started to leave when the voice practically shouted her name, this time from above. "Iowa!" It was Luke's voice, and he had been standing on top of the outcrop, following her movements and reveling in her foolishness.

"It's your conscience, Iowa. Why didn't you look up?" He was standing a few feet out of reach, and not only were his arms arrogantly folded, but he was smiling and laughing – barely able to speak because of his laughter – and all at her expense. He waved a long, slender stick at her (they had been playing a game of tag in which thin, three-foot long sticks were used to tag one another) as if to say, 'tut, tut, tut,' which enraged her and made her want to punish him all the more.

Running toward a section of the outcrop that led to the top where he was standing, Iowa charged madly up the rocks, injuring her fingertips in the process but determined to reach him once and for all. Slipping and scrambling, she somehow made it to the top, her stick still in hand, and when she was finally able to stand up and confront him, Luke smiled at her, turned, and jumped to the ground. He fell on one knee but, unhurt, jumped up and started across the field, heading into the trees toward the lake. Despite her fury and passionate desire to catch him, Iowa couldn't make the jump and so she scampered down the same way she came up. She didn't lose sight of him, however, because he was waiting for her just inside the woods and, when she was within ten feet, he turned and continued heading toward the lake.

Luke jumped over roots and bushes, stumbled on stumps, rocks, and inexplicable holes, but somehow managed to remain upright, staying comfortably ahead of Iowa, who was tiring quickly, her lungs and legs demanding a rest. Feeling sorry for her, and wishing that she would finally catch up, he slowed as he arrived at the clearing surrounding the lake and then the inexplicable happened – he tripped over a soft spot in the earth just inside the clearing and fell face forward on the open ground. Just then the other Cygnets arrived, having caught sight of him falling with Iowa only a few feet behind.

Breathing heavily, Iowa walked slowly over to where Luke was lying on the ground, face down, his head resting on his cradled arms, and stopped. She bent over for a few moments trying to catch her breath, which for a few moments seemed an impossible task, but when she finally recovered somewhat, she took a couple of steps closer to him. Luke hadn't moved. He was winded as well, but unlike Iowa he only needed to lie down and relax a bit to recover. Staring intently at him, her mind blank and animalistic, Iowa suddenly gritted her teeth and slapped him twice on the butt with her stick, just as he had slapped her earlier, although unlike his gentle tags her strokes were sharp and violent.

"Tag!" she gasped, suddenly out of breath again. Her face was red and sweaty – she was still far from recovered – and for a moment it looked like she was going to say something else to him but didn't. She stepped back and again bent forward, this time grabbing her right side.

Iowa was silent for a few moments while she tried to control her breathing and calm her nerves. When Luke finally began to stir, he rolled over and, looking up at her from over his shoulder, noticed the angry expression that clouded her beautiful face. No, it wasn't anger, it was fury, and he couldn't understand why she would be upset after the fun they were having running through the woods and climbing up and down the outcrop. But as he watched her, noticing the way she was looking at her dirty clothes and the ripped sleeve of her blouse (it must have got caught on one of the bushes or tree limbs in the forest), he could tell that her fury was increasing, not subsiding. Scowling at him with half-closed eyes, as if she couldn't stand to look at him, Iowa gripped her stick so tightly that her knuckles turned white.

Luke slowly rose to his feet and, brushing the dust and twigs off his clothes (which were completely intact), turned and looked at Iowa. He was breathing normally, but instead of calmly saying something pleasant to her (perhaps noting that she got in some good hits, perhaps suggesting that she was too difficult to elude, or perhaps apologizing for her torn clothes, even though he wasn't responsible for their condition), he couldn't say a word and remained staring, astonished that someone could be so beautiful in torn and dirty clothes. A slight breeze came up from the left, and, as he continued staring, he felt increasingly warm inside as the breeze continually tossed long strands of her golden hair across her face. Observing her delicate movements as she brushed the hair from her face with the back of her hand, he imagined stepping closer to her, gently pulling the hair back from her face, and brushing the dust off her face and lips with the tips of his fingers. Naturally, he would never attempt such a thing without a clear indication that she wanted it, and yet the idea that she did want it – that she would smile as he touched her soft face – forced a slight, involuntary smile to crease the corners of his mouth.

Still clutching her stick, Iowa returned his stare, although she didn't smile and there was nothing in her expression to indicate what she was now thinking.

Not turning away, Luke wanted to speak to her. He wanted to say something that might hint at what he was feeling. He wanted to speak her name and hear his uttered in return. But just as he opened his mouth, his courage failed him and, tongue-tied, he stood smiling and praying that she would be the first to break the silence. When she didn't immediately respond, Luke realized that it was all up to him and that if didn't say something now, he might never again get such an opportunity. Breathing deeply to settle his nerves and briefly closing his eyes to steel himself, he opened his eyes just in time to observe Iowa's ugly grimace as she swung her stick at his face, catching solidly under his right eye.

It happened so quickly that he didn't have a chance to duck, which was probably lucky, for had he moved he might have been struck in his eye. Regardless, the hit was painful, and within seconds he could feel the area around his eye begin to swell. When he put his hands to his eyes and pulled them back to look at them (a reflex action), he could see blood and, almost instantaneously, feel it trickling down his cheek. "Ouch!" he remembered shouting, while Press and Dana crowded around him and attended to his injury.

The dog shook his head and then the rest of his body, and by the time his tail stopped moving, the memories associated with the rocks had vanished. Licking the front of his nose and once more sniffing the air, he chose a narrow path between two boulders and began climbing or, rather, walking up a steep, dirt incline that was bound on either side by fat, gray rocks.

Chapter Eighteen

The climb began as easily as he had anticipated when studying the map. The path, which varied from over four feet wide to a little more than one, meandered back and forth as if it had once been the bed of an ancient stream. But while he was walking (the incline and the sometimes narrow passages made it impossible to move at a faster pace) and making progress, he was becoming a little apprehensive because he couldn't see above the walls on either side of him, while the route was so circuitous that he couldn't see much in front or behind him, either – only the black sky and, sometimes, a glowing edge of the moon were clearly visible. He couldn't sense any danger, although his sense of sight was fairly useless at that point. Wagging his tail, he told himself that his concern was unnecessary, and he congratulated himself on having chosen an easy path over the cliff.

His congratulations were short-lived, however, for no sooner had he rounded the next corner than he found himself face to face with a rock completely blocking the path. The rock was higher than all the other rocks around it, and its face was a sheer vertical, making it impossible to go around it or scale it. Since he could do nothing about the rock, the dog carefully turned around, practically bending himself in two, and followed the path back down to the base of the cliff. Back at the starting point, he began to run back and forth along the base of the cliff to find another opening that might lead him where the original path could not. Some paths looked reasonable, but when he stopped and sniffed them, he could tell that they were blocked or unsuitable in one way or another. On the other hand, there were several potentially suitable paths (that is, he couldn't see anything wrong with them), but no amount of sniffing and looking could tell him whether they led to the top or to a dead end. Whining, the dog wouldn't have been so concerned if following false leads were simply a matter of lost time, but lost time was no simple matter if he wanted to see Iowa and return home on time.

The dog had been running back and forth along the base of the cliff for nearly thirty minutes, frantically checking and rechecking each possible path or space between boulders, when he stumbled upon a strange path some thirty yards from the starting point of his aborted climb. Surprised by the unexpected appearance of this path (he was certain that he had checked each path at least once), he stopped and scanned the ground and the surrounding boulders carefully. Except for the fact that he hadn't noticed the path before, nothing about it seemed unusual. But when he sniffed around the path, he detected a rush of cool, sweet air, air that was infused with the scent of vegetation, which was absent around the base of the cliff. None of the paths had the same cool air, none had the slightest hint of greenery, which strongly suggested that this path let to the top of the cliff, where the air was probably cooler and the ground covered with lush vegetation. Confident that he had finally located the quickest way over the cliff (and certain that he could get over the cliff faster on four legs than he could scaling the face on two), he shook his body, scratched his side with his back paw, and started up the path, meandering around some large rocks and leaping over a couple of divots in the ground.

The path turned out to be much wider than the first. Indeed, some places were several feet wide, from the face of the cliff to the outside edge or wall of the path, which accompanied the path upward. It was also interesting that this wall gradually decreased in height as the path rose higher up the face of the cliff until it was no more than a few inches high, if that. In some ways, this was a blessing, for it enabled him to gauge his progress upward from the base of the cliff if he looked over it to the ground to the deep shadows below. But while he was pleased finally to have found the right path, he was nevertheless somewhat dismayed to find several places along the way that were every bit as difficult to negotiate as places along the other path; in fact, there were a couple instances in which he had troubling climbing because of the soft dirt and steepness of the path, and if it weren't for his four feet and strong nails, he would have been forced to turn around and abandon the path. It was also the case that the distance from the beginning of the path to the top of the cliff was beginning to seem much farther than he had anticipated. While his sense that he was finally on the right track gave him energy, he was nevertheless beginning to tire (moving upward, at times at a steep angle, required far more energy than moving across the open park had) and his need for water was becoming more pronounced by the minute.

Stopping to catch his breath, the dog shook his head and used his long tongue to slurp up the moisture from the sides of his mouth and whiskers. He had reached a section of the path that was nearly horizontal, although its width had shrunk so much that it was only a foot wide in some places, a far cry from the wide opening that promised to take him easily to the cliff's summit. Because the outside wall of the path was still only an inch or so high, he could peer out from time to time to see areas in the park that were illuminated by the moon's bright light and, in the distance, faint star-like lights demarcating his own neighborhood. Sniffing the air, which was still redolent of vegetation, and craning his head to detect any untoward noises, the dog continued to move forward. After a few minutes, he began to move more quickly, not as quickly as he had before he reached the cliff, but faster than any time since beginning his climb. He could sense the summit of the cliff for the first time -- the air was increasingly cooler, and the distinct smells from plants and large animals were becoming more pronounced – but just when he caught sight of what appeared to be the uppermost edge of the cliff, he followed the curve of the path and came face to face with another rock wall. Unlike the boulder he had faced on the other path, this one wasn't vertical or nearly as high. It was fairly steep, but since the top, rounded portion inclined to the right, next to the face of the cliff, he thought that he might be able to work his way around the narrow section and then continue on to the top.

It made sense, especially as he examined (sniffing the rocks and the air) the impediment and the way in which it curved to the right, leaving him a narrow opening on the left – and especially because he could see the path continuing upward on the other side of the rock – and so he decided to attempt the climb. It didn't appear to be too difficult or dangerous, although his judgment may have been clouded by the thought that if he didn't reach the top from this path, he might not have a chance to reach it from another path and still get to the zoo and back home in time. Bracing himself, he placed one paw on the outside edge of the rock and prepared to place the other next to it (pushing off with his hind feet to scale the rock's side) but then hesitated. A strange, piercing noise overhead destroyed his concentration.

Chapter Nineteen

Craning his head upward toward the dark, gray sky, the dog noticed a faint smudge floating across the Milky Way and then across the face of the moon, where its black shape was clearly outlined. The shape emitted a loud, unpleasant cawing sound, and then another and another, after which it floated out of sight. Once it was in front of the moon, he recognized it – it was a crow – which he should have recognized from the sound alone. He could sense the bird floating circling overhead for a couple of minutes before it disappeared over the summit, its cawing trailing after it before gradually fading into the black night.

The dog turned away and sniffed something on its chest. Placing his other paw onto the rock and, pulling with his front feet and pushing with his hind legs, he managed to hop onto the edge of the rock; turning his shoulders toward the cliff and readjusting his feet, he hopped up onto an adjoining rock and then onto another, moving quickly and efficiently as if he were scaling stairs. He paused on the last rock, which proved to be the end of the staircase, and, adjusting his feet so that he felt secure and steady, looked carefully across the face of the cliff for the next set of rocks or path that would take him to the top. Not more than a couple of feet in front of him, a series of narrow, elongated ledges appeared, each of which seemed to zigzag the rest of the way up the face of the cliff. Sniffing the air to confirm the existence of the ledges and their overall dimensions, the dog tightened his shoulders and repositioned his hind feet so that they could easily support his weight and, licking the end of his nose for good measure, sprang forward onto the first ledge. The ledge was no more than a couple of feet wide, somewhat narrower than it appeared before he reached it, and so he walked cautiously up the gentle incline for several feet, keeping his right shoulder against the face of the cliff, for good measure. The ledge ended on the face of a flat rock that was wide enough for him to turn and face the next ledge, which ran gently upward in the opposite direction. The dog followed this until he reached its terminus, which like the previous path, ended at a rock ledge, enabling him to turn and take the next that ran in the direction to the one immediately below it. He continued up these ledges for some time, moving closer and closer to the summit (he couldn't see the top, but he knew he was getting closer because the smell of vegetation was intensifying and he could feel cool, fresh-smelling air current from overhead circling around his nose and whiskers) and becoming more and more confident that this part of his journey was coming to an end.

This confidence was short-lived, for a few minutes later the ledge began to narrow, at first almost imperceptibly but soon after precipitously. Two feet wide was manageable, barely, but the ledge got narrower until it was only a foot wide, if that, which forced him to put one foot in front of the other carefully and push the weight of his body against the cliff as he moved up. He slowly maneuvered upward for another ten feet or so until he was forced to stop. Dirt and rocks tumbled off the cliff overhead and fell onto his head, filling his eyes and nose with dirt. He blinked several times to clear his eyes while at the same time snorting to force the dirt and dust out of his nose. When his eyes and nose felt normal again, he tried to move forward again (pressing one side of his body close to the cliff and keeping his eyes partially closed in case he was dusted again) but stopped after one step when he sneezed, three, four, five times, each one shaking his body and threatening to push him away from the cliff face.

For a moment or so, the dog stood still with his eyes closed, as if he were bracing himself for another series of sneezes (any one of which would force him off the face of the cliff), but when that didn't happen, he took two more steps until he came to a point at which the path seemed to turn around a corner (actually, the path followed a depression in the cliff to his right). Even if he wanted to, it was now impossible to turn back (he couldn't feel anything but air when he moved his left rear foot back to check the path) and, given the turn and the sliver of a path that he was on, he wasn't at all sure that he could continue. Since one direction was as bad as the other, the dog decided to press forward, for at least this direction was inching him closer to Iowa…he hoped. Sliding his right foot forward about three inches (and he could feel the dirt dribble away from him at the outer edge of his paw) and then sliding his left paw directly behind it, after which he tried to slide his hind paws in the same way, he tried to reach the curve but quickly realized that he couldn't position his rear legs as effectively as he could his front ones. As a result, his left rear foot gave way after a few moments and, unable to return to its previous position (his foot kept slipping off the edge), it hovered over the air, dangling uselessly. Stuck in this untenable position, the dog steadied himself against the side of the cliff and closed his eyes, hoping that a decision would come to him or that his problems would disappear as if by magic.

He stood still, leaning against the cliff and balancing on three feet for several minutes. The stress of the climb had exhausted the dog's mental faculties, and, no matter how hard he tried, he couldn't think of anything that would improve the situation – standing, hoping to wake up out of this nightmare, seemed the only viable alternative he had. The dog might have remained that way for some time, his mind blank, his muscles gradually weakening, but he was awoken from his slumber by a hard tap on the end of his nose and, after he opened his eyes, there were several more taps on his nose, some near the end of his nose and one between his eyes. Moving his head up slightly to avoid the sometimes painful taps, he looked up at the night sky to find the source of the rocks and dust raining downward, but there wasn't anything to see except the black sky. Moving his head down almost to his furry chest, the dog noticed that the ledge was wider than before and, instead of disappearing around the corner, it seemed to widen at the very place where his foremost paw rested. He opened and closed his eyes several times to make sure that he wasn't dreaming – to make sure that there was a ledge in front of him and that it hadn't disappeared around the corner – and each time he opened his eyes and looked carefully at the ledge in front of him, he could see that instead of disappearing around the corner, it continued straight ahead and was gradually getting wider and wider. Looking down at his front paw, he also noticed that he needed only to step forward a couple of inches to reach a section jutting out from the cliff a good two feet, which became three feet a little farther on.

Could it be real? Could a ledge have the ability to contract and widen as if it were following the dictates of its own mind, a mind that didn't have to obey natural laws? But while he observed the ledge, he noticed that its width began to change, the wide expanse narrowing and, in spots, completely disappearing, which once again left him standing precariously on the verge of a black abyss. The dog eased his front legs backwards perhaps a half an inch (he couldn't move quickly, and an inch was twice as much as he could have mustered a few minutes ago), when the ledge suddenly widened again, this time enough that he could have walked comfortably onto it. He didn't immediately attempt to reach it, however, and instead craned his head upwards, as if the answer to what was happening at his feet could be found somewhere in the sky. But when he looked into the dark night, with the full moon, twinkling stars, and dull clouds now visible, he immediately understood what was happening and what he could do as a result. A thick, dark cloud shaped like the head and neck of a floating swan was gradually moving across the face of the moon, hiding and then revealing its light so that it cast opaque shadows across the ledge, obscuring and revealing portions of it. The ledge hadn't shrunk but had been there all along. Crinkling his dusty nose and licking his dry chops, the dog pushed himself off the side of the cliff and leaped forward, landing all four legs on a portion of the ledge that was nearly three feet wide and that continued straight ahead along the face of the cliff.

Relieved, the nightmare finally over, the dog shook himself violently, forcing a horizontal roll of skin and fur to flow down from his neck and shoulders, across the entire length of his back, and then onto his rump where it disappeared at the beginning of his tail. The shake was so exuberant that it forced his rear feet to one side, causing his left rear foot to go over the edge of the path and forcing his hindquarters to squat to keep from rolling off the ledge. The dog pulled himself up and away from the edge fairly easily (a momentary burst of adrenaline flowed through his body), although the brief experience sent a shiver along his back and increased his desire for water. Breathing deeply and giving his nerves a few seconds to calm down, he licked his nose and then something on his left shoulder before venturing forward on the slightly inclined ledge. He kept his shoulder to the cliff, though, in case the ledge was actually morphing.

The dog continued along the ledge for fifteen or twenty minutes. Initially, it was fairly level from side to side (there were a couple of spots where it seemed to slope down toward the darkness), but within minutes the gently upward curve of the path quickly yielded to a sharp upward grade that was increasingly difficult to climb, especially when the dirt covering the path disappeared and left behind a smooth, hard surface that in places was almost like glass. Had he slipped on the smooth surface, there wasn't anything that could have prevented him from sliding off the edge. Somehow he managed to grip the surface by keeping his weight on the balls of his hind feet and gouging his nails into the hairline cracks that crisscrossed the ledge's surface. There were moments, of course, when he needed every ounce of his strength to keep from slipping off the ledge, but these weren't constant and, importantly, they didn't seem to weaken him so much that he couldn't continue upward. In fact, when he noticed the uppermost edge of the cliff, which was so close that it seemed almost within reach, he suddenly felt stronger, and he jumped upward and loped up the rest of the ledge until it ended at what appeared to the be the final ledge to the top.

This ledge was bathed in the moon's pale light. It looked to be at least three feet wide and no more than fifty feet or so long, and, unlike the other ledge, it inclined gently upward. Even if its surface were glass, he was confident that he could easily walk its length without slipping or holding tight to the side of the cliff. But instead of immediately charging forward and putting an end to this interminable climb, the dog stopped and stared at the ledge, his reserve of strength and energy unexpectedly dissipated as if someone had pulled the plug and released his ability to move. The ledge was certainly the beginning of the end of his journey across the face of the cliff, but to get from here to there, from where he was standing to where he needed to go, seemed extraordinarily difficult and everything that he had endured previously a complete waste of time. In the first place, the ledge didn't begin with a wide, level area which he could reach comfortably and then position himself to trot to its termination. The first couple of feet were narrow, maybe a foot and a half wide, if that, and it sloped downward, meaning that he would have to position himself carefully if he wanted to avoid sliding off. In the second place, the ledge was separated from the one he was standing on by a gap of about a foot. While this wasn't particularly troublesome (he could easily step across a foot-wide gap), it seemed almost insurmountable because the ledge in front of him was a good two feet higher, meaning that he would have to jump up and onto a sloping ledge. Finally, as if he didn't have enough to worry about, he was unexpectedly hot and thirsty, and, instead of pushing forward, he felt like lying down and resting before taking another step. Faced with what now seemed to be the greatest impediment of all, the dog leaned against the slide of the cliff and tried to rest for a few minutes before he needed to take action. Staring at the final ledge, wondering if he had the strength to jump onto it, he began to imagine how Iowa would feel if he didn't show up at the zoo. He could see her standing alone at the center of the zoo, waiting while he dithered over trivial matters, waiting while he mustered the strength to move, waiting, waiting, waiting… The dog's shoulder began slipping and, with one quick jerk, he woke up and looked at the ledge, which was so close that he could practically reach out and touch it.

Licking his nose, the dog tried to reach the ledge by placing one of his paws on it, but he couldn't quite lift his leg high enough to reach it. Taking a large breath, he tried again and again, lifting one front leg and then the other, but each time his reach was a little lower than the last time until he realized that he wasn't going to reach the ledge in this manner. Even if he could place his paws on the ledge, he wasn't certain that he had the strength to pull himself onto it and at the same time hold fast without slipping and falling down through the gap. No, it was clear that his only chance of getting onto the ledge was by jumping over the gap, which would have been easier only a few minutes ago when he felt stronger.

Now certain that there was no other choice – that is, if he wanted to see Iowa -- the dog wiggled his left ear and cautiously backed up several steps, stopping at the place where he could feel the path begin to narrow abruptly. Leaning back slightly, putting his weight on his hind legs and his nose slightly in the air, he charged at the ledge, running with every ounce of strength he could muster. Just before he reached the ledge, he stretched out his front legs and pushed off with his back legs and reached for the top of the ledge. In the dark night, he couldn't tell if his eyes were open or closed, but for the briefest instant he felt as if he were flying not just over the ledge but over the entire cliff, the air currents rushing against his nose and fur, the smell of the land beyond the cliff becoming more and more intense. It was an extraordinary sensation, and when he finally came back to earth, landing on soft dirt well beyond the curve at the end of the ledge, he felt as if he had accomplished something important, and that Iowa was now only moments away.

It had been a risky jump, given his strength and the very real possibility that had he miscalculated, there wouldn't have been a second try. But although he landed safely, his body unexpected shuddered, his muscles weakened, and he began to list toward the edge and he started to fall. His left foot slipped off the ledge, and his other legs folded beneath him, making him feel as if he were dangling over the abyss. With his strength nearly gone and his body shaking, it was practically a miracle that he didn't roll off the edge, and yet he somehow managed to lean to the right and stop his downward momentum, pull his leg back to the ledge, and finally push himself up. Even though the muscles in his legs burned and, for a few moments, couldn't stop shaking, he was nevertheless able to take a few tentative steps forward before feeling confident enough that he could make it to the summit.

He walked slowly and carefully along the final ledge until he reached to the top of the cliff and he was finally on level ground as far as he could see. He was surprised that the moon was gone and that the far end of the sky was getting brighter. Sniffing the air, he could feel the change in the temperature and taste the smells that were strongest in the early morning.

Chapter Twenty

Once the dog was safely away from the paths, ledges, and crumbling rock, he started to relax and he could feel some of his former strength and energy come back to him. It was as if the cliff had been syphoning off his vital forces, and now free from its terrible embrace he was increasingly confident that he could reach Lordan and Iowa and return home on time. Trotting quickly, he lifted his nose and breathed deeply.

The morning air was still cool, and he could smell the remnants of the moisture that had leached upward from the ground. There wasn't enough moisture around to satisfy his increasing thirst, but its presence compared to the arid land at the base of the cliff and along the cliff's face was enough to buoy his spirits and sharpen his senses for an opportunity to fill his stomach. Pausing briefly and inhaling the pleasant-smelling air, he scanned the area around him and noticed that the long, black shadows were quickly retreating and opening up a strange, new vista. There were still trees on either side of him in the distance, but they weren't as thick or densely bunched together as the forests that had practically walled the park off from the rest of the world. The ground, too, was different. It appeared to be flat, and he couldn't see anything like the deep ravines, the massive rocks, or the firm bushes that made it difficult to travel in a straight line. It was also covered by low grasses, flat weeds, and in some places dirt so soft that it felt squishy between his toes; it was almost like walking across his bed at home. Did Iowa have a bed or was she confined to a cage or a small box?

With the cliff behind him and a soothing ground upon which to travel, the dog experienced a pleasant if momentary sensation of freedom, of being able to move his body and limbs anyway he chose, without being forced to contort himself this way or that to follow the dictates of a cold-hearted cliff. The sensation was such that for a short time his muscles would wiggle now and then as if they were testing themselves after a long period of disuse or abuse. But while he began moving at a decent clip (although much slower than before he reached the cliff), he quickly began to slow down and within minutes he was walking at a snail's pace, dragging his hind paws and dangling his long tongue out the side of his mouth. Despite the comfortable air and the freedom from the constraints of the cliff, his energy was unexpectedly flagging because he desperately needed water. He was hungry, too, and there were moments when his stomach felt as though it were on fire, but he knew that he could postpone food for some time as long as he had water. The dog took two more steps and stopped, his head, tongue, and tail hanging, unable to move another inch without some moisture dampening his tongue. Barely lifting his head, the dog sniffed the air for signs of water, and then scanned the dark grass surrounding him and the clumps of bushes a couple of hundred yards to his right. There had to be water somewhere, he thought, even if the scent of moisture was faint and distant.

Instinctively, the dog slowly pawed the grass and dirt in search of moisture and, when that failed to accomplish anything, he lowered his lead slowly and began to lick the grass (he had difficulty maneuvering his tongue so that he could stroke the grass blades), hoping to find a few drops of water that might tide him over until he came across a stream or pond. The grass, however, was dry, and, even when he tried to chew it to get some moisture, there wasn't enough to wet his tongue or even allow the chewed grass to be swallowed. The dog lifted his head slightly and inhaled the air for any signs of nearby moisture, but when the closest water seemed miles away, he dropped his head and stood motionlessly, balancing his need for water and his desire to sit down and rest for a while. A few moments later, he decided to rest for a while, but when he began to tuck his left, rear leg under his body to ease himself down to the ground, bottom first, he caught sight of something moving on the ground.

Jerking his head around as quickly as he could, he noticed a small shadow dart beneath his chest and reappear on the other side, where it, too, stopped. While he desired water, the idea of food, and with it some moisture, was enough spur his remaining energy, and he turned around surprisingly quickly to locate the thing that was once again on the move – only to lose sight of it again, as it seemed to have far more energy and speed than he possessed in his current condition. But he didn't give up (he couldn't give up, if he wanted to survive and see Iowa) and turned again and again, round and round, trying to catch a glimpse of the black thing running through the grass, each time being either outhustled or outsmarted. A few moments after this, it was gone, ensconced somewhere in the thick grass around his feet. He pawed the ground several times to scare it out, but nothing moved except the grass. Turning away in search of something else, the dog caught sight of the black object again, this time five or six feet away and slowly circling him, as if it were challenging him to lunge at it. He had taken the bait and, tensing his muscles, was just about to pounce when he caught sight of something floating above him. Looking up, he saw what appeared to be a grayish hawk floating back and forth overhead.

Disappointed that he had been duped by a shadow, the dog turned away from the moon's light and, looking at the blank darkness in front of him, was about to continue his slow march to Lordan when he noticed something else. His nose twitched, and he began to sense something, a smell that was vaguely familiar, but because the smell was faint and played around with his nostrils, it took him several seconds to identify the smell – it was water. Funny that he hadn't recognized it immediately, but there was now no question that there was a fairly large body of water nearby, and where there was any sizeable body of water, there was also food. Perhaps the crow, which was now completely out of sight, had noticed it, too, since the smell was coming from the direction in the crow had flown. Sniffing intensely this time, he tried to determine the exact location and distance to the water. To his surprise, the water was only a couple hundred feet away (not close, by any means, in his condition) and, without a second thought, he turned and walked as quickly as he could to where it was located. He wasn't disappointed this time, for within a half hour he encountered a broad, shallow marsh, which from a distance was completely undistinguishable from the rest of the grassy landscape.

Nearly exhausted by the time he reached the edge of the swamp, breathing heavily and unable to hold his jaw closed, the dog slowly waded into the water and, when it completely covered all four paws, he leaned down and began to drink the precious substance. While he drank, lapping up huge mouthfuls, he noticed the gray mist hovering across the swamp, broken here and there by tall grasses and plants and the light touch of a dragonfly's feet as it bounced off the surface and disappeared in the mist. Even though the water had no taste, it was cool and he could feel its coolness flowing through his body with each drink, which not only cooled his body and increased his strength, but it also buoyed his spirits, filling him with confidence that nothing could stop him from reaching Lordan and Iowa. Minutes later, his stomach full of water, the dog waded out into the swamp until the water was up to his chest and, pushing off the bottom with his hind feet, began swimming farther out into the water. It was hard to tell how far the water extended, but it didn't really matter because it felt good, even if he had to maneuver around clumps of long, slender reeds and thick conglomerations of lily pads. Now and then, he could sense a plop in the water somewhere around him, and when he peered into the water, there were small tadpoles, fish, or whatever darting away from his shadows. Refreshed and hungry, he turned and headed back to the shore, shaking himself vigorously several times as he stepped out of the water and onto dry land.

It was now time for food. He could sense it all around the swamp, though very little of it felt readily accessible. He tried to eat some of reeds handing over the shore, but he couldn't force himself to swallow them (they were bitter and didn't feel right as he chewed on them) and, one of them, which looked like a thick, brown sausage, actually burst in his mouth, filling it with a wad of dry, tasteless cotton-like matter that he had to spit out quickly because it was getting into his nose and choking him. Shaking his head several times and snorting equally often, he drank more water until he was finally able to expel the cotton from his mouth and separate the offending plant from the rest of his body. Once he was able to concentrate on things besides the plant, he lifted his nose and turned his ears toward sections in the swamp that might have something he could actually eat. Zeroing in on a slight rustling and then on a familiar musky odor, he jumped to his left and ran around the water's edge until he spotted a large rat trying to scurry beneath a clump of thick grass. He pounced on it and, capturing it by the tail, was able to kill it within seconds and then eat sections of it. Even though it was several times the size of a field mouse (much too large to swallow whole), there wasn't much to it, mainly skin and bones. Still, this is what he needed, and he was certain that he wouldn't need anything else for quite some time.

The dog turned toward Lordan and resumed trotting, but something rustled in the grass in front of him and he jumped over to see what it was. He sniffed the ground where he thought he had seen the grass move, and despite the fact that he couldn't see anything but grass, he knew that there was something slender and inedible slithering just out of sight. His reflexes were sharp, for he was able to jump back out of reach just as a long, black snake burst through the grass and lunged for his nose. When it failed to reach its target, the snake coiled and, lifting its head toward the dog, emitted a loud, prolonged hiss.

He was surprised by the snake's presence and behavior, and he hesitated to get within range of the reptile's sharp teeth, but at the same time it presented a welcome opportunity for some play time that he couldn't resist. Sticking his nose at the snake and leaping back out of reach of its bite, he played with the offended animal for some time while it gradually tired and slowed. Several times he maneuvered around the snake and bit its back, but because it was now injured and couldn't move as quickly as before, it was unable to retaliate and desperately tried to slither out of reach. The dog barked furiously throughout the snake's ordeal, until the wounded reptile managed to elude one of his lunges and began moving into a thick clump of grass at the water's edge. However, it couldn't move quickly enough to hide completely in the grass, and the dog managed to stop its movement with his right paw and, while the snake writhed in a continuous coil throughout its body, bite it several times, each time drawing blood. This battle – joyous on the dog's part but desperate on the snake's -- might have ended seconds later, but dog was abruptly distracted by a loud cawing noise overhead. Releasing the snake, which slowly moved out of sight into the grass, he saw another crow circling overhead.

The crow cawed several more times, and soon it was joined by another crow, which cawed and circled overhead. Knowing that there was nothing to be done about the crows, even if he wanted to do something about them, the dog turned and continued on his way.

Chapter Twenty-one

The dog galloped at a leisurely pace across the soft grass. He was still eager to reach Lordan, but he also needed to conserve his energy so that he didn't get sidetracked looking for water and food. Stopping briefly to make sure he was traveling in the right direction, he was about to start again when he noticed that the sun was just below the horizon in front of him. Although the moon was still faintly visible, the sky around it was turning pale blue and there area above the horizon was bathed in shimmering, golden hues. Surprised by the night's sudden departure, the dog glanced around his surroundings to see if anything else had changed. The ground was still grassy, but the forests on either side of him were gone and in their place were large, metallic towers topped off with thick, black wires that ran from tower to tower. The dog could smell the earth coming to life, though, and as he turned his ears he could hear the plants and animals around him humming, chirping, and rustling. But after shaking his head and shoulders, and licking the tip of his nose, he noticed a faint metallic smell and heard a strange sound emanating from somewhere directly in front of him. The source of the sound, which was probably no more than a mile away, seemed to be in an area not unlike the one he was standing in, and yet it lacked the moist, organic quality of the sounds surrounding him. Indeed, it was a dull, monotonous buzzing that was punctuated from time to time by pathetic bleats and howls, all of which became louder and more insistent the closer he got to the source. After a while, these odd and increasingly unpleasant sounds became so loud that they drowned out everything else. He had reached the highway.

The dog had a fleeting recollection of a red line that bisected his map and ran roughly parallel with the cliff. Now, standing in a dust-and-gravel strewn area not more than ten feet from the line, he could see that there was not one highway but two, each one exactly parallel to the other but separated by a thin strip of dirt and weeds (not too different than the area he was standing on) probably no wider than one of the highways. Since there was nothing to block his view of the highways (the land as far as he could see was flat with only a few deformations of some kind in the distance), he could see cars, trucks, and monstrous vehicles of one kind or another speeding along the highway, each one beginning as tiny, black specs in the distance, gradually getting bigger until they were recognizable, and, once they reached their full size, blowing past him, becoming tiny, black specs as they disappeared in the distance. The dog understood from the map that he would have to cross the highways if he wanted to reach Lordan, the zoo, and eventually Iowa, but as he took a couple steps closer to the black tar that defined the highways, he couldn't fathom how he was going to get across them with the constant parade of cars and trucks whooshing back and forth in front of him.

Unable to decide what to do next, he remained motionless at the side of the highway, mindlessly observing the vehicles as they passed in front of him and feeling his fur move up and down his spine from the air they stirred up, especially the giant trucks, which sometimes pushed so much wind toward him that he had to steady himself to keep from being forced to one side. Since there was no point in trying to find another location (he could sense that one stretch of the highway was as good as another), he decided to wait until the cars and trucks were gone before crossing, ignoring as well as he could the unceasing buzz of the traffic and the disturbing honks from vehicles trying to back him away from the pavement. Finally, after about ten minutes watching and waiting, waiting and watching, the dog noticed a large gap in the traffic directly in front of him. There were darks specs in the distance, but for the moment there wasn't a single car on the near section of the highway. Even though there wasn't a corresponding gap in the traffic on the far section, he decided that this was his one chance to cross at least this half, and, if he didn't cross now, he might not have a similar opportunity for who knows how long. With only a minor hesitation, he quickly trotted across the highway until he reached the barren, dirt-covered area between the two halves of the highway.

The space between the two sections of the highway was narrower than he thought, although there was still enough room to stand comfortably and wait for the traffic in front of him to clear. The section he had just crossed, though, was once again filled with cars and trucks, and so going back the way he came to find some other way to cross both sections of the highway was impractical, to say the least. Waiting patiently for an opportunity to cross this section, he stared at the seemingly never-ending rush of traffic, wondering when it would end while being buffeted by the winds coming from the vehicles in front of him and now also in back of him. He had almost become used to the constant noise of the traffic when a gigantic truck hauling two imposing trailers was coming down the highway and wailing its loud horn (actually, it was one continuous peal that didn't end until long after the truck and its trailers passed by). Startled by the obnoxious sound, which pierced his sensitive ears like a hot poker, he jumped back away from the section of the highway he was facing. Unfortunately, this set off a chain reaction among the cars and trucks on the highway behind him, which honked their horns insistently, some even screeching their tires to avoid coming close to him. This incident, along with the continued honking from the vehicles in both directions, made the dog feel increasingly uncomfortable standing in that particular spot, and so he turned and trotted to another section that he hoped would be quieter and less sensitive to his movements.

As he moved, he noticed papers, cups, garbage of various kinds along the ground, parts of what looked like tires (large, black, quarter moon-like objects whose ragged edges seemed to reaching to the sky), as well as the remains of a deer, a cat, and two small dogs. The dog inched his nose toward a few of the carcasses, which emitted a peculiar but not entirely unpleasant odor, and he couldn't help wondering what could have destroyed parts of the bodies and, in two instances, made their eyes bulge out unnaturally. Turning away from the last carcass he encountered, he noticed that the section of the highway he still needed to cross was now open and the nearest approaching car was far off in the distance. The dog galloped across this section of the highway without a single car or truck noticing his presence, much less blowing their horns and slamming on their brakes.

Having crossed both sections safely, the dog picked up his pace and began heading toward a mass of buildings in the distance, which seemed to appear with the rising sun and the retreating shadows that once covered most of the earth. He wasn't running very hard, but he was covering large stretches of land fairly quickly until he reached an open, treeless, dirt-covered lot that was surrounded by old, shabby buildings with metal roofs, beat-up and rusting cars, and rusty, sagging fences. As far as he could tell (his view beyond the lot was limited to gaps between the old buildings), the area was filled with many lots like this one, some of which were protected by towering chain-link fences, often topped by spirals of barbed wire. Neither the lots nor this section of the town (which he didn't know was part of Lordan), seemed to be populated, and so he didn't hesitate to continue, dodging weeds, garbage, and bits of broken glass as he did so, until he came to the other side, that is, until he came to a narrow road that seemed to separate the lots from the next town (which was only a different section of Lordan). Stepping into the street between two parked or abandoned cars, the dog stretched his head out to survey the street and make sure that it was safe before venturing out any farther and, once it appeared to be safe (there weren't any moving cars to be seen), he quickly trotted across the road to reach a dirt path that separated a series of buildings and fences from the road and that was as empty of people as the road was of moving vehicles. The dog followed the path as it paralleled the road, passing a seemingly endless series of small, tired-looking buildings, whose windows were often broken out or boarded up, interspersed with additional dust-covered lots and their tall, often sagging fences. Unlike the other lots, these seemed to be filled with everything from flattened cars to piles of beat-up, gas-and-oil-clogged metal, which was rank and made his nose continually crinkle.

The sky was clear and the temperature now rapidly rising. With his increasing body temperature, and the brief moments when he felt the need for rest and sleep, the dog's pace began to slow and he longed for water, cool water, to cool his body and energize his senses. Fortunately, at the very moment he was most concerned about the heat and the absence of water, licking his lips over and over and shaking his head to throw off some of the heat, he noticed a small puddle of water inside a narrow slit of shade next to a rusted metal building on his side of the road. The water was dirty – it was nearly as brown as the surrounding soil – but water was water, and if he wanted to make it to the zoo, he needed to drink whatever came to paw or suffer the consequences. Standing in the middle of the puddle, its cool water surrounding his feet and cooling him off, he drank his fill and then licked off the pearls of water clinging to his whiskers and jowls, after which he continued onward, not once looking back at the puddle or regretting that he had not played in it a little before resuming his journey. Water (and he didn't even think of food) was now only a means to an end and, because he was so close to Iowa that he could nearly feel her presence, he was determined not to do anything unnecessary that could slow him down or subtract from the precious time that had left to see her before going back.

As the dog walked down one block after another, moving past more lots and buildings with metal roofs and broken cars either on the side of the road or in the lots, the metal-roofed buildings soon gave way to normal-looking buildings with hard roofs and unbroken windows, and the abandoned cars became running, functioning automobiles with drivers and passengers. The lots disappeared and in their place were more buildings, parking lots, and covered sidewalks where people were busily moving from one place to another, shuffling back and forth between buildings or coming and going in cars and small trucks. While the number of people walking around on the sidewalks was staggering (compared to the dearth of people only a few blocks away), they all seemed preoccupied with their own business and few of them even glanced at the dog, much less tried to help what appeared to be a lost pet wandering the streets of the city. He still had to be careful, however, for even though the traffic was slower than it was on the highway, there were more cars moving about on the roads, and there were no medians to help him if somehow he got caught in the middle of a street. His luck was good, though, because he was able to cross even the busiest streets if he followed the crowds of people crossing the direction he needed to go, although a couple of times he was nearly hit by some cars when he didn't stay close enough to these people and was compelled to run to get to the sidewalk.

Stopping briefly to rest his paws, which were hot and tired from the uncomfortable sidewalk, he sniffed the air to get his bearings. When trekking across the park, it wasn't particularly difficult to locate the smells of large animals, but in this section of the city, his senses were accosted by a variety of sensations that made it increasingly difficult to keep his focus on the zoo. There were loud, distracting noises coming from every direction -- people talking, cars moving and honking their horns, and an amazing array of unidentifiable scraping, banging, slushing, and hissing sounds -- as well as intense smells that surrounded him and threatened to engulf him. There were human smells, garbage smells, engine smells, industrial smells, unidentifiable smells, and, of course, food smells. There were restaurants and stores on both sides of the street, and the dog inhaled the scents of meat and other savory foods, in addition to an endless range of substances that he couldn't identify and that made his stomach ache with the desire to eat. Once as he crossed a street, he noticed a strong smell of raw meat (it was a butcher shop) and, instead of putting it out of his mind while he was in the center of the street, he stopped and looked over his shoulder at the shop and, for a few seconds, inhaled the smells as if he were actually eating. But he had waited too long and within seconds cars were zooming around him, honking their horns, and a few individuals leaned out their widows and shouted at him to move out of the away. "Beat it, you stupid...," yelled one young man with a dirty T-shirt and scraggly beard, leaning over the side of a beat-up, smoking car. Jumping away from the car and turning toward the direction that he needed to travel, the dog galloped the rest of the way across the street, barely escaping the screeching tires and the sounds of thin metal crunching and folding. He continued running down the sidewalk, moving in and out of people, past dogs on leashes who barked furiously at him as he passed, and finally (and after crossing several more busy streets, although he paused at each one and carefully made his way across with the pedestrians) reached a large, grassy city park, which instead of cars was filled with old, gnarled trees with leafy, sagging branches and people of all kinds strolling across the green lawn, lounging on blankets, or playing catch.

The dog observed two parallel lines of school children at the corner and followed them across the street and into the park. He was certain that the cars and their drivers wouldn't harry them as they crossed, and he thought that he could follow them in the park and not be accosted as he made his way to the zoo, which he could sense was at the other end of the park and not very far away. Once inside the park, however, he may have been a little close to the children, for several of them turned and came over to him and, crowding over him, began petting him. When the four adults who were chaperoning the children noticed the dog, two of them called the children away and the other two, tall athletic young women, ran toward him, hollering and chasing him away from the children, as if they were afraid that he might hurt them. "Scat!" one of them, a woman with dark brown hair and wearing a blue blazer, shouted several times at him, while the other woman, probably a little older but wearing the same kind of clothing, came charging at him from another angle and, waving a stick, acted as if she were going to pummel him with it. "Scat, you filthy...," the first kept yelling, and when neither one could catch him, the latter threw her stick at him, missing him by a wide range.

When he was confident that he was far enough away to slow down, he glanced back in their direction but couldn't see them; they had gone in a different direction and were hidden by the trees. Shaking his head, he turned back toward the zoo and nearly ran into a young couple behind a baby carriage. The man, who was wearing a baseball cap backwards, was clearly very protective of the baby, and he rolled up the newspaper or magazine that he had and chased the dog away and deeper into the park. He was more determined than the women, and he followed the dog for some distance before he was satisfied that he had either taught the dog a lesson or that he had made the animal afraid to come anywhere near his baby again. But the dog didn't go very far. Because the man had been chasing him away from the zoo, the dog waited until the man was far enough away that he could turn back and, moving in a huge arc to stay out of the man's sight, headed toward the sounds of large animals. Despite the commotion caused by his presence, despite the roundabout manner in which had been forced to travel through the park, the dog had somehow managed to get closer to the zoo, where the thick scent of large, dangerous animals hung over the area like a deep fog. The smells of the animals were initially pleasant, but as he got closer to their source, he became a little uneasy because the smells suggested, in many instances, large and powerful beasts that were looking for an opportunity to release their pent-up energies on something or someone. He couldn't shake the feeling, even when he reminded himself that the most dangerous of the animals were behind cages or chained to a large, metal stake in the ground. After another twenty minutes or so of walking and trotting toward the smells (always mindful of the man, the baby, the children and their teachers, and so on), the dog suddenly came upon the zoo entrance, which was a large open area partially obscured (from his position) by several large, leafy trees.

Stopping and looking around, he sniffed the thick, troubling air. At first, he could only sense the overpowering presence of the large animals, but as he quickly separated one smell from another, one large animal from another, he began to detect something familiar and less formidable – a swan, and it was Iowa. The scent created an image in his mind that hadn't changed in all these years. Yes, she was here; she was alive; he had finally found her.

Naturally, he couldn't just saunter through the entrance on four feet. Even if the zoo weren't a refactoring facility, no one would allow a dog on the premises because of the commotion it would cause among the animals, not to mention the people, who weren't used to seeing four-legged creatures outside a cage. No, he realized that his only chance of seeing Iowa would require him to change back to human form, which at the same time would make finding her among all the other animals more difficult. But since there was nothing to be done about it, nothing that he could do to change zoo rules, he would have to do his best using infinitely weaker senses, relying mainly on sight and his own voice. Shaking his head and body to brace for what he had to do, the dog scanned the area around him for a suitable place to change, one which was out of the way and which offered enough foliage to hide him from unsuspecting passersby (possibly the man with the newspaper). Spotting a thicket beneath some large trees whose long, drooping branches nearly touched the ground, the dog trotted over to it and squeezed through the branches until he reached a small clearing at their very center.

The thick foliage overhead made the area dark, and once he sat down on the thick pile of leaves covering the ground, he felt almost as if he were in bed for the evening. Rolling comfortably to his side and tucking his legs beneath him, he closed his eyes, concentrated, and changed back to human form. The change, for some reason, was difficult, as if this was the very first time he had changed, and, a few seconds into the process, his discomfort and lack of success made him wonder if he would have to stop and start over again. But somehow he managed to transition through the entire process before he was forced to make that decision, and, when he was finished, his body was sore and he was ravenously hungry. Standing up, stretching and shaking his arms and legs to loosen them up and alleviate the discomfort he felt in human form, he was ready to step out from behind the bush and walk to the zoo. It was at that moment that he noticed a young couple, probably teenagers, strolling nearby, hand in hand. It was clear that they hadn't seen anything, because they walked right past the bushes without noticing him as he stood only a few feet away.

Once the couple was gone, Luke stepped out from behind the tree and, looking around to figure out which way he needed to go, decided to follow the couple. They were probably going to the zoo, he told himself, and if not he could always ask someone along the way. He knew it was very close, and he vaguely regretted not remaining a dog until he found the entrance.

Chapter Twenty-two

Ms. Royce was sitting at her desk, tapping the end of her pencil against a large, open binder. From time to time, she glanced at the right-hand page in the binder, studied a particular passage (the same passage each time), and, after looking away, continued tapping the end of her pencil. At the same time, she stared at the closed door in front of her desk, as if she were expecting someone to open it any second.

The walls of her office were covered with pictures of people, mainly former students, and animals. There were all kinds of animals represented, although birds and raptors seemed to predominate, and more than a few of the pictures were hung side by side with the people, suggesting a connection between the two. There was also a large window behind her that covered nearly the entire wall, although it was currently covered with blinds that were tightly closed. When the blinds were open, Ms. Royce could see the broad, open area in front of the school and watch students coming and going through the front door, which was just out of sight to the left of her office. There was nothing to see today, however, because school wasn't in session, which might have been a reason for the closed blinds and the relatively dark office, which was illuminated by a lamp on the gray, metal credenza next to the wall. Perhaps, but in many ways her mood matched the dusk-like appearance of the room.

"Is this a good time?" Ms. Royce's door opened slightly and a tall woman in a business suit holding a brown portfolio appeared.

Mr. Royce looked at her with surprise. "Yes, of course. I didn't hear you enter the main doors. Yes, please come in and have a seat. Would you mind turning on the light? The switch is next to the door."

The woman who came into the office was the very same woman Luke had overheard speaking to the principal. Despite the seriousness of her expression, she seemed to be a pleasant woman, and she was carrying the portfolio tightly against the front of her jacket as if she were afraid of losing it.

"Please," insisted Ms. Royce, pointing to the cushioned chair in front of her desk when the woman hesitated. Ms. Royce also had a serious expression on her face, which over the past three years appeared to have aged somewhat. The lines on her otherwise attractive face seemed a little more prominent these days, and there were a couple of streaks of gray on the bangs of her loosely-done hair. Unlike the other woman, Ms. Royce was dressed casually, in running pants with a loose blouse, as if she had stopped by her office while running an errand, not intending to conduct business or meet with anyone.

Once the woman was seated, Ms. Royce added, "Thank you for coming today. I apologize for calling on short notice."

"You have nothing to apologize for," she replied, her expression remaining serious. "This is my job, after all." The woman, Mrs. Jacobson, was a highly placed, well-respected member of the Changers' Board, as well as the vice superintendent of the school district. "Besides, I am not sure we can wait until something happens. Do you agree?"

"Yes, I do," Ms. Royce said, her cold, unsmiling eyes locked onto the woman's, although she wasn't angry with the woman for meeting her on the weekend. "You didn't think I wanted to put it off or wait for an extension, did you?"

"No, that wasn't my meaning. It's just that the subject in this case was a student of yours…"

"You can say the subject's name. It's Luke."

"Yes, of course, and I am not implying that favoritism or…"

"Let's be clear, so there's no misunderstanding." Ms. Royce set her pencil on the desk and, after closing the large binder in front of her, looked intently at the woman. "While I personally handled Luke's case, I am quite happy if someone wants to take change of it this time. My purpose in calling you at this juncture was not to plead for special favors but to alert everyone to a possible – note that I said possible, not actual – problem. If, indeed, there is a problem, I expect it to be dealt with as expeditiously as possible, and I also expect that no special considerations will be made in this instance…"

"I'm not suggesting…"

"Please, let me finish. On the other hand, if there is a problem, I will indeed be disappointed, for I had high hopes for Luke. Nevertheless, as I said, I expect his case to be handled like any other."

"Believe me, I understand, and I think we are on the same page. Let me also say that you are doing the right thing. It's never too early to call us in on something like this. If there's a mistake, then there's no problem and we all shake hands. But if we are called after things get out of control…well, it becomes much hard to put things aright, and people suffer more. If I'm not mistaken, the situation that happened three years ago…"

Ms. Royce was certain that the woman was going to use the incident to suggest that the authorities were brought in too late last time, which would not only be a veiled criticism of Ms. Royce's handling of the incident but would also open the door for the women to insist on someone else taking control of the current case, if again there was a problem. While Ms. Royce wasn't one to deviate from regulations, she was concerned about Luke – she felt he showed great promise and feared that it would be ruined if he were punished, if it came to that, too severely – and didn't want to see him handled arbitrarily, like an animal, which happens all too often in rigidly codified systems like the one supported by the Changers' community. "You are not mistaken, but I am only interested in the potential, that is, possible, issue at hand."

"Of course, you're right. The past is past, and right now neither one of us wants anything less than the fair application of Changer law."

Ms. Royce knew that she was supposed to agree with the woman, but she was beginning to dislike the woman and didn't want to agree with anyone she potentially disliked. "Do you have the file?" she said to change the subject. She nodded to the large portfolio that the woman was holding.

The woman smiled agreeably, as if to say that she understood Ms. Royce completely. "Oh, yes, I brought it with me, as you can see." She lifted up the flap across the top of the portfolio and, fishing around for something inside it, extracted a thick stack of papers clipped together a large black clip and handed them across the desk to Ms. Royce. "Nothing superficially out of the ordinary," she said, again with a slight, knowing smile. "But if you look carefully, I am sure that you'll find some tendencies that…"

"I'm not interested in tendencies. He's been following the rules, hasn't he?" Without waiting for an answer, Ms. Royce began flipping through the pages, stopping from time to time to examine a passage or locate a footnote.

"Yes, and he continues to get excellent marks for both his academic classes and his refactoring requirements."

Although Ms. Royce wasn't looking at her, she sensed that the woman was smiling when she added these details, as if in Luke's case they meant something perverse, not positive. "He's completed community service, I believe, although I don't see any notation to that effect."

"I wasn't aware of it. If you can send me a note confirming that, I will add it to the file. Please note the date and time and any other particulars, including responses from his overseers."

"You'll have it tomorrow."

"Excellent. I'll make a note of it." The woman pulled a small, black notebook and a silver pen from the inside of her jacket pocket and made some notes.

"I don't see anything in here to suggest recidivism." She looked at the woman again, and this time her eyes were narrowed as if to suggest that she wanted nothing but the facts.

"No, nothing has been indicated."

Ms. Royce closed the papers and handed them back to the woman, who placed them back in the portfolio and closed the flap.

"Okay," Ms. Royce began and then paused, as if something suddenly came into her mind. Picking up her pencil and resting its dull point against the surface of her desk, she looked carefully at the woman across from her. The woman, who was silent at this point, looked back at her unflinchingly. Finally, turning away and looking at her desk, Ms. Royce began talking as much to herself as to the woman. "I believe I told you most of the details earlier. You have the father's statement; the mother, for some reason, didn't provide anything; and it was only last night that I found out that Luke was actually missing. The father stated that Luke was supposed to be with a friend, but when the father (or the mother, I'm not sure which) contacted the parents of Luke's friend, they didn't know anything about the arrangement."

Ms. Royce paused after she glanced up at the woman and noticed her writing in her small, black notebook.

"No need," Ms. Royce said. "I'll put it all in my report."

"Please, go on," she said without ceasing to write. "I'll only use my notes for comparison."

Ms. Royce continued looking at her for a couple of moments and then turned away and finished her statement. "The other boy seemed to be genuinely unaware of Luke's plan, if it is a plan, and his whereabouts.

Please add that Luke didn't leave a note, which might be expected if he were a runaway."

"Yes, yes, I suppose, I suppose," she replied without looking up from her notebook. When she finished scribbling something, she looked at Ms. Royce. "As I recall, there's nothing in the file to suggest a proclivity for running away. Why is that?"

"Because Luke doesn't have a proclivity for running away."

"You also stated that the boy…sorry, Luke…that is, that Luke's father told you that he never got over his initial depression. Am I correct on this point?"

Ms. Royce breathed deeply. "You are referring to whom, Luke or his father?"

"I'm sorry. Luke, of course. You said…"

"Yes, he said that, and I put it into Luke's file. It's not surprising, however. Luke is a sensitive young man, and his father is concerned about his son's emotional health, especially after the incident three years ago. I don't believe that there's anything unusual or of concern here."

"Is this the first time you heard about the boy's mental issues?"

"He doesn't have any mental health issues that I'm aware of. And, yes, this is the first that I've heard of the problem. Luke has always seemed fine around me. How he behaves at home is a matter for his parents to relate."

"Yes, of course. I'll reach out to them, too."

Ms. Royce stood up and opened the blinds. She looked out across the empty grounds in front of the school and, as if she had seen something out there that had a bearing on the case, she turned back to the woman and sat back down. "There may be something else."

"Excuse me?" the woman asked, looking up from her notebook.

"Iowa is at the Lordan facility."

The woman continued to look at Ms. Royce and then abruptly turned to her portfolio and, after opening the flap, pulled out some papers that she quickly thumbed through. Not finding what she was looking for, she looked back at Ms. Royce. "Yes, I am well aware of her situation, but how did Luke come by this information?"

"I'm not saying that he did. I only mentioned it because this is the first time since the incident that Luke has done anything to raise concerns."

"She's been there all along. Why didn't he know this earlier? Why now? Why not wait another year until he's eighteen? Do you think someone told him about her? Do you think she said anything? In Section C-1, it says…"

"I'm not interested in what Section C-1 says, and I'm not going to jump to conclusions. I simply want to point out that there was something between them a few years ago, and it may be worthwhile speaking to Iowa to see if she knows anything."

The woman put the papers back into her portfolio and, once again, closed the flap. "Unless you have something more to go on, I'm inclined to let this drop. I've been keeping tabs on Iowa, and I find absolutely no fault with her activities or services. I am certain that she's had no contact with the boy."

"Luke?"

"Yes. Let me also add that there's no way he could have learned of her whereabouts from Iowa herself. Nor could he have learned anything from other people privy to this information, and by that I mean the principal, you and me, and of course the facility officials."

"You forget the Changers on the board and…"

"Yes, yes, but I still say that there's no way he could have found out. Are you suggesting…"

"No, I'm not suggesting anything. If you say he doesn't know, then I'll take your word for it."

The woman paused for a moment, trying to fathom what was on Ms. Royce's mind. "Since you're reporting his absence only out of duty, perhaps you feel that it would be best to call in the local police to help find the boy."

"I'm reporting it out of concern, too. But, right now I think we should leave the question of the police to the parents. We still don't know if he's violated his probation…"

"If you don't mind, I'll contact his parents to see if they have any opposition to engaging the police, after which I will reach out to the Smiths. They may already have some information. If not, I'm sure they can at least locate the boy…I mean Luke."

Ms. Royce liked the Smiths. She had a great deal of respect for them both as people and as professional hunters of deviant Changers. But at the same time she hesitated to bring them in on the case (if there was a case) at this juncture because she was concerned that it could create a host of problems that could have been prevented by a few, simple phone calls. "It might be best to wait until the time when he said that he would return," she replied, knowing that if she asked for more time, the woman would see that as a special favor and would respond negatively. "Once again…"

"I share your understanding of the complexity of the issue here," she replied. She glanced at her portfolio to make sure it was properly closed and then stood up, one hand clutching the portfolio and the other reaching out to Ms. Royce. "Let's keep in touch whatever happens."

As soon as the woman closed the door behind her, Ms. Royce sat back down at her desk and, picking up her pencil, began tapping it against her desk while she stared at the back of the door. Suddenly dropping the pencil onto the desk, where it bounced a couple of times before rolling to a stop against the binder, she picked up the binder and dropped it into the large, right-hand drawer on the side of her desk. After locking the drawer and putting the key into her pocket, she again picked up the pencil with her right hand (as if she were about to write something, although there was no paper on her desk) and, with the other hand, picked up the phone on her desk and dialed a number while holding the phone with the same hand.

"Have you heard anything yet?" she asked the man on the other end as soon as he said "hello" into the line.

"No."

"All right, I guess I'm not surprised. I have a hunch."

"What do you mean?" Luke's father asked, a hint of desperation in his voice.

"Just let me know immediately if you hear anything."

"Sure, but can you tell us anything? Do you know where he is? Do you know where he's going?"

"You'll get a call from Mrs. Jacobson. She has some matters she wants to discuss with you regarding Luke. I would prefer if you didn't mention this call."

"Does she know anything? Will she be able to…"

"Look, you're just going to have to trust me, all right? When anything definitive comes up, I'll let you know. If you hear something, please contact me first, all right?"

"Of course, that's why I went to you first. You've always done right by us. I just want to know."

When the phone call was over, Ms. Royce left her office and locked the door behind her. Had someone observed her from her office window, they would have seen her leave the school building and, walk quickly toward the parking lot, which couldn't be seen from her window. Surprisingly, Ms. Royce had neglected to turn out her office lights.

Chapter Twenty-three

Luke brushed the leaves and dirt off his clothes as he followed the young couple. He kept a respectful distance from them (he didn't want them to be concerned by his presence and alert the authorities) while at the same time careful not to lose sight of them among the increasing number of people strolling and milling about the park. He followed the couple for about three or four minutes when, as he hoped, he knew they were heading to the very place he wanted to go.

They had been walking along a thick grove of trees on the right, while on the left was an open, grassy area where people were picnicking, running, kicking soccer balls, and throwing Frisbees. It surprised him how many people appeared out of nowhere and were meandering near the trees under which he changed back to human form. But while he was observing the people on his left, he noticed that the grove of trees on his right abruptly ended, revealing a large brick wall that ran on for another few yards before culminating in several large, black iron gates that marked the entrance of the zoo. Surprisingly, the gates were open (he didn't know why he had expected them to be closed), and a crowd of people young and old, including the couple, were slowing walking through the open gates into the zoo. Following the crowd and slowing walking toward the entrance, Luke noticed a large, iron sign built into the gates that said Lordan Zoo, while just underneath it was another announcing the fact that this was an entrance and that pets were not allowed on the grounds.

Luke couldn't believe how easy it was to find the entrance, and he couldn't believe his luck when he noticed another sign, to the right of the gates, which indicated the entrance was free. While he had thoughtfully brought some money with him (his allowance of five dollars – he didn't know how much he would need and was certain that five dollars would be enough for the weekend), he had mistakenly left it in his backpack. But now it didn't matter, and as he filed through the entrance with children, strollers, and parents, he was happy, happy to be alive because in a few minutes he would see Iowa again.

Walking slowly, he entered the zoo with everyone else. Actually, the crush of people was such that it was difficult to move quickly or freely, and while he gradually progressed forward, he remembered the time when Iowa called him after having been missing for over a year. She called him and no one else. She could have called any of the others, she could have called Dana, Press, and Lu, she could have called them and him, but she didn't – she called him, and the only reason that she called him and not the others must have been due to something special between them that they didn't share with the others. Admittedly, he was surprised by her call, for the last time they had spoken was shortly after she poked him beneath his eye with that stick. But as they conversed, Iowa apologizing and explaining her situation and asking him to speak to the others so that they understood, he quickly understood why she chose him to be her Aaron, and it was simply because of this special feeling that had existed between them probably since the very time they met as children. What was more important was that the feeling or special relationship between them continued after she returned and showed everyone how to change. In fact, it was at this point that she demonstrated to him and the others just how special their relationship was. While Press, Dana, and Lu ostracized him for refusing to become a swan, Iowa alone stood by him; she refused to turn away from him, even during the worst of it, before they were caught, and everyone except Iowa vilified him for Press' injury and all the rest of it. Luke was certain that had Iowa not become addicted by the power of changing and seduced by the ability to become something else, they would have stayed together and would have become even closer, possibly forgetting the Cygnets altogether. None of it mattered anymore. Really, the only thing that mattered now was that the relationship still existed and that he was here at the zoo only because she managed to communicate without words her desire to see him again.

Luke's patience was certainly put to the test as he continued to move forward – at a snail's pace, he couldn't help noting to himself -- but his irritation quickly faded when he finally reached the large, open area just inside and the crowds almost miraculously disappeared as everyone headed in different directions. Since he didn't know where to find Iowa, Luke headed straight ahead (at that moment, one direction was as good as another) and, after traveling a few yards, he was confronted by two sidewalks, one going to the left and the other to the right. The zoo was bisected by these sidewalks, which led to the various exhibits, some of which were grassy areas outside, some marshy areas that bordered the grassy areas, and some housed in large, nondescript buildings at various points on the grounds. Far from the least of the zoo's exhibits, these buildings housed a variety of animal exhibits (there was one for tropical birds, one for reptiles, one for great apes, one for large cats, and others for animals that were impossible to classify), as well as providing services for sick and injured animals and shelter for the staff, who spent long hours caring for the animals, the zoo grounds, and the exhibits. While he was standing between the sidewalks, trying to decided which direction to take (he was suddenly afraid of taking the wrong sidewalk, for the more time he spent looking for Iowa, the less time he would have to see and visit her), an old gentleman wearing a ranger suit with Lordan Zoo emblazoned on his green vest came up from behind and put his plump, hairy hand gently on Luke's shoulder. Luke turned and looked at him.

The old man was about Luke's height, although much heavier, and when he smiled, which he did when he put his hand on Luke, his face was a maze of wavy lines and shallow canyons. "Are you lost, young fella?" he asked, his voice deep and calming. "May I help you?"

Luke was startled. Even though there were people everywhere, he had a comforting feeling that he was alone, that no one way paying attention to him, but when the man appeared, seemingly as if out of nowhere, Luke had the strange sensation of being caught in the act of committing a crime. The sensation wasn't entirely misplaced, for there was a very real possibility that the rangers and other zoo officials were on the alert for people who had no business being in the zoo (people, for instance, who were searching for a friend who was now an animal, not visiting the exhibits), since this was both zoo and refactoring facility. For all Luke knew, the man could have been eyeing him because of something he observed about Luke's behavior, or maybe someone (most likely Press) informed the authorities that he was going to see Iowa; it was even possible that someone had seen him eavesdropping on the conversation after school, and therefore they knew his intentions and were now waiting for him. There were a myriad other possibilities swirling through his mind at the moment, and so Luke could only smile, hold his breath, and reply as politely as he could. "No, sir. I mean, yes. I am trying to find my way around the zoo." Luke didn't want to ask where the swans were, because he didn't want to arouse suspicions that he was here for something other than seeing all the animals.

"Well, now, I think I can help you with that. You've never been here before, I presume. Am I right, son?"

"No, sir."

"I can always tell a first timer. Are you here with your parents or a group?" He glanced around as if they might be standing somewhere nearby.

"No, sir. What I mean to say is that my parents are in the park, and they told me to have a look before they come to join me." Luke regretted having told such a silly lie (he hadn't anticipated such a question), and he was suddenly worried that the man would see through it...and him.

"I see, I see," the man replied and then paused for a moment. Luke couldn't tell whether he was waiting for him to respond – to confess – or was simply trying to make sense of what he said. "Well, perhaps you can tell me what kinds of animals you want to see first. If you tell me that, I can point out a number of things that will help you get through the zoo. There are a few exhibits here that you – and your parents – shouldn't miss."

For some reason, the man's questions didn't seem exactly straightforward. Luke was afraid that he was asking him questions to get certain answers that would confirm something that he had on his mind. "I don't want to trouble you. Maybe if you have a map..."

"Map? Sure, son. There's one over there on the wall," the man said while gesturing over his right shoulder to a map painted on the brick wall that surrounded the zoo, "and there're signposts that'll point you toward whatever kind of animal you're looking for." He gestured toward a signpost almost directly in front of Luke (he didn't know how he could have missed it) that had several pointed metal signs indicating where to find this animal or that habitat.

Luke smiled foolishly. "Thank you. I think I'll wander around for a bit, if you don't mind," he said and started to walk away from the man.

"Wait a minute, young fella," the man called out to him when he was no more than five feet away. "You sure you're not looking for something particular? I'm sure I can help you."

"No, sir," Luke replied over his shoulder and, when he turned around, bounced into the sign and, ricocheting backward, nearly knocked down a child carrying a balloon. Apologizing to the boy and his mother, who had immediately walked over, he turned to the man, who was eyeing him carefully, and informed him that he was fine and didn't need help.

The man didn't reply. With a knowing smile, he placed his hands on his hips and watched Luke as he followed a sidewalk that went up a small hill, down another, turned a corner and ended among lions, hippos, zebras, and other savannah dwellers. Luke breathed a sigh of relief when the man was out of sight, although he didn't put it past the man to follow him. Was the man connected to the refactoring program? Did the man know who Luke was and what he was doing at the zoo? Not willing to take any chances, Luke hurried through the exhibit, followed the sidewalk to another, which curved away from the major exhibits and reached out to a large, roundish lake covered with water lilies and surrounded by swamp grass.

The exhibit appeared empty and, as he looked around, he noticed a sign that said, "Under Construction." There were a couple of benches at front of the lake, and Luke decided to sit for a minute and figure out how he was going to find Iowa. It was strange, he told himself, that Changers who require rehabilitation to become humans again would be sent here. Of course, they were in an animal form, and so that part of it made sense, but to have these animals – which could be friends or loved ones – sent here so that children could laugh at them and adults could look on them as entertainment was too much. It was appalling, and it made Luke wonder at the cruelty and insensitivity of people, people who cared only for their entertainment or who simply wanted the animals kept somewhere so that their presence wouldn't be troubling. Yes, the animals had to be taken some place so they could be treated – they had broken the rules, after all – but did it have to be a place like this? It was inhuman, he told himself. Having thought all this, however, he couldn't help wondering if all the animals were Changers who had gone bad, if all the zoo officials were involved in refactoring – the process of bringing the animal back to its human form – including the man whom he had spoken to. He also wondered if Jimmy – who as one of the dogs that night at the lake had been taken for refactoring as well – were here. He didn't really care, though, because he had no intention of visiting Jimmy, even if he were in a cage right in front of him.

As he was looking blankly at the lake, Luke noticed something on the water perhaps thirty feet offshore. Initially, it looked like an odd clump of debris (grass and cattails tangled around a bright piece of wood), but the more he stared at it, the more it began to resemble something familiar – maybe an animal – although it was still too far out to be certain. This troubled Luke because it looked almost recognizable and yet he couldn't identify it – but he felt that he had to identify it because there was something important about it, something that held the keys to what he had been searching for nearly all his life. And what had he been searching for?

Luke suddenly opened his eyes. He had been traveling all night and hadn't had a chance to sleep since Thursday night. What day was it now, he asked himself? Saturday?

Standing up and, after scanning the pond to make sure he hadn't missed something, he took the sidewalk back to the entrance area where he had seen the map. Luckily, the ranger wasn't nearby, and so Luke felt a little freer to study the layout of the zoo. But while the map was large, a good five-by-four feet, he had trouble seeing anything because a gray-haired couple with a young, blond-haired boy was standing right in front of it while the boy pointed out everything he "needed" to see. It was only after they left (with the boy complaining vociferously that they were going in the wrong direction) that he could take in the entire map and search for a place where he might find Iowa. From left to right, he noticed sections of the zoo dedicated to African animals, Asian animals, Australian animals, and American (North and South) animals, while from top to bottom he found buildings housing reptiles, cats, apes, miscellaneous animals, and finally birds. Since the bird house looked promising (and it was only a short distance away), he hurried over to the building and went inside. A quick glance told him that he wasn't going to find swans amid tropical birds of the rainforests, and so he returned to the map where, with the boy and his parents out of sight, he was able to study it more leisurely.

"Aren't there swans here?" he asked himself out loud. Even though he was not alone, he didn't think that anyone would hear him or, if they did, that anyone would think to answer his query, even the blond-haired little boy who seemed to be observing him out the corner of his eyes. When Luke turned around, however, the zoo ranger was standing in front of him, only a few feet away. The man was smiling as he had been when Luke first saw him.

"Why didn't you say so earlier? You want to see some swans? Well, lookee over here." The man walked up to the map and, after looking carefully at the upper right-hand corner, jabbed his fat index finger at a small patch of blue not too far from the lake where Luke had been sitting.

"We don't keep a lot of them here, but we have a few. Look," he added, encouraging Luke to look closely at the map with him, "do you see the blue? That's a lake. They should be there." The man turned around and pointed to one of the sidewalks that bisected the zoo. "That's the direction you were going, right? Well, you had it right. Follow the path until it loops around the African rainforest. Keep following it until it ends at a small lake. There is a big sign there that says 'Under Construction.'"

"But there's nothing there…" Luke began to object.

"I see you've been out that way. Forget about the sign. We are constructing an exhibit there – hence the sign – but there are still some animals there that will be part of the exhibit when it's done. No sense moving them unless we have to. At any rate, the swans will be in that lake. Got it now?"

The man smiled at Luke, and for a few seconds he seemed like a kindly old man who only wanted to help.

"Got it. Thanks, sir."

"Word of warning, son: Don't go beyond the sign. It could be dangerous there, with construction equipment, and the like."

Luke nodded and started to walk in the direction the man had sent him when the man called out to him.

"And don't get too close," he hollered. "They're still wild animals."

Luke smiled and waved his hand. It sounded like a typical warning, until he wondered why the man would think that he would get too close to the swans. And what did he mean by saying that they were "still" wild animals? Luke shrugged his shoulders, thinking that he was reading too much into the man's words.

Chapter Twenty-four

Luke started to feel hungry as he walked along the path. He didn't know where he would get food, but he decided that he could wait to eat until he saw Iowa. By the time he had arrived at the lake with its Under Construction sign, he felt hungrier than he had only a few minutes ago, and on top of it all he had an enormous thirst. Still, he wasn't going to miss a second with Iowa to eat and drink. He could wait until this evening to eat and, after he had seen Iowa, stop at one of the water fountains in the zoo.

The pond seemed smaller than he remembered (hardly more than a few yards wide), although it appeared every bit as lifeless as it had before. He walked around it as much as he could, but because it backed up to a small, square, brick building, he couldn't see it well from every angle, especially because there were now some high bushes (he didn't remember seeing those when he was here earlier) on two sides, offering him really only one angle – straight ahead – from which to have a good view of the lake. Disappointed, he sat down on the bench and looked at the shimmering water, protecting his eyes from the reflection of the sun off the water's surface but hoping that by some miracle a swan – Iowa – would appear. He waited five minutes, ten minutes, twenty minutes, and nothing stirred – not only were there no swans, but there were no people, either. That is, the zoo, or this small section of it, seemed deserted and not even the sounds of children playing obscured the rustle of the bushes as the wind picked up. But while he sat there waiting and wondering, he noticed that the glare off the lake was becoming less intense (he didn't have to shade his eyes anymore), and instead of facing a bright, nearly colorless light, the light was no longer in his face and was now a warm, golden color, which gave everything around him a pleasant, warm hue. Luke was pleased, since he could now see parts of the lake that he couldn't see only moments before, but as he observed the warm color and noticed how the leaves and shrubs became more intensely green, he was surprised that the sun was now near the horizon, as if he had been sitting on the bench for hours, not minutes. He couldn't fathom how he could have been at the zoo for so long, especially since the gates were just opening when he arrived.

Luke's surprise turned to concern when he considered the possibility of not seeing her this day. Standing up and walking to the railing that surrounded the lake, Luke strained his eyes to find something on the surface of the water and then turned his eyes toward the grounds surrounding the lake or pond or whatever it was. But no matter how carefully he scanned the water or how intensely he observed the bushes, he saw nothing to suggest that there were birds of any kind on or near the water, much less large birds like swans, and, even more disappointing, he noticed that the shadows surrounding the building were becoming darker and more pronounced.

He decided to check out the building, for he knew that some of the buildings housed animals, and so it was quite possible that instead of floating on the water, the swans (and maybe Iowa herself) were in the building. When he reached the building, which was less than a minute's walk from where he was standing, he planned to walk up the three steps to the main door, carefully open the door and enter, and once safely inside search for Iowa. Simple, as long as he moved quickly and stealthily (he didn't want to attract attention, especially the ranger's attention), in and out without a problem, but as soon as he placed his right foot on the top step and reached for the door handle (which was shrouded in a deep shadow), he noticed that the door was padlocked and a "No Trespassing" sign was pasted to the door. Since this had been a waste of time, he walked quickly back to where he had the best view of the lake and carefully scanned the water's surface and the surrounding foliage. Nothing was visible on the mirror-like surface of the water. Frustrated, and concerned that time was running out, he picked up a small, flat rock near the railing and sent it across the surface of the water, where it left a series of distinct, concentric circles that quickly faded. Luke, certain that the ranger was mistaken about the swans, reluctantly turned away from the water and started to walk back down the path to see if there was any other place that might have swans. But no sooner was he five feet from the railing than he heard a familiar sound, the unmistakable honking of a swan.

The ranger had been right, after all. Luke leaned against the railing as he watched a swan emerge from the shadows and then slowly, effortlessly, paddle toward him, leaving in its wake two long lines that reached back to the shadows from which the animal emerged. When the swan was twenty or so feet away, he called out in a hushed tone so no one but the swan could hear, "Iowa, is that you?" The swan didn't respond, and when it was within five feet from where Luke was standing, it turned and began swimming back to the shadows where it had been hiding.

"Iowa," he cried out, this time more loudly. "Iowa! Is that you? Iowa?" When the animal had finally retreated back into the shadows from which it came, Luke realized that it wasn't Iowa (he didn't want to believe it was, for then there wouldn't be any way of communicating with her) and, turning away from the railing to seek out other places where there might be swans, he came face-to-face with the zoo ranger, almost running into him. The man was still smiling, although his smile this time seemed to have lost its pleasantness and taken on a forced, knowing quality to it.

"Who's Iowa, young man? Is that a state or species of animal?"

"I thought you said there were more swans here," Luke responded hesitantly, not quite knowing what to say.

"They were here earlier. Must have been moved to the water near the entrance. Did you see that? No? Well, maybe tomorrow. The zoo is closing and you need to hustle down to the entrance to leave." He smiled unpleasantly again, and Luke began walking quickly along the path toward the entrance. The man didn't follow him (Luke glanced over his shoulder from time to time to ascertain where he was), and by the time he finally made it to the entrance of the zoo, Luke saw quite a few people lining up and filing through the black iron gates. Stepping in line with the others, Luke was only a few feet from the gates when he casually looked to his left and noticed the small body of water the man mentioned. It seemed strange to him that he hadn't seen it earlier, especially since it was quite noticeable from where he was standing just inside the gates. He continued moving toward the gates, however, disappointed that he would have to wait until tomorrow to check it out. But just as he was about to step under the wrought-iron arch, he hesitated and again looked at the water, half of which was sparkling in the evening sun and half of which was slowly being enveloped in a thick shadow. He knew that he had no choice but to come back tomorrow morning (and he promised himself that he wouldn't return home without having seen Iowa), and yet something started nagging at him that if he didn't check it now, before he left for the night, he might lose an 'opportunity of a lifetime.' Hearing a couple of people in line ask him to move, feeling the gentle push of a young child expressing his parent's impatience, Luke jumped out of line and jogged over to the water.

It would only take a minute to locate Iowa (if she were there) and, if he indeed found her, he could at least promise to visit her tomorrow, after which he could return to the gates and at worst be one of the two or three last out of the zoo. Unfortunately, the very second he reached the railing surrounding this small body of water, he noticed the ranger, who was only a few yards away and walking swiftly toward him. The man was scowling this time.

"Just leaving," Luke called out before the man was able to reach him. Jogging back to the entrance, Luke was the last person to leave through the gates and, when he was safely outside the zoo, he heard a loud, metallic crash and then a brief train-like rush which seemed to indicate that the gates were closed and locked. Luke didn't need to verify it.

So that was that. He had come all this way to visit Iowa, and the only thing he managed to see were tourists, a few animals, an angry ranger, and a swan that was only a swan – a swan that was only a swan! Luke was disappointed, to say the least, and he was beginning to fear that he had missed the only opportunity he would have of seeing Iowa before he had to return home – and the very idea of returning home without seeing her was…well, it was very difficult to contemplate. No, it was infuriating, and he could practically see Press chiding him over his stupidity. But if this weren't bad enough, he suddenly felt extremely tired and very hungry, and it angered him to recall that he didn't have a single penny to help satisfy these or any other human needs.

Uncertain what to do or where to go next, Luke began slowly walking along the stone path that loosely encircled the zoo. He had been walking for perhaps five minutes, observing the cracks in the stone and wondering how tree roots were able to lift up or push aside whole sections of solid rock as if it were nothing, when he noticed wide, gray streaks creeping across the path. Stopping and looking at the surrounding trees, Luke was surprised by the deep shadows engulfing the trees, absorbing most of their leaves, and blanketing the ground beneath them. It seemed as if night had descended upon them even though there was still some light in the sky. But as he observed the golden glow over the zoo, he noticed that the glow was retreating as rapidly as the shadows were growing, and he realized that it would only be a matter of minutes before the sky merged with the trees, and the night would cover everything. He didn't have a lot of time. He knew that he needed to find a solution to any number of things, and yet he couldn't decide which was the most urgent and which could be postponed. Closing his eyes momentarily to concentrate, Luke suddenly lurched forward and came to an abrupt halt, nearly falling down and slamming his face against the stone path. Looking around, he could see that a large section of the stone had been pushed up by the roots of one of the trees and realized that he had tripped on the edge. He was unhurt, but as he turned back around to continue his walk, he noticed an empty park bench under a large, leafy tree and walked over to rest while he worked out these seemingly intractable problems.

'It's my lucky day,' he told himself, as he sat down on the edge of the bench. Near the center of the bench was a small, half-empty bag of popcorn, clearly a gift of providence. Luke grabbed the bag and, placing the open end over his mouth and tilting his head back, gobbled it all down in less than a minute. Nothing had ever tasted quite as good. Tossing the empty bag to the ground, he began looking around him for another bag or something else that was edible. When he failed to come up with anything at hand, Luke leaned back against the curved slats of the wooden bench and, once again, tried to find an answer to the problems that were gnawing at him almost as much as his hunger (at least his hunger was slightly less intense with the popcorn in his stomach). He couldn't go home without having seen Iowa, and waiting in the park until the zoo opened up in the morning seemed uncomfortable, especially in the cool breeze which was now blowing. The answer, however, came quicker than he expected. The sun was gone and the sky was black, and the breeze, which now and then rattled the leaves of the trees, was cooling the surrounding air to such an extent that he was shaking (he didn't have a coat, and his short-sleeve shirt didn't provide even minimal protection). Since it was too cold to leave, Luke began looking around the bushes and trees for a place that might offer some shelter from the cold and the breeze, but none of the foliage seemed to be thick enough to offer more than just a little protection.

Holding his body and stomping the ground to keep warm, Luke walked over to one patch of bushes that seemed to be thicker than any of the others he had seen in the dim light. It wasn't perfect, but at least it was enough to shelter him from prying eyes, although he couldn't see anyone either on the path or in the park. Glancing back and forth to make sure he was alone, he squeezed between two large bushes (each one nearly as tall as he was) and entered a small enclosure that was wide enough to stretch out comfortably. Luke carefully sat down on the cold, leaf-packed ground and, rolling over onto his side, he closed his eyes and changed into a dog. The transformation was a little difficult, though not as tough as the last one had been, but the extra effort it took to change was well worth it, because he could keep much warmer as a dog and use his canine senses to scour up some food; he could even get a little sleep, since he wasn't shaking any longer. The dog knew that spending the night could cost him the time he needed to return home in time, and so he resolved to push a little harder tomorrow on the return trip to ensure that he arrived when promised.

Standing up, the dog shook the earth and moisture off his fur, and lifted his nose in the air. To the left, where the zoo was located, he could smell the animals, including Iowa – he knew beyond a doubt that she was there. But because he couldn't do anything about it now, he went in search of shelter for the night, which he found a few yards away in a hollowed out log. The log appeared to be part of a play set of hollow logs for kids, but for now it would suit him perfectly. Crawling inside and rolling up, he decided to get some sleep before he went in search of water and food.

Chapter Twenty-five

He tucked his nose into his fur and, after wrapping his tail around his side and slipping it under his nose, he quickly drifted off to sleep, warm and comfortable. Every now and then some noise – the crack of a stick, the rustle of leaves, the whoosh of wind blowing through the trees – would awaken him, but after tuning his ears and sniffing the air, he would fall back to sleep knowing that the noises were a benign product of nature and not an imminent human threat.

He slept fitfully but comfortably for several hours. During one of the longest, uninterrupted periods of sleep, a procession of strange, incomprehensible, and unconnected images floated through his mind. In one of them, he was running back and forth at the edge of a small lake, barking furiously at something on its surface although quite a distance away. It was daylight, and he could see the surface of the water clearly, but there were bushes and trees on the opposite of the lake, and these covered the water at the end with deep, black, impenetrable shadows. He had just decided to swim across the lake and get whatever it was that was making him so wild, when something grabbed him by the neck and, jerking him back from the water, held him fast and even whispered to him, "Stay with me."

In another, he saw Iowa sitting on a bench in the quad at school. For some reason, they were the only ones at school, and when she spotted him walking toward her, she smiled broadly and motioned for him to come over and sit next to her. He did, but when he tried to speak to her, she turned into a swan and would only honk and twist her head up and down sideways when he asked her anything.

In the last before he woke up, he found himself alone and running through an endless, open field. It was a perfectly clear day and, except for some rocks and small clumps of bushes, nothing obstructed his vision for miles in any direction. He should have savored the endless vistas (where in the world were there such expansive views?), but he couldn't because he was nervously searching for something and, running for an hour in one direction and then an hour in another, all the time getting farther and farther from the thing he desperately needed to find. But what was worse was that this something – and he could never stop long enough to define it – was waiting for him and its very existence depending on him finding it sooner rather than later.

He woke up after this when he heard something – a high-pitched screech and a series of fading thuds – near his log. Scurrying out of the log as quickly as he could, he dashed around the log to determine the source of the sounds and, when he found nothing, he paused, listened intently, and then sniffed the air for something or someone that might have caused the sounds. When he couldn't detect anything apart from the pungent smells and peculiar grunts and snorts emanating from the zoo, he went back into the log and stretched out, resting his nose on his front paws but completely awake. This short period of sleep seemed to be all his mind and body required, for he no longer seemed tired even though he could sense that there were still several hours to go before the first light of the sun began illuminating the horizon.

While he waited for the morning light, he couldn't help wondering why he hadn't been able to find Iowa. She was there (he could sense her presence, although he couldn't quite determine her exact location), and yet when he was on the other side of the walls, he couldn't tell if she was at one location as opposed to another, or even if she were there at all. Obviously, he lacked canine senses when he was walking through the zoo on two feet, but this shouldn't have prevented him from finding her at one of the ponds – and it shouldn't have prevented her from spotting him and reaching out to him when he was within sight. Could she have been in one of the buildings and not in the water with the other swans? The ranger seemed insistent that all the swans were at the one pond, and yet there was just the one bird, a beautiful creature but unquestionably not Iowa. Maybe the ranger was mistaken about the location of the swans. He hesitated, and replayed in his mind the encounter with the beautiful white swan. It appeared to recognize him for a couple of minutes, but then it behaved as all swans do – a clear sign that it wasn't Iowa (Iowa, he was positive, would do something to let him know that she recognized him). No, he reminded himself, it wasn't Iowa. But if that wasn't Iowa, then where is she? Where are the swans that the ranger said were at the zoo?

His eyes were painfully dry, and he closed them momentarily to ease the discomfort. Just because it's a zoo doesn't mean that all the animals are on display, especially if any of them are here for refactoring, he added after a few moments. Most of them probably are, but there must be some that aren't exhibited, or some that are only visible at certain times during the day. The latter sounded slightly implausible until he remembered that reptiles often stay hidden during the day and that some of the exhibits were connected to buildings that enabled the animals to go inside for any number of reasons. Yes, he added, as if he had just stumbled onto the solution to a difficult puzzle, yes, she had to have been indoors, and so there was no way that I could have seen her. But having found what seemed to be the only reasonable answer for her absence, he was again troubled, for he realized that there was no way of finding her now unless he had access to all the buildings that she might be in – and even if he knew which building she was in, it didn't seem plausible that anyone would allow him to enter the building to find a particular swan. He also realized that if Iowa were indeed in one of the buildings, he might never locate her if he had to rely on his human senses, which naturally were dependent on sight. Having hit upon the one thing that prevented him from finding Iowa – his human limitations – he felt a strong desire to find her now if only to assure himself that she was there.

He crawled out of the log and began yawning and stretching his tired legs. Leaning back on his haunches, he stretched his front legs (his front legs were nearly level with the ground while his rear legs were upright) and then his back legs (standing normally, he extended his right rear leg and, after repositioning it, he extended his left). The dog shook himself and licked the end of his nose and the edges of his lips. But when he started to move, he abruptly stopped and, using his hind leg, scratched something on his side. He started to move again, but halted again and this time turned and used his front teeth to nibble at something in the same spot. When this didn't seem to be enough, he sat down and began furiously scratching his side with his back leg. Finally standing up, he sniffed at the offending place on his side and then shook himself from head to tail. Even though he was hungry, he felt rested and energetic and ready to find Iowa before he did anything else.

The main gates were less than a minute away. When he arrived at the familiar wrought-iron arch, he was surprised the gates were closed and that no one, not even the guards, seemed to be present. The dog didn't know why he expected the gates to be open, but as he stood looking at the gates, dumbfounded by the fact that he couldn't get through them to find Iowa, he began to recall the sound they made as they shut behind him and then the sound of a lock or bolt or something that screeched to an implacable thud behind him. Shaking his head again to put his thoughts and senses back together, he sniffed around the gates – at the base, then the sides, and then the bars – to make sure that they were indeed closed and that there weren't any inherent weaknesses in them that he could exploit. Failing to sense any weaknesses, he stuck his nose between two of the bars and tried to ascertain 1) if he could somehow angle his head and body through them or 2) if he could somehow put enough pressure on the bars to widen them enough to squeeze through. The results were negative, just as the results were negative when he scratched the stone ground beneath the gates to see if he could dig his way under them. When it was clear that he couldn't get through the entrance, he sniffed the air to determine Iowa's location which, as it turned out, was not near the gates but somewhere else in the zoo.

He turned to his left and began following her scent as it led him along the brick wall that enclosed part of the zoo. It wasn't too difficult to identify her among all the other animals in the zoo, although it wasn't easy to pinpoint her exact location because her particular scent waxed and waned and its general location drifted back and forth. He couldn't account for the variations (and, to be honest, he didn't think much about them, either), but it didn't matter because he was positive that he was heading in the right direction and that sooner or later he would arrive at the general area where he could find her.

Having followed the wall for perhaps a couple hundred yards, his nose at its base for nearly this entire distance, the dog came to the end of the wall, which was replaced by a towering fence, if you could call it that. The fence was actually a set of three fences, the front and back of which were thin, black bars too tightly spaced to squeeze through, while in the center was a chain-link fence topped with a never-ending spiral of barbed wire. Even if one somehow managed to squeeze between the bars, there was no way he could he could get through the chain-link fence or over the barbed wire, unless he had wings or nails strong enough to cut through the cement at the base of the fence. But instead of being one more impediment, the fence actually had some benefits, since he could at least see her if she were nearby. In fact, he was getting closer to her, for no sooner had he trotted a few feet along the base of the fence than he came upon something that told him that she was nearby, practically within speaking distance. Within seconds of making this discovery, he located the exact spot where she was resting, which was close to the fence and only a few feet off the ground. Running back and forth, sniffing the ground and then the air to make sure that he had indeed located her, the dog whined nervously not knowing how to contact her at night and fearing that if he couldn't locate the same spot in the morning as a human being, he might never find her.

His anxiety building, he stopped at one point and tried to dig his way through the cement at the base of the fence, but his efforts were futile and even a little painful (one of the nails on his left paw cracked). Immediately jumping back and barking twice in frustration, he was about ready to run forward a few feet to locate another way around the fence when he heard a familiar honk. It had come from a shadow-covered building twenty feet from the fence. He barked again, and the swan responded. It was Iowa.

Chapter Twenty-six

The dog became more frantic, barking and listening to the honks in return, but no matter what he did or where he looked, he couldn't find a way into the zoo. Normally, he would have run around the perimeter until he found a weakness, but he was loath to leave while he could finally communicate to her – and they did communicate, if not in words then with the sense that each one was aware of the other's presence. Finally, the honks stopped and he understood that it was time to go and that he could find a way to see her later in the morning.

He ran back to the log, stopping once along the way to drink from a little puddle of water at the base of a large tree. Crawling into the log, he curled up and, with his tail around his nose, he quickly went to sleep. He awoke just as the sun was reaching the horizon and its warm, golden light was beginning to fill the eastern portion of the sky. He was a little surprised that he slept so late, especially because everything around him seemed full of life and madly competing for attention. He could hear the twitter and whistle of birds in the trees, and as he turned his head slightly, he noticed the snarls and groans of large animals, the constant chatter of monkeys and small animals, and now and then the yelp of something that wasn't in pain but wasn't happy, either. The dog crawled out of the log and, after stretching and shaking and yawning, trotted over to the same puddle of water, which had accumulated more water during the night. Feeling strong and refreshed, he trotted over to the gates to see if they were open and, when he found them still shut, he trotted back to the log. Instead of crawling back into the log, the dog sniffed the air for the presence of people and, when he was certain that he was alone, stepped behind some bushes at the base of a large tree and changed back into a human.

The morning air was brisk, and Luke had to pat his arms and dance on his toes to keep warm. While he waited impatiently for the zoo to open, he bounced along the path, jogged short portions of it, and retraced his steps several times. For the longest time, he was alone outside the zoo (as far as he could see), which suited him just fine (and, truly, the last thing he wanted to do was to speak to someone other than Iowa), but after a while, after a couple of hours, he yearned for company of some kind – not to while away the time or assuage the loneliness he might have felt having undertaken such a significant journey all on his own (an anonymous companion might also have helped him locate the most expeditious way back home) – he wanted to see people, because their presence would help him understand the time of day and how much more time he needed to wait until he entered the zoo. In due time, however, people, mainly young people with children, started to arrive, and as they spread themselves throughout the park, he positioned himself near the gates to be the first to walk under the wrought-iron arch. It would take a couple of hours more before people (young and old alike) began hovering near the gates, and another twenty minutes after this before one of the rangers would slowly, lugubriously open the heavy gates to let the crowds push their way into the compound.

By the time this happened, Luke was nearly beside himself with anxiety, a combination of impatience to get inside and a fear that all this waiting could cost him a chance to see Iowa. After all, it had been hours since he had communicated with her, and there was no way of telling (not as a human) if she had been moved or where she was at the moment. Still, he managed to control himself, at least outwardly, and when the door did finally open, he walked slowly through the gates with the hundreds of other people doing the same thing, jostling one another as if they, too, had only one chance in a thousand, in a million, to see something extraordinary, or, as he told himself, to see something he had been waiting his whole life to see.

Once past the crowd at the inside of the gates, Luke walked quickly in the direction in which he expected to find her, the place where he had communicated with her. He quickly came to the fork in the paths, and took the left-hand path, which rose slightly and curved sharply in the same direction, passing several exhibits of what appeared to be desert dwellers, including an open area with small mounds of soil peppering the surface of the ground whose inhabitants were nowhere to be seen. Once he was past these exhibits, he stepped off the path and took a hard left, away from the exhibits located on the map, across a grassy area, and over upturned soil that appeared to have been poured down or dug up recently. Five minutes later, he arrived at a small, square, brick building. There was nothing else around it except for bushes, a few trees, and some construction equipment to one side (a cement mixer, wheelbarrows, shovels, rakes, and the like) and, because the lights were out, it appeared uninhabited. Glancing around the area, he found nothing that a swan would find habitable, and so he knew that if Iowa were still in the area, she was in the building.

Luke looked carefully around the building to make sure that no rangers were in sight (he was, after all, off the zoo trail and had passed at least one sign that warned visitors to return to the path) and, once comfortable that the area was safe for a few moments, he walked up to the building and began surveying it for windows and other openings through which he could communicate with Iowa. Besides the large, black door in the center of one of its sides (there was also a small porch above the door and a couple stone steps leading to the door), there were two small windows up near the eaves on all four of the outside walls, each window opened outward but at least seven feet off the ground and too high and small for him to reach and crawl through. By the time he had circumnavigated the building several times, he was standing at the back and, looking up at the small windows, starting to wonder if he had found the right location or if his communication last night with Iowa had simply been a dream. He didn't want to think this, and so after running around the building one more time, he walked a little farther down the grounds, following the fence to see if there was another building that he might have encountered in the night. But having trespassed the out-of-bounds are far longer than he thought prudent (not to mention wasting time that he might need when he found Iowa), Luke was fairly certain that she wasn't in this part of the zoo and decided to go back to the building and, if that proved to be a waste of time, to check out the ponds and everywhere else she might be living.

When he reached the building again, he paused and observed its nondescript exterior and the small windows which now seemed not only devoid of life but inhospitable to life. He couldn't understand how enough air could get through the windows to enable animals to thrive inside, that is, if they were meant to thrive (after all, few people actually knew what happened in refactoring facilities). But as he was turning away because nothing was apparently inside, Luke heard a faint sound coming from inside. The sound resembled something a swan might make: a honk. Of course, he wasn't positive, given all the other sounds floating and mingling throughout the air, and so he turned and walked up to the building and, standing beneath one of the windows on the side of the building, he listened carefully for additional honks. For a few moments, he couldn't hear anything other than the din from the rest of the zoo (and he regretted not being able to use his canine senses), but when he pressed his ear to the wall of the building directly underneath the window, he heard it again. This time, it was unmistakable: It was a swan's voice, and, what was more, he was positive that it was Iowa's voice.

"Iowa," Luke whispered, making sure that no one could hear him. "Iowa," he said a little louder when he didn't get a response from the first time he called her name.

"Honk!" the swan responded to Luke's call.

"Iowa, I knew you were here! Iowa, Iowa…," Luke said loudly, not knowing quite what else to say.

The swan honked several times.

"Iowa," Luke said again, and then he cupped his palms around the sides of his ear, as if this would enhance his hearing and bring him closer to Iowa. "Iowa, I just found out you were here. I didn't know until a few days ago. I would have been here sooner had I known…I would have come anywhere had I known where you were."

"Honk, squawk!"

"Iowa, what can I do? Are you okay? How long are you going to be here?" Having said this, Luke realized that she could be here for some time, especially if she hadn't changed back to human form. He had been told that some refactoring cases lasted years (which was probably the case with Jimmy), but the notion that she could be here for years – maybe all her life if she couldn't change back – filled him with a deep sorrow and brought tears to his eyes.

"Iowa," he said again, his voice thick with the emotion that flowed over him. Luke was not simply happy that he had found her: He was filled with something that could best be described as love. Yes, he loved her, and for a moment at least all the past years seemed to have evaporated and he was with Iowa, as if she never left, as if they had never parted. "Iowa," he began again, "I…I don't know what to do. Can you tell me what to do? Everything is locked, I think. Iowa, please help me. What should I do?"

"Honk, honk!"

"Look, Iowa, I need to leave soon. I have to be home this evening, but I'll come back as soon as I can. Iowa, I will never leave you." Luke glanced around to make sure that no one was within earshot. "Iowa," he began and, placing his arms and hands on the building as if he were hugging it, whispered so quietly as to be talking to himself, "I always wanted to say this – I love you."

"Squawk!"

"I'll be back as soon as I can," he added is a normal voice. "Please, don't forget me." Luke pushed away from the building and, hesitating, turned back and looked at the drab, square edifice as if he were saying goodbye to a loved one.

Reluctantly, he walked away from the building, and Iowa. When he was no more than twenty feet beyond the stairs, he spotted the zoo ranger that he had spoken to yesterday. The man came out of nowhere, and as he spotted Luke, his heavy face became angry (his lips were firm and unsmiling, while his eyes were practically slits) and he stood motionless, his legs spread out and firmly planted on the ground, his hands on the sides of his hips.

Chapter Twenty-seven

Luke tried not to look. He continued walking toward the path and even passed the ranger without saying a word. But when they were side-by-side, the man reached out and grabbed Luke by his left bicep and forced him to stop. Luke, however, looked straight ahead, as if he had merely stopped on his own accord and not because he was being held tightly.

"What are you doing here?" the ranger asked. He wasn't pleasant this time.

"Nothing," Luke replied without looking at him.

"Didn't you see the sign?"

"No, sir."

"It said, 'No Trespassing.' You can read, can't you?"

"I'm sorry. I didn't see it. I am going back to the path right now."

The man looked at Luke for a couple more seconds and then released his arm. Sidestepping in front of Luke, he stared directly into his face and, for a few additional seconds, it appeared as if he was trying to place Luke's face, which he was certain that he had seen before. "Wait a minute," he finally said. "I know you. You're the kid that was looking for swans, right?"

Luke continued to look down, trying to avoid the man's intense gaze. "I'm not looking for anything. I got lost, and I'm walking back to the path."

"No, you're that kid. What are you doing here? There aren't any swans here. I told you yesterday they're all down in the pond."

"Yes, sir. I'll check them out." Luke side-stepped the ranger, but the man stepped back in front of him. "May I please go?"

"What exactly are you doing here? And what were you doing by the building."

"I told you..."

"Yes, you told me. And now I'm going to tell you something. You're not supposed to be here. Do you understand me?"

Luke nodded, glancing at the man's face out of the corner of his eyes. "May I go now?"

The man looked at Luke for a few more seconds and, for the second time, he appeared to be churning something around in his brain. Troubled, fearing that there was something about Luke that he should know, he reluctantly stepped aside to allow Luke to continue toward the path. But as Luke carefully and quickly walked away, the man watched him, now playing with his chin and scratching the side of his face as if he had a beard. Something suddenly came to him just as Luke stepped onto the path.

"Hey," he called out to Luke. "Where's your parents? Does anyone know you're here?"

Luke hesitated and then kept walking. He knew that he should have stopped and replied to the man, but something in him told him that if he stopped, the man would catch up with him and take him into custody or whatever they do at zoos.

"Hey," the man said again, only this time more loudly. "Does anyone know you're here? Answer me."

Luke didn't wait for another response from the man and started running. He ran down the path until it came to a fork, on both sides of which people were walking and standing in front of the animal cages. Luke, afraid that the man would easily catch him if he headed directly for the gates, went toward the left, which went up a slight hill and seemed to disappear in the foliage of rainforests and large, gnarled trees commonly found in central Africa and on the African mountains. On one side was a wide open space fenced in by black railings. This was the savannah area, and Luke could see giraffes slowly moving from one spot to another or reaching up into the trees and pulling leaves off the trees and lazily chewing them with a grinding motion of their lower jaw. There were also some zebras, antelopes, and other large animals that he couldn't name. On the other side were smaller pens and cages filled with leopards, cheetahs, and other large cats. Each of the animals was pacing back and forth in their cages – each one appearing to be on edge, unlike the animals in the open area on the other side of the path – and several of them, particularly the black panthers, jumped and roared when Luke ran by, as if they were shouting warnings to him and letting the man know exactly where Luke was.

Glancing behind him as he rounded the corner, Luke didn't see the man anywhere and so he naturally assumed that he was either not following him or lacked the energy to keep up. He slowed down to a jog to conserve his own energy, Luke continued following the path until he came to a dark pond, the same pond he visited yesterday. This time, however, Luke noticed a large swan floating on the water and, as he got closer to the lake, the swan began swimming toward him. Feeling relatively safe, although he knew that he didn't have a lot of time (and, for all he knew, the man could be waiting for him at the main gates), he stopped and looked at the beautiful bird, which suddenly honked several times and continued to inch closer and closer to him.

"Hello?" Luke couldn't resist saying to the bird when it was only a few feet from him. "Do you know me?"

The swan continued to honk as if it did indeed recognize Luke, and when it came to the edge of the lake, it stepped out of the water and walked to the railing and stuck its head between the rails, reaching for Luke. As Luke watched the animal, it began to move its brilliantly white head up and down in a way that he remembered Iowa doing – Iowa alone, and not the other Cygnets, did that, he told himself. He couldn't believe it and, reaching out to it, the swan pushed its head against Luke's hand and rubbed it several times. "Iowa?" Luke gasped. "Is it you? It is you. I didn't..."

The swan honked again, only this time its sound was softer, quieter than he remember wild swans sounding.

"Iowa, I'm sorry, I thought...never mind. I came here to see you, I love you, and I'm..."

Luke didn't finish. He suddenly heard heavy footsteps bearing down on him and, glancing in the direction of the noise, he saw the ranger only feet from him. Luke turned to continue running, but before he could pull his hand away, the swan bit him and then hissed loudly. Shocked, Luke jumped out of the way as the man reached for him, and then continued down the path.

Luke's hand ached as he passed a large cage on his right that was filled with chimpanzees, all of which started screaming as Luke and the man passed them. Luke was quickly distancing himself from the man, who Luke noticed, when he glanced back, was again tiring out, but then he nearly ran into several children in a large group hovering around one of the cages. They were tightly bunched together as their chaperon shepherded them together, causing him to stumble and forcing him to squeeze by them with his back to the railing separating him from cages with monkeys and other primates. Luke, however, pushed through as quickly as he could, because the man was nearly in reach, (he was also being slowed by the children), and as he did so he could feel himself being pelted with rocks or bits of foul-smelling mud from the monkey cages. Luke managed to elude the man as he lunged for Luke and, being caught off balance, the man fell to the pavement.

Several people offered to help the man, who quickly got up, but he pulled himself away from them and, watching Luke run away, shouted at him to stop. "You, come back here. I want to talk to you."

Luke didn't respond. He continued to run toward the main gates, which were only a hundred yards or so away. He did glance over his shoulder to make sure that the ranger was unhurt, but when he did he noticed that the man was on his feet and running (a little more slowly than before and now with a decided limp) while holding a walkie-talkie to his mouth with his left hand and gesticulating toward Luke with his other hand. Luke didn't know what was going on, but he wasn't going to hang around to find out.

As he approached the gates, throngs of people started pouring through the gates, while outside a large group of people were standing and waiting their turn to force themselves beneath the arches and into the zoo. Luke couldn't believe that so many people were either trying to enter the facility or, having entered, were crowding around the entrance as if they didn't know what to do next. Sure, some of the people were studying zoo maps or looking for the signs to this or that habitat, but the majority of the people he saw acted like deer in the headlights, waiting for something happen. Very quickly, Luke reached a point that he could run no farther, and he began carefully squeezing between people or around them, sometimes jostling them, and often eliciting angry comments.

"Hey," one young man shouted at Luke. He was holding the hand of a young boy, who couldn't have been more than two years old, and when Luke squeezed passed by him, he picked up the child to keep him from falling over. "What's the matter with you?"

Luke turned to apologize when he noticed to his left another ranger, one much younger than the other, who kept glancing at Luke as he worked his way through the crowd, staying even with him as if he were a shadow. The younger man was clearly coordinating his movements with the older, who was still dogging Luke and, as he threaded his way between a small group of children, was now only a few feet away, just out of arm's reach. Luke hoped that if he could elude the rangers until he reached the gates, he could find refuge in the park, that is, 'if they don't follow me there,' he whispered to himself. 'It wouldn't make sense for them to follow me there,' he added to convince himself that he could find freedom in the park.

He didn't know how far he had been running, but it wasn't until he reached the main part of the crowd (only a few feet from the gates) that he felt his energy and strength begin to flag. He wasn't so tired that he needed to stop, not right away, but he knew that he couldn't keep up the pace for much longer, especially because his legs were beginning to weaken and the crowd was beginning to seem stronger, less willing to move aside and let him through. When he was almost within reach of the gates, he noticed a third ranger, a tall man with a straight jaw, speaking into his walkie-talkie, probably to the other two who were following Luke. The third ranger was standing right in the center of the entrance, directly under the large, wrought iron, ornamented curve on which hung the sign "Lordan Zoo." With the other rangers closing in on him, Luke's legs suddenly regained their strength and, turning his shoulder toward the ranger at the gates, Luke managed to push a number of people aside and force the ranger to one side, causing him to stumble and drop his walkie-talkie.

"You," the man with the prominent jaw hollered after he had righted himself and retrieved the unit. "You, come back here. Do you hear me? Come back here!"

The man didn't follow him, although he continued yelling as Luke sped from the zoo into the park, heading directly for the dense trees that seemed to be everywhere.

Chapter Twenty-eight

The air was cooler beneath the dense, tree canopy. It took a few moments to adjust to the dim light under the trees, but even this didn't slow him down. Luke continued running as fast as he could, dodging people, park benches, and small bushes (sometimes leaping over the bushes), until he was confident that the men were no longer following him. Even then, as he came to a halt at the base of an old, gnarled oak tree, he continued to glance nervously around just in case one of the men was honing in on him from a different, unexpected direction. As soon as he caught his breath, he noticed that he was hardly alone, for even though no one was near him under the tree, he could still see people lounging nearby on the park grass, strolling along the stone path loosely encircling the zoo, and children playing on the grass, stone walk, and beneath some of the other trees. The presence of these people was somewhat comforting, since it would be harder for the men to single Luke out of the mass of humanity in the park, but it also made things more difficult because he was compelled to look at everyone who came close to make sure it wasn't one of the men. Exhausted, his side aching from his exertions, Luke spied an empty park bench in the open a few feet away and slowly walked to it and plopped himself down.

His side continued to ache, his heart pounded unmercifully in his chest, and sweat poured off his face and into his eyes, which he tried to clear with the back of his sweaty hand. Luke tried to keep a wary eye on everyone around him, but for a few minutes he couldn't do anything but concentrate on his recovery and, when he finally began to feel better, his right shin, which had somehow been bruised while running from the men. When at last he was almost back to normal, Luke noticed that the people walking past him on the path were eyeing him, glancing at him as if there was something odd or disturbing about his appearance. One elderly woman hesitated when she came close to him and, looking at him as if she were sizing him up, asked him if he were okay and if he needed any help. When Luke replied in the negative, telling her that he felt fine and was simply a little winded from his walk, she smiled and continued walking along the path.

Luke had been sitting for some time before he felt better, back to normal and ready to run, if it came to that. But instead of getting up and leaving the park (the men could still be looking for him and he also needed to return home), he decided to sit for a little while longer to enjoy the cool air and the pleasant scent of the trees and vegetation surrounding him. Observing a wide open stretch of grassy park directly in front of him, Luke noticed a group of adolescents playing soccer, or what looked like soccer, for they didn't appear to be following the rules in terms of touching the ball and guarding the goals, wherever they were located. However, since he wasn't an expert or even much of a fan, he felt that what looked wrong or peculiar might simply be an example of his ignorance. Leaning his head back so that it rested on the bench, Luke closed his eyes for a moment (they were tired and sore from all the sweat and rubbing) and recalled the time when Iowa was exhausted and holding her side, which occurred after she chased him around the lake and before she finally struck him with the stick. Smiling at the similarity of his struggle to catch his breath, he tried to bring back some of the details of that day and instead thought about how she looked the last time she appeared in human form, how she told him things that she didn't tell Press or anyone else, and finally how there would come a time when he could see her as a human being and not a swan. It occurred to Luke that seeing her again would be difficult though not impossible, particularly if he waited a few weeks before returning. By that time, the rangers would have forgotten him, and the whole escapade (there was no better word for what set them off) would have been something that neither the rangers nor the people affected by it recalled with any clarity, certainly not enough to identify him as the culprit. Would Iowa understand?

Although he thought he informed her that he had to leave, he wasn't exactly positive and the more he considered it, the more he began to think that he hadn't said anything of the kind. Maybe, if he located her again from outside the zoo's walls, he could somehow explain to her that he needed to go away but that he would be back, that he wouldn't be gone for long, a few days or weeks perhaps…and the important thing was that he knew exactly where to find her. Luke didn't need a canine's senses to locate Iowa this time, for she was right around the corner from the gates, floating in the lake that he should have investigated first. With his arms splayed, he pressed the front of his body tightly against the brick wall to make himself invisible to the zoo staff and curious onlookers, and waited patiently, motionlessly, listening to every creak and groan, until he was certain that no one was close enough to hear him speak. "Iowa," he called in a loud whisper that seemed to echo throughout the area surrounding the zoo. "Iowa, I'll be back. I'm sorry, but I couldn't stay..." He was about to explain at least part of his problems when he heard a voice from the other side of the wall speak his name. "Luke," it said, softly and tenderly, sounding as if he were separated from it by the thickness of a couple bricks; "Luke, I understand..." Luke immediately stepped back and surveyed the wall, noticing a series of hand-sized chips, holes, and protuberances in the wall that angled upward to the top. Grasping with both hands a large brick that jutted out from the wall's surface, he pulled his body up until his toes reached a hole large enough to position both feet, after which he reached up for another projecting brick that would enable him to pull his body up another few feet until the toes of his shoes... Luke suddenly opened his eyes.

Blinking his eyes and glancing around, he noticed that everything seemed dark and that large, impenetrable shadows had pooled beneath the trees. Luke looked up at the sky and for a few moments was vaguely certain that something was wrong, for the sun was gone and the sky seemed covered by a dark curtain, punctured near the horizon by a few pin-like points of light that flickered and danced and then went out. The park around him was deserted, except for a couple of shadows in the distance that seemed to be crossing the far corner to get from one place to another as quickly as possible. For a few moments, he couldn't understand the unexpected change in his surroundings, but as his senses became more alive he realized that he had dozed off while sitting on the bench. Even this was hard to understand, though, because he couldn't remember being tired and, while he recalled closing his eyes briefly, it wasn't long enough to account for the change that now surrounded him. Well, if he had fallen asleep, then he had fallen asleep, although it also meant that he needed to start thinking about the journey back – back without having really connected with Iowa. Of course, he connected with her, but had they made any plans? Had they decided what would happen when she was done with refactoring and was a human again?

Still seated in the park bench, Luke listened to the leaves shaking in the trees, watched as one large, nearly black leaf rolled and bounced across the path in front of him before collapsing on the grass, and began to recall his behavior in the zoo. He shouldn't have tried to run from the rangers, and he shouldn't have pushed anyone to get away, especially the children. It was disgraceful the way he behaved, and he couldn't help wondering what Iowa might have thought had she seen him cavorting like a crazy person. Surprised at his behavior, he turned his attention on the dark, stone path to take his mind off his troubles, and it was then that he noticed someone or a shadow standing about fifty feet away, under one of the street lamps that dotted areas of the park, speaking into a walkie-talkie. He wasn't mistaken – there was no mistaking the large rectangular, brick-like objects that were emblazoned with small red and green light -- although it didn't make a lot of sense that the rangers would still be following him after all this time. But Luke wasn't going to take any chances, and slowly and casually standing up so as not to attract attention, he quickly walked toward the trees and merged into the deep shadows beneath them.

"Hey!" he heard a man yell. Looking in the direction of the sound, he noticed a thick mass of bushes at the base of one of the trees and not taking any chances squeezed between the bushes and squatted down beneath a large, leafy bush. A few seconds later, Luke heard the sound of heavy footsteps nearby and then the voices of men talking. They were close, maybe ten feet away, although he could only pick up snatches of their words.

"…running in here…"

"…should have…"

"…too fast, but I got a good loo…"

"…what now?"

"…back…report…follow…"

It was hard to tell if they were speaking about him, but again he wasn't going to take any chances. While he waited for the men to leave, he remained motionless, trying to be another shadow at the base of the tree. Now and then, he thought they might be gone, but then he would hear a creak or rustle and then something uttered indistinctly – "…not yet…," "for crying…" – and he would hold his breath and become another shadow like all the others surrounding him. While he waited, alternately holding his breath and inhaling and exhaling quietly, he couldn't help thinking about Iowa, and the more he thought about her, the greater his sense that he had failed to communicate something very important to her. Maybe he had communicated something to her the first time, when he was certain that he had located her from outside the zoo walls, but he couldn't decide if either of the swans he met inside the zoo were Iowa or simply swans – or even someone else undergoing intensive refactoring. Could he have been mistaken about the first swan? But it was the second swan that bit him. Was that a sign that the second swan wasn't Iowa? But he was convinced in both instances that he had found the right swan and that she, it, recognized him. Was he wrong? Were any of them Iowa – and, if they were, how was he supposed to determine which was which, unless…? Unless? And why did all the animals object to his presence as he tried to escape the ranger? Shaking his head to put these things behind him, Luke continued to listen for the men, turning his head toward each creak and groan, each sigh, emanating from somewhere nearby. When he hadn't heard them in a while, he shifted his weight and started breathing a little easier. But just as he began to think about Iowa and her life at the zoo, it occurred to him that he was running out of time – he needed to start moving if he wanted to return home before his parents began to worry – and so he stretched his legs out and rolled to his side, and changed into a dog.

One half of the large, yellow moon could be seen, while the rest was covered with dark clouds that were gradually filling the sky. The wind picked up and rattled the leaves in the tops of the trees. A few seconds after this, the wind swirled around the base of the trees, shaking the bushes, hurling a crumpled paper cup, and standing his fur on end. The movement of his fur tickled his sensitive skin, causing him to shake his body three times to force his fur down to a more comfortable position. The wind died down as quickly as it had arisen, and he stood still for a moment in the hushed surroundings listening for signs of danger. When this didn't tell him anything, he lifted his nose in the air and sniffed deeply for anything nearby that resembled human beings. Unfortunately, this didn't impart anything useful, either, because the air was especially heavy with the scents of large, uneasy animals and the greasy, metallic smells from the streets surrounding the park. The dog sneezed a fine mist out of his nose and then pressed his head into the bushes to identify any human activity before he ventured out his little enclave. When the areas around him seemed safe, he decided to push his way through the thickets and begin his journey home.

He pushed his way through the first couple of feet or so relatively easily (although he didn't like the feel of the small, narrow branches against his skin), but his forward momentum slowed and then came to a complete halt. The branches were so tightly interwoven at this point that they formed a wall that was practically impenetrable. If this weren't bad enough, many of the branches were broken, particularly the ends, which created sharp, little spears that poked and jabbed his skin. Knowing that it was futile to continue, the dog decided to back out and look for another section to squeeze through, but he was forced to stop after only moving a few inches because the spears were jabbing his stomach and groin. He tried to move forward again to alleviate the pain in stomach, but this proved as useless as moving back or to either side, and in seconds he was completely surrounded by innumerable little spears stabbing him painfully in practically every part of his body. Whimpering, the dog wanted someone to help him out of the bushes, but since the only people likely to come to his rescue were the rangers, he closed his eyes and, using every ounce of his strength, leaped up and over the bushes, landing unsteadily on the other side. He shook his body to ease the irritation the bushes caused and licked a couple of spots where the skin was broken.

Looking around, the dog started trotting quickly through the park and back toward the city streets. He couldn't tell how late it was or how much of the night he had left, but he felt certain that he needed to hurry because time was running out. But as he was nearing the end of the park, he noticed two strange, star-like lights at the end of the path bouncing up and down and moving back and forth. The lights, which were more or less at eye level, suddenly began to move more quickly and within seconds they became large and brighter. Instinctively, the dog trotted to the other side of the path and then off the path entirely, but the lights turned in his direction and they continued to grow in size and brightness until it became obvious that they were focused on him. Within seconds, he heard a man shout and then sensed a light illuminate his face and, turning around, he ran away from the lights and back toward the zoo.

The dog came to a screeching halt, however, when another set of lights shined on him and he could hear other men call out for him to stop.

"Boy, come here, boy!" one of the men was hollering. Although he couldn't see his face or distinguish his smell very clearly, the dog was certain it was one of the rangers who was chasing him earlier. Turning to the right and bounding over bushes, rocks, benches, and depressions, the dog ran with all his might to escape the men, but no sooner than he felt that he had eluded them, more lights sprang up and there were more shouts from the men. This time, however, he kept going. There was simply no other choice in his mind – he either maneuvered around them or he fell into their clutches. Luck was on his side, for one of them was caught flatfooted, enabling the dog to escape between his legs and run out of the park into the surrounding streets. The dog didn't slow down until he was several blocks away from the park and couldn't sense the rangers anymore.

Chapter Twenty-nine

The dog didn't recognize this section of town.

He also didn't understand why the rangers were chasing him when it was Luke, his human side, who had violated the rules, failed to obey the rangers, and potentially injured visitors. How could anyone connect the young man with the dog? Standing on a curb next to a neon sign that cast a shimmer of light across the dirty water in the gutter, he glanced down at the water and couldn't help admiring the canine reflection that was tenderly looking back at him. What complicated matters was that he was now some distance away from where needed to be to get home (he had entered the park from the opposite side of the zoo, about two miles from where he was standing), and he would have to make his way back without entering the park. Sniffing the fetid city air, he realized that if he veered sharply to the right and continued angling right, he would eventually meet the line that would lead him directly home. While it would add time to his travel, he didn't feel that there was any other choice.

Glancing once more at his reflection, he couldn't resist the urge to bend down and tap the image with the tip of his nose, which made sparkling, concentric circles around his nose. He lapped up a small amount of water and, turning immediately to the right, began moving at a measured trot down the street. The street was lit up on one side by small stores, restaurants, and neon signs that filled the area with a dull, pale yellow light and cast long, dark shadows that reached across the sidewalk and disappeared into the black street. The other side of the street looked more or less like this side, except that there were more people milling about, either standing near doors or walking on the sidewalk, often in pairs. There were a few people on this side of the street, although they all seemed more interested in entering the businesses and restaurants than in milling about. The streets were also lined with cars and at times the traffic was heavy.

Fortunately, no one seemed particularly interested in him as he trotted to the end of the block, crossed the street (which at the time wasn't busy) and then trotted down the next, which looked exactly like the previous block and curiously like the following one. He felt strong, even after running to escape the rangers, but he was becoming hungry and thirsty. Block after block, right on one corner and left on the next, somehow angling toward the point at which he could pick up the path home, there was nothing in terms of food and water, each gutter dry and dusty as if they were the edges of a desert. What made matters worse was that he could smell food emanating from the restaurants, strong, powerful smells of meat and other mouth-drooling delicacies, and yet he realized that he could do nothing either as a dog or a human to get so much as a scrap. Knowing that this would change when he reached the wild, barren areas between his town and this one, he pressed on, constantly licking his chops and imagining the mice he would catch and the streams he would wade in to fill his belly with cool, refreshing water.

Not more than a couple of blocks from reaching the broad, open grassland that would eventually lead him to his neighborhood, a large man stepped out from the shadows and blocked his way. He was wearing overalls, a baseball cap, and heavy boots, and he had a thick, graying mustache. He stopped at least ten feet before reaching the man, and watched him as he squatted down and stretched out his hand as if he were offering a tasty treat.

"Where you going, boy?" the man said soothingly. "You shouldn't be running here without a collar. I can see you don't have a collar. Are you a stray? I'll bet you are. Maybe you want to come home with me."

The man didn't move any closer, although he positioned his enormous body so that he occupied the center of the sidewalk, making it difficult for anything to stay on the sidewalk and get around him. Instinctively wagging his tail because of the man's soft, pleasant voice and because he was interested in what he had in his hand (and he hoped that it was something to eat), the dog eyed him cautiously, trying to determine whether or not the man was to be trusted.

"Come on, boy," the man insisted, smiling broadly and stretching his hand out further. "Come on, boy, you can trust me." He smacked his lips several times and, adjusting his feet slightly, leaned forward a little more and stretched out his hand almost to the point at which he could grab a handful of fur. "Come on, boy, or are you a girl? Come on, I'm not going to bite. Look, I've got something for you, something really special."

The man slowly began to stand up while continuing to hold out his hand. "Come here, boy," he said again, after which he took a couple of slow, careful steps forward. "There's nothing to be afraid of. Come on, boy. You can trust me." He took another couple of steps forward until he was no more than three feet away and, squatting down again, stretched his arm and hand out to within inches of the dog's nose.

The dog couldn't see the man's face very well in the dim, evening light. But as soon as he was nearly nose to nose with the man and could sense him more clearly, he couldn't help feeling that there was something peculiar about his behavior (the man was too assertively friendly, and he kept shifting his dark eyes back and forth as if he were about ready to move to one side quickly) and, when he noticed the smell of animals and pungent chemicals on the man's hand, he began to fear that he had allowed the man to get too close. Without taking his eyes off the man's eyes and hands, the dog began to slowly and smoothly inch backward until he was confident that he could turn and run around the man if he made any abrupt moves. Undeterred, the man got up and took another step toward the dog and, slowly squatting down, he reached out again and offered the dog his treat. This time, however, a bright light from a nearby doorway momentarily illuminated the man's hand, and the dog could see clearly that the man was only pinching his fingers together and didn't have a treat or anything else. The dog's tail immediately stopped wagging and, just as the man started to ask him to look at his hand, the dog turned and tried to gallop away. His path, however, was blocked by another man who was straddling the sidewalk and stretching out his arms to prevent the dog from going around him. This was one of the zoo rangers.

During that instant when the dog encountered the ranger, the first man had somehow managed to pick up a long pole at the end of which was a rope with a loop in it. While the dog began to back away from the ranger, the first man had inched closer and was slowly lowering the loop over the dog, positioning it so that he could grasp the animal around the neck. Catching sight of a shadow moving toward him, the dog jerked his body toward a parked car on the street to avoid the shadow. The man missed and nearly fell down, but he quickly steadied himself and, pivoting toward the dog, tried to reach him again with the loop. The ranger went into motion, too, moving next to the car so that the only way the dog could escape was by turning around and leaping over the first man. The man

155

lunged and managed to grab the dog's ear, but as tried to steady himself and lower the loop around the dog's neck, the dog banged into his leg and the man, losing his grip on its ear, fell to the ground. The dog leaped over the fallen man, eluded the ranger's clumsy attempt to grab his tail, and ran down the street.

The dog noticed an alley to his right and, pivoting adroitly, charged into it and continued running almost as quickly as he could. The alley was much darker than the street and suffused throughout with black shadows. It was bound on both sides by the dark, discolored, and windowless walls of tall buildings that rose and disappeared into the night overhead. There were only a few lights in the alley, most of which were pallid, yellow light bulbs centered above closed, faceless doors on the walls of the buildings. But the illumination didn't reach much beyond the doors, for it was blocked by the giant trash containers that seemed to accompany every faceless door on the buildings. There were some bright areas, though, in the center of the alley where water pooled and reflected the lights above the doors and, occasionally, the moon when not covered by clouds. Of course, the dog didn't need much light to see his way clearly through the alley, and he ran its entire length from the beginning to the end on the other side of the block, dodging bottles, papers, and other debris lying almost everywhere. For the most part, it was deserted, although he passed a man dressed in white apron heaving two large bags of trash into one of the large containers next to the buildings (there were no sidewalks) who, when he saw the dog, stopped after depositing the trash and whistled loudly. But the dog didn't turn and continued running, his nose filled with the fetid smell of trash and human waste, which seemed at odds with the wonderful smells permeating the streets.

He didn't stop once during the few minutes that it took to traverse the alley, not even to take a single drop of water, which he desperately desired. When he burst out at the other end, he was engulfed by a blaze of lurid lights and surrounded by a cacophony of human voices and human smells. He still didn't stop, and charged down one street after another, heading circuitously toward the point at which he could finally intersect the path that would take him home. However, he was forced to slow down before reaching that point, because he was tiring rapidly and he was desperate for water (his tongue was hanging out the side of his mouth and bouncing against jaw and nose); nevertheless, he continued moving, now at a brisk trot, which would slow even more as he continued. It was clear that the men were still looking for him, still lurking around the corners and prowling the streets, and so no matter how much he wanted to stop and catch his breath and take a drink, he continued on, pushing himself to his limits until city streets gave way to dark, deserted roads, which in turn gave way even darker, deserted lots with chain-linked fences surrounding metal covered buildings. There were even fewer lights here than there had been in the alley, but because the moon had pulled away from the clouds, there were fewer shadows and the roads were somewhat visible in the gray light. The dog relaxed a little in this area, for he was heading directly home and neither the men nor anyone else was in sight. Block after block seemed deserted, as if humans had built the terrible, rundown structures lining the road and had never seen fit to occupy them.

Finally, the dog slowed to a walk, moving slowly up one dark, deserted street and down another, hoping to chance on a puddle somewhere but knowing that he probably wouldn't come upon anything to eat or drink until he finally arrived at the open parkland. With his head and tail hanging lifelessly, he kept a wary eye open for men and water but tried not to think of either one, for if these things weighed too heavily on his mind, he might stop, lie down, and give up. Despite his present concerns, he didn't want to give up, not after he had seen Iowa. But had he actually seen her? The question began to trouble him more and more.

Chapter Thirty

None of it made sense, he reminded himself as he continued moving across the deserted streets, only some of which had sidewalks. First there were the swans and then there were the rangers. Why were the rangers trying to capture him? What did he do to make them leave the park and follow him through the city streets? The dog stumbled over something (he was too weak to leap over obstacles and too tired to observe everything in front of him) and then hesitated. What if the rangers were still on his trail? What if they were closing in on him this very second?

Holding his breath, he listened intently to everything around him. Within the billowing wind, he heard the gravel bounce on the ground and the fences and metal roofs of the buildings creak and groan. Turning his ears right and left, he perceived the tap-tap-tap of debris (cups, paper, and indescribable items) dancing across the streets or struggling hopelessly to free itself from the fences and walls that held it captive. For a moment, he thought he noticed patches of human sounds and smells, but as soon as he craned his head to zero in on the patches, they were gone and in their stead were areas that humans had touched or occupied at one point but were now devoid of human life. Since he didn't seem to be in danger, he began breathing normally (as normally as a tired dog could under the circumstances) and, after nibbling at his side and then scratching the area with his hind leg, resumed his slow perambulation down the deserted street.

Forgetting the men for a moment, the dog started thinking about the swans at the zoo. He really didn't want to think about them, just as he didn't want to contemplate the men or his increasing thirst and weakening stamina, but he couldn't help himself because Iowa had been the point of the trip, and the more he thought about them, the greater his concern that he had not actually seen her or knew which was the swan and which his beloved. The dog hesitated and then continued walking. Of course, there was another possibility. The two swans may have been one and the same. It was a stretch, perhaps, but it seemed possible that shortly after he left the first, it flew over to the other pond, where he encountered it as the second.

It definitely made sense, since this would have been the only way for her to maximize their time together, even though she couldn't have known that he would check out the other body of water. No, that was wrong; she could have overheard the ranger telling him the location of the lake, and she would have had no reason to doubt that he would check it out. On the other hand, he wasn't certain that swans could fly. He never saw Iowa or any of the other Cygnets fly, and he couldn't recall any of them ever speaking about flying, even when they rattled on over lunch at school about their swan activities (telling each other how much fun they had swimming and doing all the other things that swans do, speaking over his head as if he weren't there, as if he were a complete cypher). But if they had been able to fly, wouldn't they have said something about it, especially Press, who jabbered away at everything that came to mind? Then again, maybe they didn't know how to fly. It was all new to them, and so it might very well have been that they didn't fly because they didn't know how. Iowa spent more time as a swan, and if it were possible she certainly would have flown many times without giving it a second thought. Yes, it only made sense that both swans were one and that the one was Iowa.

This line of reasoning satisfied him for another couple of steps until he recalled that the swan in the lake near the gate bit him. It wasn't an accidental nibble or something done to call attention to itself. On the contrary, it was a savage bite, the kind of thing a swan does to protect itself and keep someone it doesn't like at bay. Moreover, the swan hissed at him, which, if nothing else, was an affirmation of its violent intentions. So, why did these things happen? If the swan were Iowa, then why did she attack him in such a manner? Was it because she didn't want to see him? Was it because she was too far gone and could no longer relate to humans? But if the swan wasn't Iowa, then something else didn't make sense: For a few seconds, the swan, Iowa, or whatever it was clearly appreciated his presence and tried to communicate with him before the ranger appeared. Could the swan's reaction have been caused not be something that Luke may or may not have done but by mere presence of the ranger? His presence may have startled her and, like most startled animals, she reacted blindly, attacking the first thing within reach. A reflexive action and nothing more, certainly not an indication that the swan was not Iowa and that the swan or Iowa wanted to chase Luke away. The questions were unsettling and seeming endless, and they did nothing to enhance his understanding of what had happened. To calm his nerves and help focus on what was foremost in his mind now, the dog tried to recall Iowa's kind features and her gentle personality – although this, too, was unsettling, because Iowa could also be cold and hot, angry and hurtful.

He stumbled slightly over something in the dirt, and, righting himself without injury, he recalled an incident when all the Cygnets were sitting at a lunch table at school. Press and Lu were bickering over something and, when Luke innocently tried to change the subject to get them to calm down, Press turned on him and told him to mind his own business. But as if that weren't quite enough, she accused him of meddling and interfering in "things" that he didn't understand. Luke was taken aback by Press' almost vicious response, especially because he had only wanted to prevent a bigger quarrel, and he was shocked when out of the blue she suggested...no, when she stated that he didn't belong with the Cygnets.

"I don't understand. Why are you mad at me?" he asked, trying to understand why she was suddenly fighting with him.

"What don't you understand? You're not like us. You sit and watch us with that smirk you always have, and you try to make us do things you want to do, as if anyone cares what you want to do."

"I don't...I don't know...what you're talking about. I ..." Luke tried to respond, but he was flummoxed because he couldn't understand why one of his closest friends (even if she had a temper) could speak to him in this manner, especially when he meant no harm. What was equally troubling was none of the other Cygnets came to his defense – at least not for a few moments – as if they felt that her cruel words had at least some merit.

"Cat got your tongue? Why don't you leave us alone? Why don't you go away and stop bothering us? Why don't you..." It was at this point that Press stood up and leaned over the table as if she were about to attack him.

Luke instinctively leaned back and silently, open-mouthed, stared at Press, not knowing what to do or what she was going to do.

Iowa, who must have been as surprised as Luke, quickly intervened before Press could take the next, irrevocable step. "Wait a minute," she said, staring at Press and looking as if she were about to stand up and confront the taller girl. "He's not bothering you or anyone else." Luke noticed that her face was becoming red with anger.

Press turned toward Iowa, who was sitting to her right. "Why are you always defending him? When he's not around you complain that he won't stop ogling you. That's your word, if you recall."

Iowa suddenly jumped up and, using a tone that was rare for her, told Press to back off. "Shut up!" she shouted at Press. "He's as much a Cygnet as you are, but if you're going to start picking on everyone, why don't you leave."

Press was certainly taken aback by Iowa's aggressive attitude. She certainly wasn't afraid of Iowa, since she was a good head taller and quite athletic, but there was something about Iowa's unremitting attitude that made her back down mentally and physically, and she broke into tears, which naturally encouraged everyone to reach over to console her and assure her that they were all the best of friends, which also meant that they forgot all the mean things that she had been saying to Luke. Iowa, too, petted her, although not as much as Dana and Lu and, while she was helping Press recover, she glanced at him with an expression that seemed to suggest that he was at least partly responsible for this unpleasant event. It was almost as if she had bitten him for something that he didn't do.

The dog sneezed from the dust that suddenly flew up in the breeze. When the breeze subsided and his sneezing stopped, he began to recall some of the many times that Iowa smiled at him alone, or picked him over the others in one of the seemingly endless games the Cygnets played at the lake. Until she poked him under his eye, there was never a time in his memory when she didn't exhibit some form of favoritism toward him, either choosing him for her partner in these games or, later, silently communicating her thoughts to him with winks, smiles, and blushes, all of which he understood. So while she could behave in ways that seemed arbitrary and senseless, she made it clear through her actions and sometimes her words that she had a special feeling for him, something that she didn't share with the others. Was it love? He didn't know, but he hoped she did because he loved her.

The dog sneezed again, and once more for good measure. His senses clear, he licked the tip of his nose and then the sides of his mouth, and it was then that he noticed something in the air, something that made him drool and brought back to mind the serious state he was in. The dog was standing on a patch of dirt outside a junkyard filled with huge stacks of flattened cars and row upon row of badly damaged cars that were in all likelihood destined to be flattened like the rest. He was next to the chain-link fence that surrounded the yard, and, as he sniffed the air among the greasy, gas-scented wrecks, he detected the distinct smell of water somewhere inside the yard. The absence of food in the yard didn't matter, for he needed water more than anything else.

He ran back and forth along the fence looking for an opening. He noticed one location – a square section cut into the fence and lined with thick, steep tubing – but it was locked (there was a giant, gray padlock hanging from it) and too high for him to scale. The dog didn't give up the search, though, because the heavy scent of water was making him desperate for a drink – so desperate that he failed to recognize the other scents wafting from the other side of the fence. Giving up on the fence, the dog searched the ground next to the fence for an opening or gap that he could exploit to get inside the yard (the fence was too high to jump and, in his desperation for water, he never once considered changing and climbing over) and came across a slight depression under the locked gate. The depression wasn't very deep (it opened a gap of a few inches to the bottom of the gate), but as he tested it with his front paws, he noticed that it was soft and that it easily yielded to his nails. Using his front paws, he began excavating the depression, furiously pulling the dirt out and forcing it back between his hind legs. Within seconds, the depression became a hole and, within minutes, the hole became wider and deeper.

The hole became so big that he was certain he could use it to get under the fence. After stopping and glancing around to make sure that he was still alone, the dog got down on his front knees and, leaning over onto his right shoulder, poked his head in the hole under the fence. His head easily went under, but because his shoulders and body were too big and long, he was forced to back out and deepen the hole in every direction and dimension. Five minutes later, the hole was finally big enough to poke his head under the fence and, using all four legs, push and pull his body into the junkyard.

Once inside the fence and on all four feet, the dog sniffed at something on his chest and, after sniffing the air, headed directly to the water.

Chapter Thirty-one

The source turned out to be a rusty tub filled to the brim with water. The tub was located some twenty feet inside the yard and on the other side of a towering stack of flattened cars. There was a small pole with a light on its top behind the tub, but the illumination was too weak to extend beyond the cars, and so the dog had no idea of its presence until he reached the tub. The tub, of course, was irresistible, and situated in an alcove, as it were, and illuminated by a light made it appear that it had been placed there on purpose, as if someone had anticipated his thirst and had thoughtfully accommodated it, while he (the thoughtful individual) had gone to bed. The area was deserted. Cautiously walking up to the tub and sniffing its metal edge and then the water's surface to make sure it was safe to drink, he leaned over and pressed his nose against the water's surface and began lapping up the cool, sweet-tasting liquid.

Once his belly was full – he could feel his belly sag slightly under the weight of the water he had consumed – the dog took one last slurp of the water and then trotted back to the hole under the gate. The effect of the water seemed almost miraculous. Not only did he feel alive again, but he seemed to have regained most of his strength, which had been lost because of his thirst and his efforts to escape the rangers. But just as he approached the hole under the gate (his mind was now focused on leaving and, along the way home, finding some food, for his stomach was now clamoring for attention), he noticed a vague black shadow dart in front of the fence. Since the area around the gate was poorly illuminated, he couldn't tell if there was actually something there or if his eyes and mind were playing tricks on him. Once he stopped to take a better look at the area, another shadow joined the first, this one positioning itself on the other side of the hole, and within seconds he smelled the heavy presence of other animals. It surprised him that he hadn't noticed the smell earlier, especially because the smell strongly suggested that the animals weren't friendly.

Standing motionless, he watched two large Rottweiler guard dogs slowly emerge from the darkness and position themselves at the edge of the weakly illuminated area where he stood. The animals, which were about twenty feet away and about the same distance from one another, stopped for a moment and stared at him, their watery eyes glistening and their bright teeth reflecting remnants of a distant light. Before he could respond, however, the animals started angling toward him, their movements cautious and deliberate, and he could hear their deep-throated growling as they approached. Instinctively lowering his shoulders and baring his own teeth, he watched as the animals approached and then tried to match the fierce sound of their growls. Under different circumstances, he would have backed away from the animals and taken measures to elude them just as he eluded the zoo rangers; but there was no place to elude them in the yard (behind him and to his left were stacks of flattened cars, while the area on his right was blocked by one of the Rottweilers) and going forward toward the hole was just as pointless. Observing the animals' relentless approach, he recalled the moment when Jimmy (one of the boys he taught to change) and Jimmy's friends (boys Jimmy taught to change) surrounded the Cygnets while they floated on the lake as swans. He now understood what the swans must have felt when they believed that there was no escape, and for once he was sympathetic to Press and knew why she was so angry even after escaping a pack of wild, snarling dogs.

Before he knew what was happening, the Rottweiler on his left charged and, with a speed that belied its large size, grabbed him on the back of the neck and, knocking him off balance, nearly forced him to the ground. He managed to remain on his feet, but because the animal's grip was firm and unrelenting, and because its weight and size kept his nose angled down, he was unable to fight back or even reach the animal with his teeth. Seconds later, his legs began to give way and he could feel the teeth of the animal penetrating his skin and tendons, sending a shock of pain through his body that numbed his feet and legs. And it was at that moment, while he was being forced to the ground, that the other Rottweiler joined the attack and, grabbing him on the hind quarters, knocked him off his hind feet, after which his front feet crumbled beneath him.

He tried to rise. He couldn't survive if he couldn't get to his feet. But the weight of the animals, and fury in which they were tearing into him – in addition to the fact that he couldn't turn in their direction to respond – made him fear that in a few seconds he would be dead. While the pain was intense, his sense of anger and futility over having squandered opportunities was even greater. What would Iowa think and feel when she heard of his unfortunate demise? Would she cry? Would she be able to cry, or would she float dumbly on the pond like all the other birds? Nevertheless, he tried to resist, especially when the pain began to subside and body began to grow numb, but his legs and head wouldn't move, and in seconds he sensed his eyes beginning to close while the animals' crude grunts and growls began to fade into silence. Would Iowa even hear about what had happened? Opening his eyes in one final burst of strength, he struggled to get up and turn to defend himself, but his efforts were futile. He couldn't move. His legs refused to do anything except remain motionless, absorbing whatever the Rottweilers were doing to them and him. With his head against the ground, dirt filling and clogging his nostrils, he was beginning to sense that even if the Rottweilers relented, he was too badly injured to get up, much less find the path and make it home. But just as he was about to give up and close his eyes, the dog noticed a bouncing ball coming his way. It was small, maybe a tennis ball in size, and it glowed with an intensity that hurt his eyes. He didn't turn away -- for some reason, he was mesmerized by the light – even when the ball dissolved in a searing light that practically blinded him.

"Get back, you son of a….," the man shouted as he hit one of the Rottweilers over the head with his flashlight and then grabbed it by the collar and yanked it away from the dog. Kicking the other Rottweiler in the side until it, too, released its hold, he grabbed it by the collar and dragged the furiously barking animals to a small hut a few feet away and shoved them through the open door (kicking one of them back inside when it tried to leave and attack again). Once the door was shut, the man turned and walked toward the dog, his flashlight steadier this time.

The man was never more than a giant shadow to the dog, who was now struggling to get back on his feet. Flashing the light in his face, the man squatted down in from of him, observing his struggles as if he couldn't quite believe the dog, any dog, could make it to his feet, much less begin to walk, after what happened. Surprisingly, the dog did stand up, although it took a couple of tries since his legs were still numb, and when he was able to steady himself, he took one step to the side and decided to stop for a moment or so. He was weak and, more significantly, his hind legs were throbbing with pain, especially his right leg, which was becoming unbearable as the numbness wore off. Dazed and slightly disoriented, his ears ringing with the sounds of the barking and growling

165

dogs in the shed, he knew that something was going to happen and, like a helpless spectator, he stood waiting for it to happen. But nothing happened while he waited, the seconds ticking off while the man remained on his haunches, flashing the light in the dog's face and then back and forth along his body as if he were examining the dog.

"It don't look too bad, fella," the man finally said and spit something out of the side of his mouth. "I can see some welts on your neck, although that leg of yours looks pretty raw. But I guess you ain't that bad 'cause you're standing."

Unexpectedly, the dog felt a little stronger and, as long as he didn't move, didn't seem to be on the verge of topping over. He couldn't put much weight on his hind leg because of the pain, but the rest of him, as far as he could sense, didn't seem to be seriously injured. Enjoying the brief respite from moving, the dog observed the man as he turned his head this way and that, visually examining the injured dog's body. Because the pain was still controlling most of his senses, he didn't understand what the man was doing, and he couldn't tell if he was duplicitous like the rangers or violent like the dogs. The strong, unpleasant smell of tobacco and alcohol emanating from the man was unlike the smell of the rangers, but it also confused his senses.

"Well, fella," the man said again, "I think you need some help. No question you took a beatin' from them dumb beasts in there, but at least you're upright." The dog noticed for the first time a bright light on top of a pole somewhere behind the man. As the man stood up and towered over the dog, his head blocked a lot of the light, turning him into a giant, faceless shadow. Tucking the flashlight under his arm, he pulled something out of his pocket, put it to his mouth and, after a bright flash of light, breathed deeply and blew smoke out of his mouth.

"Shut up!" he hollered, turning briefly toward the dogs in the shed, which never let up with their barking and growling. Turning back to the injured dog, he said, "But I don't understand what you're doing here." He glanced around, flashing the flashlight through the yard and, not seeing anything, tugged at his ear and blew out another puff of smoke.

"Can't figure it out, unless…" He paused and, after another puff of smoke, finished his sentence. "Yeah, unless you came for the water, I guess. Mighty hot ain't it? Tub of it around the corner, right? Well, I don't know what to tell you. You got a load of it just for a lousy drink."

166

The man put the cigarette to his mouth and inhaled deeply, after which he positioned it between the thumb and middle finger of his right hand and flicked it away into the dark. The cigarette made a reddish, comet-like arc as it sailed away and landed about ten feet away on the ground, where it erupted in a short explosion of reddish sparks.

Stepping closer and shining his flashlight in the dog's direction, which made it difficult to see the man's face clearly, the man reexamined the dog's wounds, shaking his head from time to time as if he was seeing something serious and irreparable. "Looks worse than I thought in some places, boy," he said soothingly, as much to himself as to the dog. "That leg of yours looks the worst. You gonna need some serious treatment, I s'pect." He moved a half step to the side and wagged his head. "Sorry 'bout the Rotts, fella. They're stupid, but they sure protect the yard fine. Now, you're a good boy, ain't you," he said pleasantly and soothingly. The man cautiously took a couple of half steps closer to the dog, reminding him with each step that he was a good boy and that no one was going to harm him. "I just want to take a closer look at something."

The dog couldn't resist wagging his tail slightly in response to the man's words, although he didn't entirely trust the man, especially since the rangers said pretty much the same thing to him.

When the man was close enough to reach out and touch him, the dog moved to the side a couple of steps, trying not to put a lot of weight on his injured leg. Whatever injuries the man noticed on his neck, the dog couldn't feel anything there other than some stiffness, which seemed to be quickly increasing. He could certainly feel his leg, though. It was throbbing from the pain, and each little movement of his body intensified his discomfort. The dog didn't know if he could make it home on three legs, but he knew that he couldn't stay here much longer, even if the man was as nice as he seemed to be with all his pleasant words and "good boy" talk.

"I'm not going to hurt you," the man repeated as he squatted down next to the dog's side and cautiously lifted up his right arm, the palm of his right hand raised as if he were motioning the dog to halt. There was silence for a moment, which was broken only by the dog's heavy panting and by the non-stop barking from the Rottweilers in the shed, after which the man's upraised hand began to move closer to the dog. "Now, boy," he began just as he was about to touch the dog with his raised hand, "I just want to look at something. That okay, boy? You're a pretty boy. A mighty handsome dog, I'd say."

For a moment, the dog forgot about going home, the rangers, and even Iowa.

The man cautiously stroked the top of the dog's wet neck, after which he patted him gently between the shoulders. During this time, he continued calling the dog "good boy" and "nice boy," and he promised him that no one was going to hurt him. "I just want to take a look," he said, eyeing the dog's wounds. "Is that okay, boy?" Again, the dog's tail wagged slightly as the man smoothed the dog's fur on his shoulders and back. "You're doing fine," he said as he continued to pet the dog while he shined the light on his neck and leg. The man carefully stroked the top of the dog's head and nose, and, slipping his hand under the dog's jaw, lifted his head back a little so he could see into his eyes. Releasing him, the man said as if he were speaking only to himself, "The face and eyes look good. I guess only the neck and leg are really bad. Probably heal okay, though."

The man then slid his hand lightly down the dog's back to his haunches. "Not a flinch," he said, shaking his head, and added, "Good boy." Stroking the dog lightly on the haunches, the man turned his eyes to the injuries on the dog's leg, silently making mental notes as he sized up the injuries. During this time, the dog closed his eyes to ease the pain in his leg, which was unrelenting, and savored the man's gentle words, something he hadn't experienced since leaving home. Home -- home now seemed far away, and he couldn't help thinking that he might never see it again, that he might never see Iowa again. However, it was at this very moment that the man decided to examine the dog's leg more closely. Slowly pulling his hand from the dog's shoulders (his other hand was draped across his knee), the man reached under the dog and touched a sensitive area of his wounds. Startled by the man's touch, and feeling an unexpected jab of pain (it felt as if someone had stabbed him in the wound with a large spike) where the man had touched him, the dog reeled around instinctively and bit the man's hand. He hadn't reacted angrily, and, as soon as he realized what he had done, he turned his head toward the man and, with his eyes wide open, wagged his tail to convey his apologies. But the damage was done.

The man dropped his flashlight and jumped up. Grabbing his hand and cursing the dog for having attacked him, he hopped around in a small circle alternately cursing and examining his injuries. Observing the man's behavior and now afraid of what the man might do next, the dog limped quickly to the hole beneath the fence and, dipping down and putting his head and shoulders down into the hole, he pulled himself with his good legs under the fence. Once on the other side and balancing himself on three legs, the man caught sight of the dog and, still shaking his hand, walked briskly up to the fence.

"You good for nothing…," he shouted, shaking the fence with his uninjured hand, as if that by itself would repay the dog for his kindness. "Don't you ever come back here, you hear me?" The dog turned and began trotting away as quickly as he could, holding his injured leg up to keep it from touching the ground. When he was some distance from the fence, he sensed a rushing sound and then felt a large thud erupting only a few feet from his right shoulder. The man had hurled a half-empty gas can his way, which missed only because he lost sight of the dog in the dark night.

Chapter Thirty-two

The dog could tell that the man let the Rottweilers out of the shed. Their hoarse barking was clearer, and he could sense their frantic movements along the fence and other areas where they picked up his scent. For whatever reason, the man didn't let them out of the yard or through the hole, for if he had they would have caught up with him in minutes and finished him off within seconds. After a while, the barking became quieter and less insistent, and soon after that it disappeared altogether.

The dog wasn't out of the woods, however, because he still needed to get home sooner rather than later. He knew that if he were late, his parents would begin to worry, and he was afraid that if his father began to worry, his mother would begin to panic and would no doubt call Ms. Royce for help. The last thing he needed was for Ms. Royce to get involved (he reminded himself that Press would have a field day if she found out that he had run afoul of Ms. Royce). The dog therefore pushed himself as hard as he could, but no matter how fast he tried to move, no matter how hard he pushed himself, he continued to move at a snail's pace compared to earlier in the day. It was difficult to walk effectively on three legs, and the pain was such that every movement he made jostled his injured leg and sent blinding shocks of pain throughout his body. He needed to travel quickly, he needed to cover a great distance before the sun came up, and yet there were moments when he slowed to a hobble, there were moments when he nearly fell down when he tried to step over a small rock or weed because it took too much out of him to go around, and there were moments when he feared that he would have to stop, recuperate, or else collapse altogether. He didn't want to collapse, for that would solve nothing and would eventually let everyone know when he did and what happened to him. Of course, he would have to explain his injuries when he got home (it would be hard to hide something like that), but he would deal with that when the time came and, for now, he needed to continue on, even if he moved slower than a snail.

There were a couple moments when the pain mysteriously subsided (a little, though never completely leaving his body and consciousness) in which he nearly convinced himself that he would better in the morning. Obviously, it was unrealistic to think that he would be healed any time soon, but he felt that at least by morning light he might have more use of his injured hind leg, which would enable him to pick up his speed. This hope vanished within an hour or so when he stopped to catch his breath because he couldn't continue moving without a rest. Pausing in the middle of a wide open space of dirt and small rocks and weeds, he examined his injuries, beginning with the most serious of them (as far as the pain was concerned), his hind leg. He craned his neck toward his leg (he didn't try to sit down, because the pain throbbed unmercifully when he tried to lower his haunches to a sitting position), but there wasn't enough light to see much except a few areas that were so wet that they reflected some of the full moon's soft glow. But when he put his nose near his leg and gingerly touched some of the injuries with the tip of his tongue, he could tell that he was in far worse shape than he had imagined, than even his intense pain led him to believe. From the smell, he understood that most of his leg was wet from blood, which seemed to emanate from a number of puncture and gashes, particularly one that was at least three inches long and at least as wide just above his hock, exposing some of the bone. Knowing the healing power of his saliva, the dog licked these and other injuries; when he had accomplished all he could to help his leg and body, he licked his nose and started off as before, albeit a little more slowly. Despite his rest, the pain and the idea that his body was terribly injured sapped a good deal of his strength and energy.

The dog was far from anything that suggested human habitation. He couldn't recall when he finally left the empty lots, the buildings with metal roofs, and the fences behind, but it seemed like a long time ago. Indeed, he felt as though he had been hobbling through the open land for hours, although he had trouble sensing the passage of time because of the concentration required to remain upright (every now and then he slipped on something in the dirt, and it took nearly all his strength to keep from falling over) and because of the pain, which at times shot its way through his leg and into his body. And because he couldn't accurately determine the time of night (the moon wasn't any help, for it seemed fixed overhead when it wasn't hidden by fast-moving black clouds), he couldn't tell how much longer he had to walk before he reached the cliff, or how much time he needed to reach home. It was the cliff, however, that he was desperate to reach. If he recalled correctly, it marked the halfway point between zoo and home, although descending the cliff might take time, perhaps hours. Pausing again, this time to make sure that he was traveling in the right direction, the dog licked his chops and nose several times and, breathing heavily, tried to push himself harder, as hard as he pushed himself at any point in his journey. But he wasn't able to move any faster and, in fact, was moving even slower than he had only a few minutes ago, if that were possible. The need for food and water had come over him, competing with the pain for his attention. Since there wasn't anything edible or drinkable in sight, the dog pushed on, telling himself that once he made it down the cliff, there would be any number of places to drink and things to eat.

While he was walking, his eyes, ears, and nose focused on the direction in which he needed to travel, he caught sight of something out the corner of his eyes. It seemed like a phosphorescent blur, dull orange in color, but when he hesitated and looked, there was nothing. Licking his chops, he continued moving, practically dragging his injured leg, certain that it was nothing more than his imagination and a reminder that he didn't have time to relax and chase phantoms. Shortly after this, the dog paused again after hearing a strange hissing sound in front of him. The sound clearly didn't come from anything nearby, although its peculiar sound seemed to represent something, a marker perhaps, on his journey home. While he was listening to the sound and trying to identify it by scent, he caught sight of another phosphorescent blur, this time on the other side of his body. Turning in its direction, he thought he noticed the same dull, orange blur that he had seen a few seconds ago, and just like the last time it disappeared too quickly for him to make anything of it. Giving his head a slow and partial shake (anything more would have aggravated his festering injuries), the dog took a couple of strained steps forward and stopped. Listening carefully, he suddenly recognized the sound in front of him – it was the highway, the landmark that separated one part of his journey from the other parts, and it also made sense of the phosphorescent blurs, since they were probably reflections from cars or their headlights. Indeed, the closer he got to the highway, the brighter the surrounding area appeared because of the vehicles' headlights and taillights.

Thirty minutes later, the dog was standing at the edge of the highway, as cars and trucks traveled furiously up and down the road either unaware of or unconcerned by his presence. While he stood there, every few seconds the headlights of a car or truck (or sometimes a bus) illuminated one side of his body and, in some instances, forced him to close his eyes because of the brightness of the light. And sometimes when a large truck or bus passed near him, he could feel the rush of wind hit his body and, if he weren't standing just right, he would be forced to shift his stance to keep from being pushed over. While he was pleased to have made it this far, he was nevertheless worried about his ability to cross both sides of the highway. He had trouble crossing it when he was healthy, and now with his injured leg and increasingly stiff neck (it was starting to get difficult to lift his nose in the air), it would take something special to cross without getting hit. A couple of times, a large truck would honk its horn – a loud, deep bellow that began before the truck reached him, increased in intensity when the truck was close to him, and faded into the din when the truck was passed him – startling him and causing him to lean away from the sound (he couldn't move well enough to jump back), which for some reason inspired a chorus of car horns that forced him to take a step or two away from the road.

As before, the dog knew that the only way to negotiate the highway successfully was to do it by halves, crossing one direction of traffic, resting in the median, and then crossing the other direction. It made sense, but he also expected it to be especially challenging this time given the slow pace he was moving. After waiting for a few minutes, the traffic on the section of road nearest to him thinned out, giving him an opportunity to cross at his own pace. Walking as quickly as he could, the dog crossed this section of the highway and, once safely in the dirt-covered median, waited patiently for the other side to clear.

Chapter Thirty-three

The dog stood a few feet from the edge of the highway and watched the cars and trucks racing from one end of his vision to the other. It appeared to be a never-ending stream of vehicles, which created a constantly-swirling breeze that tugged at the ends of his fur and sometimes forced him to steady his legs to remain upright. He was surprised that he still had enough strength to keep himself upright, often with a slight and painful hop to prevent his bad leg from touching the ground, but he was less surprised by the fumes surrounding him, which were repellant, and the sounds of the vehicles, the roar of the engines and the screams of the horns warning him to keep back from the pavement. Since he wasn't moving, except when he had to rebalance himself from time to time, he started to feel a little better and became a little more optimistic that that he could at least reach the cliff. His injured leg, which hung limply and was balanced against the ground by his paw, was more or less stationary, which mitigated the pain and allowed him to concentrate on things without being constantly reminded that he was hurt and that his leg hurt.

The dog had been standing in the median for quite some time, when he looked up at the night sky and noticed that the stars were disappearing and that the black canopy overhead was gradually turning gray. He didn't immediately assign any particular significance to this change – it was simply a change – probably because he was too tired and weak to understand the significance of the things surrounding him. He did, however, notice what appeared to be a hawk floating back and forth overhead, lazily catching invisible air currents as it searched for prey. It was only when the bird was momentarily out of sight that he noticed that the sky was clear and, as he turned his eyes to the land in front of him, that the dark shadows were practically gone. The dog might have become troubled by the passage of time, but the hawk came back into view and he started to wonder what it felt like floating effortlessly in the sky, relaxing as if he were in his bed at home and watching all the people and animals below him scurrying about as if they had something important to do.

The idea that people and animals might be concerned troubled him, but before he was able to delve into the matter, he began rising off the ground (first his front legs and then his hind legs) and was soon floating in the air and soaring over the land and then over a vast, blue ocean so far below that neither a wave nor wrinkle could be seen. He wondered, as he felt the cool air currents rush against his nose, what the ocean smelled like and if its scent had anything in common with the scent that permeated the pond at home, where he and Iowa spent some of the best times of their lives together. He could almost see Iowa down below, looking up at him and waving at him, as if she alone could see him so many miles beyond the visual capabilities of ordinary people. The Cygnets weren't with her, but then the Cygnets seemed to have disappeared long ago, long before he and Iowa met and became inseparable. Iowa was beautiful, he told himself, imagining what she looked like while he floated in the air; he had never seen anyone nearly as beautiful and, what's more, she reciprocated the warm feelings that he felt for her – she alone stood by him through thick and thin, and he knew that he could count on her just as she counted on him during the unpleasant times. Staring into the blue, he seemed to float higher until he slowly lost sight of her and once again the hawk came into view, floating back and forth across the blue expanse below him.

While he watched the hawk, mentally trying to pull it closer to him so that he could examine it and find out why it was so insistently flying around him, he slowly became aware of a soft buzzing sound that seemed to be enclosing him in a giant pair of soft hands, and, as it grew louder and more insistent, filled his senses and seemed to permeate his very body. It didn't make any sense, it resembled nothing that he had ever heard before, and yet its insistence seemed to be demanding something from him, even though he couldn't fathom what this something could be. Once, when the noise was nearly unbearable, he closed his eyes and shook his head several times to ease the strain on his sore ears, but when he opened them again to look at the hawk, the bird was gone. Perhaps equally strange, his body began to feel heavy, as if it were no longer light enough to continue floating, and he knew that at any moment he would begin to hurtle downward, past the hawk, past Iowa, and crash into the blue water far below. He didn't understand how this could happen; he only knew that it would happen and that for some reason it should happen. Surprisingly, it felt good to accept this fact, as if by accepting it he was relieved of all obligations to worry or even become afraid. But just as he was beginning to feel good inside because there was no reason to be afraid, the noise surrounding him became louder and a huge gust of wind pushed him from behind, and he could feel himself hurling toward the water –not floating downward as he had imagined, but falling with ever increasing speed. As he went down, he began to see sand floating past him, probably from a nearby beach, and, while it didn't exactly surprise him, it did seemed a little peculiar to see so much of it so high in the air and moving in a manner that contradicted his own direction and his own senses.

Something else began to happen as he fell. He felt pain, not the kind of pain he expected to feel while moving through the sky (even though he didn't know what kind of pain was typical for animals in the sky), but a localized pain, emanating from somewhere below almost as if the location wasn't on his body, and it seemed to increase the faster he moved – and he was moving faster and faster. The hawk must have been falling, too, for it suddenly reappeared and was now keeping pace with his downward momentum, and for a brief moment he felt sorry for the bird because it was probably feeling the same sensations he was. However, judging by the way it moved smoothly through the sky, it didn't provide any evidence to suggest that it was uncomfortable – it didn't appear to have a gritty sensation in its eyes, its tongue wasn't hanging out in a desperate search for the slightest bit of moisture, and it wasn't writhing in the grip of an invisible hand that was crushing its bones and forcing the air out of its lungs. If anything, the bird seemed to unaware of its sufferings, which made its plight all the more sad and pathetic.

There was a loud, dull sounding thud behind him. Before he could turn around and locate the source of the sound, he felt as if he were spinning around and rolling over, his body sliding across the surface of the asphalt, and his injured leg turning and folding beneath him as if all its bones had melted or turned to rubber. The dog lifted its head and looked around. On both sides, he could see narrow strips of weeds and dirt that separated one side of the highway from the other, while directly in front of him was a seemingly endless wall of cars and trucks, every one of them obscuring the beautiful open plain that he needed to reach if he was to survive. The sun was extraordinarily bright and hot, and the dog slowly pushed the upper part of his body up with his front legs and then struggled to lift his hind end with his one good leg, which unexpectedly felt sore.

When he was finally upright, he tried to back up a couple of steps, but he was unsteady, too unsteady to withstand another blast from a passing big rig, and his weak leg crumbled under him and his hind quarters fell to a sitting position. The dog pushed himself up again with a slight whimper, and this time he was able limp back a few feet from the edge of the pavement, where he was reasonably safe from the cars, trucks, and other things on the highway.

Balancing on three feet, the toes of his injured leg lightly touching the gravel on the side of the pavement, the dog breathed deeply and wagged his head a couple of times to clear his senses. Observing the line of cars and trucks in front of him (and, without looking, realizing the same things was behind him), he watched the heavy traffic and positioned himself in such a way that he could withstand the wait until it cleared.

Chapter Thirty-four

The dog didn't have long to wait. As if by magic, the traffic in front of him thinned and, seconds later, there was a long gap between the vehicles that just passed him and the specs in the distance coming toward him. The dog immediately understood that he didn't have a lot of time. He needed to cross now or wait for the next break, and who knew when that would come, if ever? He also realized that his ability to cross quickly was severely hampered by his injured leg, and no matter how quickly he tried to move, no matter how desperately he tried to move, he could only go at a certain pace which, if he didn't move now, would not be quick enough to cross before the distant specs became much bigger.

The dog started across the highway, his injured leg unable to help apart from holding up the tips of his paw that would otherwise drag on the pavement and slow his progress. Fortunately, this section wasn't particularly wide – wide enough for two vehicles side by side – and he seemed to be crossing with relative ease, although the pain in his injured leg was now shooting through him every time he hopped with the other leg, and he couldn't do anything but hop since the injured one was useless for locomotion. He had nearly made it across the pavement – his front paws were already on the gravel at the far side of the highway, and one more hop and he would be safe on the other side and able to continue his journey home when he noticed out the corner of his eye a speck that was now a monumental boulder towering above him. Before he could take one more step, or even makes sense of the obscene growth of the spec, he felt a ringing in his ears, after which he collapsed, still with his forelegs on the gravel and his hind legs on the pavement.

It wasn't clear if he had been hit or if he was simply forced to the ground from the air swirling around the vehicle. The car didn't seem to care one way or the other, for after it swerved as if to avoid the dog, it continued traveling at the same rate of speed on the highway, honking its horn several times as it turned back into a speck and finally disappeared altogether. Hit or not, the dog was hurled to the ground with enough force to slam his head against the pavement – or possibly a large, flat rock hidden beneath the gravel – and for some time thereafter he remained on his side at the edge of the roadway, his hind legs actually touching the pavement.

Amazingly, all of the passing cars succeeded in going around the dog, although several of them came close enough to ruffle his fur and, on a couple of occasions, knock gravel from the edge of the road on his prone body. Despite the injury to his head, the dog's injured leg seemed to have suffered the most in the impact. It had twisted under the weight of his body as he fell to the pavement, and there were signs that it was broken, possibly in several places. When he finally came to his senses, he struggled back to his three feet and, with the paw of his injured foot dragging on the ground, hopped off the pavement (one car barely missing him) and across an open, grassy field until he was fifty yards or so from the highway. Groggy, his head throbbing, his injured leg becoming temporarily numb, the dog somehow summoned his energy and headed in the direction that would take him to where he needed to go. He began moving again, limping and struggling to stay on his feet, without thinking about what had just happened on the highway, the results of which came back to him with every painful step he took.

Licking his chops to allay his increasing thirst, he continued on, now and then thinking about Iowa, often wondering where she was at a particular moment, wondering if her life at the zoo was satisfactory, and forgetting the possibility that it was not Iowa he had seen but some other animal, one drawn to him because he might have had food. Without truly understanding the processes in operation at a refactoring facility, he naturally imagined them to be long and painful, and the prohibitions placed on the subject after the process could be equally abhorrent. But he was also convinced that Iowa had an indomitable spirit and that if anyone could endure setbacks and come out happy and stronger because of them, it was she. Iowa was an amazing person, he told himself rhythmically, as he hobbled through the field, and if she could endure refactoring – which, he added, was far worse than anything that he was going through – then he could endure his injuries, make it home, and visit her again some other day. He would be waiting for her when she was finished and released. No matter how long it took, he told himself, he would wait and then welcome her with open arms when she was finally free.

Breathing heavily, his tongue hanging from the side of his mouth, the dog glanced to his right and noticed a long stretch of forest, some hundred yards or so away, which essentially created a wall between the open, grassy area he was walking across and the rest of the park. It was dense enough to create dark shadows at the base of each tree, while the tops of the trees and a good deal of the leafy area were intensely green, as if some wild artist had squeezed blue-green paint directly from the tube onto the trees. He turned away from the trees to concentrate on moving forward but couldn't help glancing back from time to time. The dark, moody quality of the forest reminded him of the trees in the park near his house, where the Cygnets had spent so much time climbing and chasing one another around their rough, bark bases. While he was thinking about the forest by his house, and the Cygnets and Iowa, he caught sight of something at the edge of the forest, only a few hundred feet away. Stopping and looking, he couldn't see anything for a few moments, but just as he was about to turn away and continue his slow migration toward home, he noticed a large animal of some kind half in and half out of the shadows on one of the trees. The animal, which was dark brown and had long, swept-back horns, seemed to be running in the same direction that he was headed, although it was dodging in and out of the trees as if it couldn't make up its mind to travel in the shade or sunlight. The animal's erratic movements didn't make sense, but before he could study it more carefully, it darted back into the forest and disappeared.

He turned his attention to the task at hand. He needed to focus, because he was quickly losing strength due to his increasing pain (the numbness had worn off) and the absence of water, which was weakening him and robbing him of his ability to concentrate (he was starting to obsess about water, and it was clear that there wasn't any water within an easy walking distance). As far as he could ascertain, the nearest water on this side of the cliff would likely cost him a day's travel, if he were lucky enough to withstand the effort to reach it. It was at this point, when he reminded himself that water was too far away to reach and make it home the same day – it was at this point that he suddenly slowed to a pace that was barely faster than he could crawl. His leg was dragging across the grass and dirt, causing him increasingly sharp pains, and he was having trouble mustering the will to continue on under the impossibly hot sun, which kept rising higher in the cloudless sky. A few minutes later, unable to raise his injured leg or bear the pain that resulted from dragging it, he stopped.

Breathing deeply and trying to refresh his lips by licking his dry, cracked nose, he closed his eyes and wondered if it were better to expend the energy to reach the forest in order to stay under the cool canopy until he reached the cliff. It might take some time to get there, but he was certain that once under its cover, the heat wouldn't be as intense and that he could find enough moisture to keep his mouth and nose wet. He tried to shake, but he couldn't move his neck and back very well, at least not without causing a significant amount of pain.

It was then that he heard another hawk screech, and shortly afterwards it came into view, flying back and forth in front of him, only a few yards away. At one point, it passed so close to him that had he been in better condition, he might have been able to touch it with his nose. Watching the bird fly up in the sky and then soar back down until it was almost at eye level, he couldn't help wondering why it was so close and why it screeched every time it came close to him. A few seconds later, the hawk swooped down so low and close that it seemed to hover in front of him, staring into his eyes as if he had done something wrong and unforgiveable.

Chapter Thirty-five

He hesitated, but once the hawk returned to the blue sky, he continued moving forward, although now limping on two legs (his right front leg was feeling the strain of supporting the weight of the injured leg). He desperately wanted to stop – he was exhausted, and every time he moved so much as a half-step forward, the pain rushed through his body and a couple times made him feel lightheaded and on the verge of fainting. Nevertheless, he refused to stop, because he had to reach the cliff soon if he were to have the slightest chance of…of what he couldn't say, as the thought quickly fled back to the dark recesses of his mind as if it were afraid of being recognized and examined. The dog trudged on, each rock or weed becoming a nearly insurmountable obstacle that forced him to halt, heave his body to one side (away from his injury), and laboriously walk around something that he wouldn't have given a second thought to under normal circumstances.

He continued in this manner for another fifteen minutes or so when he noticed something in the distance ahead. He stopped to stare but couldn't find anything to suggest that it hadn't been a figment of his imagination. Closing his eyes, he breathed deeply several times to build the energy needed to continue moving. But this time, when he opened his eyes and tried to pull his body forward, he couldn't move his legs enough to take even a half-step forward. The pain was now coming from all angles, as if different parts of his body were in league with his injured limb and showing their solidarity with the useless appendage. He turned to look at his injuries in the light of day. He couldn't move his head enough to perform a detailed examination of his hindquarters, but after he moved his nose partly around his shoulder, he noticed a strong, metallic scent of blood and decaying flesh. He couldn't see his injuries very well, but what little he could see was a dark, reddish color, while directly below the spot where his leg would normally have been positioned were numerous red and brown spots glistening in the sun's light.

Leaning slightly forward to keep his angry body upright, the dog tried to lick his parched lips, but his tongue was dry and it merely slid uselessly over the sides of his mouth and nose. The dog told himself that he was too tired to go on and that if he only had a few minutes of rest, he could continue nonstop for some time, maybe all the way to the cliff. But when he began to relax his body, strange thoughts began floating through his mind – thoughts telling him that it was useless to continue and that Iowa was only a swan and a swan was only a bird. After blowing snot from his nostrils to help expunge such thoughts, the dog was seized with the desire to make one hard push to reach the cliff, after which he would make another to get down the cliff, and so on. Steadying his legs and leaning forward, he heaved himself violently to one side so that he faced the right direction. An explosion of pain racked his body (his injured leg did not immediately move with the rest of his body), and he hesitated before attempting to take a step forward. When the pain subsided slightly, he carefully placed one foot slightly forward and, with a pull and a partial hop, managed to move a few inches forward, dragging his injured leg behind him. Minutes passed and then what seemed like hours as he repeated the motion, each time wincing in pain but each time moving a few more inches forward.

The dog managed to walk this way for perhaps a hundred feet, pushing himself to the limits of his endurance, when he stumbled over a large rock and nearly fell down. He had twisted his body in a desperate attempt to remain upright, but his injured leg couldn't (or wouldn't) follow his movements and somehow in the process his nose skidded briefly in the dirt. His nose filled with dirt and dust, he sneezed violently several times, each sneeze seemingly punishing his leg for having betrayed him. When his sneezing finally stopped, he didn't move and stood motionless, vacantly gazing at the ground. The pain and his weakened condition filled him with thoughts about death, about the deaths of people whose names he recognized, about the deaths of Iowa's parents, and, for the first time in his life, he began to consider his own death. He wasn't particularly troubled by the thought, since it would end the suffering he was forced to endure and he wouldn't have to justify his absence if he couldn't make it back on time. On the other hand, he wasn't certain that he wanted to die, unless of course he could die in Iowa's arms or have her by his side holding his hand as he passed from light to dark, from this world to the next.

Sluggishly moving his head to clear his thoughts, the dog attempted a couple more steps forward and then stopped. He had reached the limit of his strength; he couldn't take another step without rest and water. (Food was out of the question, since there was no way of catching anything without being able to move a little faster.) Dying briefly came to mind again, but he didn't think much about it because he lacked the mental strength to consider it fully, no matter how miserable or thirsty he was. Maybe, he told himself, when he was stronger and refreshed he would consider the matter, but now…now…now, he didn't know about now. His eyes getting heavy, he told himself that he needed to plan for the cliff, although what would happen once he reached the cliff was anyone's guess. Maybe water was the first thing…but he changed his mind and decided that what he needed most was some sleep, after which everything would be easy.

The dog adjusted his body and tried to sleep. For a few seconds, there was blackness, which by itself was a relief from the hot, blinding sun, and nothing at all floated through his tired mind. Shortly after this, Iowa took shape in his mind. She had been waiting for him, and when he arrived as Luke, she took his arm and together they strolled down the face of the cliff, following a short path that was nearly as level as the base of the cliff. The stroll didn't take very long and, for the most part, was fairly uneventful except for this one thing – the absence of pain. He felt no pain, no discomfort of any kind, and his tall, hale, and hearty self was completely normal, as if his leg and the rest of his body had miraculously restored themselves to good health. In fact, Luke never felt better or stronger, and he told himself that if she asked him, he could move the largest mountain for her (or perhaps some big rocks). Iowa wasn't weak, and she didn't scare easily, and yet her presence magnified his strength and courage and, no matter what concerned her or made her afraid, he was there to help her. However, he wasn't a "typical boy," as Press often disdainfully taunted him. He didn't see Iowa as someone who needed his help, as much as someone who inspired him to go beyond his limitations. But none of it mattered, neither his strength nor Press' jibes. What mattered was that they were together again, and together they could traverse the cliff and the rest of the park.

His mind began to drift, and he saw himself at the lake with Iowa. The other Cygnets were gone, and he and Iowa slowly strolled around the edge of the lake, laughing and talking softly; their hands touched and then their fingers intertwined. The image quickly faded, and another immediately replaced it. Luke was much older now, maybe his father's age, and although there were streaks of gray near his temples and delicate lines beneath his eyes, he didn't seem to have the tired, careworn look that had come over his father in recent years. He was coming home, just like his father did every night, but instead of going into his parents' house and immediately shutting himself up in his bedroom, he opened the door and saw Iowa coming to greet him. She was older, too, but she still had a look of youthfulness and radiance that seemed to fill the house, and she put her arms around his shoulders and kissed him. "I've been waiting for you all day," she said with a smile that told him how happy she was to see him. Reaching around her waist, he walked with her to the living room and, sitting down on a soft, down-filled couch, he turned to her and together they talked about their day. He had problems getting some orders filled, while she met with some friends and planned their upcoming vacation. The children were outside, she added, as if she knew that it was at this particular moment that he always asked about the children, if they weren't immediately present. He leaned more closely to her and, placing the tip of his right index finger against her lips, began…

The dog slowly started to list, like a ship beginning to flounder, and within seconds he fell over onto the ground. He wasn't hurt (he fell on the opposite side of his injury), although he lacked the strength to get up. He couldn't use his good hind leg because it was pinned underneath him, and he couldn't use his front legs because the soft dirt didn't provide any resistance, even if he had the strength to pull himself up. He struggled a little but not desperately, and, after failing to right himself, he gave up. He accepted the fact that he was too weak to get back onto his feet; he accepted the fact that even if he managed to stand, he lacked the strength to move more than a few steps; and he accepted the fact, which was a little nebulous at this moment, that he wasn't going to reach some point that he needed to reach now or in the future. He accepted these facts and, what's more, he didn't care. It was as if his desire to continue evaporated along with his physical strength – the two were inextricably intertwined – and he had no desire to go anywhere, to do anything, to survive, even if it were to see Iowa one more time. He wanted to see Iowa, he wanted to say goodbye, he wanted to ask her forgiveness for everything that he might have done wrong, but he accepted the fact that it wasn't going to happen, so he remembered Iowa with fondness while he awaited the end.

His eyes were closing. They might have closed completely, but he was suddenly awoken by a large, black bird with a featherless head that alighted only a few feet away. The bird, whose face seemed old and withered, hesitated for a few seconds before hopping cautiously toward him until it was only a few inches from the tip of his nose. Craning its head downward, its round, bloodshot eyes stared at him, while its head turned from side to side as if it were examining him. When the bird had apparently seen enough, it stepped back and let out a loud, piercing scream, which was probably a call for others of its ilk to have a look. He looked at the strange bird for a few more seconds and, when he had seen enough, he allowed his eyelids to droop once more, slowly closing and blackening out the bird. The dog's eyes were nearly closed (the only things he could see were black and gray blurs and shadows) when he heard a loud screech and then noticed something that sounded like rustling feet and feathers. Opening his eyes, he saw a hawk suddenly swoop down and, talons outspread, hit the much larger bird, forcing it off its feet. The hawk shot back into the sky, while the much larger bird clumsily righted itself using its broad wings. As soon as it was on its feet, the bird opened its wings and, running and flapping, tried to leave the area and return to the sky, where it felt much safer than on the ground. Before it was able to reach safety, however, the hawk returned and hit the black bird from behind, this time sending it headfirst onto the ground. In a second, the hawk was standing next to the bird and, shooting out one of it legs, grabbed the bird by the neck with its talons and held it securely against the ground. The hawk was motionless, its wings neatly folded on its sides, for several seconds before it screeched, turning its head and staring at the disabled bird with one eye. Unexpectedly, the hawk released the bird (which was helpless in the hawks' talons) and took one step back, although it kept its cold eyes on the bird. The downed bird again struggled to its feet and, turning away from the hawk, began to run and, flapping its wings, returned to the sky where it slowly flew out of sight.

The hawk didn't leave. It walked over to the dog and, tilting its head downward, looked into his eyes.

The dog listlessly looked back at the hawk, unable to fathom what it wanted, if it indeed wanted anything. But then something completely unexpected happened. The hawk turned and jumped several feet away though still within the dog's line of sight. Glancing around the area, the hawk nestled itself on the ground and rolled onto its side. Within seconds, its shape changed – its head and body stretched and distended, and its overall size increased obscenely – its feathers disappeared, and it ceased to be a hawk. It was now a human being, and the human being was Iowa.

Chapter Thirty-six

Iowa stepped quickly over to the dog and, lifting his head, whispered in its ear. "You have to change," she said. "There's no hope if you don't change. Do you understand me? Luke, can you hear me? Luke, are you in there? Luke?"

He longed to say her name, but he couldn't form the word in his present shape, and so he looked at her, the life coming back into his eyes and then fading.

"Luke! Listen to me. You're hurt and you need help, but you have to listen to me. You need to change…now! If you don't change…"

He continued to look at her and, to the degree that he was capable of reasoning at his point, he wasn't sure that he was really seeing her or simply dreaming. It didn't matter either way. She was beautiful. Her long, blond hair hung over her smooth face, and her blues eyes had the same luster that they had years ago. That hadn't changed.

"Luke, listen to me. I can help you, but you have to listen to me and do as I say. Can you hear me Luke? Luke!"

He focused as intently as he could on every word she spoke, often observing how her lips moved, turned, and twisted with each syllable, but he lacked the strength to respond to her, to let her know that he understood what she was saying. In fact, he wasn't certain that he could lift one of his front paws even if it were a matter of life and death. "Was changing a matter of life and death?' he wondered, noticing the intensity with which Iowa was speaking to him. He could see it in her eyes and in the manner in which the corners of her mouth dropped between some words.

"Okay, Luke, listen to me," Iowa continued, patting him on either side of his snout to make sure he stayed awake. "Luke, are you listening? Are you trying to stay awake? I'm going to help you."

He didn't blink. His concentration was such that had she released his head, it would have fallen and banged on the hard ground.

Iowa closed her eyes for a second and breathed deeply several times, as if she were wrestling with something, as if she had reservations about a particular decision. Opening her eyes and looking directly into his, she said, "I'm sorry to have to do this, Luke." Without taking her eyes away from his, she reached down with her left hand and prodded his injured leg with her index finger.

The dog didn't make a sound, but she could see from his eyes that he was conscious and, more than that, that he felt an intense rush of pain because of her touch.

"Listen, Luke, do exactly as I say or I will poke you again." She whispered something in his ear, and then leaned back. When nothing happened, she again leaned over and again whispered in his ear. When even this had no effect, she poked him in the injured limb again – this time harder than the previous time – and whispered once more into his ear. The dog suddenly started to move – feebly, to be sure, but his shoulders, head, and eyes, opening and squinting several times, all began to show a liveliness that seemed all but impossible only a few seconds earlier – and, when his movements started to become more pronounced (not just feeble shaking but what appeared to be an effort to respond to her commands), she poked him again and again in the injured leg, each time making sure that he could feel the pain intensely enough to respond in a way to make her stop. After a few more minutes of poking and responding, during which the dog had mustered sufficient strength to whine at the pain, something began to happen.

For a moment or two, the dog seemed to have ceased responding to Iowa's prodding, but then something else happened. His body began to get fuzzy, as if the outlines of his body were blurred by an invisible fog that had settled over him in the bright, intense sunlight, and soon sections of him – his neck and shoulders, for example, as well as his legs, even his injured leg – began to lose their distinctiveness, as if the lines and shadows that differentiated one limb from another were being erased and what was left was something that only retained a vague animal shape. Iowa lifted the dog's head and gently placed it on the ground. Standing up and stepping back a few feet, she glanced at the blue sky and noticed that a few light clouds were floating overhead, after which she turned her full attention to what was happening almost at her feet.

Once the details of the dog's shape disappeared, leaving it a vaguely recognizable canine shape, the rest of the animal began to undergo some stranger, and certainly more drastic, transformations. The thick parts of its haunches began to grow slimmer and its legs started to elongate and lengthen. The front legs, acting in unison, did pretty much the same thing, although the thickness of the elongations were less, and the ends of them began to splay in a way that differed remarkably from the distensions at the end of the lower limbs. At one point, Iowa thought she heard a soft whine coming from the animal – a sound that was neither canine nor human, a sound that because of its faintness, she wasn't entirely certain that it came from the throat of the animal as opposed to the sounds that arose from the thing's moving and scraping against the ground – and a few seconds later she observed the hips slimming, elongating and then the thing's fur disappearing and leaving flesh and clothes in its wake. Within minutes, the object in front of her began to appear something more like a human than a dog.

But just as the transformation seemed to be headed for completion, it started to slow and then stopped. Motionless, not even its breathing was discernible, the thing seemed to have reached the limit of its metamorphosis and could go further. It remained in this state for a couple of minutes, exhibiting no signs that it was going to complete the transformation, when it began to shrink and contract and the elongated sections began to appear more canine than human and its body started to compress, as if it had reached the limit of its elasticity and was forced to return to its natural shape.

Iowa realized what was happening. It was clear to her that he had either lost his will or his strength, or both, to finish the transformation, and that he was now reverting to the more familiar, comfortable shape. It happened to others, it happened to her once, and so she was determined not to let it happen to Luke. Stepping quickly toward the rapidly contracting shape, she reached down and this time, instead of poking the dog on the injured leg, she pulled the leg (which, although it was clearly injured, didn't look quite like a dog's leg or quite like a human's leg), shaking it up and down, making sure not to tear it apart, but guaranteeing that the owner of the leg felt the pain so intensely that his consciousness would be heightened to the breaking point – to the point at which all his remaining mental and physical abilities would be directed to stopping the pain, even if that meant finishing the transformation started minutes ago.

"Luke," Iowa screamed at him, screamed into his ear, "you need to change Now! Do you hear me? Now! NOW!" The regression immediately stopped, and he slowly began to complete the change that he had initially started. Within a couple of minutes all the changing stopped, all the scraping and sliding against the ground ceased, and lying on the ground was Luke, his leg visibly injured (although his injuries were hidden by his pants leg, the blood was soaking and staining his pants. There were no traces of the canine, and in its place was the grimacing and groaning Luke.

Luke remained on the ground for a few more minutes, but instead of lying on his side, he rolled over (careful not to move his injured leg too much) onto his back, where he positioned his left hand to shelter his eyes from the sun. At one point, a large, dark cloud covered the sun, and he was able to remove his hand and look directly at Iowa, who sat down next to him to shield his eyes from the burning light. Her face softened and, reaching gently under him, she cradled his head in the palm of her small, soft hand.

"Welcome back," she said and smiled briefly. Luke didn't immediately respond. He, too, briefly smiled, and fastened his eyes onto her face, as if she were a mirage that would disappear the very second his gaze fell on something else. "You're going to stay with me this time, aren't you?"

While he grimaced now and then as the pain shot electrical currents throughout his body, Luke continued to keep his eyes on her and attended to everything she said, although admittedly it was hard to concentrate both because of the pain and because of the fact that Iowa was here, in front of him, looking at him and speaking to him. It was almost too much to believe, especially after what had happened at the zoo, but he remained faithful and was rewarded by finding her (or she him) after all these years.

'Yes, it's Iowa,' he told himself, looking at her smooth face, her glowing hair, and the manner in which her teeth showed slightly below her upper lip as she talked and smiled at him. 'Luck?' he asked himself; 'it's not luck, it's a miracle. She's here, and she came to see me.' Luke couldn't help smiling at her, even when she wasn't smiling. While she was speaking, no doubt about something of vast importance, Luke's mind began to wander, and he observed the dimples (still, after all these years) on her cheeks when she spoke, the manner in which her light hair fell naturally over her ears and onto her collar, and her nondescript blouse and trousers – outdoor wear – which seemed to accentuate her slim youthfulness, the vibrant life within her. She said something pleasantly and, scooting cross-legged behind Luke, gently lifted up his head, placing it in her lap, began smoothing and caressing his sweaty hair.

Luxuriating in her presence and especially in her touch, which seemed as gentle as a snowflake, Luke felt as if he could remain like that forever, as if nothing else in life had any greater purpose. But his desire faded when he felt a surge of pain that coincided with a slight adjustment Iowa made to make his head more comfortable. He felt several electric surges of pain that forced his eyes wide open (he hadn't been aware that his eyes were sagging), and when he saw that Iowa was still next to him, still looking at him with concern, he felt as if something in his life had just changed – his life, as pleasant as it had been, would no longer be the same because Iowa was back and now an inextricable part of his life. But as he looked at her, sensing the warmth of her presence, a strange, troubling thought came to him. He had seen her change from a hawk to a human. It didn't make sense, because it was impossible to change into different animals – or, as Iowa informed the Cygnets when they were first considering what animal to assume, once you change into a swan, you can't change into anything else except a human. Luke didn't doubt that Iowa was sitting next to him, but he couldn't help wondering if he knew her as well as he thought, or if the Iowa next to him was the same Iowa that he had risked everything to see. He wanted to ask her about this anomaly, but a sudden surge of pain refocused his thoughts and, for a few moments, he could only close his eyes and grit his teeth.

"Am I alive?" he finally managed to gasp between the occurrences of pain. The question was meant to be funny, although it didn't sound very amusing.

"Yes," she replied, and couldn't help laughing that he could joke in such a situation. "Do you want me to poke your leg again to prove it to you?"

"No, I guess not," he responded, trying to smile to show that he got the joke.

"I am sorry I hurt you, Luke. I wasn't being mean. I only did it because you were reverting, and that was the only thing I could think of to stop it. If you had reverted to a dog again, I don't think I could have pulled you back. I guess it doesn't matter. But now I need to get you out of here so someone can look at that leg." Iowa looked briefly at his leg, and then turned back to Luke. This time, she was the one who tried to smile, but Luke noticed the concern in her eyes. "I'll take you to a place where you'll get fixed up pretty quickly, but first I think you need some food and water. Are you thirsty?"

Luke nodded, and then a serious look came over his face, one not associated with pain. "How did you know where to find me?"

"I sensed you were going this way. It didn't take me long to find you from overhead."

"No, wait," he began and tried to sit up. The pain in his leg was intense and he tried to repress his groan, but Iowa forcefully eased him back down again.

"It's too soon to stand. You need a few more minutes."

"I don't understand," he continued, suddenly recalling her strange change from a hawk. "You were a hawk, and that allowed you to find me. I thought…I thought that you could only be one animal. You said we couldn't change into two…"

Iowa hesitated, and the pleasantness disappeared from her face. "No, I was wrong. You can change into any kind of animal you want, no matter what. But it isn't easy, and it requires a lot of training to do it successfully. Right now, I can change into a few different kinds of animals, but I can't change into others because I don't have the knowledge yet. What's interesting is that only a few Changers know about this ability, and fewer still actually know how to do it. Most of them still think like you, that if you change into one animal, that's it. But for your own good, mister, I'm not going to show you how to do it. I got you into enough trouble just showing you how to change." She smiled, but it was clear that this part of the conversation was at an end. "Now, if you don't mind…"

"No, please wait." Luke reached across his chest and placed his hand gently on Iowa's forearm. "The swans at the zoo…which one of them…"

Iowa laughed. "Neither. They were just swans."

"I don't understand. How did you…?"

She turned away and seemed to be looking for something in the distance. "Let's just say," she replied, turning back to him, "I had a premonition you would come. I don't know how you found out that I was there, but there was a point at which I knew you were coming to see me. I didn't actually know you had arrived until I saw you in the zoo." Her expression suggested that she knew something about his activities at the zoo.

"You saw me at the zoo?" Iowa nodded, and Luke grimaced as much from a sliver of pain that cut through his leg as from the embarrassment of knowing that she had observed his behavior in the zoo.

"I was a hawk, the same one you saw a few minutes ago, only I was sitting in a tree near the entrance of the facility. I guess I didn't notice you when you came through the gate, but I saw almost everything else, except when you went around to the back of the buildings. I knew you were looking for me, but I couldn't make my presence known at that moment. I really did want to come to you when you were talking to the swans, especially the second one, but Marvin was skulking around and I didn't want to give him any ideas. It was great the way you eluded him. I'm not sure he's entirely convinced that you're gone."

"I still don't understand. Couldn't you have done something, changed somewhere, to at least let me know that I was making a mistake?"

Iowa shook her head slightly, her hair falling over the fronts of her shoulders. "It's a little hard to explain. Can we leave it at that? But I did feel that you were trying to communicate with me."

"But you couldn't let me know?"

"No."

Luke was silent for a few moments. "Did you follow me when I left the zoo?" he asked, breaking the silence.

"No, I couldn't. I had to...I just couldn't get away when you left. I knew that I could find you later on, and I was certain that everything would be fine. I started to look for you a couple of hours ago."

"A couple of hours ago? Did you know there were other hawks?"

"I'm not surprised. They're all over the place. But very few of them are Changers."

Luke squeezed his eyes shut as a surge of pain swept through his leg. When he opened them again, he was pleased to see Iowa still there, watching with a combination of affection and apprehension. "When did you first find me?" he asked, breathing deeply from the pain but at the same time clearly demonstrating that his overall strength was coming back. "I mean, how did you find me? When did you know it was me on the ground?"

"You're asking too many questions right now. Let's just say that I found you in the nick of time. Luke, I need to tell you something before we do anything else. Please, listen to me, Luke. We may be in big trouble. I don't think anyone knows I'm gone, but I'm not supposed to leave the zoo without permission. And no one is going to give me permission to help you unless I get approval from everyone from the facility officials to Ms. Royce, and that's not going to happen. Had I been smart, I would have told someone about your situation. Luke, you weren't supposed to see me until you were at least twenty-one, and you weren't supposed to change for fourteen years beyond that. You've broken some cardinal rules…"

"I just wanted to avoid your hawk laws…" Luke tried to smile, but the pain suddenly increased and made him grimace and scowl. "Ow! Ow! Ow! My leg really hurts sometimes."

"Talons. But this is serious, Luke. We need to get you home quickly, and not just because of your leg, which will be fine despite the pain you're feeling now."

"I hope so," he said more seriously now. "Do you think we can make it back before my parents…before they call someone? Do they know who to call in a case like this?"

"I'll do my best. I have to get back, too."

There was a moment of quiet while Luke wrestled with his pain. "Iowa," he began quietly and then closed his eyes again as another sliver of pain sliced through his leg. When it subsided (although his leg continued to hurt), he opened his eyes and smiled at Iowa, who seemed more like a dream than a real flesh-and-blood person. "I'm glad you found me."

"You should be happy somebody found you."

"No, I mean…"

She reached over and put the tip of her index finger to Luke's lips before he could finish his sentence. While he looked at her, she used the tip of her thumb to brush dirt off the faint scar under his eye, after which she shook her head and told him not to speak. "You talk too much. It's time to conserve some of your energy." She tried to smile, but when she noticed the look of disappointment on Luke's face, she said softly, "I'm glad I found you, too."

Luke seemed satisfied with her response. Relaxing a little, he tried to close his eyes to rest.

"Hold on, Luke. I said to conserve your energy, not fall asleep. We need to get moving in a minute if we are going to have any chance of getting back in time."

Luke opened his eyes and gazed into her face to indicate that he understood.

Iowa stood up and hovered over Luke, whose eyes were still fastened on the girl.

"Now, mister, are you ready? Do you think you can muster the strength to get going?"

Luke nodded.

"This isn't going to feel good, but right now we have no other choice." Iowa bent over Luke and, putting her arms and hands through his armpits, she began helping him get to his one good leg. "Time to stand," she added, lifting as hard as she could someone who was a good sixty pounds heavier than she was. "Keep your weight on your good leg. Maybe that goes without saying."

"Do you think you could become a gorilla or something like that? It would certainly make things easier."

"I wish I could. Sometime I'll tell you about my limitations."

Luke made it to his good leg and foot, bounced a couple of times on the good foot to balance himself (each time grimacing, as would be expected from someone with such an injury), and then draped his arm over Iowa's proffered shoulder. Having made it to his feet and holding onto Iowa, Luke felt a surge of energy flow through his body, and for a moment he felt that he understood everything.

"Okay?" she asked, after which she asked him to balance on one foot for a moment without holding onto her. "I want you to stand here for a moment while I get something."

Luke managed fairly well, but after a few seconds on his own he began to weaken and his mind started to feel foggy, and he couldn't help wondering if he could remain upright until Iowa returned. While he stood there, wobbling and bouncing now and then to keep from falling, Iowa walked a few yards to the right and retrieved a broken tree limb, which she brought back to Luke and instructed him hold onto a V-like section in the middle where two branches had veered from one another. "That will help you keep your balance," she said. Once he was ready, she again draped his large arm over her slender shoulders.

Chapter Thirty-seven

Together, Luke and Iowa started walking cautiously and unsteadily toward the cliff. Luke stumbled a few times during the first few minutes, and once nearly fell down and would have brought Iowa down with him, but he was able to right himself with the stick. The pain in that incident had been enormous, but he was able to bear it and all the other pain and discomfort with dignity as long as Iowa was with him. Neither one of them noticed the blood, which was darkening parts of one pants leg and dripping onto his dirty shoe. Soon, however, Luke got used to his limitations and, using the stick nearly as well as his leg before the injury, the two of them operated almost as one person, moving their legs (his good leg) and arms in tandem.

During the first few minutes as well, Luke had difficulty talking because of the concentration required to keep upright and because of the pain, which was now more intense because his movements pulled at the ripped flesh and severed tendons. But after a while, as he became more skillful on his feet and with the stick, the pain seemed to subside slightly (it was nearly impossible to touch the ground with the toe on his injured side, much less put any weight), and he was able to talk fairly comfortably, almost as if he had done this before and instinctively understood how to balance and where to hop. Before he said anything, he couldn't help looking at Iowa from time to time. He admired the top of her head, as she looked down at the ground to make sure they didn't stumble over anything, and he thought she was the most beautiful person he had ever seen whenever she glanced up at him and, especially, when he saw her smile, which she did often.

"How long do you think it will take?" he asked, desiring to hear her voice and look into her face and eyes. Of course, it was also a pertinent question, since the sun was directly overhead and they had quite a distance to travel.

"I don't know, but we'll make it. I know someone who can patch up your leg, but if your parents notice the injuries, it will be up to you to explain them."

"Sure."

He was silent for a moment. "Iowa, how close are we to water? I'm don't know how much longer I can to go without something to drink." Luke spoke calmly and hoarsely, speaking as if he were merely stating a fact and not worried or uncomfortable because of his thirst.

"Good question. I told you I'd get you some food and water. If I'm not mistaken, there's a little stream between those trees over there." She pointed to a clump of trees perhaps a hundred yards to their right. "I'll tell you what. Stand here – use the stick – and I'll go and bring some back if I can find something to carry it in." Without waiting for an answer, Iowa turned and jogged to the trees, where she disappeared from sight for several minutes. Luke balanced somewhat unsteadily while he waited, sometimes holding onto the stick with both hand to keep upright, sometimes taking a painful hop back or forward to keep stable. After what seemed to take an inordinate time to run to the trees and bring back water (he wasn't thinking of the logistics), Luke began to worry, wondering if she were in trouble or if he had simply imagined her, which in both cases meant that she would never return. He was relieved when he saw her in the distance and then as she got closer and closer, with a burlap bag over her shoulder and carrying a small, beat-up metal bucket filled with what proved to be clear, cool water.

Iowa handed Luke the small bucket and, while he eagerly drank the entire contents, she sat the bag down and emptied its contents. Besides the bucket, she had found several fresh apples, several unopened granola bars, a clear plastic bottle filled with water, duct tape, a long rope, a pocket knife, and a variety of other items, most of which Luke wouldn't learn about until later. When Luke had finished the water, he smiled and thanked her, and the pleasant expression on his face made him look stronger, better able to handle the trip. Iowa put the bucket back into the bag and, smiling at Luke, explained that there was an abandoned camp on the other side of the trees and that she scrounged all this stuff up there. "It's amazing," she added, noting as well that the apple didn't come from the camp but came from a small apple tree a few paces farther on.

"Wonderful," Luke added, cringing slightly from the pain. "You're amazing for having found all this stuff."

"It was there, and I was lucky to find it before the animals did. How are you feeling?" she asked, but didn't wait for an answer. "Do you see that long shadow about ten yards over there?" She pointed slightly to her right. "It's like a sink hole or something, but it's not very deep. Maybe a couple feet. Maybe more. Let go over there, and you can sit on the edge and relax your legs over the side. It will be like sitting on a chair." Iowa immediately positioned herself to Luke's side, and they walked silently over to the hole, which was more like an elongated depression in the earth than an actual hole. Iowa quickly eased Luke down on one of its rounded edges and helped him position his legs so that he felt comfortable.

"I spotted it as I was coming back from the trees," she said as she made herself comfortable beside him and pulled the bag to her side and began fishing something out of it. "Here," she said, pulling off its wrapper, and thrust two granola bars into his hands. "Eat this. You must not have eaten anything in quite a while."

Luke greedily stuffed the thin bars into his mouth. After the first bar, he ate three more granola bars and two apples before saying a thing. "I haven't had a thing in I don't know how long. Just as you said, I think. This was perfect, maybe the best meal I've ever had."

"Well, don't get used it." She hoisted the bag back over her shoulder. "Like I said, I was lucky. There may not be food for some time after this."

"It was also great to share it with you," he added and then realized that she hadn't eaten anything. The fact that she had merely watched him eat, along with the statement which suddenly sounded forward, embarrassed Luke, especially when she didn't immediately respond. After a painfully long silence during which he couldn't think of anything to say to cover his embarrassment, Luke thought he noticed tears welling in Iowa's eyes when she turned and smiled at him.

"What's the matter? Are you okay?" he asked, watching her and smiling back.

"Of course. I have some grit in my eyes, I suppose. But it's no big deal." Iowa turned as if she were going to position herself for their journey, but suddenly stopped and turned back to face Luke. She glanced at his pants leg and then at his shoe, which was covered with dark mud. "I don't know how I could have been so stupid. Unbutton your pants, and I'll help you pull them off. It's no joke. I need to look at your leg."

The process proved to be more difficult that either one anticipated. Because the tops of his pants were curled over and encrusted with dirt and mud (made from sweat), the process of unbuttoning and unzipping was a challenge, at best. But when this was accomplished and they tried to pull his pants down, the pants wouldn't descend any farther than his knees because the blood from various punctures and scrapes had dried and glued the pants to his leg (he might have yanked them off at this point, but every movement during this process tugged and aggravated his injuries lower down). Finally, in exasperation, Iowa helped him pull his pants back on and re-button them (zipping them halfway, however, because the zipper jammed and stuck on a section of fabric) and, once Luke was resettled on the edge, she reached into her bag, pulled out a small pocket knife, and cut the pants leg away from the most serious of his injuries. Luke couldn't look at his leg, which was still bleeding, but he could tell from the expression on Iowa's face that something was wrong, something more serious than he had imagined.

Squatting in front of him and keeping her eyes on his wounds, Iowa grabbed the burlap bag and dragged it to her side and, glancing only once in the bag, fished out a light-colored tee-shirt of some kind. Instead of using the knife, she locked her teeth on one section of the shirt and, pulling it away, ripped off a sleeve. After this, she ripped off the other sleeve in the same manner and then managed to shred strips of fabric from the remaining section. She placed the pieces on Luke's lap and silently, one by one, draped them across his injuries, after which she carefully tried them behind his leg. Not once during this process did she notice Luke's silent grimaces, even when she secured the strips of cloth, but when she was done, she carefully pulled his pants leg back together and, after locating a safety pin in the bag, secured the flaps. Standing back as if to admire her handiwork, Iowa looked first at Luke's pant leg and then watched him wipe the sweat from his face with the back of his hand.

"I'm really sorry, Luke. I didn't think...," she began but didn't finish. Before he could respond, she turned away, picked up the bag, and, after flinging it over her shoulder, reached over and helped Luke up onto his good leg. Holding onto her shoulder, he positioned the stick so that it was serviceable, and they walked down the slight incline and up the other side. Within an hour, they were a few feet from the top of the cliff.

Because this would be the most difficult part of their journey, Iowa pointed to a large rock a few feet from the edge and suggested a break before beginning the descent. The rock was big enough for Luke to lean back against its smooth surface, obviating the need to sit down and struggle up, both of which could exacerbate his injuries. Once they were settled, Iowa pulled a couple more granola bars and an apple out of the sack and offered them to Luke.

"Great stuff," he exclaimed as he bit into the fruit. He finished it, ate the granola bars, and, just in case they couldn't stop for water on the cliff, took several large gulps from the bottle. When he was full, he handed the bottle to Iowa, who also took a couple of drinks.

Luke wiped his mouth on his shoulder and then looked at Iowa. "I'm sorry. You're not eating anything, and I certainly took more than my share of the water. I wasn't thinking." He grimaced slightly because of the pain.

"Stop that. I managed to catch something just before I located you. Yes, I was a hawk, so please don't ask me what I ate. It's kind of disgusting to think about." She laughed while looking into Luke's eyes.

Luke couldn't help laughing, too, recalling what he did as a dog.

Having rested for twenty minutes or so, Iowa jumped off the rock and walked over to the edge of the cliff. "It's steep," she said, leaning slightly over the edge. "But that only works in our favor. Somehow or other we're going to have to get around that ledge" – she was looking at the very ledge that Luke scaled to reach the top – "but I guess we can deal with it when we get there." Iowa walked back to Luke and helped him off the rock; holding his arm tightly, she maneuvered to within a foot of the edge, where he could look down and see the ledge she mentioned. Once again, even though he had absolute faith in Iowa, he couldn't see any way of descending the cliff to the ledge or, once there, being able to climb down without slipping and falling. He imagined losing his balance on one of the narrow portions, and, as he considered what could happen as a result, his injured leg twitched savagely to remind him of the stakes. Turning back to Iowa, he noticed how small and slender she seemed, as if he were comparing her to the immensity that lay below him.

Iowa could sense Luke's concern (judging by his serious, silent, and prolonged stare over the ledge), and so she turned to him and tried to laugh. "Luke, there's nothing to be worried about. Together, we can do this, and probably do it quicker than you did coming up."

"There's no question that we can get down a lot quicker. But isn't there a better place, maybe somewhere where it's not so steep and the ledges are wider? This one gets narrower..." He looked over to Iowa, who was eyeing him tenderly.

"No," she shook her head. "The only better places are miles away, and it could take days to reach them." She helped Luke back from the edge and then over to the rock. After this, she reached into her bag and retrieved a rope.

"It's hard to believe you found all this stuff," he said, watching her doing something with the rope. "It looks like someone left all this stuff for us."

Iowa didn't respond.

"But where did you find the rope?" he asked, trying to make sense of what she was doing.

"From the same place I got everything else. I forgot to mention it."

"Got a rabbit in there, too?"

Iowa didn't respond to this, either. She reached across Luke and gently took his walking stick. Breaking it into four more or less equal pieces, she taped two of the sticks together and, when done, taped the other two together.

"Tape? Now I know you have the kitchen sink in there." Luke watched her work and, even though he didn't know what she was doing, he couldn't help admiring her confident manner and the way in which her hair fell across her forehead, which she removed now and then by blowing it off with a burst air from the corner of her mouth.

Testing the set of sticks for sturdiness, she stepped in front of him and, squatting down, glanced up at him. "I need you to hold still for a second."

Luke still didn't know what Iowa had in mind, but he did as requested and closed his eyes.

Iowa placed one set of sticks on one side of his injured leg and the other on the other side and, gently holding them against his leg, pulled a long strip of tape (she held the tape in her other hand and pulled and tore the tape using her teeth in the same way she had used them to tear the tee-shirt), began taping the sticks to his leg to make a splint. The process was quick and efficient, and while the pain was intense (the tape, unlike the soft tee-shirt, felt like a hard cord or chain being tightened against his injuries), Luke didn't say anything and even made a valiant though unsuccessful effort to smile.

"Done," she said when she had completed the splint and gingerly tested it to make sure it was secure. "I should have done this earlier. This is the second time. It doesn't hurt, does it? Well, this should keep your leg from moving if, for some rare reason, you land on this leg. It should protect the leg. It will also absorb some of the shock, if the unforeseen happens, and prevent a certain amount of pain. Clear?"

Luke's eyes were closed, and he was breathing deeply, rhythmically. When the pain had subsided enough, he looked at his leg and then at Iowa. "Clear as mud. How am I supposed to balance myself when I need to walk? I need another stick."

"Don't worry. I got that covered, too."

"More tape?"

"We'll find another stick below, or else I will hold you myself. I'll carry you, if I have to." Iowa smiled, while Luke grimaced in pain. But not wanting to waste time, Iowa immediately went to work and pulled the rope out of the bag.

"Here," she said, handing Luke one end of the rope. She took the other end and wrapped it around Luke's waist and pulled it under his crotch, after which she tied it around his waist, so that it was snug enough to hold his weight. Taking the other end of the rope over to a large boulder sticking halfway out of the ground, she wrapped the rope around its base (the base was narrower than its top, so there was little chance that the rope could slip over the top) and, when that was secure, wrapped the rope around her slim waist, which enabled her to release the slack on the ground in front of her while still retaining control of the rope should the unforeseen happen. It may not have been a perfect plan, but at least it gave her better control of the rope (she could leverage the boulder to prevent the rope from flying out her hands) and confidence that she wouldn't drop Luke.

"Now," she said to Luke, "We're going to lower you over the edge and then I'll gradually let out the rope until you touch bottom. It will be quick and easy, and a lot safer than trying to climb down."

"How do you know there's enough rope? It's a long way down."
"Don't worry. I measured it, and we have plenty to spare."
"You what?"

Chapter Thirty-eight

Luke turned to her. "I don't understand. When did you measure the rope?"

Iowa pretended that there had been a misunderstanding on Luke's part. "What I should have said is that I know how long the rope is and how far it is to the bottom of the cliff. When I grabbed the rope – which, incidentally, was all stretched out when I got it – I measured it while I was wrapping it. I was able to wrap the rope from my elbow to the center of my palm" (she pointed out both spots to Luke) "and I wrapped the rope around my arm like this" (she showed Luke how she wrapped the rope from the back of her arm over the palm of her hand) "which allowed me to determine that the length of the rope was sufficient. Okay?"

Luke could only shake his head in agreement at the moment because another spasm of pain suffused his leg. It made sense, of course, and he couldn't help admiring the way that she had prepared for this contingency in exactly the same way she prepared for the others, the food and water that he desperately needed. It almost seemed as if she had been able to prepare ahead of time, which was impossible. Perhaps it was simply a matter of having a different perspective – a bird's perspective— which enabled her to scour a broader area from the sky than he was capable of doing as a dog on the ground.

When the pain subsided, Luke turned his attention to the cliff and, holding the rope and leaning backwards a few inches over the edge of the cliff, he craned his neck to get a better view of what he was beginning to fear could be a matter of life and death for him. He examined the face of the cliff, the paths that zigzagged across its face, and the wide path, about halfway down, that he would somehow have to negotiate across to get the bottom. It was wide, certainly, but not wide enough for two, and he could see from his vantage point that it was covered with loose gravel. "You know," he said as he pulled himself upright and turned to Iowa, "I think I can rappel down most of the cliff. I'll have to push off the face here and there with my good leg, but that shouldn't be a problem. But that path in the middle – did you notice it? I don't know how I'm going to be able to cross it, and there's no way we can follow it together – it's too narrow for both of us."

Iowa assumed a calm, knowing expression. "You're worrying over nothing. I've seen it from above. All you have to do is bounce off the face of the cliff using your good leg while I lower you down. You won't have to walk or crawl over anything. But I'll give you instructions when you reach that section. You're going to have to trust me on this."

"I do. But…well, I'm a lot heavier than you, and there's going to be a lot of weight against the rope."

"Please," she said, stretching out and stroking his arm. "Don't worry. You could weigh ten times more than you do, and it wouldn't be too heavy or pull me down."

Luke smiled, and he felt good being with such an amazing, caring person. He especially appreciated her soft touches, for not only did they reassure him that she knew what she was doing, they also underlined the bond between them, which seemed as tight and secure as the rope that currently connected them. Still, he wasn't completely convinced that everything would be as easy as she seemed to suggest, although he kept his vague concerns to himself for fear of rupturing the warm atmosphere surrounding them. Together, they could solve whatever problems arose.

Iowa checked the rope to make sure there were no kinks or vulnerable spots and then made sure that it was secure around the base of the boulder. When satisfied, she tested the connections around her waist and Luke's, after which he scanned the large coil to her side to be certain that it was free of obstructions. "There," she said when all her checks were complete, "we shouldn't have any problems."

"Excuse me?" Luke uttered on mock disbelief. "Did you let me lean over the cliff without being certain that everything was safe?"

"Don't be a silly goose," she said pleasantly, gently placing the tip of her index finger over his lips. "You were safe before. Letting you lean over the edge isn't the same thing as lowering you over the side. Trust me, I know what I'm doing."

Luke felt warm because of her touch. He wanted to respond, he wanted to caress her smooth face with the back of his hand, but at that very moment she stepped closer to the boulder and, grasping the rope with both hands and bracing her right foot against the enormous rock, she instructed him to hop to the edge and turn so his back faced it. "Once you're comfortable, I'll give you the signal to lean back."

"Toward you?"

"No, silly, out over the cliff. Don't worry, I've got you. Even if you lose your balance, you won't go over the edge unless I let you."

"Lose my balance?"

"The worst that can happen is that you fall on the ground here. But if you follow my directions, even that won't happen."

"You've got my life in your hands."

"Don't worry. I know what I'm doing. Now, hop over to the edge…and keep both hands on the rope."

Luke took two painful hops to the edge. Holding tightly to the taut rope, he slowly turned around and placed his back toward the abyss. Observing Iowa who was observing him, he wanted to tell her that he loved her, but he held back because she nodded to him, as if she understood his thoughts, and then instructed him to lean back carefully.

"Wouldn't it be better if you changed into something a little bigger and heavier, say, an elephant? It would make all this a little easier," he said, half serious, half jesting. When Iowa smiled back, he offered the suggestion again, only this time more seriously. "Really, why can't you change into something bigger? How about a dragon so we could fly out of here?"

Iowa slowly began letting out the rope so that Luke began to inch backward without, however, moving his good foot, which remained planted on the edge of the cliff.

"It's a great idea," she said, her voice a little strained from the effort not to let out the rope too quickly. "But there are limits to what I can do. Others might be able to do it, but I can't. I don't have the skills yet." She was quiet for a few moments while she worked the rope. "Say," she began talking to relieve some of her own stress, "you don't think dragons are real, do you? We can only change into real animals, not…" Iowa smiled, but Luke was now concentrating on something else.

Luke stared at the ground at the base of the cliff, which now seemed farther down than he had previously thought. The boulders at the base of the cliff looked like sand pebbles, and what had seemed like a steep hill when he was climbing it now appeared to be a jagged precipice, as steep and as foreboding as Everest without the snow. Without looking up at Iowa (who was now higher than him because of his inclination), he called out to her, "I'm glad you've done this before. Did I tell you that sometimes I don't like heights?"

"I didn't say I've done this before, only that I know what I'm doing," she replied in a normal speaking voice, which because of her proximity he could hear clearly.

"What? You're telling me this now?"

"Luke, listen to me," she said in a calm voice. "Everything is going to be fine, as long as you listen to me. Okay? Now, push off with your foot, just as if you were bouncing on the moon. Trust me on this. It will be okay."

Luke hesitated for a moment and, closing his eyes, quietly did as she said. For a moment, the pain intensified in his injured leg, but at the same time he could feel his body straighten up and he suddenly felt in control, as if he wasn't going to fall to the mountainous abyss below.

"Do it again," shout Iowa, who could no longer see Luke. "And let me know if you have any problems. You're okay, right? Luke?"

"Yes, yes, I'm fine. Let out some more slack. I'm moving okay, although my leg hurts every time I bounce."

"There's no way to make things gentler."

For a while everything worked as planned. While Iowa slowly let out the rope, Luke bounced down the face of the cliff, moving lightly and easily as if he were walking on the surface of the moon. It had taken him no more than two bounces to discover (with Iowa's instructions) that if he held tightly to the rope, he could balance his body in such a way that prevented his injured leg from coming in contact with anything more substantial than air. But while his injured leg still hurt, especially if it shook in response to the movements of his body, the pain was certainly less than he experienced walking or moving around on the ground. Luke realized that this semi-pleasant situation wouldn't last for very long – the path was looming, and he knew that he wouldn't be able to bounce over it quite so easily or painlessly – but for the moment he enjoyed the sensation of floating and especially his life and death connection to Iowa. Indeed, this connection was something that he hadn't felt before, and traversing down the cliff made it seem absolute and inviolable. Every now and then, they would holler to one another as if to remind themselves of its existence and permanence. "Everything okay?" Iowa would holler from somewhere overhead and out of sight. "Fine and dandy," Luke would respond. "I wish you were here." "I will be in a few minutes." In a sense, the solitude enabled such easy exchanges, since it gave him the freedom to speak to her in a way that he couldn't have done when they were face to face. That is, in between the routine exchanges, he would ask her how she was doing, if she felt okay, if there was anything that he could to do to help, if she knew what they would do when they reached the base of the cliff. The latter question was fraught with meaning beyond the obvious. What he wanted to say was, 'What happens to you and me when we are off this cliff and when we finish this journey.' A cool breeze came from his left and blew a fine mist of soft dirt across his face and arms, after which it seemed to arch upward and move over the cliff.

"Did you feel that?" he called up to Iowa.

"Got some of it in my face, but I'm okay. You?"

"The same. I'm fine, too."

"Glad to hear it."

"So am I."

There was something in this short exchange – something in the way in which they shared a mutual, intimate feeling – that made Luke want to say more about his feelings. He recalled what he said to the swan, and he felt the urge to say something similar now, perhaps because they couldn't see each other and he wouldn't have to see her expression if she were offended by what he said. Breathing deeply to steel himself, he leaned back as he bounced off the face of the cliff and raised his voice upward, "Iowa?"

"Yes, Luke, what is it?"

"I want to tell you something."

"You're not in trouble, are you? Am I going too fast? Do you need a break?"

"No, it's not like that at all." There was a pause, while he bounced a few more times. "I just wanted to say…in fact, I always wanted to say…since, I don't know, since the very first time…what I'm try to say about the way I feel, always felt, is…"

Before he could finish his thought, his injured leg banged against a small, exposed rock and not only stopped the smooth, even flow of his bouncing, but the pain was such that he instinctively leaned forward toward his leg and let go of the rope, sending him against the cliff and banging his bad leg again. Blinded by the pain, he groped for the rope and, by the time he reached it, he was sliding down the face of the cliff as Iowa, unaware of his situation, continued to let out the rope.

"Iowa," he gasped, holding desperately to the rope with one hand and trying to stop his descent with the other, dragging it against the face of the cliff. "Iowa, I can't…my leg…"

Iowa stopped letting out the rope and, pausing, called down to him. "Is something the matter? Luke? Luke?"

"Stop! I need…"

"Luke?"

Between spasms of pain, Luke tried to explain what was happening. Iowa didn't need the full explanation, though, for she quickly understood what was happening and immediately went into action to prevent any more injuries. "Luke, listen to me," she hollered as forcefully as he ever heard he speak. "Grab the rope with both hands. Now, put your good foot against the wall. You might have to twist yourself, but you have to get that foot against the wall. Okay?"

"Okay," he replied in a small, slightly unsteady voice.

"There's no way that we can stop (I can't hold you forever), so I want you to use your good foot to keep off your bad leg, and I will slowly lower you until you reach the ledge. Once you're there, we can get you set right. Understand? How far is the ledge from you?"

After positioning his good foot, Luke carefully and painfully looked down his side to locate the ledge. "It's about ten feet. I can't say for sure."

"Okay, stay calm. I'm going to start lowering you again, and when your good foot reaches the ledge, let me know. Okay?"

"Okay." Luke eyed the ledge with apprehension, as if one false move on his part would be catastrophic. He also began to wonder what would happen once he reached the ledge, since that would also pose any number of difficult and painful problems.

Iowa needed all her strength to control the flow of the rope. Controlling the rope had not been a problem earlier, but she was losing strength, particularly because Luke's predicament was forcing her to expend more of her strength than she had earlier. On top of everything else, sweat was pouring off her face and into her eyes, forcing her to clear her eyes ineffectively with her shoulder (she didn't dare risk taking one hand off the rope to wipe her eyes). She wanted to look down at Luke, she wanted to do more for him, but she couldn't do that without tying off the rope, which would only slow their progress downward. However, once he reached the ledge and could stay upright, she felt certain that she could slacken the rope to peer at him from over the cliff. But just after she asked him how close the ledge was (about three feet this time) and again used her shoulder to wipe the sweat from her eyes, she spotted a large animal about a hundred feet to her right standing near the edge of the cliff. She couldn't see it clearly, although it appeared to be watching her as she struggled with the rope. But after she paused to clear her eyes again, it was gone. For a moment, she thought it might have been a coincidence, but a few seconds later it came back into view and then quickly disappeared, as if it didn't want to be seen.

Returning to the rope, Iowa called out over her shoulder. "How close are you now?"

"A couple feet, maybe, but I'm having trouble balancing. I keep rocking back and forth, and it's hard to keep my foot planted."

"I don't understand. Can you keep your foot against the cliff?"

"Yes, but I keep slipping. The surface is slippery."

Iowa didn't respond. She was beginning to sense what has happening through vibrations in the rope, although at this point there wasn't anything else she could do to help Luke. Her hands were sweaty and increasingly raw, her shoulders at times felt stretched to their limits, and she wasn't sure how long she could continue holding him if he didn't reach the ledge soon.

"Iowa," Luke called out from the abyss. "Iowa, it hurts, my leg…I'm not sure that even if I do stabilize…"

"Luke," she hollered, more forcefully than she intended. She knew that if he became upset, he could injure himself more and cause any number of additional problems. "Luke, you have to hold on for a little while. I can't do anything until you reach the ledge. How close now?"

The breeze again picked up and blew dirt into his eyes and nose. When he could finally speak, he gasped, "A foot, maybe. Two, I don't know. Close."

"I need to know how close, Luke."

"A foot…less."

Iowa's hands and arms were shaking from her efforts, and the sweat pouring off her face was mingling with the dust and turning into a thin film of mud, mud that she had trouble keeping out of her eyes. Her legs were also weakening, having continually used them to balance her weight and Luke's weight against the rock, and she was increasingly concerned that the slightest vibration in the rope or a loose pebble would make her lose her grip, sending her to the ground and the rope around the rock and down the cliff.

"Luke," she hollered, as the rope began slowly slipping through her hands, "Luke, brace your leg against the cliff. Do it now. Dig in." The rope stopped slipping for a moment, but Iowa could feel the ground giving way beneath her feet, and she was certain that any second something would give unless Luke steadied himself. 'Only a foot,' she told herself, 'he can handle that.' Glancing over her right shoulder, she started to tell Luke to look for a way of steadying himself once he reached the ledge, but the rope unexpectedly jerked, her hands burned, and her feet slipped out from under her. Iowa dropped to the seat of her pants and, with a single, obscene jerk, the rope leaped out of her hands.

Chapter Thirty-nine

"Luke!" she screamed as she scrambled to capture the rope that was lying limply a few feet from the rock. "Luke!" She grasped the rope and pulled it as hard as she could. "Luke," she screamed again, feeling with some relief that the rope was resisting her efforts, which suggested that he had not become separated from the rope. "Luke!"

When she couldn't pull any more, she paused and, gripping the rope as tightly as she could, turned her head to listen for sounds that Luke was still alive. It was at this moment, though, that another wind arose, whooshing up over the cliff's edge and stirring the dirt into a hot, orange cloud of dust that got into her eyes and nose. Coughing, resenting the sting of sand against the back of her bare neck, Iowa waited until the breeze moved on and the dust settled to turn her head toward the cliff and listen for sounds indicating Luke was okay. For a while there was only silence, which was broken now and then by a dull, distant rumble and a faint bird cry. Iowa was just about to call Luke's name (she had been reluctant to call out sooner, because she feared the worst and didn't want to have her fear confirmed) when she noticed a faint noise coming from just below the edge of the cliff. It sounded like a weak, muffled cough, but it faded too quickly for her to be certain that it was anything at all. She waited a couple more seconds and was just about to call Luke when the cough returned, although this time she was positive that it was a cough and that it was Luke.

"Iowa," Luke hollered weakly. "Iowa, can you hear me? I have dirt in my nose." He coughed several times in succession and then sneezed twice. "I'm also stuck. I'm about six inches from the ledge, but my good foot is stuck in a hole on the face of the cliff, and I can't pull it out."

"Luke, Luke, are you all right?" she hollered back, more joyful than concerned. At least he hadn't plummeted to the bottom.

"Yes, I'm fine, but my foot is stuck. I was holding it against the wall when the rope shook and I slipped. I'm hanging here. What do I do?"

"Luke, are you sure you're all right?" she asked, continuing to grasp the rope as if Luke's life depended on it, as if any slack would spell his demise.

"I have dirt in my nose but otherwise fine. I can't free my foot."

"Okay, okay, let me think."

"I thought you already had the answers," he said pleasantly, trying to downplay the situation he was in. "I'm joking," he added a second later. Luke knew that she was doing everything she could to help him, and he didn't want her to think that he was ungrateful no matter what happened.

"Okay," she replied after a couple of seconds. "Can you hold onto anything? Do you see a rock or a hole or something like that?"

Luke wiped the dirt and sweat from his eyes and nose while holding the rope with one hand and scanning the wall for something to hold. Spotting a brick-sized rock a couple feet away and almost at eye level, he nodded as if she could see his movements and shouted, "I see a rock I can use. I'll have to reach…"

"Excellent. Now, hold onto it, and use it to pull your body upward while I retrieve some rope. Once your weight is completely off your foot, see if you can pull it out. How deep is it, anyway? It's not wedged up to the ankle, is it? Deeper? Is that injured, too?"

She was demanding answers too quickly for him to respond. Examining the foot in question, he could see that it was ankle-deep in the hole, but because of the odd shape he needed to pull his foot upward at an acute angle to extract it from the cliff. Luckily, the foot didn't appear to be injured, and therefore Luke was positive that once he managed to free himself (with Iowa's help), he was ready to tackle the ledge.

"To my ankle," he replied, "but it feels okay. If you can pull me up a couple of feet, I think I can pull myself out. If my other leg weren't…"

"Good, good," Iowa interrupted. She immediately instructed Luke to grab the rock and "pull and balance" himself while she raised him the requisite two feet. "It's not more, is it?" she asked him, fearful that she might not have the strength to pull him another six inches beyond this.

"More what?"

"How much more do I have to raise you?"

"I think this is enough." He wiggled his foot back and forth and then up and down, and within a few seconds was able to extract his foot.

Much to his relief (and moments later to Iowa's), his foot wasn't injured, although when he finally got it free, it didn't feel quite as strong as it had before he stepped into the hole.

It was a relief to both of them when Luke finally set his good foot securely on the ledge, which he conveyed to Iowa by hollering, "the hawk has landed." Iowa told Luke to lean against the cliff and find something (a rock, a hole, a broken branch of something that might have died years ago and was now protruding through the rock and dirt) to hold onto to keep himself from falling. When Luke confirmed that he could use the same rock for this purpose, Iowa finally released the tension on the rope and, letting one hand go, wiped the sweat and dirt from her eyes using the back of her free hand. When she was sitting down and resting on the ground, breathing deeply to calm her nerves, Iowa noticed a familiar cackle overhead and looked up at the intensely blue sky.

A small flock of crows, perhaps twenty or so, were circling overhead, maybe a hundred feet above her, cawing in such a way that unless one listened carefully, one might have thought that they were saying something intelligible. The birds continued circling for another minute and then, as if being ordered, swooped down within ten feet of Iowa before returning overhead, their movements accompanied by raucous cawing. Iowa tried to ignore the crows, but when she turned away their noise increased and, for a few seconds, they sounded and acted as if they were angry, as if they were chiding her for something she did. While she tried to limber up her shoulders and hands so that she'd be ready for the final stretch down the cliff, the most vocal of the crows swooped down at her head and snatched several hairs from her scalp. Iowa lunged for the crow, which easily eluded her grasp, and when it came back and began floating lazily above her head, she picked up a rock and hurled it at the bird, missing it by several yards. Plopping back down on the soft ground, Iowa crossed her arms and legs and tried to control her anger, at the same time pretending that the crow was finally gone or that it could no longer bother her. Perhaps the animal had taken her attitude as a challenge, for no sooner did she appear relaxed than it returned and made several passes behind her head, each time coming so close that she could hear the movement of its wings and feel the air as it passed by her. Finally, the crow floated around in front of her and, flapping its wings furiously, flew directly at her face. It swerved at the last second to avoid hitting her, but it had come so close that

Iowa instinctively ducked to avoid encountering it. Having made a statement, the crow flew back to join the others, which had been circling overhead during this encounter, and after a short chorus of cawing they all flew away as quickly as they had arrived, leaving in their wake an eerie silence.

Luke had noticed the birds as well, even though none of them came very close to him, and once they were out of sight, he called up to Iowa to find out if she had seen them, too.

"They were sure acting strange," he added. "Maybe they were sick or something."

"Yeah, they were strange, all right, but there was nothing the matter with them. Just a bunch of dumb crows."

"But they seemed to be…"

"Don't worry about them, Luke. Concentrate on your footing. We need to get you off this cliff as soon as possible." There was an edge to her voice that he hadn't noticed before.

"Okay, but I just noticed something."

Iowa feared that he would prolong the discussion about the crows, but she was pleasantly surprised when he informed her that the ledge was not as wide as he thought and that he was almost positive that he could hop to the edge and, as long as she kept the rope taut, go over the side and continue downward.

"It shouldn't be too hard," he added, mentally rehearsing what he would have to do to get over the edge safely and painlessly.

"Okay, let me know when you need more rope." There was a moment of silence before she added, "and let me know when you're safely over."

Holding onto the rock with one hand and the rope with the other, Luke gradually slid his good foot back until it was at the ledge's edge, where he balanced his weight between his toes and the hand holding the rock. After closing his eyes and inhaling deeply to steady his nerves, he looked up at the top of the cliff and shouted for two feet of slack. He wobbled and nearly lost his balance when Iowa complied, but he somehow managed to hold onto the rock and then used it regain control and reposition himself. When he was ready, balancing precariously on his toes, he pushed away from the rock and, leaning back, grasped the rope with both hands so that he was ready to take another foot of rope and propel himself off the ledge. By this time, Luke was confident that he could descend with ease – and control – as long as Iowa gave him the right amount of slack and his leg, which continually ached, didn't angrily erupt as it continued to do with increasing frequency. Iowa wasn't so certain. Even though she had no reason to doubt the justification for his confidence, she worried that he might reinjure his leg on the way down or that something else would happen to turn the whole thing into a fiasco, for which she would be held completely responsible.

Iowa slowly and reluctantly (truly, there was no other choice) began lowering the rope an inch at a time. It worked, and for a few moments she was beginning to breathe a little easier, feeling increasingly confident that she wouldn't have to explain why she did this and not that, or why she chose to take this route as opposed to the other, or even staying put, since that would have been the safest and most practical course. But despite the best laid plans, mistakes (acts of God and nature) are bound to happen as they did in this case, for Luke suddenly and inexplicable lost control and, swinging wildly to his right, banged his injured leg against the cliff's rugged face. Now hanging freely, both legs dangling below him, Luke winced in pain and nearly cried out. The rope swayed back and forth, while he was pirouetting at the end of the rope, unable to control the motion. The one saving grace was that he managed to keep upright grabbing the rope with one hand and blindly reaching out with the other for something, anything, on the cliff that he could grasp to stop the spinning. Unfortunately, the cliff sloped precipitously inward under the ledge, and, despite his best efforts, there was nothing he could do to reach the face of the cliff, which receded a good ten feet beneath the ledge and completely beyond his reach.

"What's going on, Luke?" Iowa hollered. She could feel his erratic movements and periodic tugs as the rope twisted and turned.

"My leg. I can't stop spinning. The wall is too far to reach. How do I slow down?"

"Is everything else okay?"

"Yes, no…I don't know, but this is making me sick."

"Okay, okay, listen to me." Iowa readjusted herself to ease some of the increasing discomfort in her arms and legs. "Listen, I am going to pull up a foot or so, and when you reach the top of the ledge, I want you to grab it and stabilize yourself. Okay? Do you understand? Let me know when you can reach it."

"Yes," he replied. "You don't need to pull very far."

Iowa used almost every ounce of her strength to pull Luke back to the ledge. She wasn't strong enough to pull continuously, mechanically, but she was able to lift in in short, discontinuous bursts, which was enough to bring him closer to the ledge.

When the ledge was finally in reach, Luke practically lunged at it. He was able to grasp a ragged edge of it fairly easily, but the momentum of his spinning was such that he couldn't hold on to anything and continued spinning. Undaunted, he reached for the same section again, and again it slipped out of his grasp and the spinning continued. Unfortunately, he had neglected to inform Iowa that he had reached the ledge, and so she continued to pull him upward, inch by inch. While this helped Luke reach out for other sections of the ledge to hold onto, it also pulled the hand holding to rope into contact with the ledge (where it touched the ledge before arcing over and up toward Iowa), pinching his hand so severely that he momentarily let go of the rope before grasping it a foot lower down. It could have ended badly, but Luke had the presence of mind to holler out that he had reached the ledge.

"Iowa," he shouted. "Stop pulling. I made it." Luke reached upward and, grasping the ledge, held on tightly to stop his spinning.

"Did you stop spinning?"

"Yes. You can lower me down now."

"I'll lower you about a foot, and I want you to release whatever you're holding on to. You should begin spinning again, but you need to do it to let out the tension in the rope. You'll spin a few seconds in either direction, but you'll eventually stop. Let me know when you're stopped, and I'll start lowering you again."

Luke did as Iowa told him. Not surprisingly, he started to spin again, but his spinning was a little slower and after a few seconds the spinning slowed to a complete halt. But as soon as this happened, he began to spin again in the opposite direction, going around and around, each time more slowly than the last, until once again he came to a stop. Once that happened, he began to spin in the original direction, albeit slowly until he came to another halt, after which the process reversed itself. This continued for perhaps a minute, until all the pent-up energy in the rope was finally dissipated and he could hold the rope without moving significantly in any direction. Surprisingly, he wasn't sick from all the motion (a few seconds earlier, he was certain that he was going to vomit), but when he looked down and saw the base of the cliff some fifty feet or so below his feet, he felt uneasy and was certain that if he continued to look down he would either faint or heave.

"I'm okay," he shouted to Iowa, looking up at the underside of the ledge, at the same time brushing sand and grit off his face and out of his eyes that had either drifted down the edge or had been blown by the breeze. "Let's go down."

Once again, Iowa continued releasing the rope, watching it as carefully as she could and feeling for any discontinuities in the tension that could suggest something was wrong. She was relieved after ten minutes or so, because everything seemed to be going smoothly; the rope responded exactly as expected and Luke was quiet, a sign that he wasn't in trouble. Iowa would have preferred to release the rope more quickly, but she wasn't going to risk it because she wasn't certain that she still had the strength to pull him back up to stop the motion. If he did start spinning again, she could always let him spin until he reached the bottom, but that risked injury when he reached the bottom and it was always possible that the friction against the ledge could sever the rope. She decided not to worry about these problems until they occurred.

"We're almost there," Luke called out suddenly. "Don't stop now." Iowa had unexpectedly stopped lowering and, for a few seconds, Luke was suspended between the top of the ledge, which now seemed miles away, and the base of the cliff, which was no more than four feet below. "Iowa," he called again. "Can you hear me? We're almost there. Maybe another three or four feet to the bottom."

"What?" she asked. "How many feet?"

"Four, maybe a little more. We're almost there."

"Wait," she shouted.

Luke waited. One minute, two minutes, five minutes, and no response. "Is everything okay?" he hollered. When she didn't respond, Luke started to wonder if there was something wrong, if something was preventing her from answering. "Iowa," he called out one more time, and this time like the last he was surrounded by silence. He could hear the rustle of a breeze somewhere overhead, and when he looked out across the bright landscape in front of him from under the ledge, he could see a fine mist of dust floating down from the top of the cliff. For a few seconds, he felt alone and after a few more seconds, he started to think that she might have run out of rope. Why else would she stop? Any other time, he would have untied the rope and dropped to the ground. But dropping now wasn't particularly appealing: His leg was throbbing, and every couple of minutes or so an electric spasm would shoot through his leg and then the rest of his body, reminding him that even if he made it to the ground safely, the rest of the trip wasn't going to be a cakewalk. "Iowa," Luke called out again. "Is there a problem? Did we run out of rope?"

Iowa had indeed stopped lowering the rope. But she stopped not because the rope had come to an end or because she was tired and needed a few minutes to rest and rejuvenate her energy. Even though she was exhausted and her nerves strained, she still had enough strength to lower Luke to the bottom and maybe even pull him up another couple of feet, if it came to that. No, she stopped lowering him because one of the crows, the one that had brushed her hair and had flown almost into her face, had returned and was now sitting on top of the rock around which the rope holding Luke was secured. The crow was looking directly at her, flapping its wings and cawing. Iowa returned the bird's stare, although she didn't say anything, and when it stopped cawing watched it swoop back into the air and disappear. She didn't move for a few moments after the crow was gone, not until she heard Luke calling to her and trying to explain his situation.

"There's plenty of rope," she finally replied, and then lowered him the last few feet until he reached the soft dirt at the base of the cliff.

Once safely on the ground, Luke hollered for more rope and, when that was available, he hopped over to the face of the cliff (which was about ten feet from where he landed) and, leaning against the cliff in the cool shade made by the ledge, untied the rope and pulled it off his waist and legs. Tossing the rope back to where he had landed, Luke hollered that the rope was now hers and that she should hurry down. Even though he was physically beaten from the descent, Luke was nevertheless exhilarated – he made it down without serious injury and, more importantly, it was only a matter of minutes (the amount of time she needed to slide down the rope) before he would again have some direct time with Iowa. This was truly a bonding experience, even more than the time they spent above the cliff, and Luke felt closer to Iowa than he had ever felt, and he was certain that she, too, felt something similar as a result of the experience. While he rested and waited impatiently for Iowa's arrival, he called out to her several times to tell her about the soft dirt and the cool shade at the base of the cliff. He also informed her that he leg was feeling a little better (perhaps the descent had done something positive to it), although in fact his leg was aching and even the slightest movement of his body seemed to increase the pain. Luke didn't want to tell her the truth at that moment; he was pleased to be safe, and he was also concerned that if he did tell her the truth, she might rush down and…well, he didn't want to think about what might happen if she became careless.

For a few minutes, Luke waited patiently for Iowa to appear over the edge. After all, the cliff was fairly high and, even though she would be able to descend much faster than he did, it would still take some time for her to reach the base. Throughout this time, he continued to holler to her and at one point he even began speaking to her in nearly the same way he spoke to the swan at the zoo. But after a while, with no response even to his most intimate words, Luke began to worry, especially when he looked over at the rope and noticed that it was in the same place and position where he tossed it. Since it was impossible to climb down using the rope without moving it at least an inch or two, Luke began to wonder if something happened or if she returned to the zoo and left him to fend for himself. He shook his head, telling himself that he was betraying her by thinking such absurd and vile thoughts, and yet such thoughts refused to leave his mind, making him reconsider everything he said to find the exact words that might have caused her to leave. He knew it wasn't true, he knew that Iowa wouldn't do such a thing, and yet the thoughts and their embellishments increased the longer he was forced to wait. Finally, unable to wait another second, Luke pushed off the cliff and hopped several painful steps toward the rope.

He was going to hop to a place where he could look up at the top of the cliff when he was stopped mid-effort as a large, brown burlap bag floated from the sky and hit the ground at the exact spot where he landed. The bag made a muted thud upon impact, which was followed by a metallic tinkle and a slight cloud of dust Ten seconds later, a large, brown hawk swooped out of nowhere and landed on the bag. The hawk tucked its wings behind it and, while looking directly at Luke, kneaded the bag with its talons, after which it screeched, jumped off the bag, and walked a few feet to the side.

The hawk ruffled its feathers and seconds later Iowa was standing in front of him, enveloped in the dazzling, bright sunlight.

Chapter Forty

"I was starting to worry," Luke said, as Iowa walked out of the sunlight into the cool, dark shade. "I thought…"

She stood directly in front of him and, without moving her head, appeared to be examining his face. Before Luke could say anything else, she reached up and, using the tip of her right thumb, gently cleaned the dust away from the scar under his eye. But when he smiled, she abruptly turned away and looked out across the bright plain in front of them. "Sometimes, you think too much, Luke," she said without looking at him.

Luke was taken aback by her response. Her words sounded harsh, and yet she hadn't raised her voice and her tone, as far as he could tell, seemed normal. Perhaps if she had been looking at him instead of surveying the landscape in front of them, he might have been able to gauge her thoughts and emotions better. He was also surprised that she didn't immediately ask him about his leg. True, he didn't say too much about it on the way down, and so she might very well conclude that it wasn't in any worse shape than before they started out. Still, his leg was the very reason they had descended the cliff in that fashion.

"I'm sorry," he responded quietly.

Without glancing back, Iowa walked back out into the bright light to where the rope was still hanging. Grasping the rope with one hand, she looked up to the point at which it came over the ledge and then gave the rope a couple of quick, sharp tugs. She didn't say anything while she appeared to be examining that point, and a few moments later, after releasing the rope and flipping it disdainfully away from her, she turned to Luke and, with a wan smile, apologized to him. "No, I'm sorry. I had something on my mind and I…it doesn't matter. I would have been worried in your place, too." She reached over and retrieved the burlap bag and, tying a loop on its loose end, she threaded her arm through the loop and swung the bag over her shoulder as if it were a backpack. Before returning, she began to scan the ground around her until, a few seconds later, she spotted a long stick a few feet away. She picked up the stick, which looked somewhat like the stick that had served as a crutch and then later as a splint, and walked into the shadow under the ledge and handed it to Luke.

She watched intently as Luke worked to position it to hold his weight. But unlike the other stick, this one was too short to serve as a crutch and lacked a handle or a nob that might have made it useful as a cane. When Luke nodded that he was ready to go, she stepped in front of him, smiled faintly as she shook her head, and kissed him lightly on the cheek. Without a word, she took the stick and threaded it through her sack and, positioning herself on his injured side, draped Luke's arm over her shoulder and together they walked and hopped out into the light and toward Luke's home. Once his eyes adjusted to the light, Luke looked out across the wide expanse in front of them, which, for some reason, looked different than it had when he was approaching the cliff. The forests were still there, on either side of them, while the rest of the area was open and flat (except for some small hills at the farthest reach of the plain) and strewn with rocks and the occasional weed.

"Are you ready?" she asked, finally breaking the silence. This time her voice had the pleasant almost loving tone that he had expected when she came into the shadow.

Luke breathed deeply. The air was warm, and in the distance he could see the heat radiate off the overheated rocks. But because the air was filled with the scent of the trees on either side of them, it was pleasant to be outside under the sun, more pleasant in fact than the cool, stale smell under the ledge. Perhaps holding onto Iowa made a difference. "Of course, I am," he said, as they began hobbling back toward home.

For the first hour or so, neither one of them said a word as they slowly made their way over the soft, barren ground, which for some reason reminded Luke of a gigantic bowling alley, absent a gigantic set of pins at the end. The ground was as soft as sand for about a quarter of a mile, and every now and then Luke's good ankle would turn the wrong way in the soft dirt, which would cause him to lean to one side and nearly bring them both to the ground. Somehow, though, Iowa always managed to keep them upright, and it was during those moments when they were both struggling together to stay on their feet that he felt closest to her and started to wonder how he could ever do without her. Indeed, at those times, his very ability to continue depended on her, just as it did when she found him lying on the highway, listening to the cars as they sped by, waiting for the end most likely from a passing car. The sandy dirt soon gave way to hard, albeit dusty ground, and soon they were able to travel together almost as smoothly as if they were running a painful three-legged race. Having traveled on the hard ground for a couple of hours, Iowa paused and motioned to the dark, turbulent clouds coming their way.

Turning to him, she told him that it was going to rain in a few minutes. "Can you smell it? We need to find shelter."

Luke agreed – he was ready to agree with anything she said, especially because in this instance shelter would give them a chance to talk – and Iowa pointed to some large rocks near the forest to the right.

"There are some large rocks over there that should have some under-hangings where we could sit out the rain," she added, pointing to an outcrop of rocks nearly as high as a house next to the forest on the right. She noted that although the rocks were perhaps a few hundred yards away, they could beat the storm if they hurried. "How's your leg holding out?"

"It still hurts, I still get these spasms, but I'm feeling better than I did earlier." He didn't tell her that for the past hour his leg had been bothering more than before, that there were moments during which he would have happily cut it off had he been carrying a knife – he didn't want to tell her, because she had been doing everything she could to get him home (and to help), and it would sounded like a criticism of her efforts to do so, or else she might think him a baby for going on about his worthless leg. Luke agreed, and together they hobbled toward the rocks, stumbling twice (once nearly falling over) in their haste to beat the storm. They approached the first and largest of the rocks just as the first drops of rain began tentatively falling.

At first glance, the outcrop seemed to be little more than a smooth, vertical wall of gray rock. But on Iowa's insistence, they limped slowly around to the other side (by this time, Luke was exhausted, another fact which he didn't disclose to Iowa) where there was a cave-like area at the base of the rock that was high enough for them to enter without bowing their heads. Stepping into this dank, cave-like formation, they immediately stopped and waited for their eyes to adjust to the darkness before venturing any deeper. In the meantime, the rain had increased and was now pounding down furiously, and the noise it made hitting the hard ground and slamming against the slick rock was practically deafening. It was several minutes before they could have a conversation without yelling; in the meantime, they looked around at the cave, noticing the soft dirt that covered the floor and the flat, raised rocks that almost looked like chairs that were near the back wall. There were no signs of human presence, although in certain areas Luke noticed signs that a large animal had been in the cave, possibly making it a temporary home at some point in the recent past. Looking longingly at one of the flat, chair-like rocks near the back, Luke hopped over to the nearest one (and careful not to hit his head as the top of the cave began sloping inward at that point) and sat down, leaning against the wall as if it were designed for such a use. While he rested, he closed his eyes to ease one particularly violent bout of pain and, when it subsided to a dull discomfort, he couldn't bring himself to open them again. Without looking at her, he informed Iowa that he was going to close his eyes for a "just a minute" to "refresh them.'

Several flashes of bright light illuminated the cave (which Luke noticed even with his eyes shut), which were followed by a crackling sound and then a loud crash, as if a gigantic tree were being broken in half by a gargantuan beast outside of the cave. Luke had never liked the sound of thunder, especially when he was much younger, but sitting there outside of the reach of both the rain and the lightening, and with each peal of thunder his leg seemed to hurt less and less, he began to feel unusually comfortable and secure, and in no time he started to compare this event with others, particularly those when he was much younger, when he and Iowa were still Cygnets. There was one particular time when he, Iowa, and the rest of the Cygnets were playing in the woods near the lake when it started to rain, slowly and hesitantly, just as it did a few minutes earlier, and then the lightening started, streaming in all directions and thunder exploding as if were directly overhead. Without a conversation between them, they all rushed toward an outcrop of gray rocks that were centered in a clearing not too far from the lake, laughing and running wildly through the trees that surrounded the rocks, doing their futile best not to get completely soaked, especially as the rain increased until it seemed like a deluge.

He and Iowa were the first to reach the outcrops and crawl under a narrow opening that led to a large, cavern underneath them. They had been the closest to the rocks when it started raining, but they only started running when they noticed the others heading for safety, and then of course it was a mad scramble to see who could reach the rocks first. Press should have been the first to arrive, but she stumbled over something and then was cut off by either Dana or Lu, forcing her to remain behind as the other two charged their way behind Luke and Iowa. As soon as Luke and Iowa were in the cave (it was Iowa who actually entered first), both of them simultaneously walked to the back (the cave was high enough inside for even Press to stand upright) where the ground was soft and dry. The others came in shortly afterwards, and in turn each one found a spot on the ground as far away from the opening as possible, as if being close to the opening, though dry, was not enough to protect them from the fury outside.

Sitting a couple of feet from one another, he and Iowa watched the others as they tried to find some place comfortable to rest on. There was a moment when she seemed to watching the others that he stole a glance at her (there was enough light in the cave to see fairly well, particularly when lightening illuminated the sky outside), observing the tiny, globules of water on her hair and face, especially the one at the very tip of her nose that leaped to the ground when she sensed his observation and turned to face him. Luke escaped embarrassment when the cave suddenly became dark as if the lights had gone out, and with the temperature now dropping precipitously and the storm outside slamming and shouting, he could sense Iowa slowly inching closer to him until they were sitting side by side, their shirtless arms touching and transmitting both warmth and the shivering of Iowa's arms and shoulders.

He couldn't remember how long they sat in the cool darkness, but it couldn't have been very long (twenty minutes? Less?). When the storm passed and the clouds began opening for the sun's pleasant light, the Cygnets all charged out of the cave as if on command. Neither he nor Iowa mentioned the experience inside the cavern, and the next thing he recalled was racing around the lake in the warm, spring-like air.

It was deathly still when Luke awoke. He could tell that the storm had passed, because it was bright in the cave and he could see bright sunlight covering everything outside. The air was still cool and rancid, although it was not exactly unpleasant because it was the opposite of what they could expect outside. Once his head was clear, Luke noticed that Iowa was no longer next to him. Glancing casually around, he realized that she wasn't in the cave, although he thought she might be outside checking the weather or doing something practical. Unconcerned, he called her name twice, knowing that she would tell him to relax until she came back inside. But when she didn't respond, not even to the fourth and fifth bellowing of her name, Luke became concerned and started to wonder if anything had happened to her.

Remembering the stick that she had carried in her sack, Luke was going to reach for it and hobble outside to see what she was doing and find out why she didn't respond. But when he turned to the spot where she had dropped the bag, nothing was there except an empty, smoothed out spot in the dirt. He immediately looked on the other side of him, hoping that he had either forgotten where she had put it or that she had moved it for some reason or another, but that was as empty as the first space. Luke glanced hurriedly around the cave for the bag – which was the only proof he had that she hadn't left him – and, when he saw nothing, no bag or other remnants that she had even been there, he called her name loudly two more times. "Iowa, where are you?" There was no response and, when after a few minutes it was evident that there would be no response, Luke pushed himself up to his good foot (using the wall behind him for leverage) and then tried to hop to the entrance to see if he could find her. The pain in his leg, which up until that moment almost seemed gone, came back with a fury, rushing up and over his entire body and forcing him to sit back down until it subsided. His stomach became upset and he felt like vomiting. Closing his eyes and gritting his teeth, he nearly started crying as much from the pain as from the frustration that he couldn't go anywhere without help.

"Iowa," Luke called again, this time as much to find her as to evoke her memory. But unlike most other times, the pain didn't cease. While it ebbed and flowed, it was far more intense than it had ever been, and Luke began wondering if there was a large rock nearby that he could grasp and put himself at least temporarily out of his misery. There wasn't, certainly nothing that he could spot when he again glanced around the cave, and so he promised himself that when the pain subsided, he would crawl outside if he had to and find something that would stop the pain, the unending pain. Luke leaned carefully backward against the wall (even the slight movements he made angered his leg and encouraged it to torture him to remain still) and closed his eyes. "If only I can wait it out a few moments,' he told himself, "maybe it will go away. What's the matter with my leg?" Once again, Luke could feel the sweat pour off his face, and, spitting twice just to do something to take his mind off the offending limb, he quickly fell asleep (or passed out). When he finally awoke, the light was still streaming into the shelter, although it was softer, less intense, and, more important, Iowa was there, standing directly in front of him.

The pain wasn't quite as intense as it had been, and Luke wiped his moist eyes with his right forearm and smiled at her. "You're back. I was afraid you left."

"I wasn't gone long. I suppose I could have left the stick for you, but honestly I didn't want to take any chances and have you hurt yourself even more." She smiled and continued looking at him.

"Where did you go?"

Iowa reached to his side and picked up her bag, which appeared to be fuller than the last time he saw it. "I went to find food. While I was foraging around, I noticed a trail through the trees that opens up to another open area that we can use to bypass the rocky areas we're approaching." Luke remembered the depressions, bushes, and rocks that were difficult to cross even when he had four good legs.

"I'm surprised. I didn't think…"

"Don't worry about it. And don't be surprised. Dogs can't sense everything. Sometimes things are a lot clearer from a bird's point of view." She smiled and both she and Luke laughed. "Now, let's eat. I don't know about you, but I'm starved. I think you'll like what I found."

Iowa opened the bag and pulled out some apples, two bottles of water, and a cooked fish on a piece of board. From within the shadows, she pulled out a large, wooden crate and, turning it upside down, placed it down between them as a table.

"Where did you get all this? Where did the crate come from?" Luke asked with surprise as he sat up and watched her place the food on the table. She also retrieved from the bag two plastic plates, plastic forks and knives, and a couple of paper towels, which served as napkins. After arranging everything neatly, as if she were setting out a dinner at home, she sat down next to Luke and began eating an apple.

"These are the last of the apples and water that I had with me. While I was looking for a better way to travel, I noticed a small stream and plucked a fish out of the water. Piece of cake," she added, as if Luke should have understood her abilities.

"But it's cooked. How did you manage that?"

"Really, Luke, what's so difficult about making a small fire and cooking fish on a stick?"

Luke smiled and nodded. When he reached for a fork, it occurred to him that the plates, paper towels, and utensils were an even more amazing find.

"Knives, forks, plates? Where did you find all this stuff? There's not a store around here."

"There wasn't a store. I found a pile of large trash bags that someone had tossed away. Most of them were shredded and their contents gone (courtesy of our friends), but in the couple that were still intact, I found some amazing things, such as the utensils and plates. Don't worry, this stuff was still in packages. It's amazing what people will throw out..."

"And it's shocking what people will do to the environment. So what else did you find?"

"Nothing much," she smiled, took a bite of her apple, and nudged him with her narrow elbow to start eating. "Please, eat. We can talk about stuff I have in my little old bag later."

Luke ate with gusto. His pain, although still present, was less troublesome, which allowed him to move enough without discomfort to bring forkfuls of fish to his mouth. Of course, he was also extremely hungry. He couldn't clearly remember when he had last eaten, but it was long enough ago that he couldn't get enough in his mouth. Iowa, however, only nibbled at her food, trying to leave most of it for Luke, who would need the energy if they were to continue traveling.

"Why aren't you eating?" Luke asked at one point, feeling a little embarrassed that he was consuming most of their food.

Iowa smiled. An apple was enough for her, she explained, and she added that she was more concerned that he had sufficient food. "You need to keep your strength up."

Chapter Forty-one

When Luke was done eating, Iowa pulled a large, black trash bag out of her burlap bag – "something else I salvaged from the dump," she said while shaking it open – and began picking up the plates, utensils, and leftover food and tossing them into the bag. It took less than a minute to clean up. When she was done, she tied the top of the plastic bag and tossed it toward the entrance of the cave. She picked up the wooden crate, which Luke was certain was heavy given its apparent solidity, flipped it around so that the open end was up, and put it next to the bag at the entrance of the cave. Finally, she picked up her burlap bag (pulling the stick out and handing it to Luke before she did so) and dropped it and the plastic bag into the crate.

Luke was surprised. It was obvious that she was not going to leave anything behind in the cave, but it didn't make sense to take the crate and trash bag with them. He didn't like the idea of littering any more than she did, but it was reasonable to make an exception this one time (they might even be able to come back for the stuff the following week, if his leg was feeling better), even if it were left to rot or to the animals. How was she going to manage the crate, since there was no way that he could help? Surely, she didn't harbor any ideas that he could lug half of it, while she lugged the other on the opposite side? When Iowa was done and standing in front of Luke, ready to help him up, he couldn't resist asking her why they were going take the crate with them. "I don't think I can be of much help lifting it, if that's what you're thinking."

Iowa chuckled. "Don't be silly. We're leaving this stuff behind. You're right, there's no way that you and I could carry it back. It would slow us down, if nothing else."

Luke was satisfied with her response, until he remembered the burlap bag. After all, it had served as a lifeline for them, and tossing it away now almost seemed like tossing away their lifeline. Maybe she had already emptied its contents, he wondered, but wouldn't the burlap be useful by itself. "Aren't we going to keep the sack?" he asked just as she reached down and positioned her hands under his arms. "Isn't there something else in it that we can use?"

"Nah," she replied. "We used everything that was necessary. If we were going to be out for several nights, it might come in handy, but to take it with us now would be a nuisance. Now, if you're ready…"

Iowa helped Luke to his feet. Hopping to balance himself, Luke stood still while Iowa, holding him upright with one hand, reached down and retrieved the walking stick, which she handed to him across his stomach. He used that to steady himself while Iowa draped his other arm across her shoulders and then positioned her arm around his back and chest. When she was done, she tested their respective positions by adjusting her shoulders and arm, and then, turning slightly in Luke's direction, asked him if he was ready to travel.

"I think so," he said. "I feel good. My leg still hurts, but not as bad as before. Maybe the food helps. Well, let's go."

Iowa hesitated for a moment. "Luke," she began quietly, "I'm…I'm sorry for…"

"What?" he asked turning to her. "Sorry for what? If it weren't for you, I wouldn't have made it this far. I might still be lying…"

"You don't understand. I'm…I wish things were different. I wish…but, you know, we all move forward and…"

Luke smiled and he could feel tears welling up in his eyes. "I don't have a clue what you're talking about. But it doesn't matter. Forward or backward, it doesn't matter. You have nothing to be sorry about, unless it's because it took us so long to see each other again and under these circumstances. I'm sorry, too."

Iowa sniffed and, without being able to see her face clearly, Luke knew that she was holding back tears. Luke, too, was moved, both because of her tears and because he now had the opportunity of saying what he had wanted to say for some time, what he had tried to say to that stupid swan. Because of their physical closeness and the fact that neither one was looking directly into the other's face, Luke said, barely above a whisper, "Iowa, I wanted to find you because I wanted to tell you something. It's something that I've felt for maybe my whole life, or at least as long as I've known you. Do you know that I've never stopped thinking about you, never stopped dreaming about a day when I would see you again and tell you….? What I want to say is that I always believed I would see you

232

again; I never had the slightest doubt. If I doubted that, I don't think I could have gone on…"

"Luke," she gently interrupted. "I understand."

"You do?" He turned toward her to see her profile in the shadow. Her hair, which appeared to be a dark chestnut in the muted light in the cave, was hanging down and obscuring part of her chin. The manner in which her head was tilted and the soft curves that defined her forehead, nose, and lips reminded him of a famous work of art that he'd seen in a book at school. He couldn't remember the piece very well (it was a portrait of some kind), but he was positive that Iowa was even more beautiful than the most famous painting or statue in the world – she had the kind of face and inner beauty that any artist would want to depict and give up in despair of doing her justice. Had he been more mobile, he would have leaned over and kissed her on the cheek, but just thinking of attempting that kind of movement sent a sliver of pain through his leg, forcing him to close his eyes for a moment and grimace. He managed to remain upright, however, even though he felt like dropping to the ground or falling back onto his rock chair to let the pain run its course. When he finally opened his eyes, Iowa was looking directly at him.

"Are you okay?" she asked. "Are you ready to do some walking? Do you think you can walk?"

He nodded vaguely, but before he could say anything, she reached over and, with the tip of her thumb, wiped the damp and dirt from the scar beneath his eye.

"Iowa," he began but was interrupted before he could express his thoughts.

"It's time to go," she said quietly, almost sadly, as if she, too, hesitated to leave but knew that they had no choice.

"I know."

Iowa readjusted herself and him, and together they hobbled slowly out of the cave, careful not to make any sudden moves that might upset their balance before Luke felt strong enough to walk at a slightly quicker pace.

They walked into the harsh daylight, around the side of the outcrop, and continued until they had distanced themselves from the formation's shadows and had an unobstructed view of the wide-open plain before them. They paused briefly to let Iowa adjust her shirt and then readjust their arms. Just as they were about to start walking, Luke noticed the sun.

Chapter Forty-two

Luke hadn't thought much about the position of the sun when he and Iowa left the cave, but now that they were standing in the open field and he had a moment of leisure to look at things, he was disturbed by what he saw. The sun was still bright, of course, but its brightest rays had mellowed to a dark, pleasant yellow, almost gold. More to the point, the sun was low in the sky and inching closer to the horizon, which meant not only that the day was coming to an end, but also that time was running out more quickly than he had expected. Was it still possible to make it home before arousing the suspicions of his parents and practically everyone else? And what about Iowa? Would she have enough time to get back before someone noticed that she was gone?

Luke looked at the sun until spots started dancing before his eyes, and when he turned away he tried to make sense of the sun's position and the elongated shadows he noticed across the landscape. Where had all the time gone? He remembered arriving at the cave early in the afternoon, while the sun was still high overhead, and he could recall having what seemed to be lunch and…and what else? What else? What had happened to speed up the movement of the sun, for that was the only thing that could explain the time of day. Luke closed his eyes several times to remove the sun spots, and when he opened them again he suddenly remembered that he had slept for some time while Iowa had been foraging for food. But it didn't seem possible that he could have slept for hours. A few minutes, perhaps, but not hours. Okay, maybe an hour, but even this couldn't account for the sun's position.

Luke turned his head to ask her about the time. But when he observed her face and then felt the touch of her body against his, he forgot about the lost hours and the likelihood of getting home on time. He watched the movements of her head and shoulders as she got comfortable, and he noticed the manner in which the sun's golden light glistened on her light-colored hair. He felt warm inside when she blew the hair out of her eyes with a puff of air out the corner of her mouth, and then, when that proved ineffectual, pushed it back with a upward shove with the back of her hand, as if she had something on the palm of her hand that she didn't want to get into her hair. When she was ready to start walking again, which she signaled with a quick look and a nod to Luke (who reciprocated), he noticed the warm, golden color of her arms and the tops of her feet, the areas exposed to the sun's light, and then as she glanced up the smoothness of her skin and the delicate lines caused by the sweat pouring through the dust on her forehead and cheeks. He wanted to speak to her now, just as he had wanted to speak to her in the cave, because he realized that with the expiring sun, his time with Iowa was also expiring, if only temporarily (he knew that he would see her again, but he didn't know how long the interval might be between now and then).

This was the worst thing that could happen. He couldn't stand the thought of losing sight of her even for a few minutes, and he told himself that he would gladly forsake everything to spend the rest of his life with her. In fact, the more he thought about it, the more he wanted to say those very things to her, and he felt like kicking himself (strangely, the idea of kicking in his condition sounded amusing) because he had a chance to say them when they were in the cave but couldn't. He lacked the courage. He wasn't afraid that Iowa would laugh at his sentiments (she wasn't the kind of person to do such a thing), but he would have been demoralized if she were to decline his overture, or if she were to put it off until some vague time in the future, as some of the girls he knew might have done. Of course, he asked himself, if she were to put him off until some vague time in the future, how would the situation between them be any different? They would reach his home, and that would be that, possibly forever. No, he couldn't let that happen. When they began encountering large rocks and strange pock marks in the soil, both of which had to be carefully traversed, Luke tried to think of some way he could broach the subject before it was too late, before something came up (and things always come up, don't they?) and robbed him of the best chance he would ever have to speak to her about what was in his heart.

Steeling himself, he turned to Iowa and, while he was mentally fumbling with the words he would say, he didn't look where he was stepping and stumbled over a rock and fell down, bringing Iowa along with him. Luckily, he fell on his good side and, lucky, too, Iowa managed to avoid hitting his injured leg. But luck wasn't entirely with him, for while he managed to land appropriately, something in his bad leg was aggravated and sent a shockwave of pain through him as fiercely as if he had landed on the leg. Unconsciously hollering, Luke gingerly grabbed a portion of his leg that hadn't been mauled and rolled back and forth on the ground. Iowa, after she moved out of his way, scooted around behind him and held him in her arms.

"Luke, Luke, I'm so sorry. Did I hit your leg? I'm sorry, I'm sorry. Concentrate on something else. Concentrate on something happy to forget the pain. I'm so sorry."

"Iowa," Luke gasped as the pain subsided enough to stop his hollering. He closed his eyes and was silent for a few minutes, while he mentally wrestled with the agony and the sudden fear that something even more cataclysmic was happening to him. When the torment had tempered just enough to allow him to think and speak, he gasped out, "Iowa, I want to be with you forever." He growled again in pain and was silent for a few more minutes, while Iowa watched him and petted his damp hair and then placed her cheek on his head. "Iowa," he gasped when he was able to speak again, "I can wait until you're done with refactoring…I can wait. Do you….," he started to say, but had trouble articulating his words. Iowa held him tightly and, while he continued his fight with the pain, she whispered in his ear, "I'm here, Luke. I'm here."

Luke's pain eventually dulled to an agonizing throb. When he was finally able to communicate with her, they both agreed that it was time to stand up and continue on, although both of them also realized that the journey was going to become more difficult, if not because of Luke's increasing weakness then because of the light, which would begin to dim fairly soon. Iowa was able to help Luke get to his good foot (he leaned on his stick as much as on Iowa to stand and then take a few tentative steps), and he nodded that he was ready, they moved forward, this time slower than before. They were silent for a while. Iowa needed all her strength and concentration to get Luke over or around one obstacle after another, while Luke needed to divide his thoughts between his next step forward and using the stick as a substitute for his injured leg. When the bottom edge of the sun seemed only inches from the horizon, Iowa pointed out a large, flat rock a few feet ahead of them and suggested that they reach the rock and take a break. He could sit down on the rock and, because it protruded a couple of feet out of the ground, it wouldn't be difficult to lower him onto it and, since it was wide and flat, Luke might even be able to lie on his back if his leg allowed it.

"We'll both collapse from exhaustion if we don't take a break," she said as they approached the rock.

Once they were standing in front of it (it was actually the remnant of something that had been sheared off in the primordial past), Iowa turned and, facing Luke, grabbed both of his hands and gently lowered him onto its smooth surface. The process seemed quick and simple to Iowa, but it was not quite as easy for Luke, who squinted, gritted his teeth, and put his chin on his neck the entire time. He felt a little better when he was finally secure on the rock, although the pain didn't stop even if the intensity varied. Indeed, there were moments when his leg felt like it was expanding beyond his skin's ability to contain it and, just when he was certain that it would explode, whitish dots began dancing in his vision and he sense his mental processes clouding and fading. He wanted to pass out, which would relieve the torment for a while (and which he was now certain probably happened in the cave), but nothing ever seemed to happen, because as soon as he felt that he was sinking into the abyss, his eyes would open wide while he waited again for the leg to explode. During the better moments, however, when he was able to think of something other than his discomfort, Luke tried to think of some way of speaking to her about their future. He was fairly certain that he had finally managed to express his love for her and that she reciprocated, even though he couldn't recall the exact moment when he said as much. Nor could he remember her exact words in response, although he was certain that he had been moved by them.

Having made Luke as comfortable as she could, Iowa smiled at him and then walked a few feet to the side. She put the edge of her hand to her forehead to block some of the sun's glare, and began scanning the land surrounding them. It was obvious that she was looking for a practical route forward, but he couldn't help admiring her slender figure in the golden sunlight and wondering if he had actually declared his love to her. When the intensity of the pain began to diminish (it came and went now in periodic throbs), Luke managed to wipe the sweat from his eyes with the back of his shaky right hand while at the same time watching her movements and the graceful way she balanced on one hip and then craned her head to focus in on something in the distance. But as he watched her,

238

wishing that he could stand up and walk over to her, he noticed that she seemed to be nervous or anxious, as if she were looking for something or expecting something. Since he had never seen her this way before, he told himself that he was imagining things and that she was indeed scouting out their route. And when she suddenly stopped and craned her ear, Luke realized that her behavior wasn't typical and that something was troubling her.

"What's the matter?" he asked, hoping that she would turn around and explain the way they would take to reach home. But Iowa didn't turn around and, instead, she motioned to him with the palm of her right hand. Luke glanced in the direction in which she was staring and, not seeing or hearing anything, spoke to her again.

"Iowa, what's wrong? Do you see something? Are we close? We can't be that close. I can't see any houses. We didn't take a wrong turn, did we?" Iowa still didn't respond, although she was no longer using her hand to signal something to him. Craning his head to get a better view of what she was looking at, Luke couldn't see anything unusual except a faint puff of dust or something far in the distance; but since it dissipated as quickly as it had arose, he wasn't certain that he had seen anything at all. "Is there a train over there or maybe a highway?" He strained his eyes in the same direction, but he still couldn't see anything of particular interest. The dust cloud didn't reappear. "If it's a highway, maybe we can get a ride back," he muttered to himself.

"No, it's not a highway," Iowa finally responded, without however looking at him. "The only highway nearby is the one you crossed earlier, and there's no turning back and hitching a ride." She turned to him and smiled, which made him feel a little foolish for jumping at such an absurd suggestion. "By the way, did you know hitchhiking is illegal?"

Luke could feel his face redden, and so he turned away and looked back into the direction that she had been scanning. "What's out there? I don't see anything."

"I thought I saw something." She stepped over the Luke and sat down on the rock next to him. "We need to rest for a few minutes. We could keep going, but it wouldn't be long before you couldn't take another step, and then where would we be?" She leaned over and smoothed back his hair, which had become matted to his forehead.

Luke wanted to respond, but a short burst of pain distracted him. Closing his eyes and breathing deeply, he waited for it to subside enough to speak comfortably. But no sooner had this burst faded when another immediately took its place, forcing him to wait that one out so that he could focus and have a reasonable conversation. Luke had expected that the second burst would be the last for a while (there were always breaks), but a third followed on the second, and then a fourth, and then a fifth, sixth, and seventh, until he could barely think of anything apart from his pain and his increasing inability to deal with it. When there was finally a prolonged pause, he kept his eyes closed to calm his nerves while he waited for another burst. But when this didn't immediately happen, he relaxed a little and tried to think of something to say to her, something that would finally convey his feelings and encourage her to reciprocate – and she would, he was certain, because she felt the same way for him that he felt for her. If not, then why would she have taken him this far? Reminding himself that they were running out of time, he turned toward her and tried to find a way of saying something before he had to deal with another mind-numbing burst of pain.

"Iowa," he said while his eyes were still closed. "Iowa, I…I meant what I said." He opened his eyes and looked at her. Luke looked into her clear eyes for a sign that she knew what he was going to say or that she was going to say something similar in turn. But he wasn't certain that he could see anything, even though the expression in her eyes and on her face was welcoming, maybe even encouraging. Did she understand what he needed to say, or was she merely looking at him because she through he needed something or was about to relapse in pain? "Iowa," he began again after a pause, "I want to talk to you, I want to say something before we…did you understand what I was trying tell to you earlier?" Luke was desperate to get it out before the pain came back, but how much he needed to say, he realized, depended on what he may or may not have said earlier.

"About what?"

"Anything. I remember saying something, and then everything started to hurt and the rest is a fog. Didn't I tell you something? Apart from my leg, of course. I must have said something?"

"I'm sorry, Luke, I don't know what you're getting at. You're not talking about your leg, are you?" She looked at him for a moment and then her eyes narrowed, as if she was half expecting him to say something that would affect their return.

"Iowa, please, you must… Okay, let me start from the beginning, and will you promise to chime in if you remember something?"

She chuckled slightly. "Of course." But before he could continue, she abruptly turned around and stared at the area she had been scanning.

"Iowa, what is it?"

"I'm sorry, Luke," she replied, quickly turning around. "You have my full attention."

Indeed, he had her full attention. He could see it in the way she looked at him and the manner in which her body faced his, as if she were prepared to catch anything that fell from his lips. Feeling slightly intimidated by her attention, he nevertheless knew that he to tell her now before it came back, before anything stopped him from saying what he needed to say, what he was desperate to say.

"Iowa, I know we are going to part soon, but I don't want it to be forever. I mean, I want us to be together forever, even if we can't be at the same place. Do you know what I'm getting at?"

"I think so," she responded hesitantly.

Had there been more time, he might have been angry that she responded so tepidly. "Okay, you remember our promises as Cygnets, that we would always be friends and never move away, if we could help it?"

"Sure. It was a kind of silly promise, wasn't it?"

For a moment, Luke was certain that his pain was coming back, but when that didn't happen he looked more intensely at her, determined to break the gulf that suddenly seemed to have arisen between them. "I suppose, but I never forgot it, and I reached out to you when I found out where you were."

"It was nice seeing you, Luke, although…"

"Although what? Iowa, don't you understand what I'm trying to say?"

She turned away. "I only mean that I wish it could have been under different circumstances. Luke," she said, turning back to him, "I don't like seeing you in pain, and…and, Luke, you shouldn't have changed…"

"It doesn't matter. I don't care what I had to do to see you. I'll take the responsibility, but I wouldn't do anything different." It was at the moment that a slight quiver of pain rose in his leg. It subsided nearly as fast, and for a few seconds Luke was afraid that everything was going to be ruined if he succumbed to another spasm of pain. It might be impossible to start the conversation over.

"Iowa, I meant everything I said at the zoo. Did you hear me?"

She vaguely nodded her head, although he could see tears welling in her eyes.

"I told you I loved you. Okay, maybe I told a bird that I loved her, but I meant it…that is, I meant what I said when I thought I was speaking to you. Does this make sense? Iowa, I love you. I'm glad I found you. And I don't want us to be apart forever. Now, do you understand me?"

Iowa was silent for a few moments. She continued to look at Luke, although her face didn't betray any emotions (neither happiness nor unhappiness, nor even perturbation, over what he said). When it was clear that it might be a few seconds before she responded (unless she was waiting for Luke to follow up with something else), Luke turned away and looked out at the land that she had been scanning earlier.

"I'm sorry to have bothered you," he said quietly, breaking the increasingly uncomfortable silence. "I'm sorry to have put you out so much, and I truly hope that I haven't gotten you into trouble. If…if you've already stayed too long, please go, and I will find a way to get back on my own." He turned to her and, looking into her lovely, watery eyes, said, "I still mean what I said. I hope you won't hold it against me. If nothing else, I want us to remain friends."

Iowa turned her shoulders toward Luke and, putting both hands on Luke's cheeks, she carefully pulled him toward her and gently kissed his lips. Luke winced in pain but didn't turn away.

Chapter Forty-three

Something again distracted Iowa, and she turned away from Luke. Standing up, she again faced the plain that she had scanned earlier, but now her appearance, her firm jaw and straight posture, suggested that she had found something, perhaps the something that she had been searching for earlier. Luke, not making sense of her strange behavior, silently turned toward the plain, too, and tried to fathom what had now captured her attention. He didn't see anything initially, but he noticed that her eyes were still glistening, as if they were full and ready to empty themselves.

"What is it?" he asked. He gently (so as not to rouse his temperamental leg) reached over and grasped her limp hand, which was hanging by her side. She glanced back at him, but otherwise didn't seem to notice his touch.

Luke looked at her for a moment or two and then looked out at the plain, trying to figure out what she was seeing. Within a few seconds, he spotted another vague cloud of dust at the edge of the horizon, only this time the cloud didn't immediately disappear. It wasn't much, just a brownish discoloration, and for a few seconds Luke was convinced that it was a dust devil, even though he couldn't make out the spiral. 'Maybe you can't see the spiral because of all the dust it's kicking up,' he told himself. But unlike the last puff of dust, this one started to get bigger and more concentrated, and within seconds it was spreading out as if it were a giant ball rolling across the plain and heading directly toward them. A couple minutes later, the ball became a dull, brownish-colored car and it was heading their way (and since they were the only ones on the plain, it was clear that it was heading directly for them). Iowa watched the vehicle without saying anything, without moving or taking her eyes off it for a second. Luke, too, watched it for a while, after which he turned and looked up at Iowa.

"What is it? Do you know what's going on? Is it from the zoo? Are they coming for you? Iowa, if they are, please save yourself. Don't worry about me. I'll get home, and I'll come back for you. Iowa, remember, I love you, and I'll find you wherever you are."

Iowa turned her head toward Luke and, looking at him over her right shoulder, she said in a dull voice, "I'm sorry, Luke."

"There's nothing to be sorry about. If you're in trouble, I am the one who should be sorry. Iowa, listen to me, leave now while you have a chance."

Turning back to the car, Iowa and Luke watched it bounce and bang over the rocks and holes on the plan, each bump or bounce spitting up more dust in the cloud that hung over the vehicle. There was a moment when it disappeared entirely, only to reappear as it leaped upward out of a hole or valley in the ground. Luke couldn't help wondering how the occupants, if indeed there was more than one person in the car, could tolerate the wild, bumpy ride, and then he tried to visualize the kind of person who would drive such a car like that, the banging and careening were certain to damage the car until it practically fell to pieces. In fact, he was surprised that it hadn't already fallen to pieces, since it appeared to be an older vehicle (judging by its roundish shape), quite possibly a cab, given its orange color. 'Wouldn't it be funny if someone called a cab for her,' he thought.

The car, which did look like an old cab, soon came close to them and, careening in the dirt as if the driver (if there was a driver) had finally lost control or as if the vehicle had broken so that he could no longer control it, pulled up within ten feet of them and screamed to a stop, its clanking engine sputtering one last, loud metalling clank before it, too, ceased to move. A big dust cloud enveloped the car and, within seconds, Luke and Iowa were lost in the cloud, coughing and trying to brush the dust off their faces and out of their eyes.

When the dust gradually settled to the ground (the air was perfectly still and didn't disturb the microscopic particles as they floated to earth), the vehicle remained motionless, as if the occupant or occupants were reluctant or unable to step out and greet Luke and Iowa. Interestingly, while the car remained motionless, emitting a faint smell of grease and gas, neither Luke nor Iowa could see the aforementioned occupants, because the windows were covered in dust and were nearly as opaque as the body of the car.

Both Luke and Iowa remained stationary as they waited for something to happen. Iowa stared calmly and expectantly, while Luke was increasingly nervous and concerned and glanced back and forth between the car and Iowa, who remained facing the car with her back toward him. He was positive that the unexpected appearance of the car could only mean trouble, and he was equally certain that Iowa would shoulder most of the trouble, even if everything she did was done to help him. If only he hadn't changed, if only he had taken a bus to town or even had his parents drive him (and he knew that he could have kept them in the dark while he spoke to Iowa). 'If only I had used my head,' he told himself, 'everything might have been different.' Turning once more to Iowa, he couldn't help admiring her slim figure and the manner in which her long, soft hair fell over her delicate shoulders, which for some reason made him feel sorry for her. He longed to touch her glistening hair, to stroke her soft shoulders, and to whisper his love in her ear. He wanted to tell her how much he loved her, and he also wanted her to say that she forgave him and would always be waiting for him, and this time he didn't care if she didn't say anything in response.

Luke lifted his right hand and painfully reached for Iowa, who was unaware of his effort to communicate to her. But as he moved closer to her, as the tip of his middle finger came with inches of her back (or so it seemed to him), the pain suddenly rushed back into his leg and violently demanded that he return to his previous position. The intensity of his discomfort was such that he struggled between screaming and crying out Iowa's name, and yet he was determined not to lose this one last chance of connecting with her.

"Iowa," he gasped finally. "Iowa…"

Iowa turned and was surprised to see Luke hanging precariously forward, both hands now reaching out to her while the rest of him was on the verge of falling over, face down in the dirt.

"Iowa, I love you. Please run. I'm sorry I brought all this…on you."

Iowa grasped his hands and eased him back on the rock. Grimacing in pain, he looked into her eyes and tried to speak, but she shook her head and mouthed the word "no." She smiled faintly and, with the tip of her right thumb, smoothed the faint scar under his eye, where she had stabbed him when they were much younger. "Luke," she said quietly, "Luke, you don't understand."

"I understand. I understand everything. I love you, and I'll never leave you. I'll find you wherever they take you. Trust me, I'll find you.

I'm sorry I got you into…," he started to say, but the pain came over him and he nearly passed out. When it subsided somewhat, he looked at her and tried to tell her again that he loved her (saying that was the only thing that felt good just then), but he couldn't utter the words. Confident that she knew what was in his heart, Luke gasped, "Go, while you still have a chance. I'll find you. I promise."

Iowa was silent. Just then, the car doors banged open and one of the passengers tumbled out of the car and nearly fell face down in the dirt (his door, which was on the other side of the car, was apparently stuck, and when he pounded it open with his big shoulder, the door quickly gave way sending him out more quickly than he had anticipated). He jumped up and, after quickly brushing himself off, walked confidently over to the other side of the car where the other passenger was outside and waiting his arrival. The man and woman seemed to be middle-aged, and while they were average in height, both were rather bulbous. Each of them had a nice, almost humorous face, especially the man, whose thick, black mustache, which almost seemed too big for his round face, constantly twitched back and forth especially when he was contemplating something. The woman wore a grandmotherly blue floral dress that hung down to her ankles, while the man, who resembled an eccentric uncle, had a plain white shirt, covered almost entirely by a loosely fitting pair of workman's overalls, complete with a carpenter's pencil in the left-hand pocket. Inexplicably, he also wore a dust-covered bowler, which somehow managed to stay on his head when he fell. Naturally, this charming couple was Mr. and Mrs. Smith.

Mrs. Smith looked at her husband as he finally made his way around the car. "All you all right, Mr. Smith?" Her look of concern, which incised wrinkles at the corners of her eyes, was genuine.

"Yes, my dear, quite all right. I've been on the ground many times before." He brushed himself off again, although not as efficiently as last time, and then he and Mrs. Smith turned to Iowa.

Without Luke noticing, Iowa had stepped away from him when the Smiths arrived, and was now standing next to the car, where she greeted first the woman and then the man. "Hello, Mrs. and Mr. Smith," she said, proffering her hand. Her face was emotionless, although the tone of her voice was friendly, almost familiar. She didn't look at Luke, who was staring, his mouth open, at what was happening in front of his eyes.

"Oh, it's good to see you, dear," said Mrs. Smith in a charming, grandmotherly voice. "I am sorry that we didn't have a chance to get together earlier, but you were busy, I was busy, and Mr. Smith…well, you know how Mr. Smith can be at times."

Mr. Smith looked at his wife without smiling or rancor, and then looked over his shoulder at Luke, who was still speechless.

"Yes, Mrs. Smith is right, Iowa. We are sorry for having missed you, but your presence now makes up for the earlier…what word am I looking for, my dear?" he asked, turning to his wife.

"Never mind, Mr. Smith, she understands you perfectly."

Smiling faintly, Iowa responded with a nod. While she didn't look at Luke, she had a good idea what was going on in his mind.

"We can take it from here, dear Iowa," said Mrs. Smith sweetly. "My understanding is that the young man is still injured, is that correct?" She didn't look at Luke and instead focused all her attention on Iowa, who tried to answer most of the questions with a nod or shake of her head. "Is it serious? Again, my understanding is that he, Luke, needs medical treatment and that our initial goal upon returning is to ensure an examination by a physician, preferably at a hospital."

Iowa nodded.

"Very good. Mr. Smith has the paperwork, which he will go over with you in a minute. As always, we need your signature, although I've never had any doubts with you that everything will be in order." She paused and chuckled pleasantly. "My, it's good to see you again. It's been how long? Two months? More? No, I don't believe that. Mr. Smith, can you believe that? Well, time does fly sometimes. Why, I remember we first got you. It was right after your father died, do you remember? Well, of course, you do. I shouldn't have said that. Oh, you were such a little firebrand then. Naturally, you had every right to be, thrust as you were upon strangers. Everything came out all right, though, and I can't tell you how proud you make us. I know, I know, I've said this many times before, but it's absolutely true, my love. You've made our lives and program worthwhile. Well, it looks as if Mr. Smith has the paperwork." Mrs. Smith stepped back and, after glancing at Luke and smiling affectionately, turned to Mr. Smith, who was now standing in front of Iowa.

Mr. Smith pulled a wad of folded papers out of his back pocket, opened the wad all at once, and began scanning some of the pages.

Glancing at Luke, he cleared his throat and declared that everything "appeared to be in order. Page six provides a clear indication that the young man named Luke is injured and that he needs medical care. Is that right?" he asked Iowa, completely ignoring Luke.

Iowa nodded.

"Good, then. If you don't mind signing here [he pointed to a space on the last page of the packet], we can wrap this up fairly quickly. Good, very good. You're free to return."

Mr. and Mrs. Smith began to turn toward Luke when Mr. Smith hesitated and turned back to Iowa. "I know you had a good reason. It isn't like you to disobey one of the crows..."

"They're such nasty creatures," Mrs. Smith interjected sweetly. "Sometimes the only thing they can do is criticize. Of course, that's between you and me, my dear."

"Yes, of course," Mr. Smith continued, a little put off at the interruption. "Iowa, I didn't believe a word they said. They were out of order. I wouldn't have waited by the side of the road either, although I realize that once you made the decision to cross the cliff, there was no turning back, no second guesses. Look, I am not supposed to tell you this, but the crows believe your actions were premeditated – they spotted you planting supplies – and they will do their best..."

"Their darndest," Mrs. Smith interjected. "Oh, please forgive my language."

"...to convince the council. Mrs. Smith and I won't support them, if that makes any difference."

"But don't worry, my dear," Mrs. Smith said, gently patting Iowa's forearm. "You have a sterling record as a Minder and, even if they were to convince the others, no one will be upset, except the crows, of course. Mrs. Royce, above all others, will understand, given your history with Luke."

Mr. Smith gently squeezed forward and took Iowa's hand. "She's right. Even if it were a crow mark, it's not a very dark one, and it won't interfere with your work."

"Speaking of work, I believe it's time." Mrs. Smith smiled at Iowa and, leaning over, kissed her gently on the cheek. Mr. Smith did the same thing, too, and both times Iowa leaned forward to accept their kisses.

Looking at the Smiths, who suddenly seemed sad, Iowa backed up a few steps. When she was in a good place (in a clear area), she took one more look at Luke, whose unbelieving eyes were locked on her. "I'm sorry, Luke." Seconds later, a hawk hovered high overhead, circling above a dusty car while three people, two rather heavyset individuals standing and facing a much trimmer person sitting on a flat rock. For a couple of minutes, all three seemed motionless, but then as if on command one of the heavy individuals stepped over to the person on the rock, while the other heavy person walked to the car, pulled something black and square of the trunk and headed toward the person on the rock.

The wind seemed unusually heavy at that moment, and the hawk bounced this way and that trying to keep its balance in the air. Its wings appeared to be pushing back and forth on an invisible cushion of air, and when it had apparently had enough, it flew away.

Chapter Forty-four

"Luke? I'm sure I have the name correct," said Mr. Smith. He was standing directly in front of Luke and rummaging through the pages of his folded pack of papers, the ones on whose last page Iowa had inscribed her name. "Luke, Luke, let me see here, I know it's written down."

"Yes, my name is Luke," Luke said quietly, his head hanging and his eyes closed not because of the pain but because of the confusion. He wanted to hide from the world in which Iowa now seemed such an ambiguous character.

"Luke, Luke…well, this is strange, I had just been speaking about you to Iowa and…well, it has to be in the papers, but for the life of me…"

Mrs. Smith reached around Mr. Smith and put the papers back together with the first page on top. "You weren't mistaken, my dear. See, it's on the very first line, where it's supposed to be. Here it is…Luke." She smiled affably and then took a step back so that Mr. Smith stood alone in front of Luke.

"Of course. I don't know how I could have missed it. The next thing you know, I'll have to have glasses."

"But you already have them. They're in your right front pocket." She didn't move, because Mr. Smith could retrieve them, if necessary, without her help.

"Right again, Mrs. Smith. But I don't need them now. Now, where was I? Hmmm…"

"I believe you were going to speak to the young man and answer any questions he might have."

Mr. Smith looked up from the papers. Squinting as if he were examining Luke, who continued to hang his head, he answered his wife without turning away from the young man in front of him. "Quite so, quite so."

But before Mr. Smith could utter another word, Mrs. Smith stepped a little closer to Mr. Smith and whispered in his ear. "This may break protocol, but perhaps I should patch up his injuries while you speak to him. It would save time, and the poor boy does look uncomfortable."

"Yes, I agree," he whispered back. Taking out his glasses and carefully putting them on, he turned to Luke and said in a rather cool, officious tone, "Mrs. Smith is quite right. What I mean to say is that we have to attend to some formalities, but during said formalities Mrs. Smith would like to take a look at your…" He paused, turned back to his papers, and once again began flipping through them.

"Injuries," she interjected.

"Yes, yes, injuries. Thank you, Mrs. Smith. Yes, this is what I'm looking for."

"Certainly. But you should straighten your glasses first."

Mr. Smith turned back to Luke. "Now, as I intimated, Mrs. Smith will proceed while I proceed with said formalities." Glancing at the front page of the papers and then back at Luke, he visually examined the young man while Mrs. Smith picked up a large, suitcase-like black box that Mr. Smith had retrieved from the car and placed it near Luke, who didn't seem to notice anything around him. Mrs. Smith opened the box and pulled out a colorless sheet of plastic and, placing it on the ground next to Luke's feet, she carefully eased herself down on it, at the same time making sure that her dress appropriately covered her ankles. Having accomplished that feat, she began sorting through the box's contents until she found the three items that she needed.

"Now," she said pleasantly, scissors in one hand and gauze in the other, "if you don't mind, I'll patch things up a bit."

Luke nodded in agreement without looking up. While his physical pain was temporarily gone, he was now burdened with another kind pain, one which seemed stronger and more tormenting than the other.

"Very good. I'll make things a little more comfortable until we can get you to a doctor." With that she went to work, removing the sticks that Iowa had taped around his injured leg and then cutting through his pants legs on both sides to expose the full extent of his injuries.

Mr. Smith observed her handiwork and beamed with pride. After glancing one more time at his papers, he turned to Luke and began speaking to him while glancing at Mrs. Smith from time to time to make sure things were going smoothly. "Well, as I was saying about the formalities, there are a few we need to attend to before…that is, while Mrs. Smith works a miracle. Please don't take that literally. First, we need some information…and I would advise you to answer all my…our questions as a sign of good faith, if you know what I mean."

Luke didn't respond.

"Fine, right," Mr. Smith continued, a little put off by Luke's silence. "We can certainly do it the hard…"

"I believe he understands what you're saying, my dear. I also believe he will be cooperative. Won't you, Luke? But please hurry along with the formalities. His leg is in bad shape, and we need to get him to a doctor fairly quickly." Mrs. Smith hesitated, looked over at Luke, and said, "You shouldn't worry, Luke. We will get you to a doctor before things get any worse. This is just a terrible area for germs and the like."

"My dear," said Mr. Smith, "please don't derail the conversation. I promise you that I will be as quick as possible. Now, if we can all get back to business…"

"Yes, dear," she replied and went back to work. Occasionally, something she did or touched elicited a minor reaction from Luke (gritted teeth, closed eyes), but by and large she was as gentle as she was efficient.

"All right, Luke…say, you remember us, don't you? We brought our little dear Iowa to live with us after her mother died. A sad day, and Iowa had a tough time of it for a while, but she spoke often of her friends. I believe you called yourselves The Goslings, if I recall correctly. Goslings… a strange name, wouldn't you say?" Mr. Smith looked at the golden sky, as if he had something else on his mind but didn't quite know what it was.

"Perhaps we can skip this part of the formalities until we get into the car, my dear," Mrs. Smith said without looking up from her work. She reached back into her box to pull out more items (gauze, bottles of something, a scalpel, a small pair of scissors, and needle, and so on) and continued working, pausing only to wipe the sweat from her forehead with a clean, white handkerchief that she kept by her side. Occasionally she adjusted herself and exclaimed "mercy," but neither this nor anything else affected her concentration on Luke's injuries.

"You're right as always." Turning to Luke, Mr. Smith said, "Your parents are fine people, Luke. Wouldn't you agree, my dear?"

"Yes, they are lovely people."

"Well, Luke, they told us all about you, and naturally that's why we're here." Mr. Smith pulled a bright yellow handkerchief out of his back pocket and wiped his forehead. "They are concerned about you, and they only want what's best for you. You understand that, right?"

Luke slowly looked up at him but didn't respond.

"Let me tell you something, Luke. You gave your kind parents quite a scare. You ran away and, equally troubling, you violated your probation and a cardinal rule with respect to changing. Now, I hope you agree that your actions were sufficient to raise the concerns of your parents, every decent parent in your neighborhood, and of course the members of the Changer community."

"That's exactly right," responded Mrs. Smith, although it wasn't exactly clear to whom she was speaking.

"Luke," began Mr. Smith sternly, "I am required to emphasize that you violated the principles of your probation. We – your parents, your neighbors, and the Changer community – thought you understood that you were not supposed to change…," Mr. Smith droned on as if he were reading from a script. He mentioned correction, rehabilitation, and refactoring, again noting with respect to the latter that it was likely to be fairly intense. He added that Luke's parents would doubtless miss him, but that if "things" went according to plan, there was probably no reason why they couldn't write to him, as long as it wasn't too stressful for them. Eventually, if all went well (he emphasized the word "if"), he would be reunited with his parents.

Luke looked at Mr. Smith and then at Mrs. Smith, after which he glanced up at the sky, hoping to see Iowa one more time.

"It's a hot one today, dear," Mrs. Smith said to her husband, although Luke didn't pay attention. "Please don't overexert yourself."

"Not a chance, I'm afraid. Young man," he said turning back to Luke. "Do you feel okay, Luke, apart from your leg? We want to make you as comfortable as possible."

Luke nodded. He was still looking at the sky when he noticed that there was still a lot of sunlight left, as if the day had slowed down and nighttime could still be a day or two away. He also noticed that while the sky was clear, there was nothing in it, neither a cloud nor a bird. Surely, there should have been birds somewhere, just as there should have been bird sounds emanating from the sky, the trees, and the surrounding fields. Instead, there was total silence, save for the clipping, snapping, and taping sounds emanating from Mrs. Smith's work. Everything – the absence of birds, the appearance of Mr. and Mrs. Smith, Iowa's appearance and disappearance, and of course his injuries -- seemed unreal or at least contrary to experience.

Mr. Smith droned on while Luke continued to stare at the sky. From time to time, he caught a word or two, sometimes a phrase or clause, but he didn't try to put them together into any meaningful whole. They were like the blank but lifeless sky, perhaps signaling the ending of his life, at least as he understood it. Had it happened again? He had given his heart to an animal in the zoo, only to find out that he had been deceived, that the animal was only an animal, not Iowa, the person whom he had always considered the love of his life. This time he had given his heart to Iowa herself, only to find out that she wasn't the Iowa he had imagined – the Iowa he knew would never have abandoned him…would never have betrayed him…and so this Iowa, this hawk, was either Iowa gone wrong or something else, something meant to deceive him from the very beginning. Luke remembered Press and Dana, and he felt ashamed because they had been right all along. There had been too much time, and the person he thought he knew was a complete stranger, or just another animal. Shaking his head slightly, Luke started to wonder if she had tried to blind him all those years ago, just as she blinded him now about who and what she was.

"It's certainly not what we expected," Mr. Smith said when his wife stood up, took off her sterile gloves, and tossed them into the box.

"It certainly isn't," she replied and, picking up the box, turned to Luke. "It certainly isn't. Now, I've done all that I could, and it's time for a doctor to take it from here. As far as I'm able to judge, you should be okay, as long as we get you to a doctor, although there could be some side effects, some weaknesses as a result of the injury. But I'm no expert. However, I would advise you to stay clear of all dogs for a while," she added, smiling as if her statement was not only witty but actually made sense.

"Bravo, my love, well said," chirped Mr. Smith.

Luke's leg felt tight, as if someone was squeezing it and cutting off his circulation. Looking down at the leg, he noticed that the ends of his pants were severed and that something was wrapped around his leg. The pristine white bandage covered his wounds neatly (strips of white medical tape bound a thick bandage, which was spotted here and there with red spots), and in place of the sticks was a metal contraption that held his leg in place and kept his foot and the rest of his body from jiggling it, which clearly lessened the pain. He was amazed that Mrs. Smith had attended to him almost without his being aware of it, although he was now beginning to feel twinges of pain, as if he had been given an anesthetic that was beginning to wear off.

"My leg," he said, looking at Mrs. Smith, who was carting the box back to the car and carefully placing it into the trunk. When she returned a few seconds later, he looked up at her and told her that the bandage was a little too tight. "My leg is starting to hurt," he said.

"That's to be expected," responded Mrs. Smith. "Your injuries are fairly serious, and it should hurt, just a little, of course, to show that it is not dead and can be revived. I have a couple of pills for you that might do the trick." She opened her hand and handed Luke two pink tablets. When he had placed them into his mouth, she handed him a glass of water that she seemed to have pulled out of thin air.

It took a couple of minutes for the pills to take effect, and when they did he began to feel lightheaded and braced himself on the rock with both hands to keep from falling over.

"Don't be alarmed, sweetie, the pills are supposed to make you a little drowsy," she said, smiling at him in a grandmotherly way.

"It will also make the transportation much easier," Mr. Smith added, not speaking to anyone in particular. He briefly disappeared, and when he reappeared he was pushing a black, high-backed chair, which he parked next to Luke. The chair might have resembled a wheelchair except that the wheels were more like steel balls, and they were too small for an occupant to reach unless he had the oversized arms of a gorilla. Nevertheless, it looked comfortable – there were thick cushions covering the seat, back, and arms – and when the Smiths, one of either side of him, picked him up and gently lowered him into the chair (it was amazing how strong and capable they were), it felt comfortable as well. Indeed, every inch of the chair was soft and squishy, and even the straps that they tied across his chest, arms, and good leg felt pleasant. The Smiths placed an inflatable tube around Luke's injured leg (the tube was fastened to the chair), and they immobilized his head with a squishy strap across his forehead and two cushions next to each ear. Closing his eyes now and then because of the pain, he sometimes felt as if he were floating.

Having been secured, Luke was wheeled over to the rear of the car and angled so that he could see into the car. Mr. Smith opened the car's hatch, locking it in place on the opposite side of the car. Reaching into the back, he pulled out a long platform, which, after he connected one end to the bottom of the hatch, set the other end on the hard ground to create a ramp to the back of the car. With a quickness and strength that belied his bulk, Mr. Smith stepped over behind Luke and, tilting the chair backwards, pulled it over to the ramp where he turned Luke around so that he was facing the car and pushed the chair up the ramp and into the back of the car. There were some clicking and snapping sounds below and out of sight, after which the door shut with a bang, encasing Luke in nearly absolute darkness. The darkness lasted until Mr. and Mrs. Smith got inside the front seat, Mr. Smith behind the wheel, slamming the doors after them. "Are you comfy?" Mrs. Smith asked, turning around and smiling at Luke. Mr. Smith, grumbling something about the windshield, got out of the car, brushed the dirt and dust off the windshield, and then returned to his place behind the wheel.

The car roared to life with a loud clanging sound and, seconds later, turned and charged back from where it came, bouncing and banging over ruts and holes and, several times, narrowly missing large rocks. The car kicked up as much dust as it had upon arriving, and within minutes it had dissolved in a cloud of dirt and dust and finally disappeared into the dusk.

Chapter Forty-five

The hawk hadn't gone far away. It found a small, leafless tree about a mile away and settled into the top branch. From there, it had a clear view of everything that the Smiths were doing, and because its hearing was keen, it was able to hear everything that was said. The hawk desperately wanted to know what was going on in Luke's mind, but since that was impossible it had to settle with observing his movements and trying to find meaning in them.

Once the car had departed, the hawk leapt off the branch and flew back toward the rock where Luke had been sitting. The bird extended its wings and floated lazily in the invisible air currents, swooping to the right and then the left, simultaneously observing the ground and watching the car and the ball of dust that engulfed it. The hawk continued to circle the site until the car and its surrounding ball of dust were well out of sight.

Before it flew away, heading back to the zoo where it would continue to fulfill certain duties, the hawk scanned the ground one more time, watching several animals come out of the forests – on one side, an elk, several foxes, and a small bear, and on the other side a couple of wolves that timidly stepped out of the woods into the fading light. Directly below, perhaps a hundred feet down, a swarm of noisy, cawing crows began congregating and crisscrossing the site. The hawk was too high for the crows to reach comfortably, but it was obvious that their presence – as well as their insistent cacophony – was directed toward the hawk, perhaps a way of insisting that it leave and go back to where it roosted. The hawk was about to heed the crows' strident urgings, but when it took one last glance over the area, it noticed not far from the rock the remnants of the food that Iowa had given Luke, as well as a few other items which she hadn't used that were stashed behind a small, dust-covered bush. It was surprising how easily Luke had been fooled as to the origin of all the supplies, but then his love for Iowa blinded him to many things, and would continue to blind him as long as he thought she was still alive. Would he ever accept her death should it occur before his?

Iowa was, of course, a Minder. She was a Changer who watched over other Changers, a kind of Changer probation officer who monitored Changers who were on probation for having broken Changer rules. As a Minder, she quietly followed the offender (when officially requested, of course, since there are strict rules regarding all Changer actions) and, when the individual was about to violate his or her probation, she would reveal herself and help the individual step back from the precipice. There were rare cases (rare, because they were difficult to spot and correctly diagnose) in which she minded select individuals – individuals who had committed no crime – to prevent them from ending up in a facility. These were the more interesting ones, because she not only had to stop a particular action before it started; she also had to convince the Changer in question that the next step was the dividing line between living a fairly normal life and losing years to refactoring. It had been clear to everyone when Iowa first arrived at the Lordan Zoo that her ability to change and her aptitude for persuading her fellow refactorants to mend their ways made her an ideal candidate for a Minder, even though she, too, had fallen from grace. Ms. Royce intervened on her behalf, which eventually moved the others to agree, provided that Iowa didn't display any tendency toward recidivism. Ms. Royce's faith in Iowa seemed well placed.

Iowa was afraid that Luke might do something. She wasn't surprised, though, since she understood his personality quite well. But Iowa didn't have a premonition or some kind of special knowledge about Luke and what he might do. Ms. Royce phoned her shortly after she had conversations with Mrs. Jacobson, the well-placed member of the Changers' Board, and Luke's parents. Ms. Royce was not, however, commissioning Iowa to act as a Minder to Luke; on the contrary, she was merely informing her of the facts due to the close relationship Iowa once enjoyed with Luke and the other Cygnets. It was part formality, part interview: Had Iowa heard from Luke recently? Did she have an inkling of his plans? And the summation was simple: Keep me (Ms. Royce) informed, and don't speak to anyone about it unless you speak to me first. It was all very simple and fairly clear, that is, until Ms. Royce mentioned that she had commissioned the Smiths to look into the matter. Ms. Royce had been speaking casually and unemotionally, but at the mention of the Smiths, Iowa stumbled and was speechless for a couple of seconds.

"Is anything the matter?" Ms. Royce asked when she noticed Iowa's silence.

"No," Iowa finally responded. "No, nothing at all. Your statement reminded me that I haven't spoken to Mr. and Mrs. Smith in quite some time. I owe them a call and a visit."

"I see. Well, you will keep me informed, won't you?"

"Of course, I will. I only hope he hasn't…"

"So do I."

The mention of the Smiths was bound to raise conflicting emotions given her relationship with them. Initially, she hated the Smiths and early on, before she understood changing, ran away (twice), only to be found by the couple after she had been captured (she was a Changer by this time and was a swan when she was captured) by a couple of well-meaning boys, who had tied her (the swan) up in a fishing net and left her to languish at the edge of a lake, some three feet from the water. Once again, she was in the Smiths' hands, but this time instead of running away, she submitted to their ministrations, which were only designed to pull her back from the abyss and put her on the path to becoming a responsible adult Changer. It didn't take her long to lose her antipathy for the gentle couple, whom she came to regard as substitute parents and, once she was a fully functional Changer, as good friends. Iowa's concern in this instance was that Ms. Royce felt that the Smiths, who functioned in the Changer community as both police and foster parents (on occasion), needed to be called, which meant that Luke's situation was no longer theoretical and that intervention was officially required. Iowa would have been troubled by Luke's situation no matter what, but the fact that Ms. Royce thought it necessary to invoke the Smiths (and a Minder would doubtless be called in at some point, though most likely after years of refactoring when the subject was about to be freed in society) made Iowa pause and shudder.

The moon had been creeping over the horizon when the hawk started for the zoo. With slow, leisurely movements of its wings, it headed across the plain, past the cliff, and across the other plain, after which it flew over the highway and the outskirts of the city. By the time it reached the zoo, bright pins of light peppered the dark sky, except around the moon, which was casting enough light back to the earth to obliterate even the brightest star. Swooping over the zoo walls, the hawk floated down to the top of a large pole overlooking the entire zoo. With its wings tucked in its sides, it stayed there instead of going inside its house, observing the now quiet park and thinking about the swans, all of which had once been lively young people like Luke.

An hour later, Iowa walked into her small apartment at the corner of the zoo, where she had lived since the end of her refactoring. She had just completed high school (six months of intensive tutoring by zoo specialists enabled her to skip the eleventh grade) and was now studying for her entrance exams to a local university, where she was planning to major in zoology. The zoo was home for now, and while she planned to leave someday, she also planned to stay connected to the zoo and the good work it was doing to rescue and rehabilitate Changers.

Chapter Forty-six

Luke was treated well. The Smiths had taken him to a hospital where he underwent several surgeries and extensive treatment to repair the ripped muscles and tendons, the cracked bone, and the infection, which at one point cast serious doubt as to the ultimate viability of the limb. The surgeries were complicated, and the recovery was long and difficult, but within a couple of years, he regained full use of his leg. That is to say, his leg was completely functional and in no way impeded his mobility either when he was walking or running. However, he retained a slight, barely perceptible limp, which was usually noticeable during cold weather or in times of stress.

When the medical treatment was at an end and Luke was ready to leave the hospital, Mr. and Mrs. Smith arrived and brought Luke to their home, which was some distance away and surrounded by thick woods, cold streams, and sheer rocks, making it all but inaccessible to anyone but a few Changers. It was a modest house, but Luke had his own room and there was enough space for the three of them to move freely without running into one another. Luke's bedroom window overlooked a gentle, grassy hill at the bottom of which gurgled a little stream that was filled with tiny fish no bigger than one's little finger. During the winter, the stream was cold and calm, often frozen over during the height of the cold season (although one could look through the ice and see the water moving as it normally did), but during the first part of the spring it was rough and even colder, absorbing the snow melt from the mountains nearby. Luke loved the stream, he loved dipping his hands in the cool water during the day, reaching for the fish that were far quicker than his hands, and he loved the sound during the evening, because it suggested that something was right with the world.

Luke, as he was informed, was to remain with the Smiths for another six months, during which he was to return to his high school studies and begin a process of refactoring which consisted in recognizing the mistakes one has made and learning how to live without changing, even when surrounded by nature. During this time, Luke was not allowed to see or communicate with his parents or friends. Naturally, his parents understood and accepted what was happening to their son, although this did little to temper their sorrow; Luke, for his part, was satisfied with the arrangement, since he was ashamed to see his parents, knowing that they were aware of everything that he did or attempted to do. He didn't entirely understand what would happen at the end of this idyllic interlude (he knew that he couldn't stay with the Smiths forever, although they treated their young guest with such homey hospitality that it was hard to believe that he would ever be required to leave), but he was apprised of the details one ineffable spring morning when the Smiths pleasantly transported him in their rickety car, down the rugged mountain road from their house and across large stretches of wasteland, to a large, nondescript cinderblock building in the middle of nowhere. The building, which resembled a white, windowless sugar cube, was surrounded by a towering chain-link fence, which was topped by coils of glistening barbed wire. Once there and standing in front of a door that matched the exterior of the building, the Smiths bid their now-former guest heart-felt farewells and handed Luke over to two anonymous-looking individuals wearing dark sunglasses and black overcoats who opened the door. Without a word, the nameless, faceless individuals escorted Luke (one on each side lightly grasping one of his elbows) into the building, down several flights of cement stairs in a gray, damp-smelling stairwell, and through a long, white, unremarkable hallway that ended in a smooth, featureless door that was practically the same height and width as the hallway. The door opened as they approached, and Luke was ushered into the center of the brightly-lit, undecorated room and placed on a hard, uncomfortable kitchen chair that was surrounded (albeit a good fifteen feet away) by similar-looking chairs, each filled with dour looking individuals wearing dark sunglasses and black overcoats. These were Changers whose place in the community required them to serve as judges for his trial.

All of the lights in the room, except for the dozen or so directly above Luke's head, immediately dimmed, signaling the beginning of the trial. The trial was quick – probably no more than a half hour, excluding the deliberation which took less than five minutes – since the judges had plenty of time to consider the case while Luke recuperated at the Smiths, and so when Luke sat down and faced his judges, they required only a few simple answers to their simple questions before rendering a simple judgment. Prior to their judgment, however, one of the judges, a smallish man whose sunglasses seemed to weigh heavily on his face, took a moment to inform Luke of the seriousness of his crimes while checking for signs of remorse (which would be weighed in his favor) for what he had committed.

"In the first place," the man continued in a small, nasal voice, having first pushed his glasses back to the bridge of his nose. His voice seemed to echo in the dark room, even though the room was packed with shadows of people. "In the first place, you violated the terms of your probation, which had been generously worked out by Ms. Royce. According to those terms, you were forbidden – forbidden, I must emphasize – forbidden to change prior to your thirty-fifth birthday, not a minute less. You were also restricted from traveling outside your town, unless said travel was approved in advance by both Ms. Royce and your parents. Speaking of your wonderful parents, they are Changers, too; but, unlike their recalcitrant son, they sought to understand the responsibilities that come with changing, as well as the importance of following rules and directions with respect to changing. Parents aside, you did not inform Ms. Royce of your plans to see Iowa, even though you were cognizant of the restrictions on associating with active Changers."

Luke sat motionless. He looked up at the man from time, noticing his oversized glasses or undersized bald head, and couldn't help wondering if the man was observing him, possibly out the corner of his eyes, to find some mannerism or nervous tic that would be a sign of additional guilt of some kind.

The room was warm, though not uncomfortable, and yet sweat poured off his forehead and down his sides, and he was afraid the man would see his sweat as proof of something nefarious. Occasionally, he wiped the sweat from his eyes, but only with a casual move of the back of his right hand (as if it were a natural, innocent movement), and not once did he reach down for a Kleenex from the box that mysteriously appeared next to his feet.

"Do you deny that you violated your probation?" the man abruptly hollered.

Luke shook his head and looked down at his feet.

"Make sure the judges can hear you," the man whispered in Luke's ear, having leaned over to the young man and patted him familiarly on the shoulder.

"No," Luke responded.

"No?" he practically screamed. "No? And yet, you had the...the...and yet...the...," he began stumbling and then stopped. With one hand over his forehead to keep the overhead light out of his eyes, he scanned the invisible audience surrounding them. "Myrtle, Myrtle, where are you?" he asked someone in the audience. When a small, feminine voice responded affirmatively, he turned to the sound and said, "Thank goodness. Myrtle, I don't know what's come over me? Do you know what word I'm looking for? It's on the tip of my tongue. Starts with a C, I believe. Yes? Audacity? Yes, that's the one. Thank you, dear." Turning back to Luke, he continued with a stentorian tone. "And yet, you had the *audacity* [he stressed the word] to commit additional crimes."

Pushing his sunglasses to the bridge of his nose, the man paused, crossed his heavy arms, and stared at Luke, after which he glanced at the audience in the dark and winked. Turning back to Luke, he added, "You wreaked havoc at the zoo, you refused to obey zoo rangers, you avoided capture by said rangers, and...and..." Once again, he hesitated, although this time he hadn't forgotten a word. He shook his head slightly, as if he couldn't believe what he was going to say, and then took a deep breath to give himself the courage to say it. "And you bit a human being. Most of the crimes that I have graciously enumerated for your benefit are, if not forgivable, at least partly understandable, given the circumstances in which you were acting. I think most of us can agree on that. But we as a society can neither forgive nor forget an act against a human being, because animals are often imbued with extraordinary powers and sensitivities that in a blink of an eye can render the most powerful man null and void. What you need to understand, Luke, is that being an animal is a privilege, and if we abuse this privilege then we threaten not only man himself but also mankind. Luke, I am explaining this so that you understand why this is the most sacred rule among Changers -- a human animal must never attack a human being, even if that human being is a Changer."

The man ceased speaking and took a large step backward into the shadows, leaving Luke all alone under the bright, overhead light. Except for the occasional cough and sniffle emanating from somewhere in the darkness, the room was completely silent while everyone, Luke included, waited for the man to return to rest the prosecution. Several minutes passed before the man reappeared, which to Luke seemed an eternity, but when he stepped back into the light, his bald head glistening as if he had just polished it, he pushed his sunglasses back, cleared his throat and announced loudly so that even the people in the back of the hall could hear, "Luke, having heard your crimes and having, by your silence, accepted culpability, can you honestly deny that there are no mitigating circumstances in your case, other than the ones I enumerated. Fairly, I believe."

Luke looked up at the man and, in a weak voice, asked the man, as if he were the only one in the large room, "Will I be able to go home soon, sir?"

The man breathed deeply and histrionically and straightened his sunglasses. "Your statement," he said in a more tempered voice this time, "is duly noted." He suddenly twisted around backward and, pulling up the back of his white coat, fished for something in the back pocket of his trousers. After a few moments of twisting and turning and fumbling with his coat, he finally retrieved a small slip of white paper that had been neatly folded in quarters. He carefully unfolded it and read the contents, nodding and inhaling deeply as he did so. When he was finished, he turned to Luke and, holding the paper away from his body so that he could refer to it, pronounced the sentence.

"Luke," he said in a loud, firm voice, "you will undergo refactoring at a facility yet to be named for a period of one year, you will be prohibited from changing for a period of thirty years (and after this period only under direct supervision with a trained, experienced Changer), and you will be placed on supervised probation for a period of ten years. During these periods, you will not knowingly associate with active Changers, excepting Ms. Royce, the Smiths, and a few others whom we will choose or allow at our discretion. During your refactoring, Mr. and Mrs. Smith will be your advisors, and if at the end of this period they deem you sufficiently changed, you will be allowed to return to your parents. Do you understand and do you agree to these terms?"

"My parents," Luke sputtered, barely able to refrain from crying, "What will they be told?"

"They know everything, Luke. They are in the room."

There was silence as Luke nodded his head in agreement without looking up or trying to face the speaker. It was clear from the movements of his shoulders that he was crying, which pleased some of the judges as it suggested that there was still hope for the young man.

The man carefully refolded the paper and, pushing the recalcitrant coat away, reinserted it into his back pocket. Turning back to Luke, he pushed his sunglasses back on his nose and added, "Finally, you will be secretly minded – that, is watched – and any violations of these terms, no matter how insignificant, will be punished immediately and to the fullest extent. We have every hope that you will not change before the term of your abstinence expires, but should you violate the prohibition…well, we can only say that it would not be advisable. Are there any questions?" he asked Luke and everyone else in the room.

Hanging his head, Luke wondered what Press and Dana would say. Press would no doubt laugh at his predicament and, pointing her index finger at him, telling him gleefully that she told him so. His teachers and friends, if they learned the reason for his absence from school, would be ashamed of having had him attend their school, while family friends and neighbors would hector his parents and others for news about him, relishing the news as if it were the charred remains of car crash victims at the side of the road. But most of all, Luke wondered what his parents were thinking and if they would even speak to him again. He could easily imagine his mother cringing with shame over his crimes and his father gritting his teeth to keep from telling people what he thought of his own child. Luke felt sorry for himself and buried his face in his hands.

The man readjusted his sunglasses several times in succession, each time moving his head to facilitate the process, but for some reason the sunglasses would either slide down his small, button nose or hang at an odd, disconcerting angle, waiting for the slightest movement to slip down again. Irritated and impatient, the man pushed his sunglasses to their proper position and held them in place with his right index finger and walked out of the room, the sound of his shoes ringing against the hard floor as if he were the only one in the room. Soon afterwards, all the chairs of the remaining judges could be heard scraping the floor and then their footsteps rang out as they, too, left the room. While Luke remained seated and hanging his head, another set of shoes came clicking across the floor and stopped in front of his chair. Luke looked up, hoping that it was Iowa, hoping that she had been in the room all along and was now ready to take him under her wing, so to speak, but as he turned he was confronted, first,

266

with a pair of overalls and, second, a protruding stomach. It was Mr.
Smith.

Chapter Forty-seven

Despite the stern judgment, someone in the intervening moments before the arrival of Mr. Smith was able to influence the judges to be lenient with Luke, since he hadn't deliberatively flaunted the rules but had violated them out of passion for another Changer, one who was now a respected member of the Changer community. Afterwards, there were some in the community who blamed Ms. Royce for the commutation of his sentence, suggesting that she had used her influence to protect one of her favorites. But she steadfastly denied that she had anything to do with the sentence or its commutation (and she wasn't at the trial and not in direct communication with anyone who was). Nevertheless, she was pleased with the result, because she felt that the original sentence was too harsh given the crime (even the biting) and, moreover, she still believed that Luke had a strong character, unlike so many others who had succumbed to changing.

Luke stayed with the Smiths until he was deemed fit to return home to finish off the rest of his sentence. Unlike Iowa's initial response to the Smiths (that is, long before she got to know and appreciate them both as people and fellow professionals), Luke got along with them right away and eventually accepted them as surrogate parents. The speed with which he accepted the Smiths probably had something to do with the twin facts that he couldn't see his parents and that he wasn't certain that they didn't want to see him. It probably also had something to do with the kindness of the Smiths, particularly Mrs. Smith. Mrs. Smith was invariably sweet and loving and, even though there were moments when her patience was tried (particularly by her well-meaning husband), she always had a smile and a kind word for everyone, especially when Luke was feeling down or troubled by his recent actions. Mr. Smith, on the other hand, was almost as nice, although his niceness took other, often more subtle forms. At one moment, he could be a severe taskmaster, while at the next he was a soft-hearted soul helping a young man put his life back together, buoying the young man's spirits with praise and encouraging him to push himself a little harder.

Life at the Smith's house, however, was anything but chaotic, which Luke had expected when he was placed in the back seat of the Smiths' car and taken to their home – his home, too, as long as he remained in good standing, as Mr. Smith once put it. Instead of returning to the wilderness retreat, Luke was taken to a strange town and settled into a small room at the back of the Smiths' small brick rambler, which was similar to his own house back home except that it was in a different county and the people living in the houses surrounding the Smiths' home were, Luke was positive, either Changers or Minders.

For the first few weeks at the Smiths', Luke took all the formal instruction and informal life lessons that the Smiths offered, after which some (not all) of the studies tapered off and were replaced by school studies so that, as Mrs. Smith joyously put it, "your mind will remain sharp and not turn into mashed potatoes." (Mr. Smith, from his workroom in the basement, where he often repaired after dinner to carve and paint small figurines of famous people who had been Changers, called out, "I heard that, Mrs. Smith.") Over time, Luke earned a number of privileges such as going outside the Smiths' home (with or without them), where he could sit on the porch or stroll through the grass in the backyard – and just before he was allowed to return to his parents, stroll leisurely around the block, which enabled him to enjoy the smell of spring air and observe birds, rabbits, an errant fox or two, and other wildlife without desiring to return to animal form. Luke even noticed a handful of dogs, almost all of which were on leashes, without once desiring to experience the joy of the canine world, with its unusual senses and extraordinary physical capabilities. When the Smiths and a committee of Changers finally judged that Luke was ready to return to his parent's house, Luke was tempered in his enthusiasm. He would miss the Smiths, but more importantly he feared that returning to familiar things could trigger a relapse. Of course, he was also wary of his parents' reaction, even though he had been exchanging letters with them for several months.

Having again been warned about the Minders (the message was contained in a certified letter he received one day before leaving the Smiths), Luke bade a tearful goodbye to the Smiths, boarded a train to his town, and several hours later arrived at the front door of his house. His father paid the cab driver without arguing over the fare, and together he and Luke met Luke's mother at the door and entered the house and embarked on the final stages of his rehabilitation.

Luke was happy to be back with his parents, although he was surprised to see how much they had aged since he had last seen them (his father seemed slower these days and his forehead had become noticeable shiny, while his mother's eyes had become heavy and dark). At the same time, however, he was uneasy being at home in the familiar surroundings, particularly if these surroundings enabled him to become lax in terms of his rehabilitation, and there were times when he looked at his parents and couldn't help feeling betrayed by their actions. Luke learned early on that his parents had him followed when he left to find Iowa (his father called Ms. Royce, after all) – and he understood that they were only doing what every parent in their position would do to protect their child – but that was because they were Changers themselves, a fact about which they had seen fit to keep him in ignorance. One time, long after he finished his refactoring, when he was sitting at the kitchen table with his mother after his father's funeral, Luke quietly asked his mother why she never told him about changing and why neither she nor his father said anything to him while he was being tried. His mother, weighed down with the loss of her spouse of forty years, hesitated and then explained that they had kept silent for his own good and that they might have told him about changing if he hadn't got "in all that trouble. We weren't allowed to after that." She took his hands in hers and, looking into his eyes, she added, "Changers around the world face the same set of issues." Luke realized that she was too tired to speak about personal failings and that it was pointless to try to rectify the past, particularly when the only people who could rectify it were old and didn't believe the past could be rectified.

Luke had been required to repeat the final semester at his high school to complete his degree. He didn't feel odd that he was a year older than most of the students, but he was surprised that he didn't know anyone in the school, neither the students nor the teachers. Press and Dana were gone, and what was more surprising was that no one seemed to have known them or remembered them. Even Ms. Royce was gone, although in her case one of the new teachers suggested that she had moved to another district and was in administration, or at least that is what she thought. "What was her name again?" the teacher called out as Luke walked down the hall to his last class. One evening out of curiosity (but careful not to break probation), Luke dialed Dana's number to see if she and her family were still in the neighborhood. He was about to hang up after eight rings when a strange voice answered the line and complained about having been hit in the head too many times when he asked for Dana. The man hung up, and Luke never again tried to connect with Dana or Press.

Luke, however, felt free to think about Iowa because she was a Minder, an official just like Ms. Royce, and for a while he tried to fathom if she had any feelings for him (even as a friend) or if she had been acting the entire time in her capacity as a professional, unmoved by his protestations of affection. Over time, though, he realized that he needed to move on with life and that his feelings for his childhood friend were the feelings of a child, not a mature adult. Of course, there were moments when he felt angry over the way he thought she deceived him, but he eventually realized that there was no deception because there had been no feelings between them by that time. Whatever feelings they may have once shared, those were gone the moment she stabbed him beneath the eye – or, at least on her part, they were gone before then and the stab was only a reminder of what had been lost. Sometimes he couldn't believe how foolish he had been.

Having given up on the Cygnets, including Iowa, and having forgiven his parents for most of their shortcomings, Luke dedicated himself to school, college, and to the occasional refactoring assignment.

To all outward appearances, Luke was a model student and, according to the estimate of many teachers, he would go far after graduation. He graduated high school with honors, and he attended a nearby university where he studied science and education, earning credentials as a science teacher. While he was at the university, he continued to work at a local animal shelter that had been established to rescue and rehabilitate raptors injured in the wild. Several of the birds lived permanently at the facility. Their injuries had been so severe (broken wings, damaged eyesight, addled brains) that even though they survived and lived quite contentedly, there was no hope that they could return to the wild. One of the birds, a small, brown hawk whose badly damaged wings prevented it from flying, sometimes made Luke think of Iowa because of the way its black eyes followed his movements around the facility. It was a docile bird, and would stand contentedly on its perch, eyeing Luke whenever he cleaned its cage. Luke often wondered if there was something behind its eyes, if perhaps it was a human animal that had lost the ability to change, but he never found out. After graduation, he did his student teaching at a high school within walking distance of the university and, one year later, was licensed to teach anywhere in the state.

Free of the most restrictive obligations, Luke was finally able to live anywhere he wanted. He chose a small town in another state on the other side of the country and, after getting his credentials to teach in that state, found a teaching position at a well-respected high school. Unexpectedly, life seemed happy and full of promise, especially because he was finally putting behind him many of the mistakes he had made in his past. Perhaps it was possible to erase the past. Luke sometimes visited his parents (or his mother after his father passed away), but he was never completely comfortable with them because they and the house evoked things that he tried hard to forget. Whenever he returned to his small apartment and his school, they receded into the dark haze of the past.

Chapter Forty-eight

Luke enjoyed teaching, and he loved his school because it looked and operated a lot like a traditional prep school and not just a good public school. The school was composed of several moderately-sized buildings surrounding a larger building that resembled an English university because of its ornate columns in front and the English ivy growing on the walls. Between this building and the others were carefully manicured lawns and flagstone sidewalks, and, as he walked from one building to the next to teach his classes, Luke could almost believe that his former life had been a dream, a bad dream, and that whatever had happened would no longer have anything to do with this, his real life. Luke dedicated himself to his work, and because of his congenial speaking style and his ability to make even the most abstruse topic intelligible, he quickly became one of the most popular teachers at the school.

One day, after Luke had finished a lecture and had plopped a stack of papers onto his desk intending to grade them before he left for the day, he glanced at his watch and suddenly remembered that he was supposed to attend a department luncheon for a candidate who had recently applied to the school. The candidate, Sarah Phillips, was a young teacher from his state and, if he recalled correctly, she had grown up in a town not too far from the one in which he was raised. Although Luke hadn't met the young woman, he read her application, surveyed her CV, and spoke to a colleague, who had worked with her at another school, to see if she would be a good fit for the school. The colleague's professional opinion, along with the woman's credentials, suggested to Luke that she would be a solid addition to the faculty, and he was ready to vote in her favor, sight unseen. But even though he wanted to meet her personally for a quick interview, he didn't relish spending a considerable portion of the afternoon with certain members of the faculty, listening to them drone on about their theories of education, when a simple 30 minute meeting with the candidate would suffice to evaluate her fit at the school. Despite his desire to skip the event, he decided that he would attend, especially because he had skipped the last two candidate luncheons, which drew a couple of raised and bushy eyebrows from the chairman and a "constructive suggestion" from his assistant that Luke's attendance at these functions would "aid the evaluation process."

The luncheon was held at an exclusive restaurant on the other side of town. The establishment, which was restricted to restaurant members and their guests (one of the faculty was a member), was a maze of long halls and secluded dining rooms, and on several of the walls were signed pictures of local notables who were either members or who had dined there. When he arrived, Luke was met at the door by an older gentleman in a dark suit who escorted him to his table and who seemed slightly offended by the fact that Luke was twenty minutes late, which meant that he was relegated to a chair at the opposite end of the table from the chairman and the candidate. The host, always the consummate professional, helped Luke to his seat, handed him a menu, and hovered behind him while he chose his lunch. While he waited for his meal, Luke glanced at the pretentious decorations in the dining room and noticed, with some satisfaction, that many of the pictures of notables on the walls were of people unknown to him and probably everyone else except perhaps their direct descendants. Turning toward the opposite end of the table where the chairman, candidate, and some long-serving members of the faculty (two of whom wore striped bow ties) were sitting, Luke tried to focus on the discussion that seemed to engage several of them. As far as he could make out (it was a little difficult to hear what they were saying because of the competing discussions that were going on around his table and other tables nearby), the math and science teachers were insisting that unless all students dedicated themselves to math and science, our country would soon lose the ability to develop the technological entertainment that the public would need to be happy and socially cohesive. The discussion left him cold, because he already knew the opinions of his colleagues (especially the head math instructor, a large man with an even larger voice) and because he couldn't see or hear the candidate very well, and so he had no way of evaluating anything at all from the luncheon, except that the math teacher seemed to have divined the right solution for the future and wasn't going to let anyone stray from what he deemed was the only solution. Luke stayed for an hour or so, long enough that the chairman could note his presence, and then slipped out after dessert, going back to his office where he intended to grade the papers.

The school seemed unusually quiet compared to the dignified restaurant, and when Luke sat down behind his desk to start grading the papers, the quietness (he could hear the large clock ticking on the wall opposite his desk) and his desire to take a walk in the open field next to the school were overpowering. Promising himself that he would grade the papers at home in the evening, Luke stuffed the papers in an old, leather briefcase (it had been his father's briefcase), left his office, the building, and, instead of turning right to go to the parking lot, turned left, crossed the school yard (which was practically deserted), and squeezed through a broken section of the chain-link fence that separated the school grounds from an open park filled with wide-grassy sections, small hills, and tall trees.

Luke was neither tired of life nor disillusioned by the people living it, but there were times when he liked to escape to the park (and squeezing through the fence like an errant schoolboy made him feel like he was escaping) to clear his mind, forget the insignificant problems that arose some days, and simply enjoy the beauty of nature, even if it was nature on a small scale at the heart of a large city. What he liked best about the park, though, was its openness and the fact that few people seemed to use it, even though it had been at the center of the city for nearly a century – one could casually stroll for some time, crawl among the rocks and outcroppings, and stand beneath the tall, leafy trees and not encounter anyone. Sometimes, he felt that he alone knew of this wonderful place, even if from time to time he noticed a candy wrapper, names encircled with a heart carved in a log, and other remnants of nearby human habitation. Still, when he strolled through the area, he felt as if he were discovering a wild, uninhabited country for the first time, and whatever was on his mind before he entered the park, whatever troubles or inconveniences he had been forced to handle at school, when he entered the park, he left everything behind and he looked for signs of animals, noticed the small tree shoots coming up, and watched the starlings as they foraged for food or searched for nesting material. Whenever he saw the starlings, he would recall watching one particular bird gather twigs for its nest. The small, black bird picked up one twig and another and then another, but when it tried to pick up a fourth, it somehow lost control over the other twigs in its beak and dropped all of them. Having lost the twigs, it started all over – one twig, two twigs, three, and before it could keep its grip on the fourth, all would fall to the ground – and did this several times until it gave up and flew away, leaving a pile of useful twigs on the ground.

There was a small clearing deep within a grove of trees about a half mile from the school. The clearing wasn't particularly special, and there wasn't any kind of wildlife there that couldn't be seen elsewhere in the park, but Luke often went there when he was pensive or something in him wanted to remember the past for a few moments. The clearing reminded him of the clearing surrounding the lake where the Cygnets played, except that there was no lake or sandy shoreline on which to stretch out when the sun was low and feel the water tickle the heels of one's feet. Sometimes, when he was feeling particularly introspective, Luke would walk to one of the large rocks at the perimeter and, sitting down and leaning against one of the rocks, face the open area as he once faced the lake, watching the small white caps dancing across its surface and recalling how much fun they all had splashing in the water or floating across the water's usually calm surface. It was easy to float from one side of the lake, and when you reached the limits of your ability to remain motionless or wanted to play with the others on the other side of the lake, you could easily swim back across the lake (it wasn't very big) or even wade across it, since it was never more than chest high at its deepest. Sometimes, while he was looking across the clearing, Luke would try to remember all the diverse kinds of birds that inhabited the area surrounding the lake. He liked to tell himself that the diversity of avian species around the lake was extraordinary, and that the average birder could fill up book after book with all the new finds and sightings, after which Luke's thoughts would drift towards swans and how elegant they were floating effortlessly across the lake.

Of course, the advent of the swans presaged the demise of the Cygnets, and yet whenever he recalled the swans he couldn't help remembering Iowa and thinking about the beauty and grace of her movements and the manner in which she seemed to reach out to him, demonstrating perhaps more affection for him than all the others. But having recalled these things, Luke would invariably tell himself that Iowa never liked him, that all her demonstrations of affection were her way of using him, and that her efforts to help him after his leg was mauled were merely a way of delivering him to the authorities – and he began to harbor similar feelings; he began to dislike Iowa and felt embarrassed by the way he swooned over her and defended her to Press and Dana. Over time, though, his feelings toward Iowa softened, and sometimes, when his work was particularly stressful or when he spotted someone who bore a passing resemblance to Iowa (or what he thought she might look after all these years), he would think of her and wonder how things might have been different if there had been no changing, or if he had visited her legally, without violating his probation.

This afternoon, like many other afternoons when the sun was slowly inching its way toward the horizon behind the trees and casting the clearing in a cool, dark shade, Luke placed his briefcase on the top of a waist-high rock and sat down facing the clearing, placing his back against the rock. Closing his eyes, he began to recall one particular summer day when the sun was in the same position and golden clouds were floating lazily in the darkening sky and the smell of the trees filled the air and the lake, with its white caps peppering its surface, slapped the shore over and over again while a breeze suddenly came up and cooled the water on their wet heads and bodies. Luke had been imagining this one particular day, pulling more details from the past into his consciousness, for perhaps ten minutes when he heard something behind him, a sound that seemed to arise out of this past.

"Oh, hello," a woman's voice said hesitantly. Opening his eyes and turning in the direction of the sound, Luke saw a tall woman standing about fifteen feet away. He couldn't see her face clearly, because the sun was behind her back and creating glowing aura around her that cast her front in shade. Luke's abrupt movement around startled her, and she took a step back. "I'm sorry," she said. "I was just taking a walk and…I'm sorry, I didn't mean to intrude."

Luke didn't respond right away. He was surprised at the unexpected appearance of the woman and, because he couldn't make out her features with any clarity, he couldn't quite understand what she meant and therefore didn't quite know what to say. He didn't like to have his solitude disturbed, but that wasn't on his mind at the moment. On the other hand, the woman could see Luke's features clearly, and she took a step backwards when she noticed what seemed to be an expression of irritation on his face. She smiled briefly to cover her embarrassment and once again apologized, and, taking another step back, began to walk away from Luke and the clearing. Before she took a half dozen step, though, she stopped and turned back toward Luke. While the sun was descending behind the trees, she moved a few feet closer to where he could see her better. "I'm sorry," she repeated, looking directly at Luke and smiling. "I really didn't mean to intrude. It's just that I think I know you. Well, I don't really know you. What I mean to say is that I think I saw you today. You're all right, aren't you?"

Luke sat up and turned his head and shoulders toward the woman so that he could see her more clearly. She was tall and trim, and she was wearing a dark, business suit that highlighted the graceful curves of her body without making her seem flashy or tacky. She appeared to be about Luke's age and, as far as he could tell (her face was still covered by a slight shadow), she had dark eyes, a straight nose, and black hair that fell over her forehead but was not long enough to get into her eyes. For a brief moment, she reminded Luke of someone, perhaps someone he once knew or had once seen in a magazine, but he quickly dismissed this idea because he couldn't see her clearly and because he was looking at her from an odd angle. Still, Luke couldn't help thinking that he recognized the way she leaned forward and used her hands to add nuance to her words. Even the sound of her voice and confident tone she had while apologizing sounded vaguely familiar.

"You must think I'm an idiot," she added. Luke could tell from the way she tilted her head that she was embarrassed and possibly blushing.

Luke smiled and said that he wasn't surprised that she recognized him. "I have the kind of face that resembles everybody's brother."

"No, that's not it," she said and took another step forward, although she was still a good ten feet or so from him.

Luke adjusted himself so that he could see her more clearly. 'Where have I seen her before?' he asked himself. "You're not a student, are you?"

"Goodness, no. I mean, I was a student once, though not at this school. That sounds stupid. That's not what I mean to say. I mean…I saw you at the faculty luncheon today. I'm almost positive. You didn't stay very long, or else I didn't notice…well, I'm sorry. I didn't mean to disturb you." She turned again as if to leave and then immediately turned around again. "It was you, right? You're a teacher at the school here, a science teacher." She raised her hands and looked down at her shoes briefly. "I'm sorry," she said with a slight chuckle, as if she couldn't say something without embarrassing herself and annoying him. "I keep saying I'm sorry. I am. I didn't mean to intrude. I really appreciated the lunch…and what a place, too, but I have to go and…please, go back to what you were doing."

"Yes," Luke said, suddenly remembering where he had seen her. "Yes, you must be..."

"Sarah Philips. I'm the candidate."

"Yes, I remember." Luke started to get up, but Sarah put up her hands again and urged him to remain seated. "Please," she said, "I didn't come here to disturb you. Like I said, I noticed you here and, well, I guess I couldn't walk by and not say hello. So, hello, and it was a pleasure meeting you." Sarah turned to leave, but Luke stood up and asked her if she was going back to the school and, if so, would she like some company.

"I've been out here long enough," he added. "Besides, I need to go back and grade some papers." Luke stood up and brushed the twigs and dirt off his clothes.

Before he took three steps forward, Sarah motioned toward the briefcase sitting upright on the rock now behind him. "Is that yours?"

Luke turned and, to his embarrassment, noticed his briefcase. Grabbing it by the handle, he walked over to Sarah, wondering at the same time if she knew that the papers in question were in the case. "Thanks. I'd be in big trouble without this. Interested in seeing the school?"

"I'd love to." She turned and watched him over her shoulder as he came up to her.

Without looking directly at one another, Luke and Sarah walked under the trees, crunching the leaves, twigs, and dirt underfoot. For a few moments, they didn't say anything. But as Luke glanced at her feet and felt her presence next to him, he couldn't help thinking that there was something else familiar about her, something not explainable by the lunch at the restaurant. Luke was about to ask a question about her interests to break the silence when she stated that she liked the school and that, as he no doubt knew by now, the chairman told her that she had the position. "I can't tell you how excited I am by this. I'm really looking forward to teaching here, although I have to admit that I feel a little like a fish out of water."

"Good, I'm glad. I think you'll like it here." They were silent for a few more moments when it occurred to Luke to ask her how she happened to be in the park. "You have to admit that this is one of the strangest places to meet," he added with a warm smile.

"The chairman gave me a brief tour of the school, and he left me to my own devices to take a couple of calls. I saw the park and couldn't resist. I'm a nature lover."

"You've already seen the school? I thought you said…"

"Part of it," she added, trying to downplay the fact that she had already had the tour that Luke had just offered to give her. "But I didn't see much, because I was peppered with questions…"

There was an awkward moment of silence before it was broken by the acknowledgement that he understood. "Yes, he's a talker, and he demands your ear. But if you're interested in seeing it again, I would be happy to show it to you."

"Yes, of course."

While they walked through the trees and then through the open area toward the broken fence, Luke listened to Sarah tell him about her professional experience and then about her life. Her personal life was more or less what he expected from someone near his age and with more or less in line with his experience, save for the years of refactoring and the loss of what he once believed was the love of his life. It seemed funny now to think that the Cygnets had once been the focal point of his life and that he loved Iowa and would have done almost anything to marry her. In fact, the years and his experiences convinced him that most of what he remembered about Iowa wasn't real. "I guess throughout my life I've been a little like Walter Mitty," he ruminated out loud, "embellishing things and people to the point that if I were to compare them to reality, they would bear only a passing resemblance." Luke pulled the fence apart so that Sarah could squeeze through. When she was through, she stood to one side while he squeezed through. Once they were both on the school grounds, Sarah touched his arm lightly and they began walking toward the buildings.

"What do you mean 'Walter Mitty'?" she asked

He stopped and turned to her. "Do you know the story?"

"Yes," she responded pleasantly, as if she and Luke had known one another for a long time. "It's by Thurber." While she began to tell the story, Luke suddenly felt that he recognized her voice, although he couldn't identify it or say exactly why it sounded familiar. It made him warm inside, and a strange wave of nostalgia came over him without, however, making it clear to him why he felt this way. Luke turned to her and, observing her profile, stopped and stepped back a half foot from her.

Sarah released Luke's arm and turned to him. "Did I say something wrong?"

Luke had trouble saying something. It was as if his mind wanted to speak, but his mouth wouldn't let him. He stared at Sarah, observing her smooth face, the delicate lines opposite her nostrils, and the manner in which her dark fell across her forehead. If she had informed him she was Press, he would have believed it without a second thought. She looked exactly the way he imagined Press would look fifteen years after the last time he saw her. She had the same regular features, the same curve of her lips, the same gentle curve of her spine, and even the same lilt in her voice.

Chapter Forty-nine

"Press?" he whispered, as much to himself as to Sarah.

"What? What do you want me to press? I don't understand," Sarah said, noticing the strange expression on Luke's face.

Recovering quickly, Luke smiled and blurted out, "Nothing. It's just…it's just nothing, that's all."

"Are you sure I'm not bothering you?"

"I'm sorry, I'm sorry, I didn't mean to stare. You caught me off guard. I, ah, didn't expect to see anyone here. You're the first person in a long time…please, you're not bothering me in the least. Tell me more about your life, and please forget these mental slips of mine."

"Mental slips?"

"Walter Mitty. Okay, there are times, I guess, when I have trouble telling the difference between speaking to myself and thinking. It comes with being alone a lot, I suppose. When I was in college, I knew this young woman who talked to herself as she walked from class to class. There were no interior monologues; everything came out into the open, just like that. Oh, I don't know why I'm saying this. I'm not that bad, and she wasn't in the least bit nutty. It was just a quirk. She's an archeologist now." He looked into Sarah's eyes. "Do I sound like I'm justifying myself?"

"Perhaps a little, but I don't mind. We all justify ourselves at some point."

Luke led Sarah toward the building in which his office was located. But instead of going directly there, he and Sarah moved slowly and stopped now and then to discuss a particular point or to admire a school building or something on or about the school grounds. Even when they arrived at the corner of the building, they didn't head to the main doors – they traversed the circumference of the building so that, as Luke suggested, Sarah could admire the building's wonderful architecture and get a better idea of where the building fit on the campus and what the campus looked like from the building. Initially, they spoke as if they were colleagues enjoying one another's company, but after a while the camaraderie changed and, to Luke, at any rate, their conversations began to seem like the renewal of a long-lost friendship. Sarah told Luke about growing up on the other side of the country, about her friends and activities, while Luke talked about school and some of his friends, omitting all mention of his past troubles, which he was forbidden to speak of. When they had finally reached Luke's office, he pointed out some of the mementos he had collected from his time at the school. By the time they had practically exhausted the contents of the office, Sarah glanced at her watch and informed Luke that she had to leave because she had an appointment in half an hour. "I have to sign some papers for the chairman," she added. Before they exchanged goodbyes, Sarah pointed out a small picture of a hawk floating in the sky, which was half hidden behind an empty coat rack. Sarah wanted to reach for it, but Luke preempted her by dismissing it.

"It's not a very good picture. I like wildlife. I took it years ago."

"But why are you hiding it behind the rack? You probably can't see it at all when there's a coat there."

"I'll tell you about it some other time," he replied, smiling.

Sarah held out her right hand for Luke to shake. "I look forward to seeing you again," she said.

Luke took her hand, but before releasing it, he looked at her as if he was again trying to see something in her face. "You have the job, right?" he asked to make sure that his imagination wasn't deceiving him.

"Yes. I start next semester. I'm going to move down in a few weeks, but I need to go back to clear up some things."

"When are you going back?"

"Maybe in a couple of days. But that can change, depending on whether I get my hand back or not." She smiled and Luke immediately released her hand, his face reddening slightly. "I plan to scout out the area first and then look for an apartment."

"Good. Well, what I mean is…if you're free tonight, maybe you'd like to have dinner with me. If you have someone special…that is, I don't want to...I'm just asking…" Luke had trouble articulating his desire to see her, while at the same time he feared that such a beautiful woman as Sarah probably had men calling on her all the time. (He never considered Press beautiful, but the more he observed Sarah the greater his sense that he had been all wrong about the individual he once considered his nemesis.) He was surprised and then overjoyed when she agreed. He controlled his emotions, though, and after seeing her off, he rushed home (he was too preoccupied to work) and sat in his living room and through about this strange and beautiful woman.

Her resemblance to Press was indeed amazing. In fact, she was probably a dead ringer for Press, wherever she was now, although there were a couple of very minor things that were likely different in both women. Press, as he recalled, had lighter eyebrows and a sharper nose, while Sarah's hair seemed thicker and more buoyant. Sarah also had a softer voice and clearly she was more educated. As Luke tallied up the differences and then balanced them against the similarities, he couldn't quite believe that the two individuals were so alike that, at the very least, they could have been close relatives, even sisters (Press didn't have a sister). Luke's head was spinning, but he was also determined not to say a word about this to Sarah. If she weren't offended, she would doubtless think him crazy, like good old Walter Mitty. "Why did I have to mention Walter Mitty?" he asked himself out loud, fearing that he would never lose the association and that Sarah could never quite look at him as he was, which was about as far from Walter Mitty as one could go, he told himself silently. More to the point, who wouldn't be suspicious if a relative stranger suggested that she was a dead ringer for an old friend that he hadn't seen in years? However, Luke wasn't attracted to Sarah simply because of her resemblance to Press.

Luke dozed off thinking about Sarah and reliving his memories of Press and the Cygnets, and when he awoke and was clear as to where he was, he was shocked to see that he was running behind and that if he didn't hurry, he would be late to the restaurant. Luke was a little surprised that Sarah knew exactly where the restaurant was (it was close to the school, and she said that she was walking around before finding him in the park), but luckily it was close and he managed to get there at the same time Sarah arrived from the opposite direction. Seeing her, observing the beauty of her smile, Luke couldn't help smiling. They walked into the restaurant together and, after being escorted to a booth near the far end of the place, they ate and talked for hours, or at least it seemed like hours to the staff, who wanted the booth for other patrons and who later that evening wanted to leave at closing time.

Luke and Sarah spoke in animated tones about nearly everything. It was wonderful, especially to Luke, who hadn't shown any interest in women since the day he lost sight of Iowa. While he had met or seen any number of women he found attractive, he had never had enough interest to speak to them much less date them or consider them a different kind of friend than his male friends. Despite his anger and disillusionment, Luke waited a few years to hear from Iowa, although he never quite admitted it to himself. But after a while, after he considered time and again the fact that she was a Minder and that whatever feelings (if any) she may have had for him were obviously subordinate to her job, he gave up. Maybe she was brainwashed, he told himself many times, but then he realized that if this were so, if the Changers had succeeded in altering her thinking and emotional responses, then Iowa would never be approachable – she would never leave her job and would never think of him the way he thought of her. It didn't matter either way, for a number of years ago Luke had come to a point in his life when Iowa had ceased to matter except as a sometimes pleasant memory. The odd thing about this was that even though Iowa had been locked in the past, Luke for some reason still wasn't interested in other women or in dating or in marriage. There was nothing sad about this. Luke himself wasn't sad.

Everything changed when Sarah arrived. It felt good being with someone who was pleasant and attractive, who had a good sense of humor and who shared the same interests that he had (they were science teachers, of course, but they were also interested in nature, especially birds, and had similar tastes in books, music, education, and even politics) – Luke not only enjoyed being with Sarah, but he also felt empty whenever she wasn't around, as if her presence was integral to his enjoyment of life, and this was something that he hadn't felt since that day he believed that he loved Iowa and that there was a chance she loved him. But what he refused to acknowledge to himself was that to a certain extent, he was attracted to Sarah because of her resemblance to Press. He had forgotten the acrimony that suffused his last conversations with Press, and after seeing Sarah for a few months, he came to believe that Press had been right all along – that it had been a mistake to see out Iowa – and that if anyone appreciated him, it was Press (and perhaps Dana, whom he rarely thought about). Indeed, as time went on, the more he noticed aspects of Sarah that reminded him of Press, albeit an older and more mature Press. When Sarah smiled or laughed, the corners of her mouth curled up just like Press', and the manner in which she pronounced certain words, especially those with sibilants, were exactly like the former Cygnet's. Even the way that Sarah stretched, ran, or flexed her muscles was so like Press' mannerisms that Luke sometimes had to shake his head slightly to make sure he didn't confuse the two or accidently call Sarah by his friend's name. There were other things, too (Sarah was sometimes obsessed with winning a game or a competition of some sort), but over time as they saw more of one another, these striking similarities seemed to dissolve, and Sarah became Sarah, with all the distinctiveness that endeared her to Luke and ultimately separated her from all the other women he had ever known.

One night about six months after Sarah had settled into her new apartment and life at the school, Luke took her to dinner at a small restaurant that was only a few blocks from her apartment. Later that evening, after sitting across from each other over dinner for nearly an hour and hardly saying a word to one another, Luke walked Sarah home. There, in front of her door, he began a conversation about life that was so intense, so interesting, so important, that for nearly forty-five minutes neither one of them had the urge to move, much less come into her small apartment lest the intensity of the discussion was lost, possibly lost forever. It turned out to be the right moment, for while they hadn't known each other for very long, they both felt as if the months had been years and that two people could never be as close or as perfectly matched as they were. Not long after this, the prediction that Mrs. Kilgore, one of the school's English teachers, made to a colleague in the history department seemed about to come true. "By this time next year, *I Promessi* something – what is the name of the Manzoni book, you know the one about marriage? Maybe that's not right. It didn't end happy, did it? Well, I never read it myself, but I wouldn't be surprised to see Sarah sporting a nice diamond ring. Now, what kind of taste do you think Luke has?"

Luke and Sarah didn't disappoint either Mrs. Kilgore or her colleague. Three weeks before the start of Sarah's second year at the school, Luke and Sarah honeymooned in Hawaii.

Chapter Fifty

Luke and Sarah had been married nearly three years before they finally visited Luke's mother. Sarah met the old woman for the first time at their wedding, and she had flown across the country several times to visit Luke and Sarah, but Luke always seemed to be putting off the return trip for one reason or another. What was different this time was his mother's illness, which didn't appear to be life-threatening but was serious enough to call off his mother's expected trip to visit them. Luke had always regretted not visiting his mother before then, but he harbored mixed feelings about his home town because of the refactoring, the incident at the lake, and the possibility of running into someone who once knew him. However, given his years of absence, this was deemed as good a time as any.

Luke and Sarah stayed with Luke's mother during the visit, which lasted one week. Everything went better than expected – Luke admitted on the third day that he was having a good time (particularly because his mother was showing strong improvement) and that he was looking forward to visiting again – that is, until the last day of their stay. While the old woman was visibly improving each day, on the final day she was a little more tired than usual and went to bed shortly after dinner, giving Luke and Sarah an evening to themselves.

"She's looking so much better," Sarah whispered to Luke after his mother went to her room, "but I still worry about her being all alone out here. She doesn't seem to have many friends and, if it weren't for us, I don't think she would go out of the house." Sarah whispered because the walls were thin and because she was genuinely concerned for the old woman, whom she loved like her own mother. "At least my parents have each other, though Dad isn't much of a help with anything," she added a few minutes later, recalling the trip they had made to see them last year.

"I suppose," he responded, recalling with a twinge in his left shoulder his father-in-law's peculiar habit of slapping him on the shoulder to agree with him about one thing or another.

"No, really, we should do something. I'm worried about her."

"I'm not sure what we could do right now, other than making plans to come back."

"I've got a couple of ideas," she said, smiling. "But first, let's go for a walk. You promised to show me the neighborhood."

During their walk, they discussed buying a large house so that his mother could move in with them. Luke was in an expansive mood (the night sky was clear, the moon glistened overhead, and for a few moments all seemed right with the world), and as they strolled through the neighborhood speaking about his mother and other plans for the future, Luke pointed out the houses of his childhood friends and some of the places (a small baseball field, the local community center) where some of the kids used to congregate. Sarah seemed fascinated by all the details Luke provided and, after pausing and looking at the bright moon, Luke told Sarah about the Cygnets, explained the genesis of the name, and tried to convey the closeness of their relationship. Naturally, he omitted a detailed description of Press, and he didn't mention his past feelings for Iowa, which he realized was only a pathetic attempt to recapture one of the happiest times in his early life. But he talked about her, just as he talked about Press, Dana, and Lu, adding that they failed to keep in touch as they grew up and went their separate ways. Luke couldn't remember if he violated any rule or prohibition in speaking about them, but as long as he had Sarah by his side it didn't matter. Besides, Ms. Royce and the others had no doubt forgotten about him years ago.

"I'm sure you could find them today, if you wanted," Sarah said, feeling the nostalgia that had washed over her husband. She threaded her arm through his as they continued walking.

"No," Luke replied with a wan smile and a shake of his head. "No, it's the past, and the last thing I'd ever do is try to recreate it by calling them. I've grown up." He paused and, turning to his wife, kissed her briefly on the lips. "I'm sure that it wasn't as happy as I remember it. It doesn't matter, though, because you've made me happier than I've ever been in my life." He held her in his arms and kissed her again, after which he pulled her close to his side and put his arm around her. When they came back to Luke's mother's house, they sat down in the bench on the front porch instead of going into the house. The air was cool and comfortable, and, as they sat silently thinking about their conversations and their future together, they could hear the chirruping of the peepers and see fireflies blinking on and off.

Since the evening was still young, Luke suggested that they see one more thing before going inside. The additional thing was the high school he attended, which was only a couple of blocks away. Pausing in front of the old building and its now unkempt lawn, Luke couldn't help mentioning Ms. Royce and informed Sarah, without going into detail, that she had been one of the decisive influences in his life. Since they were near the park, Luke suddenly decided to add one more stop to the itinerary. Without explaining, he took Sarah's hand and together they walked two blocks away from the school and his mother's house, turned up one street and walked another couple of blocks until they were at the edge of the woods and the path that led to the lake.

Turning to Sarah, Luke said, "I'm going to show you something else." Luke held both of her hands and stepped over the small wooden fence that blocked off the park from the neighborhood and encouraged her to follow him.

"I think we should go back. It's getting late and it's too dark to be walking in a forest," she said only slightly resisting his pull.

Luke was ready to give in when he noticed the moon over Sara's right shoulder. It seemed bigger now and its color was no longer white but an intense orange. From somewhere in the park, he could hear the faint cawing of crows, and then a cool breeze came up, rustling the leaves and branches of the trees. Feeling a strong desire to visit the past one more time before permanently shutting it out of his life, he looked at his wife's lovely face and urged her to join him. "I have to show you one more thing and then we're done."

"We should go back, Luke. It's too dark to go out there."

"No, it's fine. Trust me. I know these woods like the back of my hand."

"Really…"

"Please," he insisted, keeping his eyes on her.

"All right, if you think it's okay. But only for a few minutes," she added, eyeing him and trying to understand his strange desire. "Are you sure it's safe?"

"Darling, I wouldn't take you anywhere that wasn't safe." Luke smiled and helped Sarah over the fence, and together they walked carefully along the old path through the dark woods.

Luckily, the moon's light filtered in through parts of the woods, and so they were able to follow the path much better than Sarah anticipated. As they walked, Luke observed the weeds, leaves, and rubble that now covered the path, which suggested that it had not been used for some time, perhaps not since the Cygnets used it regularly. In some places, thick branches reached out across the path, forcing them to push the branches aside or duck beneath them or, in one instance, climb over one that had fallen across the path, while in other places the path became so narrow (because the trees had begun colonizing its edges) that it was hard to believe that the Cygnets had been able to walk on the path side by side or that large animals had once stomped along it. They passed an even narrower area bound by stone walls, which forced them to squeeze through. Finally, after ten minutes of trudging, Luke and Sarah came upon a small rock outcrop. It was perhaps six feet high and, because of its crags and deformations, it looked something like a giant deer head lying on its side, staring blindly at the woods.

Luke dropped Sarah's hand and, running around to the back of the outcrop where he disappeared for a few seconds, emerged on the top looking down at the most beautiful woman he had ever seen.

"Isn't this wonderful?" he called out and then leaped off the smooth top down to where Sarah was standing. Unfortunately, Luke wasn't as agile as he once had been, and when he landed he fell onto the seat of his pants. Sarah reached down and helped him to his feet, after which he brushed off his pants and rubbed his leg, the same leg that had been injured years ago.

"Okay, so I'm not a kid anymore. We used to play on this rock, and we ran through the woods day and night. That's why I know it's safe. No one ever came here but us, and judging from the looks of the path, no one has been here since."

"Us?"

"I'm sorry. I mean the Cygnets. This is where we spent most of our time. I can almost hear the screams and shouts when we were running through the woods or hiding among the rocks here." Looking at the outcrop, Luke paused. "I remember being chased by one of the Cygnets around this rock, and hiding on top just like I did a second ago. I jumped down that time, too. It's funny the things you remember." Luke turned and was about to go back down the path when he noticed a golden reflection between the trees. It was the lake, and he couldn't resist running out to the edge of the water.

When Sarah arrived, she noticed Luke standing, his arms at his sides, gazing across the rippling surface of the water. For a couple of minutes, he stood silently, watching the golden beams of light from the moon dancing across the surface of the black water, and, as he scanned the dark shadows at the far side of the lake, he recalled how much he and the Cygnets loved playing in and around the lake, splashing and screaming in the cool water. He started to turn around when he noticed the shadows at the opposite end of the lake, which somehow resembled the shadows that swans make and he could almost see a pristine white swan, its head rhythmically moving up and down as its invisible feet paddled under the surface, slowly moving toward him. Iowa was now part of a distant past, but the thought of her filled him with a gentle sadness and he wondered what happened to her. Was she still at the zoo? Was she still a Minder? Was she even alive after all these years? Luke was awoken from this reverie by the distant sound of crows cawing and then Sarah's gentle touch on his shoulder, suggesting that it was time to leave.

"It's late, dear," she said. Let's go."

Luke turned and started walking, but he suddenly stopped and stepped back a couple of feet from Sarah. Staring at her beautiful face, which was illuminated by the moon's bright light, he couldn't help feeling the past surround him and engulf both of them. "Let me show you something," he said. "It's a very special part of me and my past."

Sarah eyed him carefully as he sat down on the ground and rolled to his side. "Now, don't be afraid," he added.

Sarah's eyes narrowed and her expression became serious. Before Luke could change, she reached down, grasped his hand, and helped him back to his feet. Standing face to face, Luke looked into her eyes and tried to understand why she stopped him and why her normally soft, moist eyes were now dark and cold. Sarah reached around her husband and pulled him close to her. Placing her cheek next to his, she put her lips against his left ear while fingering the scar beneath his eye with the tip of her thumb and whispered, "No, Luke. Stay with me."

Luke immediately pulled back. Staring at Sarah, his eyes were wide open and his jaw was slack. For a moment, as he stared into her dark eyes, he thought he saw images of his past, images of a time when life seemed innocent and uncomplicated. Neither Luke nor Sarah said anything as they turned and walked back to the house. Once outside the park, Luke's right leg became sore and he started walking with a noticeable limp.

- - - -))) - -)) – ((- - (((- - - -

www.ingramcontent.com/pod-product-compliance
Lightning Source LLC
Chambersburg PA
CBHW062123170626
46813CB00002B/556